THE
AND O

JOSEPH CONRAD
Korzeniowski in the Ru...
His parents were punished by the Russian...
nationalist activities and both died while Conrad was still
a child. In 1874 he left Poland for France and in 1878
began a career with the British merchant navy. He spent
nearly twenty years as a sailor before becoming a full-time
novelist. He became a British citizen in 1886 and settled
permanently in England during the 1890s, marrying Jessie
George in 1896.

Conrad is a writer of graphic richness and of extreme
subtlety and sophistication; *Heart of Darkness*, *Lord Jim*,
and *Nostromo* display technical complexities which have
established Conrad as one of the first English 'Modernists'.
He is also noted for the unprecedented vividness with
which, in such works as *The Secret Agent*, *Under Western
Eyes*, and *Victory*, he expresses a searching pessimism. Despite the immediate critical recognition that they received in
his lifetime, Conrad's major novels did not sell well until
in 1914 the commercial success of *Chance* secured for him
a wider public and an assured income. In 1923 he visited
the United States, with great acclaim; and in England he was
offered a knighthood (which he declined) shortly before his
death in 1924. Since then his reputation has steadily grown,
and he is now seen as a writer who greatly extended the
resources of English fiction and offered prophetically intelligent insights into the problems and preoccupations of
the twentieth century.

WILLIAM ATKINSON is an associate professor at Appalachian State University in North Carolina. He was educated
in England and then pursued his graduate studies in the
United States. He has published mostly on twentieth-
century British literature.

THE LAGOON
AND OTHER STORIES

JOSEPH CONRAD was born Józef Teodor Konrad Korzeniowski in the Russian-held part of Poland in 1857. His parents were punished by the Russians for their Polish nationalist activities and both died while Conrad was still a child. In 1874 he left Poland for France and in 1878 began a career with the British merchant navy. He spent nearly twenty years as a sailor before becoming a full-time novelist. He became a British citizen in 1886 and settled permanently in England during the 1890s, marrying Jessie George in 1896.

Conrad is a writer of graphic richness and of extreme subtlety and sophistication. Heart of Darkness, Lord Jim, and Nostromo display technical complexities which have established Conrad as one of the first English 'Modernists'. He is also noted for the unprecedented 'vividness' with which, in such works as The Secret Agent, Under Western Eyes, and Victory, he expresses a searching pessimism. Despite the immediate critical recognition that they received in his lifetime, Conrad's major novels did not sell well until in 1914 the commercial success of Chance secured for him a wider public and an assured income. In 1923 he visited the United States, with great acclaim; and in England he was offered a knighthood (which he declined) shortly before his death in 1924. Since then his reputation has steadily grown, and he is now seen as a writer who greatly expanded the resources of English fiction and offered prophetically intelligent insights into the problems and preoccupations of the twentieth century.

WILLIAM ATKINSON is an associate professor at Appalachian State University in North Carolina. He was educated in England and then pursued his graduate studies in the United States. He has published mostly on twentieth-century British literature.

THE WORLD'S CLASSICS

JOSEPH CONRAD

The Lagoon
and Other Stories

Edited with an Introduction and Notes by
WILLIAM ATKINSON

Oxford   New York
OXFORD UNIVERSITY PRESS
1997

Oxford University Press, Great Clarendon Street, Oxford OX2 6DP

Oxford New York

Athens Auckland Bangkok Bogota Bombay Buenos Aires
Calcutta Cape Town Dar es Salaam Delhi Florence Hong Kong Istanbul
Karachi Kuala Lumpur Madras Madrid Melbourne Mexico City
Nairobi Paris Singapore Taipei Tokyo Toronto Warsaw
and associated companies in
Berlin Ibadan

Oxford is a trade mark of Oxford University Press

Editorial Matter © William Atkinson 1997

First published as a World's Classics paperback 1997

British Library Cataloguing in Publication Data
Data available

Library of Congress Cataloging in Publication Data
Conrad, Joseph, 1857–1924.
The lagoon and other stories / Joseph Conrad ; edited with an
introduction and notes by William Atkinson.
(World's classics)
Includes bibliographical references (p.   ).
Contents: The idiots—The lagoon—To-morrow—An anarchist—
The informer—The brute—Il conde—Prince Roman—The Inn of
the Two Witches—Laughing Anne—The warrior's soul—The tale.
1. Adventure stories, English. I. Atkinson, William, 1953–
II. Title. III. Series.
PR6005.04A6 1997   823'.912—dc21   97–9268
ISBN 0–19–283222–0 (pbk.)

1 3 5 7 9 10 8 6 4 2

Typeset by Graphicraft Typesetters Ltd., Hong Kong
Printed in Great Britain by
Caledonian International Book Manufacturing Ltd.
Glasgow

CONTENTS

ACKNOWLEDGEMENTS

I would like to thank the librarians and graduate students who helped me prepare this edition: Cynthia Adams, Dianna Moody, Glenn Ellen Starr, Lenora Eason, Thomas Moore, Kari May, and Ashley Nation. Special thanks are due to Kathryn Kirkpatrick. All errors and solecisms, however, are entirely my own. I am also grateful to Appalachian State University, which was able to help with research expenses.

INTRODUCTION

Few writers have a more complicated personal history than Joseph Conrad. He was born of the minor Polish aristocracy in the Ukraine, which at the time was under Russian control. His parents were both fervent Polish nationalists, but after they died he came under the influence of his uncle, who was more willing to toe the Russian line. Thus while Conrad was formally a Russian, emotionally he was Polish, although his country had not really existed for half a century. His uncle, Tadeusz Bobrowski, tended to talk about Conrad as if he were the site of some Manichaean struggle between the hopeless idealism of his paternal blood and the down-to-earth common sense of the Bobrowski family.

At the age of 17 Conrad left Poland for France and became a seaman. Four years later he joined his first British ship, and in due course he qualified as a captain. He completed his first novel at the age of 37 and never went to sea again, earning his living entirely from writing for the rest of his life. Even though his spoken English was always imperfect, all his publications were in English. So Conrad looks like a very contemporary figure: a cultural hybrid.

Robert J. C. Young defines hybridity, 'at its simplest', as implying 'a disruption and forcing together of any unlike living things, grafting a vine or a rose on to a different root stock, making difference into sameness'.[1] Joseph Conrad the English novelist was a graft onto Captain Józef Teodor Konrad Korzeniowksi, a Pole whose second language was French. The graft was a good one, but as Young points out, if the plant is neglected, it will revert to its original state. There is frequently a sense of instability in Conrad's fiction, as if it is about to revert to something else—the motif of anarchy that spreads across four of his narratives[2] may well hint at

---

[1] *Colonial Desire: Hybridity in Theory, Culture and Race* (London and New York: Routledge, 1995), 26.

[2] 'An Anarchist' (1906), 'The Informer' (1906), *The Secret Agent* (1907), *Under Western Eyes* (1911).

Conrad's anxiety about his own unstable identity. In some of his early works, even the language sometimes seems to be straining towards French.

Indeed, the most suggestive form of hybridity for a reading of Conrad may well be Mikhail Bakhtin's theory of linguistic hybridity. In *The Dialogic Imagination*, Bakhtin argues that any text which contains elements of more than one language —the word is to be understood in both a strictly linguistic sense and in a sociological one—is hybridized.[3] Each discrete language carries in the denotations of its word store and the mental style of its syntax a view of the world. And dialects and registers with their lexical and syntactic variations mark the world-views of their speakers. The language of a completely unhybridized individual would contain nothing that is not strictly identifiable with his or her class, region, and occupation. The authority behind the language is never questioned because, there being only one language in use, only one authority need be acknowledged. Such language is profoundly conservative and non-confrontational, and Bakhtin finds little to interest him there; he prefers hybrid language, relishing it for 'the collision between differing points of views on the world that are embedded in these forms'.[4] Young tells how 'within a single "pidgin" utterance, the voice divides into two voices, two languages. This double-voiced, hybridized discourse serves a purpose, whereby each voice can unmask the other'.[5]

Conrad's narratives are nearly always at least double-voiced. Sometimes, in *The Secret Agent* for instance, his narrative voice is profoundly ironic, undermining everything he writes as he writes it. But his favourite technique, used in all but one of the stories in this collection, is the framed narrative: the text is an account of one or more narratives recounted by characters in the text. Since Conrad is not telling the story, he is not even identified as the frame narrator, and we

[3] *The Dialogic Imagination: Four Essays*, ed. Michael Holquist, trans. Caryl Emerson and Michael Holquist (Austin, Tex.: University of Texas Press, 1981).
[4] Ibid. 360.   [5] *Colonial Desire*, 21.

cannot assume that the story-tellers are reliable and vested with the author's authority. Instead, we are left uncertain which voice to attend to, with no sure sense of a single, coherent world-view.[6]

'An Anarchist', for example, is narrated by a travelling Englishman who encounters the protagonist, Paul, on a South American river. Paul is a victim of narrative. He was a quiet man and a steady worker until one evening, carried away by wine and companionship, he expressed himself in solidarity with those who work so that the rich may live in comfort. Thereafter, four different narrative powers took him over: the French judicial system, an anarchist, Henry Gee, and finally the frame narrator himself. The keyword of the story, 'anarchist', has now one meaning, now another, depending on who is using it and why. The initiating moment of drunkenness could be called the essential anarchy—a moment when wine loosens Paul's control over his social and political self. For the French authorities, the matter is simple: Paul has questioned the laws of property without which society as they know it will collapse. The anarchists, on the other hand, seem to employ the word as a justification for common theft. Henry Gee, manager of the B.O.S. cattle ranch, uses the term to enslave Paul. Gee, realizing that he has escaped from the Cayenne penal colony, labels him an anarchist from Barcelona, a tag that will keep him from finding work anywhere else in the area. The story opens with the frame narrator's fulminations against the B.O.S. advertising, so the theme of dishonest labelling is introduced at the outset.[7] So far, Gee and the anarchists have used the word 'anarchist' for their own profit, and it seems that even the French courts were plainly too literal and hasty.

The narrator's final opinion is that Paul was more of an anarchist than he admitted. If this is true, the story must be

---

[6] Contemporary students of Conrad rejoice in such textual indeterminacy. See e.g. Daphna Erdinast-Vulcan, Robert Hampson, Bruce Henricksen, Jakob Lothe, and Suresh Ravel.

[7] My reading of this story owes much to Jennifer Shaddock's 'Hanging a Dog: The Politics of Naming in "An Anarchist"', *Conradiana*, 26 (1994), 56–69.

reinterpreted, since Paul would no longer be an unfortunate victim but someone who brought his misfortunes upon himself. However, the narrator offers no evidence in support of his judgement, so why should we believe him? He is a butterfly collector, an avocation which implies a prejudice in favour of the exotic over the everyday—indeed, he is in that particular part of South America in search of 'an extremely rare and gorgeous' specimen. An anarchist is surely more 'gorgeous' than a mechanic who has got himself into trouble through a drunken brawl. Paul's account of himself is thus less exotic than the narrator's. Gee insists on calling the narrator a 'desperate butterfly-slayer'. While Gee is plainly unreliable, there may be a fragment of truth in his characterization.

'The Informer', which Conrad wrote later in the same month, also hinges on a word. Again we have an anarchist who may not be what he seems, and an enthusiast for exotica. This one collects Chinese porcelain and bronzes, some of which, he confesses, are so rare that they approach 'the monstrous'. He keeps them in a display room so cold that visitors must wear overcoats. The main character, X, is a leading figure in the international anarchist movement. The narrator is appalled by his cynicism and complains to the 'friend' who introduced them. The latter agrees but suggests that X 'likes to have his little joke'. The narrator cannot imagine what he means, and the reader is similarly puzzled. But the word 'joke' immediately opens up the whole story for reinterpretation. Nothing is necessarily what it was before; everything has become 'double-accented', as Bakhtin puts it. Jokes offer an alternative denotation which undermines the apparently authoritative meaning. Jokes delight in their hybridity.

Conrad's personal history goes a long way towards explaining the kind of stories he wrote. However, there is another important factor which contributed to the polyvocality of his narratives: the fiction market. Without it Conrad might have succeeded in establishing a single voice in peaceful but dull harmony with its language.

In 1894 Tadeusz Bobrowski died and Conrad's first novel was accepted for publication. Two years later his second book appeared and he married Jessie George. The way seemed open to a new career. But it is hard to imagine that Uncle Tadeusz would have given Conrad much encouragement, particularly when he had opposed his nephew's original ambition to go to sea. So with his uncle gone and two well-received novels to his name, literature at last looked feasible. However, Conrad had a wife, and soon a family, to provide for and had no private income. He was going to have to come to terms with the market.

In the late nineteenth century, the market-place for fiction underwent a major shift, and Conrad's short stories are a product of this development.[8] Populations in Europe and America had been growing rapidly throughout the century, while free schooling had recently begun to raise literacy levels. At the same time, improvements in paper manufacture and printing technology had very considerably reduced the price of printed material. A novel cost perhaps half what it had twenty years earlier, and it became possible for a magazine to sell for a sixpence (2½p) or a shilling (5p)—ten or fifteen cents in the USA. An extensive variety of literary magazines appeared in the 1880s and 1890s, so a writer had a wide choice of markets.

With the proliferation of magazines came the rise of the short story. The *Cornhill Magazine*, in 1860, was one of the first to move away from novels in instalments to essays and short stories. By 1910, the American *Harper's Magazine* ran only one serial and seven or eight stories in each issue.[9] Most British writers of Conrad's time produced both novels and short stories, and the relationship between the two was symbiotic. Short stories kept a writer's name before the public during the relatively long period of silence when she or he

---

[8] The following sketch of the magazine market during Conrad's career is heavily indebted to accounts by Brian Spittles, Cedric Watts, and Lawrence Graver.

[9] This vigorous short-story market began to weaken after World War I, and the popular magazines went into decline or moved away from fiction. The reason was presumably related to the rise of the cinema and, later, radio and television, which came to fulfil the need for one- or two-hour narrative experiences. In 1919, as if sensing which way the wind was blowing, Conrad sold the film rights to his works for £3,000—a very considerable sum at the time.

was working on a larger work, and novels, even if not big sellers, could generate enough critical attention to make the writer's name a selling-point for the magazine. Conrad's first two published works, the novels *Almayer's Folly* and *An Outcast of the Islands*, were critically well received, but together they earned him less than £100 for 171,000 words. His first three short stories, which he sold largely on the strength of his critical reputation, together brought him £104 for 25,500 words. He was paid again when they were collected in a single volume and republished. Later in his career, he was often able to sell a story two or three times: once in England, again in the USA, and yet again in Europe—his works were well represented in French and German translations. The American market could be very lucrative: in 1912 Conrad reported that *Harper's* was paying him £105 per short story.

Money was important to Conrad. Coming late to the career of writing, he was not willing to make sacrifices to Bohemianism and live in a garret. Short stories were relatively quick to write and fairly easy to sell, so during his honeymoon, although he was working on a novel, he wrote three short stories ('The Idiots', 'An Outpost of Progress', and 'The Lagoon'). The same pattern of producing shorter pieces while working on longer projects occurred through much of Conrad's career. The novel *Chance* is an interesting case-study.

Conrad began a story variously called 'Dynamite' or 'Explosives' in early 1905. It finally became *Chance*, his first commercially successful novel, but in the course of its production he broke off to write five stories which remained short ('An Anarchist', 'The Informer', 'The Brute', 'Il Conde', and 'Prince Roman'); seven long stories ('Gaspar Ruiz', 'The Duel', 'The Black Mate', 'A Smile of Fortune', 'The Secret Sharer', 'Freya of the Seven Islands', and 'The Partner'); several pieces of journalism; and a volume of autobiography (*A Personal Record*). While working on *Chance*, he also conceived two other short stories, 'Verloc' and 'Razumov', which grew into the novels *The Secret Agent* and *Under Western Eyes*. He finally completed *Chance* in March of 1912, five months after the publication of *Under Western Eyes*.

In 1899 J. B. Pinker became Conrad's literary agent. Conrad had already got himself published in the conservative *Blackwood's Edinburgh Magazine*, but Pinker started placing his material more widely. Several stories appeared in the *Metropolitan Magazine of New York*, which billed itself 'The liveliest magazine in America'. The biographical reminiscences later collected as *The Mirror of the Sea* appeared wherever Pinker could sell them—the prestigious *English Review*, the polyglot and sophisticated *Cosmopolis*, or the popular *Daily Mail*, which occupied much the same journalistic space then as now.

But Conrad's idea of living decently pushed him deeply into debt to his agent. Conrad, who came of the Polish squirearchy, had been kept on a loose financial rein by his uncle, but even so, his notion of an acceptable standard of living was rather remarkable. In 1907 he made an agreement with Pinker to be paid £600 a year; Pinker required written words in exchange.[10] Such an income placed Conrad in the top 2 per cent of the population, yet he still failed to live within his means. His improvidence seems to have been a mixture of faulty arithmetic and plain extravagance. He certainly felt deeply uncomfortable about his debts, so the market was always a shadowy presence in the corner of his study, whispering the urgency of writing something, anything so long as it resulted in text. His attitude towards the market was, understandably, ambivalent.

Conrad's letters are peppered with deprecatory references to popular magazines. Part of his distaste may well have been plain snobbery—a feeling that popular magazines were simply not select enough. Squire Conrad reveals himself in a letter of 1913 to George Blackwood, who originally published *Lord Jim*. He points out that the novel is now out of print and goes on to write: 'I would much prefer a new edition at 6/- [30p] leaving the Democracy of the book-stall to cut its teeth on something softer'.[11] Before publishing it in book form, Blackwood had serialized some of Conrad's early work

[10] Zdzisław Najder, *Joseph Conrad: A Chronicle* (New Brunswick, NJ: Rutgers University Press, 1983), 369.

[11] Frederick R. Karl and Laurence Davies, eds., *The Collected Letters of Joseph Conrad* (Cambridge: Cambridge University Press, 1983–96), v. 173.

in the magazine. The writer observes to Pinker: 'One was in decent company there and had a good sort of public'.[12] *Blackwood's Edinburgh Magazine* was a long-established publication with a fairly small circulation of about 10,000 copies a month, and Conrad regarded it as an alternative to ' "the market"—confound *it* and all its snippety works'.[13] Cedric Watts characterizes 'Maga' as 'staid, sober, rational and unadventurous' and likens the presence of *Heart of Darkness* in its pages to a shark in a carp pond.[14] Blackwood had his market as much as any other editor; it was merely more establishment-oriented and conservative than most.

However, Conrad's attitude was not unusual. The editor of *Harper's Magazine* (New York), in a year when he printed two of the stories included here, contrasts *Blackwood's* with his own publication, which he described as being 'addressed to all readers of average intelligence, having for its purpose their entertainment and illumination'. Like Conrad, the editor does not doubt that *Blackwood's* readers are highly cultivated and the magazine's material, therefore, at the highest literary level.[15] But we have seen that this was not the case. Wealth and education are not invariable markers of high culture.

The editor of the *Pall Mall Magazine* (London) was even harsher in his assessment. In the March 1913 issue he declared that nobody without bias could find the popular magazines—his own excepted—anything other than 'wholly bad'; they are despised by anyone with intelligence and offer fare for which there is no real demand.[16] One of the editors of the *Metropolitan Magazine* (New York) echoes his colleague at *Harper's*. In a private letter to Conrad's American publisher, he writes expressing a desire to publish some of Conrad's work, so long as it does not soar too high above the readers' heads. He asks for something like 'The Brute', one

---

[12] *Letters*, iv. 506.

[13] Quoted in Lawrence Graver, *Conrad's Shorter Fiction* (Berkeley: University of California Press, 1969), 21.

[14] *Joseph Conrad: A Literary Life* (New York: St Martin's Press, 1989), 79, 81.

[15] Graver, *Conrad's Shorter Fiction*, 137.   [16] p. 439.

of Conrad's recent stories, and concludes, 'Doubtless they would read it without realizing how good it was'.[17]

Conrad saw this letter and was furious, in spite of the writer's unqualified praise for him as an artist. 'You may tell them since they are so anxious', he wrote, 'that *Because of the Dollars* ['Laughing Anne'] will be something in the *Brute* style they are crying out for but that Conrad wants special terms for prostituting his intellect to please the Metropolitan'.[18] And yet a few years earlier Conrad had asked Pinker to send him a newspaper review of *A Set of Six*, one of his short-story collections: 'It isn't for the glory of the thing, you understand; and anyhow criticism as done in the daily press is of not much use to one; but all the same it is sometimes possible to get a hint of what pleases the general public and I am adaptable enough to profit by it'.[19]

Conrad's attempts to find a voice which would please the public, combined with the sense that he was prostituting himself, account for the forked quality of many stories, in which he uses the conventions of the adventure-romance to anatomize that very genre.[20] While Maupassant and Flaubert were important models, Conrad also admitted to a genuine fondness for the popular romantic fiction of his childhood: he had felt 'enslaved' by the novels of Captain Marryat; the sea stories of Victor Hugo and Fenimore Cooper and accounts of African, Pacific, and polar explorers had bored into his childhood consciousness. Conrad's own contemporaries also offered significant models of the exotic adventure-romance: Ian Watt lists Stevenson, Kipling, Rider Haggard, Louis Becke, and Carlton Dawes.[21] But as in both 'An Anarchist' and 'The Informer', Conrad highlights and questions the very process of exoticization, of creating an other who is interesting or desirable for his or her otherness.

[17] Graver, *Conrad's Shorter Fiction*, 168–9.   [18] *Letters*, v. 322.
[19] Ibid. iv. 102.
[20] Andrea White's study, *Joseph Conrad and the Adventure Tradition: Constructing and Deconstructing the Imperial Subject* (Cambridge: Cambridge University Press, 1993), is one of the most recent to elaborate this idea.
[21] *Conrad in the Nineteenth Century* (Berkeley: University of California Press, 1979), 43.

'The Lagoon' is very much within the exotic tradition. One of the world's oldest and most widespread stories is that of the young couple who decide to marry against their parents' wishes. Since in so many cultures marriage is about family property rather than individual desire, this romance motif can be read as fundamentally subversive of the *status quo*. The young couple, by choosing for themselves, deny the foundations of their society: that those who hold the property decide propriety. In 'The Lagoon', Arsat falls in love with Diamelen, the servant of the powerful Inchi Midah. 'There is a time when a man should forget loyalty and respect,' Arsat tells the white man who is listening to his story (p. 34); so, with his brother's help, he elopes with Diamelen, and the lovers find a place far from their ruler's anger. There, time seems to stop—even the forest is 'bewitched into an immobility perfect and final' (p. 27).

Henry Rider Haggard's *She* was published a decade before 'The Lagoon' and set the standard for the exotic romance. Haggard's immortal Ayesha lives in the land of Kôr, waiting for the fulfilment of her love. For her, time has halted until she is reunited with her beloved. But her apparent death at the end of the novel suggests that the material world prevails over the ideal. The conclusion of 'The Lagoon' implies something similar: Diamelen is dead, the trees and creepers of the jungle are stirring again, and Arsat is thinking about returning to the world to avenge his brother. When Diamelen was alive and their love was everything to them, the material world simply suspended the business of living and dying. But Arsat had to pay a price: to turn away from the social relationships with ruler and brother that generated his sense of self and manhood. The narrative suggests that love pulls a man out of the world of action where he truly fulfils himself. Marlow in *Heart of Darkness*, speaks of the importance of work: 'the chance to find yourself. Your own reality—for yourself, not for others'. Some readers have seen the ending of the short story—Arsat staring beyond the little world of the lagoon—as suggesting the possibility of redemption with the return to the everyday realm of making and doing. But Conrad describes him as looking 'into the hopeless darkness of the world' (p. 40). A world without hope does not suggest much chance of redemption. Is the world of manly honour and action truly superior to the realm of romance? In the later novella, Conrad takes us to the heart of the hopeless darkness, and again the forest will be silent and unmoving. But Kurtz's evil comes from idealism freed to fulfil itself far from the restraints of western daily life.

Conrad returned to the theme of reality and romance in a much later story, 'Prince Roman'. As a small boy, the narrator met the aged Prince Roman. He knew that the Prince came of an ancient and powerful line of Polish magnates. 'But what concerned me most was the failure of the fairy tale glamour. It was shocking to discover a prince who was deaf, bald, meagre, and so prodigiously old' (p. 159). Two different narrative traditions have collided: the princes of history are set against those of fairy-tale lore, men who do not live in this world and therefore do not grow old. The Prince's spell in fairyland ended with the premature death of his wife. Whereas Arsat's love forces him against his ruler and draws his brother into mortal danger, Prince Roman's marriage was approved by both his Polish family and the Russian noble establishment. But Poland was under the heel of Russia, so following his family's wishes meant compromising with the enemy. The death of Prince Roman's beloved wife 'removed the brilliant bandage of happiness from his eyes' (p. 166), and he finally joins his countrymen when they rise up against the wicked Tzar of Russia. At that point, he seems to come out of mourning and rejoin the world, where he recreates an identity for himself. In his rebirth, he becomes a common soldier, as if to acknowledge the authority of his national history over the compromised princely narrative that brought him his other-worldly marriage.

Prince Roman is an admirable man: he now devotes his life to the welfare of his neighbours and returned exiles. But the narrator's childish memory of the aged man lingers with the reader, and Conrad leaves us with the judgement of Roman's daughter, who considers her father too much guided by sentiment to be a good judge of men, as if he had learned nothing in the world of action and had spent his entire life in the realm of romance where princes were good and people were what they seemed.

'To-morrow', a middle-period story which Conrad wrote with the popular magazine market in mind, also casts a quizzical eye on the very tradition within which it seems to be operating. Captain Hagberd has not seen or heard from his son, Harry, for years. He expects him tomorrow, however. In the mean time, like an eccentric old patriarch, he is planning a marriage between his son and his neighbour's daughter, with due transfer of property. He knows that she will make his son a good wife because he sees her wait hand and foot on her blind father. The story turns upside-down when someone calling himself Harry Hagberd arrives. He is full of sailors' tales and the glamour of the exotic places he has visited. All seems to be working out well in that Bessie is falling in love with the man it is planned she will marry.

The interesting element of the story lies in Captain Hagberd's reaction to the young man. The reader is persuaded that Harry is who he claims to be, but the Captain will not acknowledge him. He has so exoticized his son that his prodigality is now what appeals to him: the exotic, the prodigal, will cease to be such when it is domesticated. In this, father and son see eye to eye, and Harry's attitude to Bessie changes when he learns that she was intended for him —she has become a domestic entrapment, altogether at odds with his own exotic view of himself.

Harry is not prepared to give up his self-narrative. In 'Il Conde',[22] on the other hand, we read of another man like Paul the 'anarchist', who allows his story to be narrated. Indeed, he seems to be living out that famous instance of civic boosterism: 'see Naples and die'. At face value, the story concerns a man of patrician refinement who is overwhelmed by the voice of the Neapolitan underworld—a parallel to Conrad and the popular magazines. However, as is so often the case in these stories, all is not necessarily what it seems.

[22] The title, which means 'The Count', is itself a hybrid of Italian (*il*) and Spanish (*conde*).

By the Count's own telling, a young man tried to rob him and then called him names when he found the old man had accidentally held back some money. The narrator reads the story as being about the irruption of the vulgar and brutal into the Count's elegant life, an event that causes a haemorrhaging of the sensibilities. The Count has been visiting Italy for many years and regards it as essential for his health. Now suddenly the picturesque and sustaining has become dangerous: the beasts have emerged from the jungle. But what if the Count meant to leave his gold watch and most of his money in a safe place, if he had in mind an encounter with a prostitute, of whichever sex, and was taking sensible precautions? If he did intend more than some music and a stroll in the gardens of the Villa Nazionale, then the awfulness of his experience comes from having it more or less correctly labelled—accurately told. *Almayer's Folly*, *An Outcast of the Islands*, *Heart of Darkness* all chronicle the sexual appeal and the danger of the exotic. That the Count's health will suffer in the north is not in question—he will not live much longer, but it may also be true that he cannot live there the kind of emotional and sexual life that he desires. The forbidden grants him life, yet it must not be spoken. 'Life' is very much a double-voiced word.

In all four stories, the conflict is between the attraction of the familiar and domestic on the one hand and of the variously exotic on the other, but the narratives do not offer clear choices. Arsat's dilemma is that he loves Diamelen and wants her to be as much a part of him as is his brother, but much of her appeal presumably lies in her being forbidden to him; Prince Roman's choice is between Russia and his native Poland, but his own parents urge accommodation with the Russian court; while the Count is not a native of Italy, he must live there for his health, attracted yet repelled by the natives; Captain Hagberd both wants and does not want his son to return—he is locked into a narrative of eternal deferral. As long as tomorrow is never today, time is at a standstill as it was for Arsat and Diamelen, for Prince Roman and his wife, for the dying Count in Italy.

Conrad's last story, 'The Tale', returns to the same issues: the exotic and the domestic, the self and the other, and the role of narrative. The difference is that this story was topical, as it was written and published during World War I. Its protagonist is neither foreign nor eccentric, but an officer in the British naval reserve. While on coastal patrol, he comes upon a neutral ship which he suspects may have been resupplying a German submarine. At this stage in the war, German predation on the British merchant fleet was so severe that the nation's ability to continue the war came into question. Conrad highlights the conflict between one's own and the alien. The question is whether a neutral captain is truly neutral or effectively German and, therefore, wholly other. We are never certain of the answer, and much of the story is an account of how the protagonist reaches his decision.

The tale is elaborately framed. A third-person narrator tells of two lovers. The woman asks the man to tell her a story, and he begins a narrative about a Commander and a Northman. By the end of the account it is clear that he is the Commander. The very titles he uses suggest a simple story of 'us' and 'them', of good and evil, yet such black-and-white morality turns to grey before our eyes. It is hard not to conclude that the Commander sent a possibly innocent man and his crew to their deaths. Readers of the time could have satisfied themselves with the thought that the submarine threat was so serious that any means of overcoming it were acceptable. Such would have been the popular voice. But international opinion had turned against the Germans for sinking neutral shipping and attacking passenger liners carrying civilians—the loss of 139 American lives with the sinking of the *Lusitania* in May 1915 did much to turn American opinion against Germany. The Commander of Conrad's story appears, in effect, to have followed the policy advocated by the leaders of the German navy. He becomes what he is struggling against, so again we see the dark attraction of the exotic. The man is finally a moral hybrid.

'The Tale' appeared in the *Strand Magazine*, probably the most popular of all the British periodicals. Conrad must have been well pleased to see such a story in such a magazine.

But what of the tale's first audience? We do not learn what the nameless woman of the narrative makes of her lover's account, but the 'coercion to speak', as Aaron Fogel puts it,[23] is a mark of her authority, the authority of the interrogator or the confessor. When questioned by Kurtz's fiancée at the end of *Heart of Darkness*, written almost twenty years earlier, Marlow had prevaricated and not told her the truth about Kurtz; it was, he explained to his listeners, altogether too dark for her to hear. Perhaps 'the Intended' would have revealed herself as less tender-minded than Marlow thought. The woman of the later story certainly seems able to look at the complicated truth without blinking, and at the end of the narrative she puts her arms around the man's neck, offering absolution in love. But the Commander responds coldly, as if the mixing of the domestic and the worldly, the romantic and the practical, had shrivelled up their love. The Commander, like Marlow before him, is the true idealist, believing it possible to separate principles from actions. A morality which is not frequently and openly tested in the world is as unreal as that which Marlow projected upon the women of his story.

The nineteenth-century notion of the separation of spheres had placed women securely in the domestic realm, which was represented as a haven for men after their daily business in the world of action: a woman's place was supposed to be in the home, and those who refused to accept their sphere were regarded as unruly and dangerous. The moral of 'The Tale' might be that women should not even enquire into the worldly activities of men. But had his lover not insisted on the story, the Commander would not have been forced to make explicit just how equivocal his action was. Thus the domestic sphere is set to interrogate the public realm, and it is interesting to see that the woman is better able to deal with the result than is the man.

But Conrad is no gender essentialist. Not all his female characters are tough-minded realists. They are a varied group,

[23] *Coercion to Speak: Conrad's Poetics of Dialogue* (Cambridge, Mass.: Harvard University Press, 1985).

as one would expect from a man so sceptical of all theory. In *Almayer's Folly*, his first work of fiction, Conrad represents Almayer's Malay wife as a sort of Spartan mother, advising her daughter to hand her young husband his knife and send him off to war. Almost a quarter of a century later, in 'The Warrior's Soul', Conrad writes about a similar woman; this one, a leading figure of French salon society, functions as a kind of high priestess of the warrior faith. The story concerns the collision between ideal warfare and the reality of the French retreat from Moscow in 1812.

'The Lagoon' was about a love-match. 'The Idiots', a story from the same year, tells of a peasant farmer in Brittany who decides that he needs a wife; in the next paragraph he and Susan are entering the farm gates. This hard-headed approach to marriage contrasts with the story of Arsat and Diamelen, but it affords no more happiness. Susan is no exotic, and it is her husband's all too domestic desire that leads to disaster. She is an instance of a domestic figure who, denied authority, becomes dangerous. The gypsy woman of 'The Inn of the Two Witches' is both exotic and menacing. Yet she and the two old women of the title use an item charged with domestic sexuality to do violence. 'The Brute' concerns another domestic peril: an uncontrollable ship which 'kills' at least one crewman on every voyage. The vessel was built with comfort and safety in mind, so it is more like a house than a ship: one of the background characters tells us more than once that it carried an ugly house on its deck. The feminine personal pronoun is traditionally used to refer to ships, so the ship is like a woman, but one who carries her domesticity with her rather than lives within a stationary domestic sphere.

'Laughing Anne' is perhaps the most thoroughgoing of Conrad's reversals of expectation. One assumes that Anne was at one time or another a prostitute, but Hollis, the narrator, says that she 'was ready to stick to any half-decent man if he would only let her' (p. 210). Hers really is a sad story because she wanted to be a good little Victorian wife, but she evidently 'fell', so respectable wifehood was not possible. Conrad developed the idea behind the story both here and in the novel *Victory*, although Lena, the novel's female protagonist, is merely poised at the top of the slippery slope. Each woman saves the male protagonist's life and dies in the process. The short story introduces an element absent from the novel: Davidson's wife, a domestic figure to balance the unruly Anne. Davidson adores his wife, but she is revealed at the end as a mean-spirited domestic tyrant. She refuses to look after Anne's orphan and, believing her husband to have been the father, returns to Australia. When the child grows up, he wants to become a Catholic priest, as if to repudiate domesticity and all its ills.

Conrad's tendency to represent the domestic sphere as perilous may well derive from the fact that as a sailor and an expatriate he would have found English women and their world unfamiliar and alien. Furthermore, he must have known that those he came to live amongst regarded him as exotic. The very word 'exotic' was thus double-accented, hybridized: he was a foreigner in England, yet everyone whom he knew was a foreigner to him. Conrad learned in the bone what it meant to assign and be assigned a label, so the process is always deeply problematic in his works—Nostromo literally means 'our man', but who are the implied 'we'? Characters like Kurtz, Jim, or Razumov change shape as they glide between narrative perspectives. There is the same polyvocality in the short stories—anarchists who are police spies and fanatics, fallen women who are good, British officers who behave like the enemy. Bringing unity to our responses can be like herding cats. Conrad's hybridity consists not in an amalgam of his selves but in a number of identities held together in parallel or in series, never quite speaking as one. The energy that holds them together also keeps them from fusing into a single, unequivocal persona. For each authoritative voice in a story, there is another, explicit or implicit, that denies its authority.

NOTE ON THE TEXTS

This collection consists of Conrad's dozen shortest narratives.[1] Seven of the stories fall into three groups. 'The Idiots' and 'The Lagoon' were written in Brittany in 1896 while Conrad was on his honeymoon. He published *An Outcast of the Islands* in the same year and *The Nigger of the Narcissus* in the next. 'An Anarchist', 'The Informer', and 'The Brute' were written between December 1905 and February 1906 and form a group with *The Secret Agent* (the novel and 'The Informer' even share a character, the Professor), which was published in 1907. 'The Warrior's Soul' and 'The Tale' were both written in 1916. The other stories date from various times in Conrad's career.

Conrad's practice was to publish each story in a London or New York magazine—both if possible—and then to collect about half a dozen in a single volume. This is the form in which the stories are known because standard editorial practice gives priority to the author's preferred version of any text; but in recent years many scholars have come to regard texts as almost communal entities. These stories were written for the popular market, so the decision to present them here in their earliest published form gives the nod to the popular aesthetic. The magazine versions of the stories have not been republished in a collection before.

Conrad would always make some revisions for the book collections. These are seldom more than second thoughts on word choice, and on the whole the book versions are a little more verbose. There are major revisions in five of the stories: 'The Lagoon', 'An Anarchist', 'The Inn of the Two Witches', 'Laughing Anne', and 'The Tale'. The revisions are indicated below. All spellings have been brought back into line with British practice, a few conventions of punctuation changed to house style, and obvious misprints silently corrected. Otherwise the texts are as they originally appeared.

[1] A thirteenth, 'An Outpost of Progress', is already available in Oxford World's Classics—see *Typhoon and Other Stories*.

'The Idiots'

Finished May 1896. First published in the *Savoy* (London), October 1896. Republished in *Tales of Unrest*, 1898. Conrad's first short story to appear in print. Arthur Symons, the editor, particularly admired the vague suggestiveness of Conrad's style. The *Savoy* was associated with the Decadents and Symbolists, and Conrad seems to have felt uncomfortable in such company. He would have preferred to publish elsewhere, but the story had been rejected three times by 'safer' magazines, so he let it go.

'The Lagoon'

Written August 1896. Published in the *Cornhill* (London), January 1897. Reprinted in *Tales of Unrest*, 1898, with the final sentence amended to: 'He stood lonely in the searching sunshine; and he looked beyond the great light of a cloudless day into the darkness of a world of illusions.'

'To-morrow'

Completed 16 February 1902. Published in the *Pall Mall Magazine* (London), August 1902. Republished in *Typhoon, and Other Stories*, 1903. In 1904 Conrad transformed the story into a one-act play entitled *One Day More*. It had a run of five performances the following year.

'An Anarchist'

Completed December 1905. First published in *Harper's Monthly Magazine* (New York), August 1906. Republished in *A Set of Six*, 1908, with the sixth paragraph cut.

'The Informer'

Written 27 December 1905–1 January 1906. First published in *Harper's Monthly Magazine* (New York), December 1906. Republished in *A Set of Six*, 1908.

'The Brute'

Written January–February 1906. Published in the Christmas number of the *Daily Chronicle* (London), 1906, and *McClure's Magazine* (New York), November 1907. Republished in *A Set of Six*, 1908. The *McClure's* text is used here.

'Il Conde'

Completed early December 1906. Published in *Cassell's Magazine* (London), August 1908, and *Hampton's Magazine* (New York), February 1909. Republished in *A Set of Six*, 1908.

'Prince Roman'

Based on an episode in the memoirs of Conrad's uncle and foster-parent, Tadeusz Bobrowski; see also Conrad's own memoir, *A Personal Record* (1912), chapter 2. A draft was ready by December 1908; completed and sent to his agent in September 1910. Published in the *Oxford and Cambridge Review* (London), October 1911 and, under the title 'The Aristocrat', in the *Metropolitan Magazine* (New York), January 1912. Republished in *Tales of Hearsay*, 1925.

The 'old adherent's' bits of Latin were corrupted in Doubleday's edition of *Tales of Hearsay* (1925): *affulget patriæ serenitas* became *affulget patride serenitas* and *Eripit verba dolor* became *Cripit verba dolor*. These errors were preserved in the major editions, including Dent (1946–55). Doubleday and Dent amend *ordonnance* to *ordnance*, but this does not help much since it now suggests that Prince Roman was an artillery officer rather than an aide-de-camp (see note to p. 163).

'The Inn of the Two Witches'

Written December 1912. Published in the *Pall Mall Magazine* (London), March 1913, and *Metropolitan Magazine* (New York), May 1913. Republished in *Within the Tides*, 1915. Conrad added sixty-four words to the first paragraph in the version in *Within the Tides*, between 'a romantic view of themselves' and 'I suppose it was the romanticism':

Their very failures exhale a charm of peculiar potency. And indeed the hopes of the future are a fine company to live with, exquisite forms, fascinating if you like, but—so to speak—naked, stripped for a run. The robes of glamour are luckily the property of the immovable past which, without them, would sit, a shivery sort of thing, under the gathering shadows.

Forty-eight words were added to the third paragraph, after 'the Find declared in the sub-title':

The title itself is my own contrivance (can't call it invention), and has the merit of veracity. We will be concerned with an inn here. As to the witches that's merely a conventional expression, and we must take our man's word for it that it fits the case.

'Laughing Anne'

In May 1912 Conrad began writing a story with the working title 'Dollars'. In due course it bifurcated into the novel *Victory* (published 1915) and the short story 'Laughing Anne' (completed 8 January 1914), which was published by the *Metropolitan Magazine* in September 1914 and republished as 'Because of the Dollars' in *Within the Tides*, 1915. Although Conrad disliked the magazine title, his friend R. B. Cunninghame Graham still referred to the story as 'Laughing Anne' in his obituary essay on Conrad.

The title 'Because of the Dollars' was possibly suggested by a play written in 1857–8 by Apollo Korzeniowski, Conrad's father, called *Dla miłego grosza* (For the Sake of Money). While money functions as a social contaminant in both narratives, the plots bear no resemblance to each other. In 1921 Conrad adapted the story as a two-act play, now entitled *Laughing Anne*. 'Because of the Dollars', the version published in *Within the Tides*, is about two thousand words (20 per cent) longer than the story printed here.

'The Warrior's Soul'

Suggested by an anecdote in the memoirs of Philippe de Ségur; see also Conrad's own memoir, *A Personal Record* (1912), chapter 2. Written February–March 1916. Conrad sent the story to his agent at the end of April 1916, calling it 'The Humane Tomassov'. Published in *Land and Water*, 29 March 1917. Republished in *Tales of Hearsay*, 1925.

'The Tale'

Conrad's last short story. Completed 30 October 1916. Published in the *Strand Magazine*, October 1917. Republished in *Tales of Hearsay*, 1925, with the fifth paragraph cut.

Conrad has not been particularly well served by textual scholars. There is still no complete scholarly edition, although Cambridge University Press is in the process of bringing out a scholarly collected works, complete with variants. At present the situation is bewildering. The most widely cited edition is probably *The Collected Edition of the Works of Joseph Conrad* (21 vols.; London: Dent, 1946–55); but readers also have available Dent's Uniform Edition of 1923–8, and two or three collected editions published by Doubleday in the 1920s. In addition, there are excellent editions by Oxford, Penguin, Norton, and others.

SELECT BIBLIOGRAPHY

The secondary literature on Conrad is very extensive, so this bibliography is indeed selective. I have included the works cited in the introduction and notes, the major sources for the notes, and some recent studies and articles that discuss the stories in this collection.

Biography

Baines, Jocelyn, *Joseph Conrad: A Critical Biography* (New York: McGraw-Hill, 1960).

Karl, Frederick R., *Joseph Conrad: The Three Lives* (New York: Farrar, 1979).

Meyers, Jeffrey, *Joseph Conrad: A Biography* (New York: Charles Scribner's Sons, 1991).

Najder, Zdzislaw, *Joseph Conrad: A Chronicle* (New Brunswick, NJ: Rutgers University Press, 1983).

Letters

Karl, Frederick R. and Davies, Laurence, eds., *The Collected Letters of Joseph Conrad*, vols. 1–5 (Cambridge: Cambridge University Press, 1983–96).

Criticism and Background

Ambrosiani, Richard, *Conrad's Fiction as Critical Discourse* (Cambridge: Cambridge University Press, 1991).

Bakhtin, M. M., *The Dialogic Imagination: Four Essays*, ed. Michael Holquist, trans. Caryl Emerson and Michael Holquist (Austin, Tex.: University of Texas Press, 1981).

Bonney, William W., *Thorns & Arabesques: Context for Conrad's Fiction* (Baltimore: Johns Hopkins University Press, 1980).

Busza, Andrzej, *Conrad's Polish Literary Background and Some Illustrations of the Influence of Polish Literature on His Work*, *Antemurale* (Rome), 10 (1966).

Erdinast-Vulcan, Daphna, *Joseph Conrad and the Modern Temper* (Oxford: Clarendon Press, 1991).

Fogel, Aaron, *Coercion to Speak: Conrad's Poetics of Dialogue* (Cambridge, Mass.: Harvard University Press, 1985).

Graver, Lawrence, *Conrad's Shorter Fiction* (Berkeley: University of California Press, 1969).

Hampson, Robert, *Joseph Conrad: Betrayal and Identity* (New York: St Martin's Press, 1992).

Henricksen, Bruce, *Nomadic Voices: Conrad and the Subject of Narrative* (Urbana, Ill.: University of Illinois Press, 1992).

Lothe, Jakob, *Conrad's Narrative Method* (Oxford: Clarendon Press, 1989).

Nadelhaft, Ruth L., *Joseph Conrad* (Atlantic Highlands, NJ: Humanities Press International, 1991).

Oliver, H., *The International Anarchist Movement in Late Victorian London* (London: Croom Helm, 1983).

Raval, Suresh, *The Art of Failure: Conrad's Fiction* (Boston: Allen & Unwin, 1986).

Sherry, Norman, *Conrad's Western World* (Cambridge: Cambridge University Press, 1971).

Spittles, Brian, *Joseph Conrad: Text and Context* (New York: St Martin's Press, 1992).

Watt, Ian, *Conrad in the Nineteenth Century* (Berkeley: University of California Press, 1979).

Watts, Cedric, *Joseph Conrad: A Literary Life* (New York: St Martin's Press, 1989).

White, Andrea, *Joseph Conrad and the Adventure Tradition: Constructing and Deconstructing the Imperial Subject* (Cambridge: Cambridge University Press, 1993).

Wollaeger, Mark A., *Joseph Conrad and the Fictions of Skepticism* (Stanford, Calif.: Stanford University Press, 1990).

Woodcock, George, *Anarchism: A History of Libertarian Ideas and Movements* (Cleveland, Oh.: Meridian, 1962).

Young, Robert J. C., *Colonial Desire: Hybridity in Theory, Culture and Race* (London and New York: Routledge, 1995).

Articles

D'Elia, Gaetano, 'Let us Make Tales, Not Love: Conrad's "The Tale"', *Conradian*, 12/1 (1987), 50–8.

Erdinast-Vulcan, Daphna, 'Where does the Joke Come in?: Ethics and Aesthetics in Conrad's "The Informer"', *L'Époque conradienne*, 19 (1993), 37–46.

Gillon, Adam, 'Conrad's Satirical Stance in *Under Western Eyes*: Two Strange Bedfellows—Prince Roman and Peter Ivanovitch', *Conradiana*, 18 (1986), 119–28.

Hinchcliffe, Peter, 'Fidelity and Complicity in Kipling and Conrad: "Sea Constables" and "The Tale"', *English Studies in Canada*, 9 (1983), 350–62.

Hobson, Robert W., and Pfeiffer, William S., 'Conrad's First Story and the *Savoy*: Typescript Revisions of "The Idiots"', *Studies in Short Fiction*, 18 (1981), 267–72.

Hollywood, Paul, 'Conrad and Anarchist Theories of Language', in Keith Carabine, Owen Knowles, and Wiesław Krajka, eds., *Contexts for Conrad* (*Conrad: Eastern and Western Perspectives*, vol. ii; Boulder, Colo.: East European Monographs, distributed New York: Columbia University Press, 1993), 243–63.

Nelson, Ronald J., 'Conrad's "The Lagoon"', *Explicator*, 40/1 (1981), 39–41.

Ruppel, Richard, ' "The Lagoon" and the Popular Exotic Tradition', in Keith Carabine, Owen Knowles, and Wiesław Krajka, eds., *Contexts for Conrad* (*Conrad: Eastern and Western Perspectives*, vol. ii; Boulder, Colo.: East European Monographs, distributed New York: Columbia University Press, 1993), 177–87.

Rivoallan, Anatole, 'Joseph Conrad and Brittany', *Conradian*, 8/2 (1983), 14–18.

Richardson, Donna, 'Art of Darkness: Imagery in Conrad's "The Lagoon"', *Studies in Short Fiction*, 27 (1990), 247–55.

Said, Edward, 'Conrad: The Presentation of Narrative', in *The World, the Text, and the Critic* (Cambridge, Mass.: Harvard University Press, 1983).

Shaddock, Jennifer, 'Hanging a Dog: The Politics of Naming in "An Anarchist"', *Conradiana*, 26 (1994), 56–69.

Williams, Porter, 'Story and Frame in Conrad's "The Tale"', *Studies in Short Fiction*, 5 (1968), 179–85.

A CHRONOLOGY OF
JOSEPH CONRAD

1857 (3 Dec.) Born Józef Teodor Konrad Korzeniowski, of Polish parents in Berdyczow (Berdichev) in the Polish Ukraine. Family moves almost immediately to Terechowa.

1861 (Oct.) Korzeniowskis move to Warsaw. Conrad's father, the poet and translator Apollo Korzeniowski, arrested by the Russian authorities for patriotic conspiracy.

1862 (May) Parents sentenced to exile. Family leaves for Vologda, Russia, in June.

1865 (Apr.) Conrad's mother, Ewa, dies.

1868 (Feb.) Moves with his father to Lwów in Austrian Poland.

1869 (Feb.) Moves with his father to Kraków (Cracow). (May) Apollo Korzeniowski dies. Conrad's uncle, Tadeusz Bobrowski, becomes his guardian.

1874 Leaves Poland for Marseilles to become a trainee seaman with the French merchant marine.

1876 As a 'steward' on the *Sainte-Antoine*, becomes acquainted with Dominic Cervoni (who appears in *The Mirror of the Sea*, *A Personal Record*, and *The Arrow of Gold*, and who is a source for Nostromo and for Peyrol in *The Rover*).

1877 Possibly involved in smuggling arms from Marseilles to the 'Carlists' (Spanish royalists).

1878 (Mar.) Shoots himself in the chest in Marseilles but is not seriously injured; as a direct result of this suicide attempt, Conrad's uncle clears his debts. (Apr.) The Russian consul refuses to extend Conrad's passport as he is liable for Russian military service. Forbidden to remain in France, he joins his first British ship, the *Mavis*. (July) Joins another British ship, the *Skimmer of the Sea*.

1886 (Aug.) Becomes a British subject. (Nov.) Passes the examination for Ordinary Master of the British merchant marine.

1887 Spends time in a hospital in Singapore with an injury sustained on the *Highland Forest*. Begins to become acquainted with the Malay Archipelago as an officer of the *Vidar*.

1888 Master of the barque *Otago*, his only command. (The *Otago* voyages provided a basis for 'Falk', 'The Secret Sharer', *The Shadow-Line*, and 'A Smile of Fortune'.)

1889 Resigns from the *Otago*, settles briefly in London, and begins to write *Almayer's Folly*. Begins a lasting friendship with Marguerite Poradowska.

1890 Works in the Belgian Congo for the Société Anonyme pour le Commerce du Haut-Congo.

1891 Begins his most pleasant experience at sea, as first mate on board the passenger clipper *Torrens*.

1892 Still the first mate of the *Torrens*, Conrad meets John Galsworthy, who is among the passengers and becomes a loyal friend.

1893 (Autumn) Meets Jessie George.

1894 (Jan.) Leaves his last position as a seaman. (Feb.) Death of Tadeusz Bobrowski. (Apr.) Finishes the draft of *Almayer's Folly*. (Oct.) *Almayer's Folly* accepted by Unwin. Meets Edward Garnett, Unwin's reader and an influential literary friend.

1895 *Almayer's Folly* published; adopts 'Joseph Conrad' as his pen-name.

1896 *An Outcast of the Islands* published. Becomes acquainted with H. G. Wells. Begins work on *The Rescue* and initiates correspondence with Henry James. (24 Mar.) Marries Jessie George.

1897 Corresponds with R. B. Cunninghame Graham (to be a close friend and a source for Gould in *Nostromo*). *The Nigger of the 'Narcissus'* published. Meets Henry James.

1898 Borys Conrad born. *Tales of Unrest* ('Karain', 'The Idiots', 'An Outpost of Progress', 'The Return', 'The Lagoon') published. Begins collaboration with Ford Madox Hueffer (later F. M. Ford) and takes over from him the lease of a Kent farmhouse, 'The Pent', near Ashford. Beginning of a friendship with Stephen Crane.

1899 'Heart of Darkness' finished and serialized in *Blackwood's Magazine*. J. B. Pinker becomes Conrad's literary agent. *Lord Jim* begins to be serialized in *Blackwood's*.

1900 *Lord Jim* published as a book. Stephen Crane dies. Conrad receives *The Bobrowski Memoirs*—a probable source for 'Prince Roman'—shortly before publication.

1901 *The Inheritors* (a collaboration with Ford) published.

1902 *Youth: A Narrative; and Two Other Stories* ('Youth', 'Heart of Darkness', 'The End of the Tether') published. *Typhoon* published in New York.

1903 *Typhoon and Other Stories* ('Typhoon', 'Amy Foster', 'Falk', 'To-morrow') and *Romance* (a collaboration with Ford) published. Nevertheless, Conrad's indebtedness to his agent, Pinker, continues to increase.

1904 Jessie Conrad injures her knees and is partially disabled for life. *Nostromo* published.

1905 Writes 'Autocracy and War'.

1906 Meets Arthur Marwood, who becomes a close friend. John Conrad born. *The Mirror of the Sea* published.

1907 The Conrads move to The Someries, Luton Hoo. *The Secret Agent* published.

1908 *A Set of Six* ('Gaspar Ruiz', 'The Informer', 'The Brute', 'An Anarchist', 'The Duel', 'Il Conde') published.

1909 Quarrels with Ford over his contribution to the *English Review*. The Conrads move to a cottage at Aldington, near 'The Pent'.

1910 Completion of *Under Western Eyes* accompanied by a nervous breakdown; Conrad lies in bed holding 'converse with the characters' of the novel. On his recovery the Conrads move to Capel House, Orlestone, Kent.

1911 *Under Western Eyes* published.

1912 *Some Reminiscences*, later renamed *A Personal Record*, appears in book form. *'Twixt Land and Sea* ('A Smile of Fortune', 'The Secret Sharer', 'Freya of the Seven Isles') published. *Chance* serialized in the *New York Herald*.

1913 *Chance* published as a book.

1914 *Chance* has very good sales, especially in America; the earlier works now find a larger public. The Conrads visit Poland and are trapped there for a few weeks by the outbreak of the war.

1915 *Within the Tides* ('The Planter of Malata', 'The Partner', 'The Inn of the Two Witches') and *Victory* published.

1917 *The Shadow-Line* published. Conrad begins to write 'Author's Notes' for a collected edition of his works.

1919 *The Arrow of Gold* published. The Conrads move to Oswalds, Bishopsbourne, near Canterbury.

1920 *The Rescue* published, twenty-four years after it was begun.

1921 Visit to Corsica for research on *Suspense*. Conrad in poor health. *Notes on Life and Letters* published.

1923 Conrad visits America and is lionized. *The Rover* published.

1924 (May) Declines the offer of a knighthood. (3 Aug.) Dies of a heart attack at Oswalds. Buried at Canterbury. *The Nature of a Crime* (a collaboration with Ford) published.

1925 *Tales of Hearsay* ('The Warrior's Soul', 'Prince Roman', 'The Tale', 'The Black Mate') and *Suspense* (an unfinished novel) published.

1926 *Last Essays* published.

1928 *The Sisters* (a fragment) published.

THE LAGOON
AND OTHER STORIES

THE IDIOTS

WE were driving along the road from Treguier to Kervanda. We passed at a smart trot between the hedges topping an earth wall on each side of the road; then at the foot of the steep ascent before Ploumar* the horse dropped into a walk, and the driver jumped down heavily from the box. He flicked his whip and climbed the incline, stepping clumsily uphill by the side of the carriage, one hand on the footboard, his eyes on the ground. After a while he lifted his head, pointed up the road with the end of the whip, and said—

'The idiot!'

The sun was shining violently upon the undulating surface of the land. The rises were topped by clumps of meagre trees, with their branches showing high on the sky as if they had been perched upon stilts. The small fields, cut up by hedges and stone walls that zigzagged over the slopes, lay in rectangular patches of vivid greens and yellows, resembling the unskilful daubs of a naïve picture. And the landscape was divided in two by the white streak of a road stretching in long loops far away, like a river of dust crawling out of the hills on its way to the sea.

'Here he is,' said the driver, again.

In the long grass bordering the road a face glided past the carriage at the level of the wheels as we drove slowly by. The imbecile face was red, and the bullet head with close-cropped hair seemed to lie alone, its chin in the dust. The body was lost in the bushes growing thick along the bottom of the deep ditch.

It was a boy's face. He might have been sixteen, judging from the size—perhaps less, perhaps more. Such creatures are forgotten by time, and live untouched by years till death gathers them up into its compassionate bosom: the faithful death that never forgets in the press of work the most insignificant of its children.

'Ah! There's another,' said the man, with a certain satisfaction in his tone, as if he had caught sight of something expected.

There was another. That one stood nearly in the middle of the road in the blaze of sunshine at the end of his own short shadow. And he stood with hands pushed into the opposite sleeves of his long coat, his head sunk between the shoulders, all hunched up in the flood of heat. From a distance he had the aspect of one suffering from intense cold.

'Those are twins,' explained the driver.

The idiot shuffled two paces out of the way and looked at us over his shoulder when we brushed past him. The glance was unseeing and staring, a fascinated glance; but he did not turn to look after us. Probably the image passed before the eyes without leaving any trace on the misshapen brain of the creature. When we had topped the ascent I looked over the hood. He stood in the road just where we had left him.

The driver clambered into his seat, clicked his tongue, and we went down hill. The brake squeaked horribly from time to time. At the foot he eased off the noisy mechanism and said, turning half round on his box:

'We shall see some more of them by-and-by.'

'More idiots? How many of them are there, then?' I asked.

'There's four of them—children of a farmer near Ploumar here. . . . The parents are dead now,' he added, after a while. 'The grandmother lives on the farm. In the daytime they knock about on this road, and they come home at dusk along with the cattle. . . . It's a good farm.'

We saw the other two: a boy and a girl, as the driver said. They were dressed exactly alike, in shapeless garments with petticoat-like skirts. The imperfect thing that lived within them moved those beings to howl at us from the top of the bank, where they sprawled amongst the tough stalks of furze. Their cropped black heads stuck out from the bright yellow wall of countless small blossoms. The faces were purple with the strain of yelling; the voices sounded blank and cracked like a mechanical imitation of old people's voices; and suddenly ceased when we turned into a lane.

I saw them many times in my wanderings about the country. They lived on that road, drifting along its length here and there, according to the inexplicable impulses of their monstrous darkness. They were an offence to the sunshine, a reproach to empty heaven, a blight on the concentrated and purposeful vigour of the wild landscape. In time the story of their parents shaped itself before me out of the listless answers to my questions, out of the indifferent words heard in wayside inns or on the very road those idiots haunted. Some of it was told by an emaciated and sceptical old fellow with a tremendous whip, while we trudged together over the sands by the side of a two-wheeled cart loaded with dripping seaweed. Then at other times other people confirmed and completed the story: till it stood at last before me, a tale formidable and simple, as they always are, those disclosures of obscure trials endured by ignorant hearts.

When he returned from his military service Jean-Pierre Bacadou found the old people very much aged. He remarked with pain that the work of the farm was not satisfactorily done. The father had not the energy of old days. The hands did not feel over them the eye of the master. Jean-Pierre noted with sorrow that the heap of manure in the courtyard before the only entrance to the house was not so large as it should have been. The fences were out of repair, and the cattle suffered from neglect. At home the mother was practically bedridden, and the girls chattered loudly in the big kitchen, unrebuked, from morning to night. He said to himself: 'We must change all this.' He talked the matter over with his father one evening when the rays of the setting sun entering the yard between the outhouses ruled the heavy shadows with luminous streaks. Over the manure heap floated a mist, opal-tinted and odorous, and the marauding hens would stop in their scratching to examine with a sudden glance of their round eye the two men, both lean and tall, talking together in hoarse tones. The old man, all twisted with rheumatism and bowed with years of work, the younger bony and straight, spoke without gestures in the indifferent manner of peasants, grave and slow. But before the sun had set the father had submitted to the sensible arguments of the son. 'It is not for me that I am speaking,' insisted Jean-Pierre. 'It is for the land. It's a pity to see it badly used. I am not impatient for myself.' The old fellow nodded over his stick. 'I dare say; I dare say,' he muttered. 'You may be right. Do what you like. It's the mother that will be pleased.'

The mother was pleased with her daughter-in-law. Jean-Pierre brought the two-wheeled spring-cart with a rush into the yard. The grey horse galloped clumsily, and the bride and bridegroom, sitting side by side, were jerked backwards and forwards by the up and down motion of the shafts, in a manner regular and brusque. On the road the distanced wedding guests straggled in pairs and groups. The men advanced with heavy steps, swinging their idle arms. They were clad in town clothes: jackets cut with clumsy smartness, hard black hats, immense boots, polished highly. Their women all in simple black, with white caps and shawls of faded tints folded triangularly on the back, strolled lightly by their side. In front the violin sang a strident tune, and the biniou* snored and hummed, while the player capered solemnly, lifting high his heavy clogs. The sombre procession drifted in and out of the narrow lanes, through sunshine and through shade, between fields and hedgerows, scaring the little birds that darted away in troops right and left. In the yard of Bacadou's farm the dark ribbon wound itself up into a mass of men and women pushing at the door with cries and greetings. The wedding dinner was remembered for months. It was a splendid feast in the orchard. Farmers of considerable means and excellent repute were to be found sleeping in ditches, all along the road to Treguier, even as late as the afternoon of the next day. All the countryside participated in the happiness of Jean-Pierre. He remained sober, and, together with his quiet wife, kept out of the way, letting father and mother reap their due of honour and thanks. But the next day he took hold strongly, and the old folks felt a shadow—precursor of the grave—fall upon them finally. The world is to the young.

When the twins were born there was plenty of room in the house, for the mother of Jean-Pierre had gone away to dwell under a heavy stone in the cemetery of Ploumar. On that day, for the first time since his son's marriage, the elder Bacadou, neglected by the cackling lot of strange women who thronged the kitchen, left in the morning his seat under the mantel of the fire-place, and went into the empty cow-house, shaking his white locks dismally. Grandsons were all very well, but he wanted his soup at midday. When shown the babies, he stared at them with a fixed gaze, and muttered something like: 'It's too much.' Whether he meant too much happiness, or simply commented upon the number of his descendants, it is impossible to say. He looked offended—as far as his old wooden face could express anything; and for days afterwards could be seen, almost any time of the day, sitting at the gate, with his nose over his knees, a pipe between his gums, and gathered up into a kind of raging concentrated sulkiness. Once he spoke to his son, alluding to the newcomers with a groan: 'They will quarrel over the land.' 'Don't bother about that, father,' answered Jean-Pierre, stolidly, and passed, bent double, towing a recalcitrant cow over his shoulder.

He was happy, and so was Susan, his wife. It was not an ethereal joy welcoming new souls to struggle, perchance to victory. In fourteen years both boys would be a help; and, later on, Jean-Pierre pictured two big sons striding over the land from patch to patch, wringing tribute from the earth beloved and fruitful. Susan was happy too, for she did not want to be spoken of as the unfortunate woman, and now she had children no one could call her that. Both herself and her husband had seen something of the larger world—he during the time of his service; while she had spent a year or so in Paris with a Breton family; but had been too home-sick to remain longer away from the hilly and green country, set in a barren circle of rocks and sands, where she had been born. She thought that one of the boys ought perhaps to be a priest, but said nothing to her husband, who was a republican,* and hated the 'crows,' as he called the ministers of religion. The christening was a splendid affair. All the commune came to it, for the Bacadous were rich and influential, and, now and then, did not mind the expense. The grandfather had a new coat.

Some months afterwards, one evening when the kitchen had been swept, and the door locked, Jean-Pierre, looking at the cot, asked his wife: 'What's the matter with those children?' And, as if these words, spoken calmly, had been the portent of misfortune, she answered with a loud wail that must have been heard across the yard in the pig-sty; for the pigs (the Bacadous had the finest pigs in the country), stirred and grunted complainingly in the night. The husband went on grinding his bread and butter slowly, gazing at the wall, the soup-plate smoking under his chin. He had returned late from the market, where he had overheard (not for the first time) whispers behind his back. He revolved the words in his mind as he drove back. 'Simple! Both of them. . . . Never any use! . . . Well! May be, may be. One must see. Would ask his wife.' This was her answer. He felt like a blow on his chest, but said only: 'Go, draw me some cider. I am thirsty!'

She went out moaning, an empty jug in her hand. Then he rose, took up the light, and moved slowly towards the cradle. They slept. He looked at them sideways, finished his mouthful there, went back heavily, and sat down before his plate. When his wife returned he never looked up, but swallowed a couple of spoonfuls noisily, and remarked, in a dull manner:

'When they sleep they are like other people's children.'

She sat down suddenly on a stool near by, and shook with a silent tempest of sobs, unable to speak. He finished his meal, and remained idly thrown back in his chair, his eyes lost amongst the black rafters of the ceiling. Before him the tallow candle* flared red and straight, sending up a slender thread of smoke. The light lay on the rough, sunburnt skin of his throat; the sunk cheeks were like patches of darkness, and his aspect was mournfully stolid, as if he had ruminated with difficulty endless ideas. Then he said, deliberately:

'We must see . . . consult people. Don't cry. . . . They won't be all like that . . . surely! We must sleep now.'

After the third child, also a boy, was born, Jean-Pierre went about his work with tense hopefulness. His lips seemed more narrow, more tightly compressed than before; as if for fear of letting the earth he tilled hear the voice of hope that murmured within his breast. He watched the child, stepping up to the cot with a heavy clang of sabots* on the stone floor, and glanced in, along his shoulder, with that indifference which is like a deformity of peasant humanity. Like the earth they master and serve, those men, slow of eye and speech, do not show the inner fire; so that, at last, it becomes a question with them as with the earth, what there is in the core: heat, violence, a force mysterious and terrible—or nothing but a clod, a mass fertile and inert, cold and unfeeling, ready to bear a crop of plants that sustain life or give death.

The mother watched with other eyes; listened with otherwise expectant ears. Under the high hanging shelves supporting great sides of bacon overhead, her body was busy by the great fireplace, attentive to the pot swinging on iron gallows, scrubbing the long table where the field hands would sit down directly to their evening meal. Her mind remained by the cradle, night and day on the watch, to hope and suffer. That child, like the other two, never smiled, never stretched its hands to her, never spoke; never had a glance of recognition for her in its big black eyes; which could only stare fixedly at any glitter, but failed hopelessly to follow the brilliance of a sun-ray slipping slowly along the floor. When the men were at work she spent long days between her three idiot children and the childish grandfather, who sat grim, angular, and immovable, with his feet near the warm ashes of the fire. The feeble old fellow seemed to suspect that there was something wrong with his grandsons. Only once, moved either by affection or by the sense of proprieties, he attempted to nurse the youngest. He took the boy up from the floor, clicked his tongue at him, and essayed a shaky gallop of his bony knees. Then he looked closely with his misty eyes at the child's face and deposited him down gently on the floor again. And he sat, his lean shanks crossed, nodding at the steam escaping from the cooking-pot with a gaze senile and worried.

Then mute affliction dwelt in Bacadou's farmhouse, sharing the breath and the bread of its inhabitants; and the priest of the Ploumar parish had great cause for congratulation. He called upon the rich landowner, the Marquis de Chavanes, on purpose to deliver himself with joyful unction of solemn platitudes about the inscrutable ways of Providence. In the vast dimness of the curtained drawing-room, the little man, resembling a black bolster, leaned towards a couch, his hat

on his knees, and gesticulated with a fat hand at the elongated, gracefully-flowing lines of the clear Parisian toilette* from
within which the half-amused, half-bored marquise* listened
with gracious languor. He was exulting and humble, proud
and awed. The impossible had come to pass. Jean-Pierre
Bacadou, the enraged republican farmer, had been to mass
last Sunday—had proposed to entertain the visiting priests at
the next festival of Ploumar! It was a triumph for the Church
and for the good cause. 'I thought I would come at once to
tell Monsieur le Marquis. I know how anxious he is for the
welfare of our country,' declared the priest, wiping his face.
He was asked to stay to dinner.

The Chavanes returning that evening, after seeing their guest
to the main gate of the park, discussed the matter while they
strolled in the moonlight, trailing their elongated shadows
up the straight avenue of chestnuts. The marquis, a royalist*
of course, had been mayor of the commune that includes
Ploumar, the scattered hamlets of the coast, and the stony
islands that fringe the yellow flatness of the sands. He had
felt his position insecure, for there was a strong republican
element in that part of the country; but now the conversion
of Jean-Pierre made him safe. He was very pleased. 'You have
no idea how influential those people are,' he explained to
his wife. 'Now, I am sure, the next communal election will
go all right. I shall be re-elected.' 'Your ambition is perfectly
insatiable, Charles,' exclaimed the marquise, gaily. 'But, ma
chère amie,'* argued the husband, seriously, 'it's most important that the right man should be mayor this year, because
of the elections to the Chamber.* If you think it amuses
me. . . .'

Jean-Pierre had surrendered to his wife's mother. Madame
Levaille was a woman of business known and respected
within a radius of at least fifteen miles. Thickset and stout,
she was seen about the country, on foot or in an acquaint-
ance's cart, perpetually moving, in spite of her fifty-eight years,
in steady pursuit of business. She had houses in all the hamlets, she worked quarries of granite, she freighted coasters
with stone—even traded with the Channel Islands.* She was
broad-cheeked, wide-eyed, persuasive in speech: carrying her

point with the placid and invincible obstinacy of an old woman who knows her own mind. She very seldom slept for two nights together in the same house; and the wayside inns were the best places to inquire in as to her whereabouts. She had either passed, or was expected to pass there at six; or somebody, coming in, had seen her in the morning, or expected to meet her that evening. After the inns that command the roads, the churches were the buildings she frequented most. Men of liberal opinions would induce small children to run into sacred edifices to see whether Madame Levaille was there, and to tell her that so-and-so was in the road waiting to speak to her—about potatoes, or flour, or stones, or houses; and she would curtail her devotions, come out blinking and crossing herself into the sunshine; ready to discuss business matters in a calm sensible way across a table in the kitchen of the inn opposite. Latterly she had stayed for a few days several times with her son-in-law; arguing against sorrow and misfortune with composed face and gentle tones. Jean-Pierre felt the convictions imbibed in the regiment torn out of his breast—not by arguments, but by facts. Striding over his fields he thought it over. There were three of them. Three! All alike! Why? Such things did not happen to everybody—to nobody he ever heard of. One yet—it might pass. But three! All three. For ever useless, to be fed while he lived and. . . . What would become of the land when he died? This must be seen to. He would sacrifice his convictions. One day he told his wife:

'See what your God will do for us. Pay for some masses.'

Susan embraced her man. He stood unbending, then turned on his heels and went out. But afterwards when a black *soutane** darkened his doorway he did not object; even offered some cider himself to the priest. He listened to the talk meekly; went to mass between the two women; accomplished what the priest called 'religious duties' at Easter. That morning he felt like a man who had sold his soul. In the afternoon he fought ferociously with an old friend and neighbour who had remarked that the priests had the best of it and were going now to eat the priest-eater. He came home dishevelled and bleeding, and happening to catch sight of his children (they were kept generally out of the way), cursed and swore incoherently, banging the table. Susan wept. Madame Levaille sat serenely unmoved. She assured her daughter that 'It will pass;' and taking up her thick umbrella, departed in haste to see after a schooner* she was going to load with granite from her quarry.

A year or so afterwards the girl was born. A girl! Jean-Pierre heard of it in the fields, and was so upset by the news that he sat down on the boundary wall and remained there till the evening, instead of going home as he was urged to do. A girl! He felt half cheated. However, when he got home he was partly reconciled to his fate. One could marry her to a good fellow—not a good for nothing, but to a fellow with some understanding and a good pair of arms. Besides, the next may be a boy, he thought. Of course they would be all right. His new credulity knew of no doubt. The ill luck was broken. He spoke cheerily to his wife. She was also hopeful. Three priests came to that christening, and Madame Levaille was godmother. The child turned out an idiot too.

Then on market days Jean-Pierre was seen bargaining bitterly, quarrelsome and greedy; then getting drunk with taciturn earnestness; then driving home in the dusk at a rate fit for a wedding, but with a face gloomy enough for a funeral. Sometimes he would insist for his wife to come with him; and they would drive in the early morning, shaking side by side on the narrow seat above the helpless pig, that, with tied legs, grunted a melancholy sigh at every rut. The morning drives were silent; but in the evening, coming home, Jean-Pierre, tipsy, was viciously muttering, and growled at the confounded woman who could not rear children that were like anybody else's. Susan, holding on against the erratic swayings of the cart, pretended not to hear. Once, as they were driving through Ploumar, some obscure and drunken impulse caused him to pull up sharply opposite the church. The moon swam amongst light white clouds. The tombstones gleamed pale under the fretted shadows of the trees in the churchyard. Even the village dogs slept. Only the nightingales, awake, spun out the thrill of their song above the silence of graves. Jean-Pierre said thickly to his wife:

'What do you think is there?'

He pointed his whip at the tower—in which the big dial of the clock appeared high in the moonlight like a pallid face without eyes—and getting out carefully, fell down at once by the wheel. He picked himself up and climbed one by one the few steps to the iron gate of the churchyard. He put his face to the bars and called out indistinctly:

'Hey there! Come out!'

'Jean! Return! Return!' entreated his wife in low tones.

He took no notice, and seemed to wait there. The song of nightingales beat on all sides against the high walls of the church, and flowed back between stone crosses and flat grey slabs, engraved with words of hope and sorrow.

'Hey! Come out!' shouted Jean-Pierre loudly.

The nightingales ceased to sing.

'Nobody?' went on Jean-Pierre. 'Nobody there. A swindle of the crows. That's what this is. Nobody anywhere. I despise it. Allez! Houp!'*

He shook the gate with all his strength, and the iron bars rattled with a frightful clanging, like a chain dragged over stone steps. A dog near-by barked hurriedly. Jean-Pierre staggered back, and after three successive dashes got into his cart. Susan sat very quiet and still. He said to her with drunken severity:

'See? Nobody. I've been made a fool! Malheur!* Somebody will pay for it. The next one I see near the house I will lay my whip on . . . on the black spine . . . I will. I don't want him in there . . . he only helps the carrion crows to rob poor folk. I am a man. . . . We will see if I can't have children like anybody else . . . now you mind. . . . They won't be all . . . all . . . we see. . . .'

She burst out through the fingers that hid her face:

'Don't say that, Jean; don't say that, my man!'

He struck her a swinging blow on the head with the back of his hand and knocked her into the bottom of the cart, where she crouched, thrown about lamentably by every jolt. He drove furiously, standing up, brandishing his whip, shaking the reins over the grey horse that galloped ponderously, making the heavy harness leap upon his broad quarters. The

country rang clamorous in the night with the irritated bark-
ing of farm dogs, that followed the rattle of wheels all along
the road. A couple of belated wayfarers had only just time
to step into the ditch. At his own gate he caught the post
and was shot out of the cart head first. The horse went on
slowly to the door. At Susan's piercing cries the farm hands
rushed out. She thought him dead, but he was only sleeping
where he fell, and cursed his men who hastened to him for
disturbing his slumbers.

Autumn came. The clouded sky descended low upon the
black contours of the hills; and the dead leaves danced in
spiral whirls under naked trees till the wind, sighing profoundly, laid them to rest in the hollows of bare valleys. And
from morning till night one could see all over the land black
denuded boughs, the boughs gnarled and twisted, as if con-
torted with pain, swaying sadly between the wet clouds and
the soaked earth. The clear and gentle streams of summer days
rushed discoloured and raging at the stones that barred the
way to the sea, with the fury of madness bent upon suicide.
From horizon to horizon the great road to the sands lay
between the hills in a dull glitter of empty curves, resembling
an unnavigable river of mud.

Jean-Pierre went from field to field, moving blurred and
tall in the drizzle, or striding on the crests of rises, lonely and
high upon the grey curtain of drifting clouds, as if he had
been pacing along the very edge of the universe. He looked
at the black earth, at the earth mute and promising, at the
mysterious earth doing its work of life in death-like stillness
under the veiled sorrow of the sky. And it seemed to him
that to a man worse than childless there was no promise in
the fertility of fields, that from him the earth escaped, defied
him, frowned at him like the clouds, sombre and hurried
above his head. Having to face alone his own fields, he felt
the inferiority of man who passes away before the clod that
remains. Must he give up the hope of having by his side a
son who would look at the turned-up sods with a master's
eye? A man that would think as he thought, that would
feel as he felt; a man who would be part of himself, and
yet remain to trample masterfully on that earth when he was

gone! He thought of some distant relations, and felt savage enough to curse them aloud. They! Never! He turned homewards, going straight at the roof of his dwelling visible between the enlaced skeletons of trees. As he swung his legs over the stile a cawing flock of birds settled slowly on the field; dropped down, behind his back, noiseless and fluttering, like flakes of soot.

That day Madame Levaille had gone early in the afternoon to the house she had near Kervanion.* She had to pay some of the men who worked in her granite quarry there, and she went in good time because her little house contained a shop where the workmen could spend their wages without the trouble of going to town. The house stood alone amongst rocks. A lane of mud and stones ended at the door. The sea-winds coming ashore on Stonecutter's point, fresh from the fierce turmoil of the waves, howled violently at the unmoved heaps of black boulders holding up steadily short-armed, high crosses against the tremendous rush of the invisible. In the sweep of gales the sheltered dwelling stood in a calm resonant and disquieting, like the calm in the centre of a hurricane. On stormy nights, when the tide was out, the bay of Fougère, fifty feet below the house, resembled an immense black pit, from which ascended mutterings and sighs as if the sands down there had been alive and complaining. At high tide the returning water assaulted the ledges of rock in short rushes, ending in bursts of livid light and columns of spray, that flew inland, stinging to death the grass of pastures.

The darkness came from the hills, flowed over the coast, put out the red fires of sunset, and went on to seaward pursuing the retiring tide. The wind dropped with the sun, leaving a maddened sea and a devastated sky. The heavens above the house seemed to be draped in black rags, held up here and there by pins of fire. Madame Levaille, for this evening the servant of her own workmen, tried to induce them to depart. 'An old woman like me ought to be in bed at this late hour,' she good-humouredly repeated. The quarrymen drank, asked for more. They shouted over the table as if they had been talking across a field. At one end four of them played cards, banging the wood with their hard knuckles, and swearing at every lead. One sat with a lost gaze, humming a bar of some song, which he repeated endlessly. Two others, in a corner, were quarrelling confidentially and fiercely over some woman, looking close into one another's eyes as if they had wanted to tear them out, but speaking in whispers that promised violence and murder discreetly, in a venomous sibillation of subdued words. The atmosphere in there was thick enough to slice with a knife. Three candles burning about the long room glowed red and dull like sparks expiring in ashes.

The slight click of the iron latch was at that late hour as unexpected and startling as a thunder-clap. Madame Levaille put down a bottle she held above a liqueur glass; the players turned their heads; the whispered quarrel ceased; only the singer, after darting a glance at the door, went on humming with a stolid face. Susan appeared in the doorway, stepped in, flung the door to, and put her back against it, saying, half aloud:

'Mother!'

Madame Levaille, taking up the bottle again, said calmly: 'Here you are, my girl. What a state you are in!' The neck of the bottle rang on the rim of the glass, for the old woman was startled, and the idea that the farm had caught fire had entered her head. She could think of no other cause for her daughter's appearance.

Susan, soaked and muddy, stared the whole length of the room towards the men at the far end. Her mother asked:

'What has happened? God guard us from misfortune!'

Susan moved her lips. No sound came. Madame Levaille stepped up to her daughter, took her by the arm, looked into her face.

'In God's name,' she said shakily, 'what's the matter? You have been rolling in mud. . . . Why did you come? . . . Where's Jean?'

The men had all got up and approached slowly, staring with dull surprise. Madame Levaille jerked her daughter away from the door, swung her round upon a seat close to the wall. Then she turned fiercely to the men:

'Enough of this! Out you go—you others! I close.'

One of them observed, looking down at Susan collapsed on the seat: 'She is—one may say—half dead.'

Madame Levaille flung the door open.

'Get out! March!' she cried, shaking nervously.

They dropped out into the night, laughing stupidly. Outside, the two Lotharios* broke out into loud shouts. The others tried to soothe them, all talking at once. The noise went away up the lane with the men, who staggered together in a tight knot, remonstrating with one another foolishly.

'Speak, Susan. What is it? Speak!' entreated Madame Levaille, as soon as the door was shut.

Susan pronounced some incomprehensible words, glaring at the table. The old woman clapped her hands above her head, let them drop, and stood looking at her daughter with disconsolate eyes. Her husband had been 'deranged in his head' for a few years before he died, and now she began to suspect her daughter was going mad. She asked, pressingly:

'Does Jean know where you are? Where is Jean?'

Susan pronounced with difficulty:

'He knows . . . he is dead.'

'What!' cried the old woman. She came up near, and peering at her daughter, repeated three times: 'What do you say? What do you say? What do you say?'

Susan sat dry-eyed and stony before Madame Levaille, who contemplated her, feeling a strange sense of inexplicable horror creep into the silence of the house. She had hardly realized the news, further than to understand that she had been brought in one short moment face to face with something unexpected and final. It did not even occur to her to ask for any explanation. She thought: accident—terrible accident—blood to the head—fell down a trap door in the loft. . . . She remained there, distracted and mute, blinking her old eyes.

Suddenly, Susan said:

'I have killed him.'

For a moment the mother stood still, almost unbreathing, but with composed face. The next second, she burst out into a shout:

'You miserable madwoman . . . they will cut your neck. . . .'*

She fancied the gendarmes* entering the house, saying to her: 'We want your daughter; give her up:' the gendarmes with the severe, hard faces of men on duty. She knew the brigadier well—an old friend, familiar and respectful, saying heartily, 'To your good health, madame!' before lifting to his lips the small glass of cognac—out of the special bottle she kept for friends. And now! . . . She was losing her head. She rushed here and there, as if looking for something urgently needed—gave that up, stood stock still in the middle of the room, and screamed at her daughter:

'Why? Say! Say! Why?'

The other seemed to leap out of her strange apathy.

'Do you think I am made of stone?' she shouted back, striding towards her mother.

'No! It's impossible . . .' said Madame Levaille, in a convinced tone.

'You go and see, mother,' retorted Susan, looking at her with blazing eyes. 'There's no mercy in heaven—no justice. No! . . . I did not know. . . . Do you think I have no heart? Do you think I have never heard people jeering at me, pitying me, wondering at me? Do you know how some of them were calling me? The mother of idiots—that was my nickname! And my children never would know me, never speak to me. They would know nothing; neither men—nor God. Haven't I prayed! But the Mother of God herself would not hear me. A mother! . . . Who is accursed—I, or the man who is dead? Eh? Tell me. I took care of myself. Do you think I would defy the anger of God and have my house full of those things—that are worse than animals who know the hand that feeds them? Who blasphemed in the night at the very church door? Was it I? . . . I only wept and prayed for mercy . . . and I feel the curse at every moment of the day— I see it round me from morning to night . . . I've got to keep them alive—to take care of my misfortune and shame. And he would come. I begged him and Heaven for mercy. . . . No! . . . Then we shall see. . . . He came this evening. I thought to myself: "Ah! again!" . . . I had my long scissors. I heard him shouting. . . . I saw him near. . . . I must—must I? . . . Then take! . . . And I struck him in the throat above the breast-bone.

. . . I never heard him even sigh. . . . I left him standing. . . . It was a minute ago. . . . How did I come here?'

Madame Levaille shivered. A wave of cold ran down her back, down her fat arms under her tight sleeves, made her stamp gently where she stood. Quivers ran over the broad cheeks, across the thin lips, ran amongst the wrinkles at the corners of her steady old eyes. She stammered:

'You wicked woman—you disgrace me. But there! You always resembled your father. What do you think will become of you . . . in the other world? In this . . . Oh misery!'

She was very hot now. She felt burning inside. She wrung her perspiring hands—and suddenly, starting in great haste, began to look for her big shawl and umbrella, feverishly, never once glancing at her daughter, who stood in the middle of the room following her with a gaze distracted and cold.

'Nothing worse than in this,' said Susan.

Her mother, umbrella in hand and trailing the shawl over the floor, groaned profoundly.

'I must go to the priest,' she burst out passionately. 'I do not know whether you even speak the truth! You are a horrible woman. They will find you anywhere. You may stay here —or go. There is no room for you in this world.'

Ready now to depart, she yet wandered aimlessly about the room, putting the bottles on the shelf, trying to fit with trembling hands the covers on cardboard boxes. Whenever the real sense of what she had heard emerged for a second from the haze of her thoughts she would fancy that something had exploded in her brain without, unfortunately, bursting her head to pieces—which would have been a relief. She blew the candles out one by one without knowing it, and was horribly startled by the darkness. She fell on a bench and began to whimper. After a while she ceased, and sat listening to the breathing of her daughter, whom she could hardly see, still and upright, giving no other sign of life. She was becoming old rapidly at last, during those minutes. She spoke in tones unsteady, cut about by the rattle of teeth, like one shaken by a deadly cold fit of ague.

'I wish you had died little. I will never dare to show my old head in the sunshine again. There are worse misfortunes

than idiot children. I wish you had been born to me simple
—like your own. . . .'

She saw the figure of her daughter pass before the faint
and livid clearness of a window. Then it appeared in the
doorway for a second, and the door swung to with a clang.
Madame Levaille, as if awakened by the noise from a long
nightmare, rushed out.

'Susan!' she shouted from the doorstep.

She heard a stone roll a long time down the declivity of
the rocky beach above the sands. She stepped forward cautiously, one hand on the wall of the house, and peered down
into the smooth darkness of the empty bay. Once again she
cried:

'Susan! You will kill yourself there.'

The stone had taken its last leap in the dark, and she
heard nothing now. A sudden thought seemed to strangle her,
and she called no more. She turned her back upon the black
silence of the pit and went up the lane towards Ploumar,
stumbling along with sombre determination, as if she had
started on a desperate journey that would last, perhaps, to
the end of her life. A sullen and periodic clamour of waves
rolling over reefs followed her far inland between the high
hedges sheltering the gloomy solitude of the fields.

Susan had run out, swerving sharp to the left at the door,
and on the edge of the slope crouched down behind a boulder.
A dislodged stone went on downwards, rattling as it leaped.
When Madame Levaille called out, Susan could have, by
stretching her hand, touched her mother's skirt, had she had
the courage to move a limb. She saw the old woman go away,
and she remained still, closing her eyes and pressing her side
to the hard and rugged surface of the rock. After a while a
familiar face with fixed eyes and an open mouth became
visible in the intense obscurity amongst the boulders. She
uttered a low cry and stood up. The face vanished, leaving
her to gasp and shiver alone in the wilderness of stone heaps.
But as soon as she had crouched down again to rest, with
her head against the rock, the face returned, came very near,
appeared eager to finish the speech that had been cut short
by death, only a moment ago. She scrambled quickly to her

feet and said: 'Go away, or I will do it again.' The thing wavered, swung to the right, to the left. She moved this way and that, stepped back, fancied herself screaming at it, and was appalled by the unbroken stillness of the night. She tottered on the brink, felt the steep declivity under her feet, and rushed down blindly to save herself from a headlong fall. The shingle seemed to wake up; the pebbles began to roll before her, pursued her from above, raced down with her on both sides, rolling past with an increasing clatter. In the peace of the night the noise grew, deepening to a rumour, continuous and violent, as if the whole semicircle of the stony beach had started to tumble down into the bay. Susan's feet hardly touched the slope that seemed to run down with her. At the bottom she stumbled, shot forward, throwing her arms out, and fell heavily. She jumped up at once and turned swiftly to look back, her clenched hands full of sand she had clutched in her fall. The face was there, keeping its distance, visible in its own sheen that made a pale stain in the night. She shouted, 'Go away'—she shouted at it with pain, with fear, with all the rage of that useless stab that could not keep him quiet, keep him out of her sight. What did he want now? He was dead. Dead men have no children. Would he never leave her alone? She shrieked at it—waved her outstretched hands. She seemed to feel the breath of parted lips, and, with a long cry of discouragement, fled across the level bottom of the bay.

She ran lightly, unaware of any effort of her body. High sharp rocks that, when the bay is full, show above the glittering plain of blue water like pointed towers of submerged churches, glided past her, rushing to the land at a tremendous pace. To the left, in the distance, she could see something shining: a broad disc of light in which narrow shadows pivoted round the centre like the spokes of a wheel. She heard a voice calling, 'Hey! There!' and answered with a wild scream. So, he could call yet! He was calling after her to stop. Never! . . . She tore through the night, past the startled group of seaweed-gatherers who stood round their lantern paralysed with fear at the unearthly screech coming from that fleeing shadow. The men leaned on their pitchforks staring fearfully.

A woman fell on her knees, and, crossing herself, began to pray aloud. A little girl with her ragged skirt full of slimy seaweed began to sob despairingly, lugging her soaked burden close to the man who carried the light. Somebody said: 'The thing ran out towards the sea.' Another voice exclaimed: 'And the sea is coming back! Look at the spreading puddles. Do you hear—you woman—there! Get up!' Several voices cried together. 'Yes, let us be off! Let the accursed thing go to the sea!' They moved on, keeping close round the light. Suddenly a man swore loudly. He would go and see what was the matter. It had been a woman's voice. He would go. There were shrill protests from women—but his high form detached itself from the group and went off running. They sent an unanimous call of scared voices after him. A word, insulting and mocking, came back, thrown at them through darkness. A woman moaned. An old man said gravely: 'Such things ought to be left alone.' They went on slower, now shuffling in the yielding sand and whispering to one another that Millot feared nothing, having no religion, but that it would end badly some day.

Susan met the incoming tide by the Raven islet and stopped, panting, with her feet in the water. She heard the murmur and felt the cold caress of the sea, and, calmer now, could see the sombre and confused mass of the Raven on one side and on the other the long white streak of Molène sands that are left high above the dry bottom of Fougère Bay at every ebb.* She turned round and saw far away, along the starred background of the sky, the ragged outline of the coast. Above it, nearly facing her, appeared the tower of Ploumar church; a slender and tall pyramid shooting up dark and pointed into the clustered glitter of the stars. She felt strangely calm. She knew where she was, and began to remember how she came there—and why. She peered into the smooth obscurity near her. She was alone. There was nothing there; nothing near her, either living or dead.

The tide was creeping in quietly, putting out long impatient arms of strange rivulets that ran towards the land between ridges of sand. Under the night the pools grew bigger with mysterious rapidity, while the great sea, yet far off, thundered in a regular rhythm along the indistinct line of the horizon. Susan splashed her way back for a few yards without being able to get clear of the water that murmured tenderly all around and, suddenly, with a spiteful gurgle, nearly took her off her feet. Her heart thumped with fear. This place was too big and too empty to die in. To-morrow they would do with her what they liked. But before she died she must tell them—tell the gentleman in black clothes that there are things no woman can bear. She must explain how it happened. . . . She splashed through a pool, getting wet to the waist, too preoccupied to care. . . . She must explain. 'He came in the same way as ever and said, just so: "Do you think I am going to leave the land to those people from Morbihan* that I do not know? Do you? We shall see! Come along, you creature of mischance!" And he put his arms out. Then, Messieurs, I said: "Before God—never!" And he said, striding at me with open palms: "There is no God to hold me! Do you understand, you useless carcase. I will do what I like." And he took me by the shoulders. Then I, Messieurs, called to God for help, and next minute, while he was shaking me, I felt my long scissors in my hand. His shirt was unbuttoned, and, by the candle-light, I saw the hollow of his throat. I cried: "Let go!" He was crushing my shoulders. He was strong, my man was! Then I thought: No! . . . Must I? . . . Then take!— and I struck in the hollow place. I never saw him fall. Never! Never! . . . Never saw him fall. . . . The old father never turned his head. He is deaf and childish, gentlemen. . . . Nobody saw him fall. I ran out. . . . Nobody saw. . . .'

She had been scrambling amongst the boulders of the Raven and now found herself, all out of breath, standing amongst the heavy shadows of the rocky islet. The Raven is connected with the main land by a natural pier of immense and slippery stones. She intended to return home that way. Was he still standing there? At home. Home! Four idiots and a corpse. She must go back and explain. Anybody would understand. . . .

Below her the night or the sea seemed to pronounce distinctly:

'Aha! I see you at last!'

She started, slipped, fell; and without attempting to rise, listened, terrified. She heard heavy breathing, a clatter of wooden clogs. It stopped.

'Where the devil did you pass?' said an invisible man, hoarsely.

She held her breath. She recognized the voice. She had not seen him fall. Was he pursuing her there dead, or perhaps . . . alive?

She lost her head. She cried from the crevice where she lay huddled, 'Never, never!'

'Ah! You are still there. You led me a fine dance. Wait, my beauty, I must see how you look after all this. You wait. . . .'

Millot was stumbling, laughing, swearing meaninglessly out of pure satisfaction, pleased with himself for having run down that fly-by-night. 'As if there were such things as ghosts! Bah! It took an old African soldier to show those clodhoppers. . . . But it was curious. Who the devil was she?'

Susan listened, crouching. He was coming for her, this dead man. There was no escape. What a noise he made amongst the stones. . . . She saw his head rise up, then the shoulders. He was tall—her own man! His long arms waved about, and it was his own voice sounding a little strange . . . because of the scissors. She scrambled out quickly, rushed to the edge of the causeway, and turned round. The man stood still on a high stone, detaching himself in dead black on the glitter of the sky.

'Where are you going to?' he called roughly.

She answered, 'Home!' and watched him intensely. He made a striding, clumsy leap on to another boulder, and stopped again, balancing himself, then said:

'Ha! ha! Well, I am going with you. It's the least I can do. Ha! ha! ha!'

She stared at him till her eyes seemed to become glowing coals that burned deep into her brain, and yet she was in mortal fear of making out the well-known features. Below her the sea lapped softly against the rock with a splash, continuous and gentle.

The man said, advancing another step:

'I am coming for you. What do you think?'

She trembled. Coming for her! There was no escape, no peace, no hope. She looked round despairingly. Suddenly the whole shadowy coast, the blurred islets, the heaven itself, swayed about twice, then came to a rest. She closed her eyes and shouted:

'Can't you wait till I am dead!'

She was shaken by a furious hate for that shade that pursued her in this world, unappeased even by death in its longing for an heir that would be like other people's children.

'Hey! What?' said Millot, keeping his distance prudently. He was saying to himself: 'Look out! Some lunatic. An accident happens soon.'

She went on, wildly:

'I want to live. To live alone—for a week—for a day. I must explain to them. . . . I would tear you to pieces, I would kill you twenty times over rather than let you touch me while I live. How many times must I kill you—you blasphemer! Satan sends you here. I am damned too!'

'Come,' said Millot, alarmed and conciliating. 'I am perfectly alive! . . . Oh, my God!'

She had screamed, 'Alive!' and at once vanished before his eyes, as if the islet itself had swerved aside from under her feet. Millot rushed forward, and fell flat with his chin over the edge. Far below he saw the water whitened by her struggles, and heard one shrill cry for help that seemed to dart upwards along the perpendicular face of the rock, and soar past, straight into the high and impassive heaven.

Madame Levaille sat, dry-eyed, on the short grass of the hill side, with her thick legs stretched out, and her old feet turned up in their black cloth shoes. Her clogs stood near by, and further off the umbrella lay on the withered sward like a weapon dropped from the grasp of a vanquished warrior. The Marquis of Chavanes, on horseback, one gloved hand on thigh, looked down at her as she got up laboriously, with groans. On the narrow track of the seaweed-carts four men were carrying inland Susan's body on a handbarrow, while several others straggled listlessly behind. Madame Levaille looked after the procession. 'Yes, Monsieur le Marquis,' she said dispassionately, in her usual calm tone of a reasonable old woman. 'There are unfortunate people on this earth. I had only one child. Only one! And they won't bury her in consecrated ground!'

Her eyes filled suddenly, and a short shower of tears rolled down the broad cheeks. She pulled the shawl close about her. The Marquis leaned slightly over in his saddle, and said:

'It is very sad. You have all my sympathy. I shall speak to the Curé.* She was unquestionably insane, and the fall was accidental. Millot says so distinctly. Good-day, Madame.'

And he trotted off, thinking to himself: I must get this old woman appointed guardian of those idiots, and administrator of the farm. It would be much better than having here one of those other Bacadous, probably a red republican, corrupting my commune.

THE LAGOON

THE white man, leaning with both arms over the roof of the little house in the stern of the boat, said to the steersman—
'We will pass the night in Arsat's clearing. It is late.'

The Malay only grunted, and went on looking fixedly at the river. The white man rested his chin on his crossed arms and gazed at the wake of the boat. At the end of the straight avenue of forests cut by the intense glitter of the river, the sun appeared unclouded and dazzling, poised low over the water that shone smoothly like a band of metal. The forests, sombre and dull, stood motionless and silent on each side of the broad stream. At the foot of big, towering trees, trunkless nipa palms rose from the mud of the bank, in bunches of leaves enormous and heavy, that hung unstirring over the brown swirl of eddies. In the stillness of the air every tree, every leaf, every bough, every tendril of creeper and every petal of minute blossoms seemed to have been bewitched into an immobility perfect and final. Nothing moved on the river but the eight paddles that rose flashing regularly, dipped together with a single splash; while the steersman swept right and left with a periodic and sudden flourish of his blade describing a glinting semicircle above his head. The churned-up water frothed alongside with a confused murmur. And the white man's canoe, advancing up stream in the short-lived disturbance of its own making, seemed to enter the portals of a land from which the very memory of motion had for ever departed.

The white man, turning his back upon the setting sun, looked along the empty and broad expanse of the sea-reach. For the last three miles of its course the wandering, hesitating river, as if enticed irresistibly by the freedom of an open horizon, flows straight into the sea, flows straight to the east —to the east that harbours both light and darkness. Astern of the boat the repeated call of some bird, a cry discordant and feeble, skipped along over the smooth water and lost itself, before it could reach the other shore, in the breathless silence of the world.

The steersman dug his paddle into the stream, and held hard with stiffened arms, his body thrown forward. The water gurgled aloud; and suddenly the long straight reach seemed to pivot on its centre, the forests swung in a semicircle, and the slanting beams of sunset touched the broadside of the canoe with a fiery glow, throwing the slender and distorted shadows of its crew upon the streaked glitter of the river. The white man turned to look ahead. The course of the boat had been altered at right-angles to the stream, and the carved dragon-head of its prow was pointing now at a gap in the fringing bushes of the bank. It glided through, brushing the overhanging twigs, and disappeared from the river like some slim and amphibious creature leaving the water for its lair in the forests.

The narrow creek was like a ditch: tortuous, fabulously deep; filled with gloom under the thin strip of pure and shining blue of the heaven. Immense trees soared up, invisible behind the festooned draperies of creepers. Here and there, near the glistening blackness of the water, a twisted root of some tall tree showed amongst the tracery of small ferns, black and dull, writhing and motionless, like an arrested snake. The short words of the paddlers reverberated loudly between the thick and sombre walls of vegetation. Darkness oozed out from between the trees, through the tangled maze of the creepers, from behind the great fantastic and unstirring leaves; the darkness, mysterious and invincible; the darkness scented and poisonous of impenetrable forests.

The men poled in the shoaling water. The creek broadened, opening out into a wide sweep of a stagnant lagoon. The forests receded from the marshy bank, leaving a level strip of bright-green, reedy grass to frame the reflected blueness of the sky. A fleecy pink cloud drifted high above, trailing the delicate colouring of its image under the floating leaves and the silvery blossoms of the lotus. A little house, perched on high piles, appeared black in the distance. Near it, two tall nibong palms, that seemed to have come out of the forests in the background, leaned slightly over the ragged roof, with a suggestion of sad tenderness and care in the droop of their leafy and soaring heads.

The steersman, pointing with his paddle, said, 'Arsat is there. I see his canoe fast between the piles.'

The polers ran along the sides of the boat glancing over their shoulders at the end of the day's journey. They would have preferred to spend the night somewhere else than on this lagoon of weird aspect and ghostly reputation. Moreover, they disliked Arsat, first as a stranger, and also because he who repairs a ruined house, and dwells in it, proclaims that he is not afraid to live amongst the spirits that haunt the places abandoned by mankind. Such a man can disturb the course of fate by glances or words; while his familiar ghosts are not easy to propitiate by casual wayfarers upon whom they long to wreak the malice of their human master. White men care not for such things, being unbelievers and in league with the Father of Evil, who leads them unharmed through the invisible dangers of this world. To the warnings of the righteous they oppose an offensive pretence of disbelief. What is there to be done?

So they thought, throwing their weight on the end of their long poles. The big canoe glided on swiftly, noiselessly and smoothly, towards Arsat's clearing, till, in a great rattling of poles thrown down, and the loud murmurs of 'Allah be praised!' it came with a gentle knock against the crooked piles below the house.

The boatmen with uplifted faces shouted discordantly, 'Arsat! O Arsat!' Nobody came. The white man began to climb the rude ladder giving access to the bamboo platform before the house. The juragan* of the boat said sulkily, 'We will cook in the sampan,* and sleep on the water.'

'Pass my blankets and the basket,' said the white man curtly.

He knelt on the edge of the platform to receive the bundle. Then the boat shoved off, and the white man, standing up, confronted Arsat, who had come out through the low door of his hut. He was a man young, powerful, with a broad chest and muscular arms. He had nothing on but his sarong.* His head was bare. His big, soft eyes stared eagerly at the white man, but his voice and demeanour were composed as he asked, without any words of greeting—

'Have you medicine, Tuan?'*

'No,' said the visitor in a startled tone. 'No. Why? Is there sickness in the house?'

'Enter and see,' replied Arsat, in the same calm manner, and turning short round, passed again through the small doorway. The white man, dropping his bundles, followed.

In the dim light of the dwelling he made out on a couch of bamboos a woman stretched on her back under a broad sheet of red cotton cloth. She lay still, as if dead; but her big eyes, wide open, glittered in the gloom, staring upwards at the slender rafters, motionless and unseeing. She was in a high fever, and evidently unconscious. Her cheeks were sunk slightly, her lips were partly open, and on the young face there was the ominous and fixed expression—the absorbed, contemplating expression of the unconscious who are going to die. The two men stood looking down at her in silence.

'Has she been long ill?' asked the traveller.

'I have not slept for five nights,' answered the Malay, in a deliberate tone. 'At first she heard voices calling her from the water and struggled against me who held her. But since the sun of to-day rose she hears nothing—she hears not me. She sees nothing. She sees not me—me!'

He remained silent for a minute, then asked softly—

'Tuan, will she die?'

'I fear so,' said the white man sorrowfully. He had known Arsat years ago, in a far country in times of trouble and danger, when no friendship is to be despised. And since his Malay friend had come unexpectedly to dwell in the hut on the lagoon with a strange woman, he had slept many times there, in his journeys up or down the river. He liked the man who knew how to keep faith in council and how to fight without fear by the side of his white friend. He liked him— not so much perhaps as a man likes his favourite dog—but still he liked him well enough to help and ask no questions, to think sometimes vaguely and hazily in the midst of his own pursuits, about the lonely man and the long-haired woman with audacious face and triumphant eyes, who lived together hidden by the forests—alone and feared.

The white man came out of the hut in time to see the enormous conflagration of sunset put out by the swift and stealthy shadows that, rising like a black and impalpable vapour above the tree-tops, spread over the heaven, extinguishing the crimson glow of floating clouds and the red brilliance of departing daylight. In a few moments all the stars came out above the intense blackness of the earth, and the great lagoon gleaming suddenly with reflected lights resembled an oval patch of night-sky flung down into the hopeless and abysmal night of the wilderness. The white man had some supper out of the basket, then collecting a few sticks that lay about the platform, made up a small fire, not for warmth, but for the sake of the smoke, which would keep off the mosquitos. He wrapped himself in his blankets and sat with his back against the reed wall of the house, smoking thoughtfully.

Arsat came through the doorway with noiseless steps and squatted down by the fire. The white man moved his out-stretched legs a little.

'She breathes,' said Arsat in a low voice, anticipating the expected question. 'She breathes and burns as if with a great fire. She speaks not; she hears not—and burns!'

He paused for a moment, then asked in a quiet, incurious tone—

'Tuan . . . will she die?'

The white man moved his shoulders uneasily, and muttered in a hesitating manner—

'If such is her fate.'

'No, Tuan,' said Arsat calmly. 'If such is my fate. I hear, I see, I wait. I remember . . . Tuan, do you remember the old days? Do you remember my brother?'

'Yes,' said the white man. The Malay rose suddenly and went in. The other, sitting still outside, could hear the voice in the hut. Arsat said: 'Hear me! Speak!' His words were succeeded by a complete silence. 'O! Diamelen!' he cried suddenly. After that cry there was a deep sigh. Arsat came out and sank down again in his old place.

They sat in silence before the fire. There was no sound within the house, there was no sound near them; but far away on the lagoon they could hear the voices of the boat-men ringing fitful and distinct on the calm water. The fire in the bows of the sampan shone faintly in the distance with

a hazy red glow. Then it died out. The voices ceased. The
land and the water slept invisible, unstirring and mute. It
was as though there had been nothing left in the world but
the glitter of stars streaming, ceaseless and vain, through the
black stillness of the night.

The white man gazed straight before him into the darkness
with wide-open eyes. The fear and fascination, the inspiration
and the wonder of death—of death near, unavoidable and
unseen, soothed the unrest of his race and stirred the most
indistinct, the most intimate of his thoughts. The ever-ready
suspicion of evil, the gnawing suspicion that lurks in our
hearts, flowed out into the stillness round him—into the stillness profound and dumb, and made it appear untrustworthy
and infamous, like the placid and impenetrable mask of an
unjustifiable violence. In that fleeting and powerful disturbance of his being the earth enfolded in the starlight peace
became a shadowy country of inhuman strife, a battle-field
of phantoms terrible and charming, august or ignoble, struggling ardently for the possession of our helpless hearts. An
unquiet and mysterious country of inextinguishable desires
and fears.

A plaintive murmur rose in the night; a murmur sadden-
ing and startling, as if the great solitudes of surrounding
woods had tried to whisper into his ear the wisdom of their
immense and lofty indifference. Sounds hesitating and vague
floated in the air round him, shaped themselves slowly into
words; and at last flowed on gently in a murmuring stream
of soft and monotonous sentences. He stirred like a man waking up and changed his position slightly. Arsat, motionless
and shadowy, sitting with bowed head under the stars, was
speaking in a low and dreamy tone.

'. . . for where can we lay down the heaviness of our
trouble but in a friend's heart? A man must speak of war and
of love. You, Tuan, know what war is, and you have seen
me in time of danger seek death as other men seek life! A
writing may be lost; a lie may be written; but what the eye
has seen is truth and remains in the mind!'

'I remember,' said the white man quietly. Arsat went on
with mournful composure.

'Therefore I shall speak to you of love. Speak in the night. Speak before both night and love are gone—and the eye of day looks upon my sorrow and my shame; upon my blackened face; upon my burnt-up heart.'

A sigh, short and faint, marked an almost imperceptible pause, and then his words flowed on, without a stir, without a gesture.

'After the time of trouble and war was over and you went away from my country in the pursuit of your desires, which we, men of the islands, cannot understand, I and my brother became again, as we had been before, the sword-bearers of the Ruler. You know we were men of family, belonging to a ruling race, and more fit than any to carry on our right shoulder the emblem of power. And in the time of prosperity Si Dendring* showed us favour, as we, in time of sorrow, had showed to him the faithfulness of our courage. It was a time of peace. A time of deer-hunts and cock-fights; of idle talks and foolish squabbles between men whose bellies are full and weapons are rusty. But the sower watched the young rice-shoots grow up without fear, and the traders came and went, departed lean and returned fat into the river of peace. They brought news too. Brought lies and truth mixed together, so that no man knew when to rejoice and when to be sorry. We heard from them about you also. They had seen you here and had seen you there. And I was glad to hear, for I remembered the stirring times, and I always remembered you, Tuan, till the time came when my eyes could see nothing in the past, because they had looked upon the one who is dying there—in the house.'

He stopped to exclaim in an intense whisper, 'O Mara bahia!* O Calamity!' then went on speaking a little louder.

'There's no worse enemy and no better friend than a brother, Tuan, for one brother knows another, and in perfect knowledge is strength for good or evil. I loved my brother. I went to him and told him that I could see nothing but one face, hear nothing but one voice. He told me: "Open your heart so that she can see what is in it—and wait. Patience is wisdom. Inchi Midah may die or our Ruler may throw off his fear of a woman!" ... I waited! ... You remember the lady with the veiled face, Tuan, and the fear of our Ruler before her cunning and temper. And if she wanted her servant, what could I do? But I fed the hunger of my heart on short glances and stealthy words. I loitered on the path to the bath-houses in the daytime, and when the sun had fallen behind the forest I crept along the jasmine hedges of the women's courtyard. Unseeing, we spoke to one another through the scent of flowers, through the veil of leaves, through the blades of long grass that stood still before our lips: so great was our prudence, so faint was the murmur of our great longing. The time passed swiftly . . . and there were whispers amongst women—and our enemies watched—my brother was gloomy, and I began to think of killing and of a fierce death. . . . We are of a people who take what they want—like you whites. There is a time when a man should forget loyalty and respect. Might and authority are given to rulers, but to all men is given love and strength and courage. My brother said, "You shall take her from their midst. We are two who are like one." And I answered, "Let it be soon, for I find no warmth in sunlight that does not shine upon her." Our time came when the Ruler and all the great people went to the mouth of the river to fish by torchlight. There were hundreds of boats, and on the white sand, between the water and the forests, dwellings of leaves were built for the households of the Rajahs.* The smoke of cooking-fires was like a blue mist of the evening, and many voices rang in it joyfully. While they were making the boats ready to beat up the fish, my brother came to me and said, "To-night!" I made ready my weapons, and when the time came our canoe took its place in the circle of boats carrying the torches. The lights blazed on the water, but behind the boats there was darkness. When the shouting began and the excitement made them like mad we dropped out. The water swallowed our fire, and we floated back to the shore that was dark with only here and there the glimmer of embers. We could hear the talk of slave-girls amongst the sheds. Then we found a place deserted and silent. We waited there. She came. She came running along the shore, rapid and leaving no trace, like a leaf driven by the wind into the sea. My brother said gloomily, "Go and take her; carry her into our boat." I lifted her in my arms. She panted. Her heart was beating against my breast. I said, "I take you from those people. You came to the cry of my heart, but my arms take you into my boat against the will of the great!" "It is right," said my brother. "We are men who take what we want and can hold it against many. We should have taken her in daylight." I said, "Let us be off;" for since she was in my boat I began to think of our Ruler's many men. "Yes. Let us be off," said my brother. "We are cast out and this boat is our country now—and the sea is our refuge." He lingered with his foot on the shore, and I entreated him to hasten, for I remembered the strokes of her heart against my breast and thought that two men cannot withstand a hundred. We left, paddling downstream close to the bank; and as we passed by the creek where they were fishing, the great shouting had ceased, but the murmur of voices was loud like the humming of insects flying at noonday. The boats floated, clustered together, in the red light of torches, under a black roof of smoke; and men talked of their sport. Men that boasted, and praised, and jeered—men that would have been our friends in the morning, but on that night were already our enemies. We paddled swiftly past. We had no more friends in the country of our birth. She sat in the middle of the canoe with covered face; silent as she is now; unseeing as she is now—and I had no regret at what I was leaving because I could hear her breathing close to me—as I can hear her now.'

He paused, listened with his ear turned to the doorway, then shook his head and went on.

'My brother wanted to shout the cry of challenge—one cry only—to let the people know we were freeborn robbers that trusted our arms and the great sea. And again I begged him in the name of our love to be silent. Could I not hear her breathing close to me? I knew the pursuit would come quick enough. My brother loved me. He dipped his paddle without a splash. He only said, "There is half a man in you now—the other half is in that woman. I can wait. When you are a whole man again, you will come back with me here to shout defiance. We are sons of the same mother." I made no answer. All my strength and all my spirit were in my hands that held the paddle—for I longed to be with her in a safe place beyond the reach of men's anger and of women's spite. My love was so great, that I thought it could guide me to a country where death was unknown, if I could only escape from Inchi Midah's spite and from our Ruler's sword. We paddled with fury, breathing through our teeth. The blades bit deep into the smooth water. We passed out of the river; we flew in clear channels amongst the shallows. We skirted the black coast; we skirted the sand beaches where the sea speaks in whispers to the land; and the gleam of white sand flashed back past our boat, so swiftly she ran upon the water. We spoke not. Only once I said, "Sleep, Diamelen, for soon you may want all your strength." I heard the sweetness of her voice, but I never turned my head. The sun rose and still we went on. Water fell from my face like rain from a cloud. We flew in the light and heat. I never looked back, but I knew that my brother's eyes, behind me, were looking steadily ahead, for the boat went as straight as a bushman's dart, when it leaves the end of the sumpitan.* There was no better paddler, no better steersman than my brother. Many times, together, we had won races in that canoe. But we never had put out our strength as we did then—then, when for the last time we paddled together! There was no braver or stronger man in our country than my brother. I could not spare the strength to turn my head and look at him, but every moment I heard the hiss of his breath getting louder behind me. Still he did not speak. The sun was high. The heat clung to my back like a flame of fire. My ribs were ready to burst, but I could no longer get enough air into my chest. And then I felt I must cry out with my last breath, "Let us rest!" "Good!" he answered; and his voice was firm. He was strong. He was brave. He knew not fear and no fatigue . . . My brother!'

A rumour powerful and gentle, a rumour vast and faint; the rumour of trembling leaves, of stirring boughs, ran through the tangled depths of the forests, ran over the starry smoothness of the lagoon, and the water between the piles lapped the slimy timber once with a sudden splash. A breath of warm

air touched the two men's faces and passed on with a mournful sound—a breath loud and short like an uneasy sigh of
the dreaming earth.

Arsat went on in an even, low voice.

'We ran our canoe on the white beach of a little bay close
to a long tongue of land that seemed to bar our road; a
long wooded cape going far into the sea. My brother knew
that place. Beyond the cape a river has its entrance. Through
the jungle of that land there is a narrow path. We made a
fire and cooked rice. Then we slept on the soft sand in the
shade of our canoe, while she watched. No sooner had I
closed my eyes than I heard her cry of alarm. We leaped up.
The sun was halfway down the sky already, and coming in
sight in the opening of the bay we saw a prau* manned by
many paddlers. We knew it at once; it was one of our Rajah's
praus. They were watching the shore, and saw us. They beat
the gong, and turned the head of the prau into the bay. I
felt my heart become weak within my breast. Diamelen sat
on the sand and covered her face. There was no escape by
sea. My brother laughed. He had the gun you had given
him, Tuan, before you went away, but there was only a
handful of powder. He spoke to me quickly: "Run with her
along the path. I shall keep them back, for they have no
firearms, and landing in the face of a man with a gun is certain death for some. Run with her. On the other side of that
wood there is a fisherman's house—and a canoe. When I
have fired all the shots I will follow. I am a great runner, and
before they can come up we shall be gone. I will hold out
as long as I can, for she is but a woman—that can neither
run nor fight, but she has your heart in her weak hands."
He dropped behind the canoe. The prau was coming. She and
I ran, and as we rushed along the path I heard shots. My
brother fired—once—twice—and the booming of the gong
ceased. There was silence behind us. That neck of land is
narrow. Before I heard my brother fire the third shot I saw
the shelving shore, and I saw the water again: the mouth of
a broad river. We crossed a grassy glade. We ran down to
the water. I saw a low hut above the black mud, and a small
canoe hauled up. I heard another shot behind me. I thought,

"That is his last charge." We rushed down to the canoe; a man came running from the hut, but I leaped on him, and we rolled together in the mud. Then I got up, and he lay still at my feet. I don't know whether I had killed him or not. I and Diamelen pushed the canoe afloat. I heard yells behind me, and I saw my brother run across the glade. Many men were bounding after him. I took her in my arms and threw her into the boat, then leaped in myself. When I looked back I saw that my brother had fallen. He fell and was up again, but the men were closing round him. He shouted, "I am coming!" The men were close to him. I looked. Many men. Then I looked at her. Tuan, I pushed the canoe! I pushed it into deep water. She was kneeling forward looking at me, and I said, "Take your paddle," while I struck the water with mine. Tuan, I heard him cry. I heard him cry my name twice; and I heard voices shouting, "Kill! Strike!" I never turned back. I heard him calling my name again with a great shriek, as when life is going out together with the voice—and I never turned my head. My own name! . . . My brother! Three times he called—but I was not afraid of life. Was she not there in that canoe? And could I not with her find a country where death is forgotten—where death is unknown?'

The white man sat up. Arsat rose and stood, an indistinct and silent figure above the dying embers of the fire. Over the lagoon a mist drifting and low had crept, erasing slowly the glittering images of the stars. And now a great expanse of white vapour covered the land: flowed cold and grey in the darkness, eddied in noiseless whirls round the tree-trunks and about the platform of the house, which seemed to float upon a restless and impalpable illusion of a sea; seemed the only thing surviving the destruction of the world by that undulating and voiceless phantom of a flood. Only far away the tops of the trees stood outlined on the twinkle of heaven, like a sombre and forbidding shore—a coast deceptive, pitiless and black.

Arsat's voice vibrated loudly in the profound peace.

'I had her there! I had her! To get her I would have faced all mankind. But I had her—and——'

His words went out ringing into the empty distances. He
paused, and seemed to listen to them dying away very far—
beyond help and beyond recall. Then he said quietly—

'Tuan, I loved my brother.'

A breath of wind made him shiver. High above his head,
high above the silent sea of mist the drooping leaves of the
palms rattled together with a mournful and expiring sound.
The white man stretched his legs. His chin rested on his
chest, and he murmured sadly without lifting his head—

'We all love our brothers.'

Arsat burst out with an intense whispering violence—

'What did I care who died? I wanted peace in my own
heart.'

He seemed to hear a stir in the house—listened—then
stepped in noiselessly. The white man stood up. A breeze
was coming in fitful puffs. The stars shone paler as if they
had retreated into the frozen depths of immense space. After
a chill gust of wind there were a few seconds of perfect calm
and absolute silence. Then from behind the black and wavy
line of the forests a column of golden light shot up into the
heavens and spread over the semicircle of the eastern horizon.
The sun had risen. The mist lifted, broke into drifting patches,
vanished into thin flying wreaths; and the unveiled lagoon
lay, polished and black, in the heavy shadows at the foot of
the wall of trees. A white eagle rose over it with a slanting
and ponderous flight, reached the clear sunshine and appeared
dazzlingly brilliant for a moment, then soaring higher, became
a dark and motionless speck before it vanished into the blue
as if it had left the earth for ever. The white man, standing
gazing upwards before the doorway, heard in the hut a confused and broken murmur of distracted words ending with
a loud groan. Suddenly Arsat stumbled out with outstretched
hands, shivered, and stood still for some time with fixed
eyes. Then he said—

'She burns no more.'

Before his face the sun showed its edge above the tree-tops,
rising steadily. The breeze freshened; a great brilliance burst
upon the lagoon, sparkled on the rippling water. The forests
came out of the clear shadows of the morning, became

distinct, as if they had rushed nearer—to stop short in a great stir of leaves, of nodding boughs, of swaying branches. In the merciless sunshine the whisper of unconscious life grew louder, speaking in an incomprehensible voice round the dumb darkness of that human sorrow. Arsat's eyes wandered slowly, then stared at the rising sun.

'I can see nothing,' he said half aloud to himself.

'There is nothing,' said the white man, moving to the edge of the platform and waving his hand to his boat. A shout came faintly over the lagoon and the sampan began to glide towards the abode of the friend of ghosts.

'If you want to come with me, I will wait all the morning,' said the white man, looking away upon the water.

'No, Tuan,' said Arsat softly. 'I shall not eat or sleep in this house, but I must first see my road. Now I can see nothing—see nothing! There is no light and no peace in the world; but there is death—death for many. We were sons of the same mother—and I left him in the midst of enemies; but I am going back now.'

He drew a long breath and went on in a dreamy tone.

'In a little while I shall see clear enough to strike—to strike. But she has died, and . . . now . . . darkness.'

He flung his arms wide open, let them fall along his body, then stood still with unmoved face and stony eyes, staring at the sun. The white man got down into his canoe. The polers ran smartly along the sides of the boat, looking over their shoulders at the beginning of a weary journey. High in the stern, his head muffled up in white rags, the juragan sat moody, letting his paddle trail in the water. The white man, leaning with both arms over the grass roof of the little cabin, looked back at the shining ripple of the boat's wake. Before the sampan passed out of the lagoon into the creek he lifted his eyes. Arsat had not moved. In the searching clearness of crude sunshine he was still standing before the house, he was still looking through the great light of a cloudless day into the hopeless darkness of the world.*

TO-MORROW

WHAT was known of Captain Hagberd in the little seaport of Colebrook* was not exactly in his favour. He did not belong to the place. He had come to settle there under circumstances not at all mysterious—he used to be very communicative about them at the time—but extremely morbid and unreasonable. He was possessed of some little money, evidently, because he bought a plot of ground, and had a pair of ugly yellow brick cottages run up very cheaply. He occupied one of them himself and let the other to Josiah Carvil—blind Carvil, the retired boat-builder—a man of evil repute as a domestic tyrant.

These cottages had one wall in common, shared in a line of iron railing dividing their front gardens; a wooden fence separated their back gardens. Miss Bessie Carvil was allowed, as it were of right, to throw over it the tea-cloths, blue rags, or an apron that wanted drying.

'It rots the wood, Bessie my girl,' the Captain would remark mildly, from his side of the fence, each time he saw her exercising that privilege.

She was a tall girl; the fence was low, and she could spread her elbows on the top. Her hands would be red with the bit of washing she had done, but her forearms were white and shapely, and she would look at her father's landlord in silence —in an informed silence which had an air of knowledge, expectation and desire.

'It rots the wood,' repeated Captain Hagberd. 'It is the only unthrifty, careless habit I know in you. Why don't you have a clothes line out in your back yard?'

Miss Carvil would say nothing to this—she only shook her head negatively. The tiny back yard on her side had a few stone-bordered little beds of black earth, in which the simple flowers she found time to cultivate appeared somehow extravagantly overgrown, as if belonging to an exotic clime; and Captain Hagberd's upright, hale person, clad in No. 1 sail-cloth from head to foot, would be emerging knee-deep out of

rank grass and the tall weeds on his side of the fence. He
appeared, with the colour and uncouth stiffness of the extraordinary material in which he chose to clothe himself—'for
the time being,' would be his mumbled remark to any obser-
vation on the subject—like a man roughened out of granite,
standing in a wilderness not big enough for a decent billiard-
room. A heavy figure of a man of stone, with a red, handsome
face, a blue wandering eye, and a great white beard flowing
to his waist and never trimmed as far as Colebrook knew.

Seven years before, he had seriously answered 'Next month,
I think,' to the chaffing attempt to secure his custom made
by that distinguished local politician, the Colebrook barber,
who happened to be sitting insolently in the tap-room* of the
New Inn near the harbour, where the Captain had entered
to buy an ounce of tobacco. After paying for his purchase
with three halfpence extracted from the corner of a handkerchief which he carried in the cuff of his sleeve, Captain
Hagberd went out. As soon as the door was shut the barber
laughed. 'The old one and the young one will be strolling
arm in arm to get shaved in my place presently. The tailor
shall be set to work, and the barber, and the candlestick maker;
high old times are coming for Colebrook: they are coming,
to be sure. It used to be "next week," now it has come to
"next month," and so on,—soon it will be next spring, for
all I know.'

Noticing a stranger listening to him with a vacant grin,
he explained, stretching out his legs cynically, that this queer
old Hagberd, a retired coasting-skipper, was waiting for the
return of a son of his. The boy had been driven away from
home, he shouldn't wonder; run away to sea and never heard
of since. Put to rest in Davy Jones's locker this many a day,
as likely as not. That old man came flying to Colebrook
three years ago all in black broadcloth* (had lost his wife
lately then), getting out of a third-class smoker as if the devil
had been at his heels; and the only thing that brought him
down was a letter—a hoax probably: some joker had written
him about a seafaring man with some such name who was
supposed to be hanging about some girl or other, either in
Colebrook or in the neighbourhood. 'Funny, ain't it?' The old

chap had been advertising in the London papers for Harry
Hagberd, and offering rewards for any sort of likely information. And the barber would go on to describe, with sardonical
gusto, how that stranger in mourning had been seen exploring the country, in carts and on foot, taking everybody into
his confidence, visiting all the inns and alehouses for miles
around, stopping people on the road with his questions, looking into the very ditches almost; first in the greatest excitement,
then with a plodding sort of perseverance, growing slower
and slower; and he could not even tell you plainly how his
son looked. The sailor was supposed to be one of two that
had left a timber ship, and to have been dangling after some
girl; but the old man described a boy of fourteen or so—'a
clever-looking, high-spirited boy.' And when people only smiled
at this he would rub his forehead in a confused sort of way
before he slunk off, looking offended. He found nobody, of
course; not a trace of anybody—never heard of anything worth
belief, at any rate; but he had not been able somehow to
tear himself away from Colebrook.

'It was the shock of this disappointment, perhaps, coming
soon after the loss of his wife, that had driven him crazy on
that point,' the barber suggested, with an air of great psychological insight. After a time the old man abandoned the active
search. His son had evidently gone away; but he settled himself to wait. His son had been once at least in Colebrook in
preference to his native place. There must have been some
reason for it, he seemed to think, some very powerful induce-
ment, that would bring him back to Colebrook again.

'Ha, ha, ha! Why, of course, Colebrook. Where else? That's
the only place in the United Kingdom for your long-lost sons.
So he sold up his old home in Colchester, and down he
comes here. Well, it's a craze, like any other. Wouldn't catch
me going crazy over any of my youngsters clearing out. I've
got eight of them at home.' The barber was showing off his
strength of mind in the midst of a laughter that shook the
tap-room.

Strange, though, that sort of thing, he would confess, with
the frankness of a superior intelligence, seemed to be catching.
His establishment, for instance, was near the harbour, and

whenever a sailorman came in for a hair-cut or a shave—if
it was a strange face he could not help thinking directly,
'Suppose he's the son of old Hagberd.' He laughed at himself
for it. It was a strong craze—so strong that it came off on you
like too much blue dye. He could remember the time when
the whole town was full of it. But he had his hopes of the
old chap yet. He would cure him by a course of judicious
chaffing. He was watching the progress of the treatment. Next
week—next month–next year! When the old skipper had put
off the date of that return till next year, he would be well on
the way of not saying any more about it. In other matters
he was quite rational, so this, too, was bound to come. Such
was the barber's firm opinion.

Nobody contradicted him; his own hair had gone grey
since that time, and Captain Hagberd's beard had turned
quite white, and had acquired a majestic flow over the No.
1 canvas suit, which he had made for himself secretly with
tarred twine, and had assumed suddenly, coming out in it
one fine morning, whereas the evening before he had been
seen going home in his mourning of broadcloth. It caused
a sensation in the high street—shopkeepers coming to their
doors, people in the houses snatching up their hats to run
out—a stir at which he seemed strangely surprised at first,
and then scared; his only answer to the wondering questions
was that startled and evasive 'For the present.'

That sensation had been forgotten long ago; and Captain
Hagberd himself, if not forgotten, had come to be disregarded
—the penalty of dailiness—as the sun itself is disregarded
unless it makes its power felt heavily. Captain Hagberd's
movements showed no infirmity: he walked stiffly in his garb
of canvas, a quaint and hale figure; only his eyes wandered
more furtively perhaps than of yore. His manner abroad
had lost its excitable watchfulness; it had become puzzled and
diffident, as though he had suspected that there was somewhere about him something slightly compromising, some
embarrassing oddity; and yet had remained unable to discover
what on earth this something wrong could be.

He was unwilling now to talk with the townsfolk. He had
earned for himself the reputation of an awful skinflint, of a

miser in the matter of living. He mumbled regretfully in the shops, bought inferior scraps of meat after long hesitations; and discouraged all allusions to his garb. It was as the barber had foretold. For all one could tell, he had recovered already from the disease of hope; and only Miss Bessie Carvil knew that he said nothing about his son's return because with him it was no longer 'next week,' 'next month,' or even 'next year.' It was 'to-morrow.'

In their intimacy of back yard and front garden he talked with her paternally, reasonably, and dogmatically, with a touch of arbitrariness. They communed on the ground of unreserved confidence. It was authenticated by an affectionate wink now and then, and Miss Carvil had come to look forward rather to these winks. At first they had discomposed her: the poor fellow was mad. Then she had laughed at them: there was no harm in him. Now she was aware of an unacknowledged, pleasurable, incredulous emotion, expressed by a faint blush. He winked not in the least vulgarly; his thin red face with a well-modelled curved nose, had a sort of high air—the more so that when he talked to her he looked with a steadier and more intelligent glance. A handsome, hale, upright, capable man, with a white beard. You did not think of his age. His son, he affirmed, had resembled him amazingly from his earliest babyhood.

Harry would be one-and-thirty next July, he declared. Proper age to get married with a nice, sensible girl that could appreciate a good home. He was a very high-spirited boy. High-spirited husbands were the easiest to manage. These mean, soft chaps, that you would think butter wouldn't melt in their mouths, were the ones to make a woman thoroughly miserable. And there was nothing like home—a fireside—a good roof: no turning out of your warm bed in all sorts of weather. 'Eh, my dear?'

Captain Hagberd had been one of those sailors that pursue their calling within sight of land. One of the children of a bankrupt farmer, he had been apprenticed hurriedly to a coasting skipper, and had remained on the coast all his sea life. It must have been a hard one at first: he had never taken to it; his affection turned to the land, with its innumerable houses, with its quiet lives gathered round its firesides. Many sailors feel and profess a dislike to the sea, but his was a profound and emotional animosity—as if the love of the stabler element had been bred into him through many generations.

'People did not know what they let their boys into when they let them go to sea,' he expounded to Bessie. 'As soon make them convicts at once.' He did not believe you ever got used to it. The weariness of it got worse as you got older. What sort of life was it in which more than half your time you did not put your foot inside your house? Directly you got out to sea you had no means of knowing what went on at home. One might have thought him weary of distant passages; and the longest he had ever made lasted a fortnight, of which the most part had been spent at anchor, sheltering from the weather. As soon as his wife had inherited a house and enough to live on (from a bachelor uncle who had made some money in the coal business) he threw up his command of an East-coast collier* with a feeling as though he had escaped from the galleys; and after all these years he might have counted on the fingers of his two hands all the days he had been out of sight of England. He had never known what it was to be out of soundings. 'I have never been further than eighty fathoms from land,' was one of his boasts.

Bessie Carvil heard all these things. In front of their cottage grew an under-sized ash; and on summer afternoons she would bring out a chair on the grass plot and sit down with her sewing. Captain Hagberd, in his canvas suit, leaned on a spade. He dug every day in his front plot. He turned it over and over several times every year, but was not going to plant anything 'just at present.'

To Bessie Carvil he would state more explicitly: 'Not till our Harry comes home to-morrow.' And she had heard this formula of hope so often that it only awakened the vaguest pity in her heart for that old man.

Everything was put off in that way, and everything was being prepared likewise for to-morrow. There was a boxful of packets of various seeds to choose from, for the front garden. 'He will doubtless let you have your say about that, my dear,' Captain Hagberd intimated to her across the railing.

Miss Bessie's head remained bowed over her work. She had heard all this so many times. But now and then she would rise, lay down her sewing, and come slowly to the fence. There was a charm in these gentle ravings. He was determined that his son should not go away again for the want of a home all ready for him. He had been filling the other cottage with all sorts of furniture. She imagined it all new, fresh with varnish, piled up as in a warehouse. There would be tables wrapped up in sacking; rolls of carpets thick and vertical like fragments of columns, the gleam of white marble tops in the dimness of the drawn blinds. Captain Hagberd always described his purchases to her, carefully, as to a person having a legitimate interest in them. The overgrown yard of his cottage could be laid over with concrete . . . after to-morrow.

'We could just as well do away with the fence. You could have your drying-line out, quite clear of your flowers.' He winked, and she would blush faintly.

This madness that had entered her life through the kindness of her heart had reasonable details. What if his son returned? But she could not even be quite sure that he ever had a son; and if he existed anywhere he had been too long away. And when Captain Hagberd got excited she would steady him by a pretence of belief, laughing a little to salve her conscience.

Only once she had tried pityingly to throw some doubt on that hope doomed to disappointment, but the effect of her attempt had scared her very much. All at once over that man's face there came an expression of horror and incredulity, as though he had seen a crack open out in the firmament.

'You—you—you don't think he's drowned!'

For a moment he seemed to her ready to go out of his mind, for in his ordinary state she thought him more sane than people gave him credit for. On that occasion the violence of the emotion was followed by a most paternal and complacent recovery.

'Don't alarm yourself, my dear,' he said a little cunningly: 'the sea can't keep him. He does not belong to it. None of us Hagberds ever did belong to it. Look at me; I didn't get drowned. Moreover, he isn't a sailor at all; and if he is not a

sailor he's bound to come back. There's nothing to prevent
him coming back . . . !'

His eyes began to wander.

'To-morrow.'

She never tried again, for fear the man should go out of
his mind on the spot. He depended on her. She seemed the
only sensible person in the town; and he would congratulate
himself frankly before her face upon having secured such a
level-headed wife for his son. The rest of the town, he con-
fided to her once, in a fit of temper, was certainly queer. The
way they looked at you—the way they talked to you! He had
never got on with any one in the place. Didn't like the people.
He would not have left his own country if it had not been
clear that his son had taken a fancy to Colebrook.

She humoured him in silence, listening patiently by the
fence; crocheting with downcast eyes. Blushes came with difficulty on her dead-white complexion, under the negligently
twisted opulence of mahogany-coloured hair. Her father was
frankly carroty.

She had a full figure; a tired, unrefreshed face. When Captain Hagberd vaunted the necessity and propriety of a home
and the delights of one's own fireside, she smiled a little, with
her lips only. Her home delights had been confined to the
nursing of her father during the ten best years of her life.

A bestial roaring coming out of an upstairs window would
interrupt their talk. She would begin at once to roll up her
crochet-work or fold her sewing, without the slightest sign of
haste. Meantime the howls and roars of her name would go
on, making the fishermen strolling upon the sea-wall on the
other side of the road turn their heads towards the cottages.
She would go in slowly at the front door, and a moment afterwards there would fall a profound silence. Presently she would
reappear, leading by the hand a man, gross and unwieldy like
a hippopotamus, with a bad-tempered, surly face.

He was a widowed boat-builder, whom blindness had over-
taken years before in the full flush of business. He behaved
to his daughter as if she had been responsible for its incur-
able character. He had been heard to bellow at the top of
his voice, as if to defy Heaven, that he did not care: he had

made enough money to have ham and eggs for his breakfast every morning. He thanked God for it, in a fiendish tone. He also used the name of God several times every day for the purpose of damning his daughter.

Captain Hagberd had been so unfavourably impressed by his tenant, that once he told Miss Bessie, 'He is a very extravagant fellow, my dear.'

She was knitting that day, finishing a pair of socks for her father, who expected her to keep up the supply dutifully. She hated knitting, and, as she was just at the heel part, she had to keep her eyes on her needles.

'Of course it isn't as if he had a son to provide for,' Captain Hagberd went on a little vacantly. 'Girls, of course, don't require so much—h'm—h'm. They don't run away from home, my dear.'

'No,' said Miss Bessie, quietly.

Captain Hagberd, amongst the mounds of turned-up earth, chuckled. With his maritime rig, his weatherbeaten face, his beard of Father Neptune, he resembled a deposed sea-god who had exchanged the trident for the spade.

'And he must look upon you as already provided for, in a manner. That's the best of it with the girls. The husbands . . .' He winked. Miss Bessie, absorbed in her knitting, coloured faintly.

'Bessie! my hat!' bellowed out old Carvil, who had been sitting under the tree mute and motionless, like an idol of some remarkably monstrous superstition. He never opened his mouth but to howl for her, at her, sometimes about her; and then he did not moderate the terms of abuse. Her system was never to answer him at all; and he kept up his shouting till he got attended to—till she took him by the arm, or thrust the mouthpiece of his pipe between his teeth. He was one of the few blind people who smoke. When he felt the hat being put on his head, he stopped his noise at once. Then he rose, and they passed together through the gate.

He weighed heavily on her arm. During their slow, toilful walks she appeared to be dragging with her for a penance the burden of that infirm bulk. Usually they crossed the road at once (the cottages stood in the fields near the harbour, two hundred yards away from the end of the street), and for a long, long time they would remain in view, ascending imperceptibly the flight of wooden steps that led to the top of the sea-wall. It ran on from east to west, shutting out the Channel like a neglected railway embankment, on which no train had ever rolled within memory of man. Groups of sturdy fishermen would emerge upon the sky, walk along for a bit, and sink without haste. Their brown nets, like the cobwebs of gigantic spiders, lay on the shabby grass of the slope; and, looking up from the end of the street, people would recognise the two Carvils from afar, by the creeping slowness of their gait. Captain Hagberd, pottering aimlessly about his cottages, would raise his head to see how they got on in their promenade.

He advertised still in the Sunday papers for Harry Hagberd. These sheets were read in foreign parts to the end of the world, he informed Bessie. At the same time he seemed to think that his son was in England—so near to Colebrook that he would of course turn up 'to-morrow.' Bessie, without committing herself to that opinion in so many words, argued that in that case the expense was unnecessary: Captain Hagberd had better spend that half-crown on himself. She declared she did not know what he lived on. Her argumentation would puzzle him and cast him down for a time. 'They all do it,' he pointed out. There was a whole column devoted to appeals after missing relatives. He would bring the newspaper to show her. He and his wife had done it for years; only she was an impatient woman. The news from Colebrook had arrived the very day after her funeral; if she had not been so impatient she might have been here now, with no more than one day more to wait. 'You are not an impatient woman, my dear.'

'I've no patience with you sometimes,' she would say.

If he still advertised for his son he did not offer rewards for information any more; for, with the muddled lucidity of a mental derangement he had reasoned himself into a conviction as clear as daylight that he had already attained all that could be expected in that way. What more could he want? Colebrook was the place, and there was no need to ask for more. Miss Carvil praised him for his good sense, and he was soothed by the part she took in his hope, which had become his delusion; in that idea which blinded his mind to truth and probability, just as the other old man in the other cottage had been made blind by another disease to the light and beauty of the world.

But anything he could interpret as a doubt—any coldness of assent, or even a simple inattention to the development of his projects of a home with his returned son and his son's wife—would irritate him into flings and jerks and wicked side glances. He would dash his spade into the ground and walk to and fro before it. Miss Bessie called it his tantrums. She shook her finger at him. Then, when she came out again, after he had parted with her in anger, he would watch out of the corner of his eyes for the least sign of encouragement to approach the iron railings and resume his paternal and patronising relations.

For all their intimacy, which had lasted some years now, they had never talked without a fence or a railing between them. He described to her all the splendours accumulated for the setting-up of their housekeeping, but had never invited her to an inspection. No human eye was to behold them till Harry had his first look. In fact, nobody had ever been inside his cottage; he did his own housework, and he guarded his son's privilege so jealously that the small objects of domestic use he bought sometimes were smuggled in rapidly across the front garden under his canvas coat. Then, coming out, he would remark apologetically, 'It was only a kettle, my dear.'

And, if not too tired with her drudgery, or worried beyond endurance by her father, she would laugh at him with a blush, and say: 'That's all right, Captain Hagberd; I am not impatient.'

'Well, my dear, you haven't long to wait now,' he would answer with a sudden bashfulness, and looking about uneasily, as though he had suspected that there was something wrong somewhere.

Every Monday she paid him his rent over the railings. He clutched the shillings greedily. He grudged every penny he had to spend on his maintenance, and when he left her to make his purchases his bearing changed as soon as he got into the street.

Away from the sanction of her pity, he felt himself exposed without defence. He brushed the walls with his shoulder. He mistrusted the queerness of the people; yet, by then, even the town children had left off calling after him, and the trades-men served him without a word. The slightest allusion to his clothing had the power to puzzle and frighten especially, like something utterly unwarranted and incomprehensible.

In the autumn, the driving rain drummed on his sailcloth suit saturated almost to the stiffness of sheet iron, with its surface flowing with water. When the weather was too bad, he retreated under the tiny porch, and, standing close against the door, looked at his spade left planted in the middle of the yard. The ground was so much dug up all over, that as the season advanced it turned to a quagmire. When it froze hard, he was disconsolate. What would Harry say? And as he could not have so much of Bessie's company at that time of the year, the roars of old Carvil, that came muffled through the closed windows, calling her indoors, exasperated him greatly.

'Why don't that extravagant fellow get you a servant?' he asked impatiently one mild afternoon. She had thrown some-thing over her head to run out for a while.

'I don't know,' said the pale Bessie, wearily, staring away with her heavy-lidded, grey, and unexpectant glance. There were always smudgy shadows under her eyes, and she did not seem able to see any change or any end to her life.

'You wait till you get married, my dear,' said her only friend, drawing closer to the fence. 'Harry will get you one.'

His hopeful craze seemed to mock her own want of hope with so bitter an aptness that in her nervous irritation she could have screamed at him outright. But she only said in self-mockery, and speaking to him as though he had been sane, 'Why, Captain Hagberd, your son may not even want to look at me.'

He flung his head back and laughed his throaty, affected cackle of anger.

'What! That boy? Not want to look at the only sensible girl for miles around? What do you think I am here for, my dear—my dear—my dear? . . . What? You wait. You just wait. You'll see to-morrow. I'll soon——'

'Bessie! Bessie! Bessie!' howled Carvil inside. 'Bessie!—my pipe!' That fat blind man had given himself up to a very lust of laziness. He would not lift his hand to reach for the things she took care to leave at his very elbow. He would not move a limb; he would not rise from his chair, he would not put one foot before another, in that parlour where he knew his way as well as if he had his sight, without calling her to his side and hanging all his atrocious weight on her shoulder. He would not eat one single mouthful of food without her close attendance. He had made himself helpless beyond his affliction, to enslave her better. She stood still for a moment, setting her teeth in the dusk, then turned and walked slowly indoors.

Captain Hagberd went back to his spade. The shouting stopped, and after a while the window of the parlour downstairs was lit up. A man coming from the end of the street with a firm leisurely step passed the first cottage, but seemed to have caught sight of Captain Hagberd, because he turned back a pace or two. A cold white light lingered in the western sky. The man leaned over the gate in an interested manner.

'You must be Captain Hagberd,' he said, with easy assurance.

The old man spun round, pulling out his spade, startled by the strange voice.

'Yes, I am,' he answered nervously.

The other, smiling straight at him, uttered his words very slowly: 'You've been advertising for your son, I believe?'

'My son Harry,' mumbled Captain Hagberd, off his guard for once. 'He's coming home to-morrow.'

'The devil he is!' The stranger marvelled greatly, and then went on, with only a slight change of tone: 'You've grown a beard like Father Christmas himself.'

Captain Hagberd drew a little nearer, and leaned forward over his spade. 'Go your way,' he said, resentfully and timidly at the same time, because he was always afraid of being laughed at. Every mental state, even madness, has its equilibrium based upon self-esteem. Its disturbance causes unhappiness; and Captain Hagberd lived amongst a scheme of settled notions which it pained him to feel disturbed by people's grins. Yes, people's grins were awful. They hinted at something wrong: but what? He could not tell; and that stranger was obviously grinning—had come on purpose to grin. It was bad enough on the streets, but he had never before been outraged like this.

The stranger, unaware how near he was of having his head laid open with a spade, said seriously: 'I am not trespassing where I stand, am I? I fancy there's something wrong about your news. Suppose you let me come in.'

'*You* come in!' murmured old Hagberd, with inexpressible horror.

'I could give you some real information about your son— the very latest tip, if you want to hear.'

'No,' shouted Hagberd, 'I don't want to hear!' He began to pace wildly to and fro, he shouldered his spade, he gesticulated with his other arm. 'Here's a fellow—a grinning fellow, who says there's something wrong. I've got more information than you're aware of. I've all the information. I've had it for years—for years—for years—enough to last me till to-morrow. Let you come in, indeed! What would Harry say?'

Bessie Carvil's figure appeared in black silhouette on the parlour window; then, with the sound of an opening door, flitted out before the other cottage, all black, but with something white over her head. These two voices talking suddenly outside (she had heard them indoors) had given her such an emotion that she could not utter a sound.

Captain Hagberd seemed to be trying to find his way out of a cage. His feet squelched in the puddles left by his industry. He stumbled in the holes of the ruined grass-plot. He ran blindly against the fence.

'Here, steady a bit!' said the man at the gate, stretching his arm over and catching him by the sleeve. 'Somebody's been trying to get at you. Hallo! what's this rig you've got on? Storm canvas, by George!' He had a big laugh. 'Well, you *are* a character.'

Captain Hagberd jerked himself free, and began to back away shrinkingly. 'For the present,' he muttered, in a crest-fallen tone.

'What's the matter with him?' The stranger addressed Bessie with the utmost familiarity, in a deliberate, explanatory tone. 'I didn't want to startle the old man.' He lowered his voice as though he had known her for years. 'I dropped into a barber's on my way, to get a twopenny shave, and they told me there he was something of a character. The old man had been a character all his life.'

Captain Hagberd, daunted by the allusion to his clothing, had retreated inside, taking his spade with him; and the two at the gate, startled by the unexpected slamming of the door, heard the bolts being shot, the snapping of the lock, and the echo of an affected gurgling laugh within.

'I didn't want to startle him,' the man said, after a short silence. 'What's the meaning of all this? He isn't quite crazy.'

'He has been waiting a long time for his son,' said Bessie, in a low apologetic tone.

'Well, I am his son.'

'Harry!' she cried—and was profoundly silent.

'Know my name? Friends with the old man, eh?'

'He's our landlord,' Bessie faltered out, catching hold of the iron railing.

'Owns both them rabbit-hutches, does he?' commented young Hagberd scornfully: 'just the thing he would be proud of. Can you tell me who's that chap coming to-morrow? You must know something of it. I tell you, it's a swindle on the old man—nothing else.'

She did not answer, helpless before an insurmountable difficulty, appalled before the necessity, the impossibility and the dread of an explanation in which she and madness seemed involved together.

'Oh—I am so sorry,' she murmured.

'What's the matter?' he said, with serenity. 'You needn't be afraid of upsetting me. It's the other fellow that'll be upset when he least expects it. I don't care a hang; but there will be some fun when he shows his mug to-morrow. I don't care *that* for the old man's pieces, but right is right. You shall see me put a head on that coon—whoever he is!'

He had come nearer, and towered above her on the other side of the railings. He glanced at her hands. He fancied she

was trembling, and it occurred to him that she had her part
perhaps in that little game that was to be sprung on his old
man to-morrow. He had come just in time to spoil their sport.
He was entertained by the idea—scornful of the baffled plot.
But all his life he had been full of indulgence for all sorts
of women's tricks. She really was trembling very much; her
wrap had slipped off her head. 'Poor devil!' he thought. 'Never
mind about him. I daresay he'll change his mind before to-
morrow. But what about me? I can't loaf about the gate till
the morning.'

She burst out: 'It is *you*—you yourself that he's waiting
for. It is *you* who come to-morrow.'

He murmured. 'Oh! It's me!' blankly, and they seemed to
become breathless together. Apparently he was pondering over
what he had heard; then, without irritation, but evidently
perplexed, he said: 'I don't understand. I hadn't written or
anything. It's my chum who saw the paper and told me—
this very morning. . . . Eh? what?'

He bent his ear; she whispered rapidly, and he listened for
a while, muttering the words 'yes,' and 'I see' at times. Then,
'But why won't to-day do?' he queried at last.

'You didn't understand me!' she exclaimed impatiently. The
white streak under the clouds died out of the west. Again
he stooped slightly to hear better; and the deep night buried
everything of the whispering woman and the attentive man,
except the familiar contiguity of their faces, with its air of
secrecy and caress.

He squared his shoulders; the broad-brimmed shadow of a
hat sat cavalierly on his head. 'Awkward this, eh?' he appealed
to her. 'To-morrow? Well, well! Never heard tell of anything
like this. It's all to-morrow, then, without any sort of to-day,
as far as I can see.'

She remained still and mute.

'And you have been encouraging this funny notion,' he
said.

'I never contradicted him.'

'Why didn't you?'

'What for should I?' she defended herself. 'He would have
been miserable. He would have gone out of his mind.'

'His mind?' he muttered, and heard a short nervous laugh from her.

'Where was the harm? Was I to quarrel with the poor old man? It was easier to half believe it myself.'

'Aye, aye,' he meditated intelligently. 'I suppose the old chap got around you somehow with his soft talk. You are good-hearted.'

Her hands moved up in the dark nervously. 'And it might have been true. It was true. It has come. Here it is. This is the to-morrow we have been waiting for.'

She drew a breath, and he said good-humouredly: 'Aye, with the door shut. I wouldn't care if . . . And you think he could be brought round to recognise me . . . Eh? What? . . . You could do it? In a week, you say? H'm, I daresay you could—but do you think I could hold out a week in this dead-alive place? Not me! I want either hard work, or an all-fired racket, or more space than there is in the whole of England. I have been in this place, though, once before, and for more than a week. You don't want to hear that story. The old man was advertising for me then, and a chum I had with me had a notion of getting a couple of quid out of him by writing a lot of silly nonsense in a letter. That lark did not come off, though. We had to clear out—and none too soon. But this time I've a chum in London, and besides . . .'

Bessie Carvil was breathing quickly.

'What if I tried a knock at the door?' he suggested.

'Try,' she said.

Captain Hagberd's gate squeaked, and the shadow of his son moved on, then stopped with another deep laugh in the throat, like the father's, only soft and gentle, thrilling to the woman's heart, awakening to her ears.

'He isn't frisky—is he? I would be afraid to get hold of him. The chaps are always telling me I don't know my own strength.'

'He's the most harmless creature that ever lived,' she interrupted.

'You wouldn't say so if you had seen him chasing me with a hard leather strap,' he said; 'I haven't forgotten it in sixteen years.'

She got warm from head to foot under another soft subdued laugh. At the rat-tat-tat of the knocker her heart flew into her mouth.

'Hey, dad! Let me in. I am Harry, I am! Straight! Come back home a day too soon.'

One of the windows upstairs ran up.

'A grinning, information fellow,' said the voice of old Hagberd, up in the darkness. 'Don't you have anything to do with him. It will spoil everything.'

She heard Harry Hagberd say, 'Hallo, dad,' then a clanging clatter. The window rumbled down, and he stood before her again.

'It's just like old times. Nearly walloped the life out of me to stop me from going away, and now I come back he throws a confounded shovel at my head to keep me out. It grazed my shoulder.'

She shuddered.

'I wouldn't care,' he began, 'only I spent my last shillings on the railway fare and my last twopence on a shave—out of respect for the old man.'

'Are you really Harry Hagberd?' she asked swiftly. 'Can you prove it?'

'Can I prove it? Can any one else prove it?' he said jovially. 'Prove with what? What do I want to prove? There isn't a single corner in the world, barring England, perhaps, where you could not find some man, or more likely a woman, that would not remember me for Harry Hagberd. I am more like Harry Hagberd than any man alive; and I can prove it to you in a minute, if you will let me step inside your gate.'

'Come in,' she said.

He entered then the front garden of the Carvils. His tall shadow strode with a swagger; she turned her back on the window and waited, watching the shape, of which the footfalls seemed the most material part. The light fell on a tilted hat; a powerful shoulder, that seemed to cleave the darkness; on a leg stepping out. He swung about and stood still, facing the illuminated pane of the parlour window at her back, turning his head from side to side, laughing softly to himself.

'Just fancy, for a minute, the old man's beard stuck on to my chin. Hey? Now say. I was the very spit of him from a boy.'

'It's true,' she murmured to herself.

'And that's about as far as it goes. He was always one of your domestic characters. Why, I remember how he used to go about looking very sick for three days before he had to leave home on one of his trips to South Shields* for coal. He had a standing charter from the gas-works. You would think he was off on a whaling cruise—three years and a tail. Ha, ha! Not a bit of it. Ten days on the outside. The *Skimmer of the Seas* was a smart craft. Fine name, wasn't it? Mother's uncle owned her. . . .'

He interrupted himself, and in a lowered voice, 'Did he ever tell you what mother died of?' he asked.

'Yes,' said Miss Bessie, bitterly: 'from impatience.'

He made no sound for a while; then brusquely: 'They were so afraid I would go, that they fairly drove me away. Mother nagged at me for being idle, and the old man said he would cut my soul out of my body rather than let me go to sea. Well, it looked as if he would do it too—so I went. It looks to me sometimes as if I had been born to them by a mistake —in that other hutch of a house.'

'Where ought you to have been born by rights?' Bessie Carvil interrupted him defiantly.

'In the open, upon a beach, on a windy night,' he said, quick as lightning. Then he mused slowly. 'They were characters, both of them, by George; and the old man keeps it up well—don't he? A damned shovel on the——Hark! who's that making that row? "Bessie, Bessie." It's in your house.'

'It's for me,' she said with indifference.

He stepped aside, out of the streak of light. 'Your husband?' he inquired, with the tone of a man accustomed to unlawful trysts. 'Fine voice for a ship's deck in a thundering squall.'

'No: my father. I am not married.'

'You seem a fine girl, Miss Bessie dear,' he said at once. She turned her face away.

'Oh, I say,—what's up? Who's murdering him?'

'He wants his tea.' She faced him, still and tall, with averted head, with her hands hanging clasped before her.

'Hadn't you better go in?' he suggested, after watching for a while the illuminated nape of her neck, a patch of dazzling white skin and soft shadow above the sombre line of her shoulders. Her wrap had slipped down to her elbows. 'You'll have all the town coming out. I'll wait here a bit.'

Her wrap fell to the ground, and he stooped to pick it up; she had vanished. He threw it over his arm, and approaching the window squarely he saw a monstrous form of a fat man in an armchair, an unshaded lamp, the yawning of an enormous mouth in a big flat face encircled by a ragged halo of hair—Miss Bessie's head and bust. The shouting stopped; the blind ran down. He lost himself in thinking how awkward it was. Father mad; no getting into the house. No money to get back; a hungry chum in London who would begin to think he had been given the go-by. 'Damn!' he muttered. He could break the door in, certainly; but they would perhaps bundle him into chokey for that without asking questions—no great matter, only he was confoundedly afraid of being locked up, even in mistake. He turned cold at the thought. He stamped his feet on the sodden grass.

'What are you?—a sailor?' said an agitated voice.

She had flitted out, a shadow herself, attracted by the reckless shadow waiting under the wall of her home.

'Anything. Enough of a sailor to be worth my salt before the mast. Came home that way this time.'

'Where do you come from?' she asked.

'Right away from a jolly good spree,' he said, 'by the London train—see? Ough! I hate being shut up in a train. I don't mind a house so much.'

'Ah,' she said: 'that's lucky.'

'Because in a house you can at any time open the blamed door and walk away straight before you.'

'And never come back?'

'Not for sixteen years at least,' he laughed. 'To a rabbit-hutch, and get a confounded old shovel . . .'

'A ship is not so very big,' she taunted.

'No, but the sea is great.'

She dropped her head, and as if her ears had been opened to the voices of the world, she heard beyond the rampart of sea-wall the swell of yesterday's gale breaking on the beach with monotonous and solemn vibrations, as if all the earth had been a tolling bell.

'And then, why, a ship's a ship. You love her and leave her; and a voyage isn't a marriage.' He quoted the sailor's saying lightly.

'It is not a marriage,' she whispered.

'I never took a false name, and I've never yet told a lie to a woman. What lie? Why, *the* lie——. Take me or leave me, I say; and if you take me, then it is . . .' He hummed a snatch very low, leaning against the wall.

> Oh, ho, ho, Rio!
> And fare thee well,
> My bonnie young girl,
> We're bound to Rio Grande.

'Capstan song,' he explained. Her teeth chattered.

'You are cold,' he said. 'Here's that affair of yours I picked up.' She felt his hands about her, wrapping her closely. 'Hold the ends together in front,' he commanded.

'What did you come here for?' she asked, repressing her shudders.

'Five quid,' he answered promptly. 'We let our spree go on a little too long.'

'You've been drinking?' she said.

'Blind three days; on purpose. I am not given that way —don't you think. There's nothing and nobody that can get over me unless I like. I can be as steady as a rock. My chum sees the paper this morning, and he says to me: "Go on, Harry: loving parent. That's five quid, sure." So we scraped all our pockets for the fare. Devil of a lark!'

'You have a hard heart, I am afraid,' she sighed.

'What for? For running away? Why! he wanted to make a lawyer's clerk of me—just to please himself. Master in his own house; and my poor mother egged him on——for my good, I suppose. Well, then—so long; and I went. No, I tell you: the day I cleared out, I was all black and blue from his great fondness for me. Ah! he was always a bit of a character. Look at that shovel, now. Off his chump?* Not much. That's just exactly like my dad. He wants me here just to have somebody to order about. However, we two were hard up; and what's five quid for him—once in sixteen hard years?'

'Oh, but I am sorry for you. Did you never want to come back home?'

'Be a lawyer's clerk and rot here—in some such place as this?' he cried in contempt. 'What! if the old man set me up in a home, I would kick it down about my ears—or else die there before the third day was out.'

'And where else is it that you hope to die?'

'In the bush somewhere; in the sea; on a blamed mountain-top for choice. At home? Yes! the world's my home; but I expect I'll die in a hospital some day. What of that? Any place is good enough, as long as I've lived; and I've been everything almost but a tailor or a soldier. I've been a boundary rider; I've sheared sheep; and humped my swag;* and harpooned a whale. I've rigged ships; and prospected for gold; and skinned dead bullocks,—and turned my back on more money than the old man would have scraped in his whole life. Ha, ha!'

He overwhelmed her. She pulled herself together and managed to utter, 'Time to rest now.'

He straightened himself up away from the wall, and in a severe voice said, 'Time to go.'

But he did not move. He leaned back again, and hummed thoughtfully a bar or two of an outlandish tune.

She felt as if she were about to cry. 'That's another of your cruel songs,' she said.

'Learned it in Mexico—in Sonora.' He talked easily. 'It is the song of the Gambucinos.* You don't know? The song of restless men. Nothing could hold them in one place—not even a woman. You used to meet one of them now and again, in the old days, on the edge of the gold country, away north there beyond the Rio Gila.* I've seen it. A prospecting engineer in Mazatlan* took me along with him to help look after the waggons. A sailor's a handy chap to have about you anyhow. It's all a desert: cracks in the earth that you can't see the bottom of; and mountains—sheer rocks standing up high like walls and church spires, only a hundred times bigger. The valleys are full of boulders and black stones. There's not a blade of grass to see; and the sun sets more red over that country than I have seen it anywhere—blood-red and angry. It *is* fine.'

'You do not want to go back there again?' she stammered.

He laughed a little. 'No. That's the gold country. It gave me the shivers sometimes to look at it—and we were a big lot of men together, mind; but these Gambucinos used to wander alone. They knew that country before anybody had ever heard of it. They had a sort of gift for prospecting, and the fever of it was on them too; and they did not want the gold. They would find some rich spot, and then turn their backs on it; pick up perhaps something—enough for a spree —and then be off again, looking for more. They never stopped long where there were houses. They had no wife, no chick, no home, never a chum. You couldn't be friends with a Gambucino; they were too restless—here to-day, and gone, God knows where, to-morrow. They told no one of their finds, and there has never been a Gambucino well off. It was not for the gold they cared; it was the wandering about looking for it in the stony country that got into them and wouldn't let them rest; so that no woman could hold a Gambucino for more than a week. That's what the song says. It's all about a pretty girl that tried hard to keep a Gambucino lover, so that he should bring her lots of gold. No fear! Off he went, and she never saw him again.'

'What became of her?' she breathed out.

'The song don't tell. Cried a bit, I daresay. They were the fellows: kiss and go. But it's the looking for a thing—a something . . . Sometimes I think I am a sort of Gambucino myself.'

'No woman can hold you, then,' she began in a brazen voice, which quavered suddenly before the end.

'No longer than a week,' he joked, playing upon her very heartstrings with the gay, tender note of his laugh; 'and yet I am fond of them all. Anything for a woman of the right sort. The scrapes they got me into, and the scrapes they got me out of! I love them at first sight. I've fallen in love with you already, Miss—Bessie's your name—eh?'

She backed away a little, and with a trembling laugh: 'You haven't seen my face yet.'

He bent forward gallantly. 'A little pale: it suits some. But you are a fine figure of a girl, Miss Bessie.'

She was all in a flutter. Nobody had ever said as much as that to her before.

His tone changed. 'I am getting middling hungry, though. Had no breakfast. Couldn't you scare up some bread from that tea, or——'

She was gone. He had been on the point of asking her to let him come inside. No matter. Anywhere would do. Devil of a fix! What would his chum think?

'I didn't ask you as a beggar,' he said jestingly, taking a piece of bread-and-butter from the plate she held before him. 'I asked as a friend. My dad is rich, you know.'

'He starves himself for your sake.'

'And I have starved for his whim,' he said, taking up another piece.

'All he has is yours,' she pleaded.

'Yes, if I come here to sit on it like a dam' toad in a hole. Thank you; and what about the shovel, eh? He always had a queer way of showing his love.'

'I could bring him round in a week,' she said timidly.

He was too hungry to answer her; and, holding the plate submissively to his hand, she began to whisper up to him in a quick, panting voice. He listened, amazed; eating slower and slower, till at last his jaws stopped altogether. 'That's his game, is it?' he said, in a rising voice of scathing contempt. An ungovernable movement of his arm sent the plate flying out of her fingers. He shot out a violent curse.

She shrank back, putting her hand against the wall.

'No!' he raged. 'He expects! Expects *me*—for his rotten money! . . . Who wants his home! Mad—not he! Don't you think. He wants his own way . . . . He wanted to turn me into a miserable lawyer's clerk, and now he wants to make of me a blamed tame rabbit in a cage. Of me! Of me!' His subdued laugh frightened her now.

'The whole world ain't a bit too big for me to spread my elbows in, I can tell you—what's your name—Bessie—let alone a dam' parlour in a hutch. Marry! He wants me to marry and settle! And as likely as not he has looked out the girl too—dash my soul! And do you know the Judy, may I ask?'

She shook all over with noiseless dry sobs; but he was busy fuming and fretting too much to notice that. He bit his thumb with rage at the mere idea. A window rattled up.

'A grinning, information fellow,' pronounced old Hagberd dogmatically, in measured tones. And the sound of his voice seemed to Bessie to make the night itself mad—to pour insanity and disaster on the earth. 'Now I know what's wrong with the people here, my dear. Why, of course! With this mad chap going about. Don't you have anything to do with him, Bessie. Bessie, I say!'

They stood as if dumb. The old man fidgeted and mumbled to himself at the window. Suddenly he cried aloud: 'Bessie—I see you. I'll tell Harry.'

She made a movement as if to run away, but stopped and raised both her hands to her temples. Young Hagberd, shadowy and big, stirred no more than a man of bronze. Over their heads the crazy night whimpered and scolded in an old man's voice.

'Send him away, my dear. He's only a vagabond. What you want is a good home of your own. That chap has no home—he's not like Harry. He can't be Harry. Harry is coming to-morrow. Do you hear? One day more,' he babbled more excitedly: 'never you fear—Harry shall marry you.'

His voice rose very shrill and mad against the regular deep soughing of the swell coiling heavily about the outer face of the sea-wall.

'He will have to. I shall make him, or if not'—he swore a great oath—'I'll cut him off with a shilling to-morrow, and leave everything to you. I shall. To you. Let him starve.'

The window rattled down.

Harry drew a deep breath, and took one step towards Bessie. 'So it's you—the girl,' he said, in a dispassionate voice. She had not moved, and she remained half turned away,

holding her head in the palms of her hands. 'My word!' he
continued, with an invisible half-smile on his lips, 'I have a
great mind to stop . . .'

Her elbows shook violently.

'For a week,' he finished without a pause.

She clapped her hands to her face.

Coming up quite close, he took hold of her wrists gently.
She felt his breath on her ear.

'It's a scrape I am in—this, and it is you that must see me
out of it.' He was trying to uncover her face. She resisted.
He let her go then, and stepping back a little, 'Have you got
any money?' he asked. 'I must be off now.'

She nodded quickly her shamefaced head, and he waited,
looking away from her, while, trembling all over and bowing
her neck, she tried to find the pocket of her dress.

'Here it is!' she whispered. 'Oh, go away! go away! If I
had more—more—I would give it all to forget—to make you
forget.'

He extended his hand. 'No fear! I haven't forgotten a
single one of you in the world. Some gave me more than
money—but I am a beggar now—and you women always
had to get me out of my scrapes.'

He swaggered up to the parlour window, and in the dim
light filtering through the blind, looked at the coin in his
palm. It was a half-sovereign. He slipped it into his pocket.
She stood a little on one side, with her head drooping as if
wounded; with her arms hanging passive by her side, as if
dead.

'You can't buy me in,' he said, 'and you can't buy yourself out.'

He assured his hat with a little tap, and suddenly she felt
herself enfolded in the powerful embrace of his arms. Her feet
lost the ground; her head hung back; he showered kisses
on her face with a silent and overmastering ardour, as if in
haste to get back his own. He kissed her white cheeks, her
hard forehead, her heavy eyelids, her faded lips; and the
measured blows and sighs of the rising tide accompanied
the enfolding power of his arms, the overwhelming might of
his caresses. It was as if the sea, breaking down the wall

protecting all the homes of the town, had sent a wave over her head. It passed on; she staggered backwards, with her shoulders against the wall, exhausted, as if she had been stranded there after a storm and a shipwreck.

She opened her eyes without moving. Her ears pursued the firm, leisurely footsteps going away with their conquest. She began to gather her skirts, staring all the time before her. Suddenly she darted out of the open gate.

'Stop!' she cried after him.

And listening with an attentive poise of the head, she could not tell whether it was the beat of the swell or his fateful tread that seemed to fall cruelly upon her heart. Presently every sound grew fainter, as though she were slowly turning into stone. A fear of silence came to her—worse than the fear of death. She called upon her ebbing strength for the final appeal:

'Harry!'

Not even the dying echo of a footstep. Nothing. The roll of the surf, of the unconquerable sea itself, seemed stopped. There was not a sound—no whisper of life, as though she were alone, lost in that stony country of which she had heard, where madmen go looking for gold and spurn the find.

Captain Hagberd, inside his dark house, had kept on the alert. A window ran up; and in the silence of the stony country a voice alone survived, high up in the black air—the voice of madness, lies, despair—the voice of inextinguishable hope. 'Is he gone yet—that information fellow? Do you hear him yet, my dear?'

She burst out into uncontrolled tears. 'No! no! no! I don't hear him any more.'

He chuckled up there triumphantly. 'You frightened him away. Good girl. Now we shall be all right. Don't you be impatient, my dear. One day more.'

In the other house old Carvil, wallowing regally in his arm-chair, with a globe lamp burning by his side on the table, was yelling her name, in a fiendish voice: 'Bessie! Bessie! Bessie!'

She heard him at last, and, as if overcome by fate, began to totter silently back towards her stuffy little inferno of a cottage. It had no lofty portal, no terrific inscription* of forfeited hopes—she did not understand wherein she had sinned.

Captain Hagberd had gradually worked himself into a state of noisy happiness up there.

'Go in! Be quiet!' she turned upon him tearfully, from the doorstep below.

He rebelled against her in his great joy at having got rid at last of that 'something wrong.' It was as if all the hopeful madness of the world had broken out to bring terror upon her heart, with the voice of that old man shouting of his trust in an everlasting to-morrow.

AN ANARCHIST*

THAT year I spent the best two months of the dry season on one of the estates—in fact on the principal cattle estate—of a famous meat-extract manufacturing company.

B.O.S. Bos.* You have seen the three magic letters on the advertisement pages of magazines and newspapers, in the windows of provision merchants, and on calendars for next year you receive by post in the month of November. They scatter pamphlets also, written in a sickly enthusiastic style and in seven languages, giving statistics of slaughter and bloodshed enough to make a Turk turn faint. The 'art' illustrating that 'literature' represents in vivid and shining colours a large and enraged black bull stamping upon a yellow snake* writhing in emerald-green grass, with a cobalt-blue cloudless sky for a background. It is atrocious and it is an allegory. The snake symbolizes disease, weakness—perhaps even mere hunger, which last is the chronic disease of the majority of mankind. Of course everybody knows the B.O.S. Ltd, with its unrivalled products: Vino-bos, Jelly bos, and the latest unequalled perfection, Tribos,* whose nourishment is offered to you not only highly concentrated, but already half digested. Such apparently is the love that Limited Company bears to its fellow men—even as the love of the father and mother penguin for their hungry fledglings.

Of course the capital of a country must be productively employed. I have nothing to say against the company. But being myself animated by feelings of affection towards my fellow men, I am saddened by the modern system of advertising. Whatever evidence it offers of enterprise, ingenuity, impudence, and resource in certain individuals, it proves to my mind the wide prevalence of that form of mental degradation which is called gullibility.

In various parts of the civilized and uncivilized world I have had to swallow B.O.S. with more or less benefit to myself, though without great pleasure. Prepared with hot water and abundantly peppered to bring out the taste, this extract is not

really unpalatable. But I have never swallowed its advertise-
ments. Perhaps they have not gone far enough. As far as I
can remember, they make no promise of everlasting youth to
the users of B.O.S., nor yet have they claimed the power of
raising the dead for their estimable products. Why this austere
reserve, I wonder! But I don't think it would have had me
even on these terms. Whatever form of mental degradation I
may (being but human) be suffering from, it is not the popular form. I am not gullible.

I have been at some pains to bring out distinctly this
statement about myself in view of the story which follows.
I have checked the facts as far as possible. I have turned up
the files of French newspapers, and I have also talked with
the officer who commands the military guard on the Ile Royale,
when in the course of my travels I reached Cayenne.* I believe
the story to be in the main true. It is the sort of story that
no man, I think, would ever invent about himself, for it is
neither grandiose nor flattering, nor yet funny enough to
gratify the most perverted vanity.

What makes it interesting is its imbecility. In that it is
not singular. The whole of the public and private records of
humanity, history and story alike, are made interesting precisely by that priceless defect, under which we all labour—to
our everlasting discomfiture, but to each other's entertainment and edification. The story contains all the elements of
pathos and fun, of tragedy and comedy, of sensation and
surprise—whereas from rational conduct there is nothing to
be expected of a touching, instructive, and amusing nature.
I am sure to be misunderstood, but I disdain to labour a
point which to me seems absolutely self-evident. I will only
remark that the whole body of fiction bears me out. Its main
theme, I believe, is love. But it has never entered any writer's
head to take rational love for a subject. We should yawn.
Only the complicated absurdities of that psychophysiological
state can rouse our interest and sympathy. However, there
is nothing loving or lovable in what I am going to relate.

It concerns the engineer of the steam-launch belonging to
the Marañon* cattle estate of the B.O.S. Co., Ltd. This estate
is also an island—an island as big as a small province, lying

in the estuary of a great South-American river. It is wild and
not beautiful, but the grass growing on its low plains seems
to possess exceptionally nourishing and flavouring qualities.
It resounds with the lowing of innumerable herds—a deep
and distressing sound under the vast open sky, rising like a
monstrous protest of prisoners condemned to death. On the
mainland, across twenty miles of discoloured muddy water,
there stands a city whose name, let us say, is Horta.*

But the most interesting characteristic of this island (which
seems like a sort of penal settlement for condemned cattle)
consists in its being the only known habitat of an extremely
rare and gorgeous butterfly. The species is even more rare
than it is beautiful, which is not saying little. I have already
alluded to my travels. I travelled at that time, but strictly
for myself and with a moderation unknown in our days of
round-the-world tickets. I even travelled with a purpose. As
a matter of fact, I am—'Ha, ha, ha!—a desperate butterfly-
slayer. Ha, ha, ha!'

This was the tone in which Harry Gee, the manager of
the cattle station, alluded to my pursuits. He seemed to consider me the greatest absurdity in the world. On the other
hand, the B.O.S. Co., Ltd, represented to him the acme of
the nineteenth century's achievement. I believe he slept in
his leggings and spurs. His days he spent in the saddle flying
over the plains, followed by a train of half-wild horsemen,
who called him Don Enrique, and who had no definite idea
of the B.O.S. Co., Ltd, which paid their wages. He was an
excellent manager, but I don't see why, when we met at
meals, he should have thumped me on the back, with loud,
derisive inquiries: 'How's the deadly sport to-day? Butterflies
going strong? Ha, ha, ha!'—especially as he charged me two
dollars per day for the hospitality of the B.O.S. Co., Ltd (capital £2,000,000, fully paid up), in whose balance-sheet for
that year those moneys are no doubt included. 'I don't think
I can make it anything less in justice to my company,' he
had remarked, with extreme gravity, when I was arranging
with him the terms of my stay on the island.

His chaff would have been harmless enough if intimacy of
intercourse in the absence of all friendship were not a thing

detestable in itself. Moreover, his facetiousness was not very amusing. It consisted in the wearisome repetition of descriptive phrases applied to people with a burst of laughter. 'Desperate butterfly-slayer. Ha, ha, ha!' was one sample of his peculiar wit which he himself enjoyed so much. And in the same vein of exquisite humour he called my attention to the engineer of the steam-launch, one day, as we strolled on the path by the side of the creek.

The man's head and shoulders emerged above the deck, over which were scattered various tools of his trade and a few pieces of machinery. He was doing some repairs to the engines. At the sound of our footsteps he raised anxiously a grimy face with a pointed chin and a tiny fair mustache. What could be seen of his delicate features under the black smudges appeared to me wasted and livid in the greenish shade of the enormous tree spreading its foliage over the launch moored close to the bank.

To my great surprise, Harry Gee addressed him as 'Crocodile,' in that half-jeering, half-bullying tone which is characteristic of self-satisfaction in his delectable kind:

'How does the work get on, Crocodile?'

I should have said before that the amiable Harry had picked up French of a sort somewhere—in some colony or other,—and that he pronounced it with a disagreeable, forced precision as though he meant to guy the language. The man in the launch answered him quickly in a pleasant voice. His eyes had a liquid softness and his teeth flashed dazzlingly white between this thin drooping lips. The manager turned to me, very cheerful and loud, explaining:

'I call him Crocodile because he lives half in, half out of the creek. Amphibious—see? There's nothing else amphibious living on the island except crocodiles; so he must belong to the species—eh? But in reality he's nothing less than *un citoyen anarchiste de Barcelone.*'

'A citizen anarchist from Barcelona?'* I repeated, stupidly, looking down at the man. He had turned to his work in the engine-well of the launch and presented his bowed back to us. In that attitude I heard him protest, very audibly,

'I do not even know Spanish.'

'Hey? What? You dare to deny you come from over there?' the accomplished manager was down on him truculently.

At this the man straightened himself up, dropping a spanner* he had been using, and faced us; but he trembled in all his limbs.

'I deny nothing, nothing, nothing!' he said, excitedly.

He picked up the spanner and went to work again without paying any further attention to us. After looking at him for a minute or so, we went away.

'Is he really an anarchist?' I asked, when out of ear-shot.

'I don't care a hang what he is,' answered the humorous official of the B.O.S. Co. 'I gave him the name because it suited me to label him in that way. It's good for the company.'

'What!' I exclaimed, stopping short.

'Aha!' he triumphed, tilting up his hairless pug face and straddling his thin long legs. 'That surprises you. I am bound to do my best for my company. They have enormous expenses. Why—our agent in Horta tells me they spend more than a hundred thousand pounds every year in advertising! One can't be too economical in working the show. Well, I'll tell you. When I took charge here the estate had no steam-launch. I asked for one, and kept on asking by every mail till I got it; but the man they sent out with it chucked up his job at the end of two months, leaving the launch moored at the pontoon in Horta. Got a better screw at a sawmill up the river—blast him! And ever since it has been the same thing. Any Scotch or Yankee vagabond that likes to call himself a mechanic out here gets eighteen pounds a month, and the next thing you know he's cleared out, after smashing something as likely as not. I give you my word that some of the objects I've had for engine-drivers couldn't tell the boiler from the funnel. But this fellow understands his trade, and I don't mean him to clear out. See?'

And he struck me lightly on the chest for emphasis. Disregarding his peculiarities of manner, I wanted to know what all this had to do with the man being an anarchist.

'Come!' jeered the manager. 'If you saw suddenly a barefooted, unkempt chap slinking amongst the bushes on the sea face of the island, and at the same time observed, less than a mile from the beach, a small schooner full of niggers hauling off in a hurry, you wouldn't think the man fell there from the sky, would you? And it could be nothing else but either that or Cayenne. I've got my wits about me. Directly I sighted this queer game I said to myself—"Convict." I was as certain of it as I am of seeing you standing here this minute. So I spurred on straight at him. He stood his ground for a bit on a sand hillock crying out at me: "*Monsieur! Monsieur. Arrêtez!*"* then at the last moment broke and ran for life. Says I to myself, 'I'll tame you before I'm done with you.' So without a single word I kept on, heading him off here and there. I rounded him up towards the shore, and at last I had him corralled on a spit, his heels in the water and nothing but sea and sky at his back, with my horse pawing the sand and shaking his head within a yard of him.

'He folded his arms on his breast then and stuck his chin up in a sort of desperate way; but I wasn't to be impressed by the beggar's posturing.

'Says I, "You're a runaway convict."

'When he heard French, his chin went down and his face changed.

'"I deny nothing," says he, panting yet, for I had kept him skipping about in front of my horse pretty smartly. I asked him what he was doing there. He had got his breath by then, and explained that he had meant to make his way to a farm which he understood (from the schooner's people, I suppose) was to be found in the neighbourhood. At that I laughed aloud and he got uneasy. Had he been deceived? Was there no farm within walking distance?

'I laughed more and more. He was on foot, and of course the first bunch of cattle he came across would have stamped him three feet into ground under their hoofs. A dismounted man caught on the feeding-grounds hasn't got the ghost of a chance.

'"My coming upon you like this has certainly saved your life," I said. He remarked that perhaps it was so; but that for his part he had imagined I had wanted to kill him under the hoofs of my horse. I assured him that nothing would have been easier had I meant it. And then we came to a sort of dead stop. For the life of me I didn't know what to do with this convict, unless I chucked him into the sea. It occurred to me to ask him what he had been transported for. He hung his head.

'"What is it?" says I. "Theft, murder, or what?" I wanted to hear what he would have to say for himself, though of course I expected it would be some sort of lie. But all he said was:

'"Make it what you like. I deny nothing. It is no good denying anything."

'I looked him over carefully and a thought struck me.

'"They've got anarchists there, too," I said. "Perhaps you're one of them."

'"I deny nothing whatever, monsieur," he repeats.

'This answer made me think that perhaps he was not an anarchist. I believe those damned lunatics are rather proud of themselves. If he had been one, he would have probably confessed straight out.

'"What were you before you became a convict?" I asked.

'"*Ouvrier*,"* he says. "And a good workman, too."

'At that I began to think he must be an anarchist, after all. That's the class they come mostly from, isn't it? I hate the cowardly bomb-throwing brutes. I almost made up my mind to turn my horse short round and leave him to starve or drown where he was, whichever he liked best. As to crossing the island to bother me again, the cattle would see to that. I don't know what induced me to put another question:

'"What sort of workman?"

'I didn't care a hang whether he answered me or not. But when he said at once, "*Mécanicien, monsieur*,"* I nearly jumped out of the saddle with excitement. The launch had been lying disabled and idle in the creek for three weeks. My duty to the company was clear. He noticed my start, too, and there we were for a minute or so staring at each other as if bewitched.

'"Get up on my horse behind me," I told him. "You shall put my steam-launch to rights."'

These are the words in which the worthy manager of the
Marañon estate related to me the coming of the anarchist.
At the same time he made no secret of his doubt as to the
man being an anarchist at all. He meant to keep him—out
of a sense of duty to the company,—and the name he had
given him would prevent the fellow from obtaining employ-
ment anywhere in Horta. The vaqueros* of the estate, when
they went on leave, spread it all over the town. They did not
know what an anarchist was, nor yet what Barcelona meant.
They called him Anarchisto de Barcelona,* as if it were his
Christian name and surname. But the people in town had
been reading in their papers about the anarchists in Europe
and were very much impressed. Over the jocular addition of
'de Barcelona' Mr Harry Gee chuckled immensely. 'That breed
is particularly murderous, isn't it? It makes the sawmills crowd
still more afraid of having anything to do with him—see?' he
exulted, candidly, to me. 'I hold him by that name better
than if I had him chained up by the leg to the steam-launch.

'And mark,' he added, after a pause, 'he does not deny
it. I am not wronging him in any way. He is a convict of
some sort, anyhow.'

'But I suppose you pay him some wages, don't you?' I
asked.

'Wages! What does he want with money? He gets his food
from my kitchen and his clothing from the store. Of course
I'll give him something at the end of the year, but you don't
think I'd employ a convict and give him the same money I
would give an honest man? I am looking after the interests
of my company first and last.'

I admitted that, for a company spending a hundred thousand pounds every year in advertising, the strictest economy
was obviously necessary. The manager of the Marañon Estancia
grunted approvingly.

'And I'll tell you what,' he continued: 'if I were sure he's
an anarchist and he had the cheek to ask me for money, I
would give him the toe of my boot. However, let him have
the benefit of the doubt. I am perfectly willing to take it
that he has done nothing worse than to stick a knife into
somebody—with extenuating circumstances—French fashion,

don't you know. But that subversive sanguinary rot of doing away with all law and order in the world makes my blood boil. It's simply cutting the ground from under the feet of every decent, respectable, hard-working person. I tell you that the consciences of people who have them, like you or I, must be protected in some way; or else the first low scoundrel that came along would in every respect be just as good as myself. Wouldn't he, now? And that's absurd!'

He glared at me. I nodded slightly and murmured that doubtless there was much subtle truth in his view.

The principal truth discoverable in the views of Paul the engineer was that a little thing may bring about the undoing of a man.

'*Il ne faut pas beaucoup pour perdre un homme*,'* he said to me, thoughtfully, one evening.

I report this reflection in French, since the man was of Paris, not of Barcelona at all. At the Marañon he lived apart from the station, in a small shed with a metal roof and straw walls, which he called *mon atelier*.* He had a bench there. They had given him several horse-blankets and a saddle,—not that he ever had occasion to ride, but because no other bedding was used by the working-hands, who were all vaqueros— cattlemen. And on this horseman's gear, like a son of the plains, he used to sleep amongst the tools of his trade, in a litter of rusty scrap-iron, with a portable forge at his head and the work-bench sustaining his grimy mosquito-net.

Now and then I would bring him a few candle ends saved from the scant supply of the manager's house. He was very thankful for these. He did not like to lie awake in the dark, he confessed. He complained that sleep eluded him. '*Le sommeil me fuit*,'* he declared, with his habitual air of subdued stoicism, which made him sympathetic and touching. I made it clear to him that I did not attach undue importance to the fact of his being a convict.

Thus it came about that one evening he was led to talk about himself. As one of the bits of candle on the edge of the bench burned out to the end, he hastened to light another.

He had done his military service in a provincial garrison and returned to Paris to follow his trade. It was a well-paid one. He told me with some pride that in a short time he was earning no less than fifteen francs a day. He was thinking of setting up for himself by and by and of getting married.

Here he sighed deeply and paused. Then with a return to his stoical note,

'It seems I did not know enough about myself.'

On his twenty-fifth birthday two of his friends in the repairing-shop where he worked proposed to stand him a dinner. He was immensely touched by this attention.

'I was a steady man,' he remarked, 'but I am not less sociable than any other body.'

The entertainment came off in a little café on the Boulevard de la Chapelle. At dinner they drank some special wine. It was excellent. Everything was excellent. And the world—in his own words—seemed a very good place to live in. He had good prospects, some little money laid by, and the affection of two excellent friends. He proposed to pay for all the drinks after dinner, which was only proper on his part.

They drank more wine; they drank liqueurs, cognac, beer, then more liqueurs and more cognac. Two strangers sitting at the next table looked at him, he said, so sympathetically that he invited them to join the party.

He had never drunk so much in his life. His elation was extreme, and so pleasurable that whenever it flagged he hastened to order more drinks.

'It seemed to me,' he said, in his quiet tone and looking on the ground in the gloomy shed full of shadows, 'that I was on the point of just attaining a great and wonderful felicity. Another drink, I felt, would do it. The others were holding out well with me, glass for glass.'

But an extraordinary thing happened. He seemed to be slipping back. Gloomy ideas—*des idées noires*—rushed into his head. All the world outside the café appeared to him as a dismal evil place where a multitude of poor wretches had to work and slave to the sole end that a few individuals should ride in carriages and live riotously in palaces. The pity of mankind's cruel lot oppressed his heart. In a voice choked

with sorrow he tried to express these sentiments. He thinks
he wept.

The two new acquaintances hastened to console him by
their sympathetic assent. Yes. Such injustice was indeed scan-
dalous. There was only one way of dealing with the rotten
state of society. Demolish the whole *sacrée boutique*.*

Their heads hovered over the table as they whispered to
him eloquently. I don't think they quite expected the result.
He was extremely drunk. Mad drunk. With a howl of rage
he leaped suddenly upon the table. Kicking over bottles and
glasses, he yelled: '*Vive l'anarchie!** Death to the capitalists!'
He yelled this again and again. All round him broken glass
was falling, chairs were swung high in the air, people were
taking each other by the throat. The police dashed in. He
hit, bit, scratched and struggled, till something crashed upon
his head.

He came to himself in a cell, locked up on a charge of
assault, seditious cries, and anarchist propaganda.

He looked at me fixedly with his liquid, shining eyes, that
seemed very big in the dim light.

'That was bad. But even then I might have got off somehow, perhaps,' he said, slowly.

I doubt it. But whatever chance he had was done away
with by a young socialist lawyer who undertook his defence.
In vain he assured him that he was no anarchist; that he was
a quiet, respectable mechanic, only too anxious to work ten
hours per day. He was presented at the trial as the victim
of society. His cry of revolt was the expression of infinite
suffering. The young lawyer had his way to make, and this
was his start. The speech for the defence was pronounced
magnificent.

He paused, swallowed, and brought out the statement,
'I got the maximum penalty applicable to a first offence.'
I made a sympathetic murmur. He hung his head and
folded his arms.

'When I got out of prison,' he began, gently, 'I made tracks,
of course, for my old workshop. My *patron** had a particular liking for me before; but when he saw me he turned green
with fright and showed me the door with a shaking hand.'

While he stood in the street, uneasy and disconcerted, he was accosted by a middle-aged man who introduced himself as an engineer's fitter, too. 'I know who you are,' he said. 'I have attended your trial. You are a good comrade and your ideas are sound. But the devil of it is that you shall not be able to get work now anywhere. These bourgeois'll conspire to starve you. That's their way. Expect no mercy from them.'

To be spoken to so kindly in the street had comforted him very much. His seemed to be the sort of nature needing support and sympathy. The idea of not being able to find work had knocked him over completely. If his *patron*, who knew him so well for a quiet, orderly, competent workman, would have nothing to do with him now—then surely nobody else would. That was clear. The police, keeping their eye on him, would hasten to warn every employer inclined to give him a chance. He felt suddenly very helpless, alarmed, and idle; and he followed the middle-aged man to the *estaminet**round the corner to meet some other good companions. They assured him that he would not be allowed to starve, work or no work. They had drinks all round to the discomfiture of all employers of labour and to the destruction of society.

He sat biting his lower lip.

'That is, monsieur, how I became a *compagnon*,'* he said. The hand he passed over his forehead was trembling. 'All the same, there's something wrong in a world where a man can get lost for a glass more or less.'

He never looked up, though I could see he was getting excited under his dejection. He slapped the bench with his open palm.

'No!' he cried. 'It was an impossible existence! Watched by the police, watched by the comrades! I did not belong to myself any more. Why, I could not even go to draw a few francs from my savings-bank without a comrade hanging about the door to see that I didn't bolt! And most of them were neither more nor less than housebreakers. The intelligent, I mean. They robbed the rich; they were only getting back their own, they said. When I had had some drink I believed them. There were also the fools and the mad. *Des exaltés—quoi!**

When I was drunk I loved them. When I got more drink I was angry with the world. That was the best time. I found refuge from misery in rage. But one can't be always drunk—*n'est-ce pas, monsieur?** And when I was sober I was afraid to break away. They would have stuck me like a pig.'

He folded his arms again and raised his sharp chin with a bitter smile.

'By and by they told me it was time to go to work. The work was to rob a bank. Afterwards a bomb would be thrown to wreck the place. My beginner's part would be to keep watch in a street at the back and to take care of a black bag with the bomb inside* till it was wanted. After the meeting at which the affair was arranged a trusty comrade did not leave me an inch. I had not dared to protest; I was afraid of being done away with quietly in that room; only, as we were walking together I wondered whether it would not be better for me to throw myself suddenly into the Seine. But while I was turning it over in my mind we had crossed the bridge, and afterwards I had not the opportunity.'

In the light of the candle end, with his sharp features, fluffy little mustache, and oval face, he looked at times delicately and gayly young, and then appeared quite old, decrepit, full of sorrow, pressing his folded arms to his breast.

As he remained silent I felt bound to ask:

'Well! And how did it end?'

'In Cayenne,' he answered.

He seemed to think that somebody had given the show away. As he was keeping watch in the back street, bag in hand, he was set upon by the police. 'These imbeciles' had knocked him down without noticing what he had in his hand. He wondered how the bomb failed to explode as he fell. But it didn't explode.

'I tried to tell my story in court,' he continued. 'The president was amused. There were in the audience some idiots who laughed.'

I expressed the hope that some of the others had been caught too. He shuddered slightly before he told me that there were two—Simon, called also Biscuit, the middle-aged fitter who spoke to him in the street, and a fellow of the name of Mafile, one of the sympathetic strangers who had applauded his sentiments and consoled his humanitarian sorrows when he got drunk in the café.

'Yes,' he went on, with an effort, 'I had the advantage of their company over there on St Joseph's Island, amongst some eighty or ninety other anarchists. We were all classed as dangerous.'

St Joseph's Island is the prettiest of the Iles de Salut.* It is rocky and green, with shallow ravines, bushes, thickets, groves of mango-trees, and many feathery palms. Six warders armed with revolvers and carbines are in charge of the convicts kept there.

An eight-oared galley keeps up the communication in the daytime, across a channel a quarter of a mile wide, with the Ile Royale, where there is a military post. She makes the first trip at six in the morning. At four in the afternoon her service is over, and she is then hauled up into a little dock on the Ile Royale and a sentry put over her and a few smaller boats. From that time till next morning the island of St Joseph remains cut off from the rest of the world, with the warders patrolling in turn the path from the warders' house to the convict huts, and a multitude of sharks patrolling the waters all round.

Under these circumstances the convicts planned a mutiny.* Such a thing had never been known in the penitentiary's history before. But their plan was not without some possibility of success. The warders were to be taken by surprise and murdered during the night. Their arms would enable the convicts to shoot down the people in the boat as she came alongside in the morning. The galley once in their possession, other boats were to be captured, and the whole company was to row away up the coast.

At dusk two warders came over to muster the convicts as usual. Then they proceeded to inspect the huts to ascertain that everything was in order. In the second they entered they were set upon and absolutely smothered under the numbers of their assailants. The darkness fell rapidly. It was a new moon; and a heavy black squall gathering over the coast increased the profound darkness of the night. The convicts assembled in the open space, deliberating upon the next step to be taken, quarrelled in low voices.

'You took part in it too?' I asked.

'No. I knew what was going to be done, of course. But why should I kill these warders? I had nothing against them. But I was afraid of the others. Whatever happened, I could not escape from them. I sat alone on the stump of a tree with my head in my hands, sick at heart at the thought of a freedom that could be nothing but a mockery to me. Suddenly I was startled to perceive the shape of a man on the path near by. He stood perfectly still, then his form became effaced in the night. It must have been the chief warder coming to see what had become of his two men. No one noticed him. The convicts kept on quarrelling over their plans. The leaders could not get themselves obeyed. The fierce whispering of that dark mass of men was very horrible.

'At last they divided into two parties and moved off. When they had passed me I rose, weary and hopeless. The path to the warders' house was dark and silent, but on each side the bushes rustled slightly. Presently I saw a faint thread of light before me. The chief warder, followed by his three men, was approaching cautiously. But he had failed to close his dark lanthorn properly. The convicts had seen that faint gleam too. There was an awful savage yell, a turmoil on the dark path, shots fired, blows, groans, and with the sound of smashed bushes, the shouts of the pursuers and the screams of the pursued, the man-hunt, the warder-hunt, passed by me into the interior of the island. I was alone. And I assure you, monsieur, I was indifferent to everything. After standing still for a while, I walked on along the path till I kicked something hard. I stooped and picked up a warder's revolver. I felt with my fingers that it was loaded in five chambers. In the gusts of wind I heard the convicts calling to each other far away, and then a roll of thunder would cover the soughing and rustling of the trees. A big light ran across my path very low along the ground, and it showed a woman's skirt with the edge of an apron.

'I knew it was the wife of the head warder. They must have forgotten all about her. A shot rang out in the interior of the island, and she cried out to herself as she ran. She passed on. I followed, and presently I saw her again. She was pulling at the cord of the big bell which hangs at the end of the landing-pier with one hand, and with the other was swinging the heavy lanthorn to and fro. That is the signal for the Ile Royale should assistance be required at night. The wind carried the sound away from our island and the light was hidden on the shore side by the few trees that grow near the warders' house.

'I came up quite close to her from behind. She went on without stopping, without looking aside, as though she had been all alone on the island. A brave woman, monsieur. I put the revolver inside the breast of my blue blouse and waited. A flash of lightning and a clap of thunder destroyed both sound and light for an instant, but she never faltered, pulling at the cord and swinging the lanthorn as regularly as a machine. She was a comely woman of thirty—no more. I thought to myself, "All that's no good on a night like this." And I made up my mind that if a body of my fellow convicts came down to the pier—which was sure to happen soon— I would shoot her through the head before I shot myself. I knew the "comrades" well. This idea of mine gave me quite an interest in life, monsieur; and at once, instead of remaining stupidly exposed on the pier, I crouched behind a bush. I did not intend to let myself be pounced upon unawares and prevented perhaps from rendering a supreme service to at least one human creature before I died myself.

'But we must believe the signal was seen, for the galley from the Ile Royale came over in an astonishingly short time. The woman kept right on till the light of her lanthorn flashed upon the officer in command and the bayonets of the soldiers in the boat. Then she sat down and began to cry.

'She didn't need me any more. I did not budge. Some soldiers were only in their shirt-sleeves, others without boots, just as the call to arms had found them. They passed by my bush at the double. The galley had been sent away for more; and the woman sat all alone crying at the end of the pier, with the lanthorn standing on the ground near her.

'Then suddenly I saw appear in the light the red pantaloons of two more men. I was overcome with astonishment.

They too started off at a run. Their tunics flapped unbuttoned
and they were bare-headed. One of them panted out to the
other, 'Straight on, straight on!'

'Where on earth did they come from, I wondered. Slowly I
walked down the short pier. I saw the woman's form shaken
by sobs and heard her moaning more and more distinctly,
"Oh, my man! my man! my man!" I stole on quietly. She could
neither hear nor see anything. She had thrown her apron
over her head and was lost in her grief. But I remarked a
small boat fastened to the end of the pier.

'Those two men—they looked like *sous-officiers**—must
have come in it, after being too late, I suppose, for the
galley. It is incredible that they should have thus broken the
regulations from a sense of duty. And it was a stupid thing
to do. I could not believe my eyes in the very moment I was
stepping into that boat.

'I pulled along the shore slowly. A black cloud hung
over the Iles de Salut. I heard firing, shouts. Another hunt
had begun—the convict-hunt. The oars were too long to
pull comfortably. I managed them with difficulty, though the
boat herself was light. But when I got round to the other
side of the island the squall broke in rain and wind. I was
unable to make head against it. I let her drift ashore and
secured her.

'I knew the spot. There was a tumble-down old hovel standing near the water. Cowering in there, I heard through the
noises of the wind and the falling downpour some people tearing through the bushes. They came out on the strand. Soldiers
perhaps. A flash of lightning threw everything near me into
violent relief. Convicts.

'And directly a voice said, "It's a miracle." It was the voice
of Simon, otherwise Biscuit.

'And another voice growled, "What's a miracle?"

' "Why, there's a boat lying here!"

' "You must be mad, Simon! But there is, after all. . . . A
boat."

'They seemed awed into complete silence. The other man
was Mafile. He spoke again, cautiously.

' "It is fastened up. There must be somebody here."

'I spoke from within the hovel: "I am here."

'They came in then, and soon gave me to understand that the boat was theirs, not mine. "There are two of us," said Mafile, "against you alone."

'I got out into the open to keep clear of them for fear of getting a treacherous blow on the head. I could have shot them both where they stood. But I said nothing. I kept down the laughter rising in my throat. I made myself very humble and begged to be allowed to go. They consulted in low tones about my fate, while with my hand on the revolver in the bosom of my blouse I had their lives in my power. I let them live. I meant them to pull that boat. I represented to them with abject humility that I understood the management of a boat, and that, being three to pull, we could get a rest in turns. That decided them at last. It was time. A little more and I would have gone into screaming fits at the drollness of it.'

At this point his excitement broke out. He jumped off the bench and gesticulated. The great shadows of his arms darting over roof and walls made the shed appear too small to contain his agitation.

'I deny nothing,' he burst out. 'I was elated, monsieur. I tasted a sort of felicity. But I kept very quiet. I took my turns at pulling all through the night. We made for the open sea, putting our trust in a passing ship. It was foolhardy. I persuaded them to it. When the sun rose the immensity of water was calm, and the Iles de Salut appeared only like dark specks from the top of each swell. I was steering then. Mafile, who was pulling bow, let out an oath and said, "We must rest."

'The time to laugh had come at last. And I took my fill of it, I can tell you. I held my sides and rolled, they had such startled faces. "What's got into him, the animal?" cries Mafile.

'And Simon, who was nearest to me, says over his shoulder to him, "Devil take me if I don't think he's gone mad!"

'Then I produced the revolver. Aha! In a moment they both got the stoniest eyes you can imagine. Ha, ha! They were frightened. But they pulled. Oh yes, they pulled all day, sometimes looking wild and sometimes looking faint. I lost nothing of it because I had to keep my eyes on them all the time, or else—crack!—they would have been on top of me in a second. I rested my revolver hand on my knee all ready and steered with the other. Their faces began to blister. Sky and sea seemed on fire round us and the sea steamed in the sun. The boat made a sizzling sound as she went through the water. Sometimes Mafile foamed at the mouth and sometimes he groaned. But he pulled. He dared not stop. His eyes became bloodshot all over, and he had bitten his lower lip to pieces. Simon was as hoarse as a crow.

' "Comrade—" he begins.

' "There are no comrades here. I am your *patron*."

' "*Patron*, then," he says, "in the name of humanity let us rest."

'I let them. There was a little rainwater washing about the bottom of the boat. I permitted them to snatch some of it in the hollow of their palms. But as I said *"En route"* I caught them exchanging significant glances. They thought I would have to go to sleep sometime! Aha! But I did not want to go to sleep. I was more awake than ever. It is they who went to sleep as they pulled, tumbling off the thwarts head over heels suddenly, one after another. I let them lie. All the stars were out. It was a quiet world. The sun rose. Another day. *Allez! En route!**

'They pulled badly. Their eyes rolled about and their tongues hung out. In the middle of the forenoon Mafile croaks out: "Let us make a rush at him, Simon. I would just as soon be shot down as to die of thirst, hunger, and fatigue at the oar."

'But while he spoke he pulled. And Simon kept on pulling too. It made me smile. Ah! They loved their life, these two, in this evil world of theirs, just as I used to love my life, too, before they spoiled it for me with their phrases. I let them go on to the point of exhaustion, and only then I pointed at the sails of a ship on the horizon.

'Aha! You should have seen them revive and buckle to their work! For I kept them at it to pull right across that ship's path. They were changed. The sort of pity I had felt for them left me. They looked more like themselves every minute. They looked at me with the glances I had known so well. They were happy. They smiled.

' "Well," says Simon, "the energy of that youngster has saved our lives. If he hadn't made us, we could never have pulled so far out into the track of ships. Comrade, I forgive you. I admire you."

'And Mafile growls from forward: "We owe you a famous debt of gratitude, comrade. You are cut out for a chief."

'Comrade! Monsieur! Ah, what a good word! And they, such men as these two, had made it accursed. I looked at them. I remembered their lies, their promises, their menaces, and all my days of misery. Why could they not have left me alone after I came out of prison? I looked at them and thought that while they lived I could never be free. Never. Neither I nor others like me with warm hearts and weak heads. For I know I have not a strong head, monsieur. A black rage came upon me—the rage of extreme intoxication, —but not against injustice or society. Oh no!

' "I must be free!" I cried, furiously.

' "*Vive la liberté!*" yells that ruffian Mafile. "*Mort aux bourgeois** who send us to Cayenne! They shall soon know that we are free."

'The sky, the sea, the whole horizon, seemed to turn red to me, blood red all round the boat. My temples were beating so loud that I wondered they did not hear. How is it that they did not? How is it they did not understand?

'I heard Simon ask, "Have we not pulled far enough out now?"

' "Yes. Far enough," I said. I was sorry for him; it was the other I hated. He hauled in his oar with a loud sigh, and as he was raising his hand to wipe his forehead with the air of a man who had done his work, I pulled the trigger of my revolver and shot him like this, off the knee, right through the heart.

'He tumbled down, with his head hanging over the side of the boat. I did not give him a second glance. The other cried out piercingly. Only one shriek of horror. Then all was still.

'He was slipping down off the thwart on to his knees and raised his joined hands before his face in an attitude of

supplication. "Mercy," he whispered, faintly. "Mercy for me!
—comrade."

' "Ah, comrade," I said, in a low tone. "Yes, comrade, of
course. Well, then, shout *Vive l'anarchie*."

'He flung up his arms, his face up to the sky and his
mouth wide open in a great shout of despair. "*Vive l'anarchie! Vive*—"

'He collapsed all in a heap, with a bullet through his
head.

'I flung them both overboard. I threw away the revolver,
too. Then I sat down quietly. I was free at last! At last. I
did not even look towards the ship. I did not care. Indeed,
I think I must have gone to sleep, because all of a sudden
there were shouts and I found the ship almost on top of me.
They hauled me on board and secured the boat astern. They
were all blacks, except the captain, who was a mulatto. He
alone knew a few words of French. I could not find out where
they were going nor who they were. They gave me something
to eat every day; but I did not like the way they used to
discuss me in their language. Perhaps they were deliberating
about throwing me overboard in order to keep possession
of the boat. How do I know? As we were passing this island
I asked whether it was inhabitable. I understood from the
mulatto that there was a house on it. A farm, I fancied. So
I asked them to put me ashore there and keep the boat for
their trouble. This, I imagine, was just what they wanted.
The rest you know.'

After pronouncing these words he lost suddenly all control over himself. He paced to and fro, quicker and quicker,
till he broke into a run; his arms went like a windmill and
his ejaculations became very much like raving. The burden
of them was that he 'denied nothing, nothing!' I could only
let him go on, and sat out of his way, repeating, '*Calmez
vous,* calmez vous*,' at intervals till his agitation exhausted
itself.

I must confess, too, that I remained there long after he had
crawled under his mosquito-net. He had adjured me not to
leave him; so, as one sits up with a nervous child, I sat up
with him—in the name of humanity—till he fell asleep.

On the whole, my idea is that he was much more of an anarchist than he confessed to me or to himself; and that, the special features of his case apart, he was very much like many other anarchists. Warm heart and weak head—that is the word of the riddle; and it is a fact that the bitterest contradictions and the deadliest conflicts of the world are carried on in every individual breast capable of feeling and passion.

From personal inquiry I can vouch that the story of the convict mutiny was in every particular as stated by him.

When I got back to Horta from Cayenne and saw the 'anarchist' again, he did not look well. He was more worn, still more frail, and very livid indeed under the grimy smudges of his calling. Evidently the meat of the company's main herd (in its unconcentrated form) did not agree with him at all.

It was on the pontoon* in Horta that we met; and I tried to induce him to leave the launch moored there and follow me to Europe there and then. It would have been delightful to think of the excellent manager's surprise and disgust at the poor fellow's escape. But he refused with unconquerable obstinacy.

'Surely you don't mean to live always here!' I cried. He shook his head.

'I shall die here,' he said. Then added, moodily, 'Away from them.'

Sometimes I think of him lying open-eyed on his horseman's gear in the low shed full of tools and scraps of iron —the anarchist slave of the Marañon estate, waiting with resignation for that sleep which eluded him, as he used to say, in such an unaccountable manner.

THE INFORMER

MR X came to me with a letter of introduction from a good friend of mine in Paris, specifically to see my collection of Chinese bronzes and porcelain.

My friend in Paris is a collector too. He collects neither porcelain, nor bronzes, nor pictures, nor medals, nor stamps, nor anything that could be profitably dispersed under an auctioneer's hammer. He would reject, with unaffected surprise, the name of a collector. Nevertheless, that is what he is by temperament. He collects acquaintances. It is delicate work. He brings to it the patience, the passion, the determination of a true collector of curiosities. His collection does not contain any royal personages. I don't think he considers them sufficiently rare and interesting; but, with that exception, he has met and talked with every one worth knowing on any conceivable ground. He observes them, listens to them, penetrates them, measures them, and puts the memory away in the galleries of his mind. He has schemed, plotted, and travelled all over Europe in order to add to his collection of distinguished personal acquaintances.

As he is wealthy, well connected, and unprejudiced, his collection is pretty complete, including objects (or should I say subjects?) whose value is unappreciated by the vulgar, and often unknown to popular fame. Of those specimens my friend is naturally the most proud.

He wrote to me of X. 'He is the greatest insurgent (*révolté*) of modern times. The world knows him as a revolutionary writer whose savage irony has laid bare the rottenness of the most respectable institutions. He has scalped every venerated head, and has mangled at the stake of his wit every received opinion and every recognized principle of conduct and policy. Who does not remember those flaming red revolutionary pamphlets whose sudden swarmings used to overwhelm the powers of every Continental police like a sudden plague of crimson gadflies? But this extreme writer has been also a man of action, the inspirer of secret societies, the mysterious unknown Number One* of desperate conspiracies suspected and unsuspected, matured or baffled. And the world at large has never had an inkling of that fact. This accounts for him going about amongst us to this day, a veteran of many subterranean campaigns, standing aside now, safe within his reputation of merely the greatest destructive publicist that ever lived.'

Thus wrote my friend, adding that Mr X was an enlightened connoisseur of bronzes and china, and asking me to show him my collection.

X turned up in due course. My treasures are disposed in three large rooms without carpets and curtains. There is no other furniture than the glass cases and the étagères* whose contents shall be worth a fortune to my heirs. I allow no fires to be lighted, for fear of accidents, and a fire-proof door separates them from the rest of the house.

It was a bitter cold day. We kept on our overcoats and hats. Middle-sized and spare, his eyes alert in a long, Roman-nosed countenance, X walked on neat little feet, with short steps, and looked at my collection intelligently. I hope I looked at him intelligently too. A snow-white mustache and imperial* made his nutbrown complexion appear darker than it really was. In his fur coat and shiny tall hat that terrible man looked fashionable. I believe he belonged to a noble family, and could have called himself Vicomte X de la Z if he chose. We talked nothing but bronzes and porcelain.* He was remarkably appreciative. We parted on cordial terms.

Where he was staying I don't know. I imagine he must have been a lonely man. Anarchists, I suppose, have no families—not, at any rate, as we understand that social relation. Organization into families may answer to a need of human nature, but in the last instance it is based on law, and therefore must be something odious and impossible to an anarchist. But, indeed, I don't understand anarchists. Does a man of that—of that—persuasion still remain an anarchist when alone, quite alone and going to bed, for instance? Does he lay his head on the pillow, pull his bedclothes over him, and go to sleep with the necessity of the *chambardement général*, as the French slang has it, of the general blow-up, always present to his mind? And if so, how can he? I am sure that if such a faith (or such a fanaticism) once mastered my thoughts I would never be able to compose myself sufficiently to sleep or eat or perform any of the routine acts of daily life. I would want no wife, no children; I could have no friends, it seems to me; and as to collecting bronzes or china, that, I should say, would be quite out of the question. But I don't know. All I know is that Mr X took his meals in a very good restaurant which I frequented also.

I used to sit with him at a little table. With his head uncovered, the silver topknot of his brushed-up hair completed the character of his physiognomy, all bony ridges and sunken hollows, clothed in a perfect impassiveness of expression. His meagre brown hands emerging from large white cuffs came and went breaking bread, pouring wine, and so on, with quiet mechanical precision. His head and torso above the table-cloth had a rigid immobility. This firebrand, this great agitator, exhibited the least possible amount of warmth and animation. His voice was rasping, cold, and monotonous in a low key. He could not be called a talkative personality; but with his detached calm manner he appeared as ready to keep the conversation going as to drop it at any moment.

And his conversation was by no means commonplace. To me, I own there was some excitement in talking quietly across a dinner-table with a man whose venomous pen-stabs had sapped the vitality of at least one monarchy. That much was a matter of public knowledge. But I knew more. I knew of him—from my friend—as a certainty what the guardians of social order in Europe had at most only suspected, or dimly guessed at.

He had had what I may call his underground life. And as I sat, evening after evening, facing him at dinner, a curiosity in that direction would naturally arise in my mind. I am a quiet and peaceable product of civilization, and know no passion other than the passion for collecting things which are rare, and must remain exquisite even if approaching to the monstrous. Some Chinese bronzes are monstrously precious. And here (out of my friend's collection), here I had before me a kind of rare monster. It is true that this monster was polished and in a sense even exquisite. His beautiful unruffled manner was that. But then he was not of bronze. He was not even Chinese, which would have enabled one to contemplate him calmly across the gulf of racial difference. He was alive and European; he had the manner of good society, wore a coat and hat like mine, and had pretty near the same taste in cooking. It was too frightful to think of.

One evening he remarked, casually, in the course of conversation, 'There's no amendment to be got out of mankind except by terror and violence.'

You can imagine the effect of such a phrase out of such a man's mouth upon a person like myself, whose whole scheme of life had been based upon a suave and delicate discrimination of social and artistic values. Just imagine! Upon me, to whom all sorts and forms of violence appeared as unreal as the giants, ogres, and seven-headed hydras whose activities affect, fantastically, the course of legends and fairy-tales!

I seemed suddenly to hear above the festive bustle and clatter of the brilliant restaurant the mutter of a hungry and seditious multitude.

I suppose I am impressionable and imaginative. I had a disturbing vision of darkness, full of lean jaws and wild eyes, amongst the hundred electric lights of the place. But somehow this vision made me angry, too. The sight of that man, so calm, breaking bits of his bread, exasperated me. And I had the audacity to ask him how it was that the hungry proletariat of Europe to whom he had been preaching revolt and violence had not been made indignant and angry by his openly luxurious life. 'At all this,' I said, pointedly, with a glance round the room and at the bottle of champagne we generally shared between us at dinner.

He remained unmoved.

'Do I feed on their toil and their heart's blood? Am I a speculator or a capitalist? Did I steal my fortune from a starving people? No! They know this very well. And they envy me nothing. The miserable mass of the people is generous to its leaders. What I have acquired has come to me through my writings; not from the millions of pamphlets distributed gratis to the hungry and the oppressed, but from the hundreds of thousands of copies sold to the well-fed bourgeois. You know that my writings were at one time the rage, the fashion —the thing to read with wonder and horror, to turn your eyes up at my pathos . . . or else to laugh in ecstasies at my wit.'

'Yes,' I admitted. 'I remember, of course; and I confess frankly that I could never understand that infatuation.'

'Don't you know yet,' he said, 'that an idle and selfish class loves to see mischief being made, even if it is made at its own expense? Its own life being all a matter of vestment and gesture, it is unable to realize the power and the danger of real ache and of words that have no sham meaning. It is all fun and sentiment. It is sufficient, for instance, to point out the attitude of the old French aristocracy towards the philosophers whose words were preparing the Great Revolution. Even in England, where you have some common sense, a demagogue has only to shout loud enough and long enough to find some backing in the very class he is shouting at. You too like to see mischief being made. The demagogue gets the amateurs of emotion with him. Amateurism in this, that, and the other thing is a delightfully easy way of killing time, and of feeding one's own vanity—the silly vanity of being abreast with the ideas of the day after to-morrow. Just as good and otherwise harmless people will join you in ecstasies over your collection without having the slightest notion in what its marvellousness really consists.'

I hung my head. It was a crushing illustration of the sad truth he advanced. The world is full of such people. And that instance of the French aristocracy before the Revolution was extremely telling, too. I could not traverse his statement, though its cynicism—always a distasteful trait—took off much of its value, to my mind. However, I admit I was impressed. I felt the need to say something which would not be in the nature of assent and yet would not invite discussion.

'You don't mean to say,' I observed, airily, 'that extreme revolutionists have ever been actively assisted by the infatuation of such people?'

'I did not mean exactly that by what I said just now. I generalized. But since you ask me, I may tell you that such help has been given to revolutionary activities, more or less consciously, in various countries. And even in this country.'

'Impossible!' I protested with firmness. 'We don't play with fire to that extent.'

'And yet you can better afford it than others, perhaps. But let me observe that most women, if not always ready to play with fire, are generally eager to play with a loose spark or so.'

'Is that a joke?' I asked, smiling.

'If it is, I am not aware of it,' he said, woodenly. 'I was thinking of an instance. Oh! mild enough in a way. . . .'

I became all expectation at this. I had tried many times to approach him on his underground side, so to speak. The very word had been pronounced between us. But he had always met me with his impenetrable calm.

'And at the same time,' Mr X continued, 'it will give you a notion of the difficulties that may arise in what you are pleased to call underground work. It is sometimes difficult to deal with them. Of course there is no hierarchy amongst the affiliated. No rigid system.'

My surprise was great, but short-lived. Of course amongst the extreme anarchists there could be no hierarchy; nothing in the nature of a law of precedence. The idea of anarchy ruling among anarchists was comforting, too. It could not possibly make for efficiency.

Mr X startled me by asking, abruptly, 'You know Hermione Street?'

I nodded doubtful assent. Hermione Street has been, within the last three years, improved out of any man's knowledge. The name exists still, but not one brick or stone of the old Hermione Street is left now. It was the old street he meant, for he said:

'There was a row of two-storied brick houses on the left, with their backs against the wing of a great public building—you remember. Would it surprise you very much to hear that one of these houses was for a time the centre of anarchist propaganda and of what you would call underground action?'

'Not at all,' I protested. Hermione Street had never been particularly respectable, as I remembered it.

'The house was the property of a distinguished government official,'* he added, sipping his champagne.

'Oh, indeed!' I said, this time not believing a word of it.

'Of course he was not living there,' Mr X continued. 'But from ten till four he sat next door to it, the dear man, in his well-appointed private room in the wing of the public building I've mentioned. To be strictly accurate, I must explain that the house in Hermione Street perhaps did not really belong to him. It belonged to his grown-up children*—a daughter and a son. The girl, a fine figure, was by no means vulgarly pretty. To more personal charm than mere youth could account for, she added the seductive appearance of enthusiasm, of independence, of courageous thought. I suppose she put them on as she put on her picturesque dresses and for the same reason: to assert her individuality at any cost. You know, women would go to any length almost for such a purpose. She went to a great length. She had acquired all the appropriate gestures* of revolutionary convictions;—the gestures of pity, of anger, of indignation against the anti-humanitarian vices of the social class to which she belonged herself. All this sat on her striking personality as well as her slightly original costumes. Very slightly original; just enough to mark a protest against the philistinism of the overfed taskmasters of the poor. Just enough, and no more. It would not have done to go too far in that direction—you understand. But she was of age, and nothing stood in the way of her offering her house to the revolutionary workers.'

'You don't mean it!' I cried.

'I assure you,' he affirmed, 'that she made that extremely effective gesture. How else could they have got hold of it? The cause is not rich. And, moreover, there would have been difficulties with any ordinary house-agent, who would have wanted references and so on. The group she came in contact with through going about in the poor quarters of the town (you know the gesture of charity and personal service which was so fashionable some years ago) accepted with gratitude. The first advantage was that Hermione Street is, as you know, miles away from the suspect part of the town, specially watched by the police.

'The ground floor consisted of a little Italian restaurant, of the flyblown sort. There was no difficulty in buying the proprietor out. A woman and a man belonging to the group took it on. The man had been a cook. The comrades could get their meals there, unnoticed amongst the other customers. This was another advantage. The first floor was occupied by a shabby Variety Artists' Agency—an agency for performers in inferior music-halls, you know. A fellow called Bomm, I remember. He was not disturbed. It was rather favourable than otherwise to have a lot of foreign-looking people, jugglers, acrobats, singers of both sexes, and so on, going in and out all day long. The police paid no attention to new faces, you see. The top floor happened, most conveniently, to stand empty then.'

X interrupted himself to attack impassively, with measured movements, a *bombe glacée** which the waiter had just set down on the table. He swallowed carefully a few spoonfuls of the iced stuff, and asked me, 'Did you ever hear of Stone's Dried Soup?'

'Hear of what?' I asked, completely put off.

'It was,' X pursued evenly, 'a comestible article, once rather prominently advertised in the dailies, but which never, somehow, gained the favour of the public. The enterprise fizzled out, as you say here. Parcels of their stock could be picked up at auctions at considerably less than a penny a pound. The group bought some of it, and an agency for Stone's Dried Soup was started on the top floor. A perfectly respectable enterprise. The stuff, a yellow powder of extremely unappetizing aspect, was put up in large square tins, of which six went to a case. If anybody ever came to give an order, it was, of course, executed. But the advantage of the powder was this, that things could be concealed in it very conveniently. Now and then a special case got put on a van and sent off to be exported abroad under the very nose of the policeman on duty at the corner. You understand?'

'Perfectly,' I said, with an expressive nod at the remnants of the *bombe* melting slowly in the dish.

'Exactly. But the cases were useful in another way, too. In the basement, or in the cellar at the back, rather, two printing-presses were established. A lot of revolutionary literature of the most extreme kind was got away from the house in Stone's Dried Soup cases. The brother of our anarchist young lady found some occupation there. He wrote articles, helped to set up type and pull off the sheets, and generally assisted the man in charge, a very able young fellow called Sevrin.

'The guiding spirit of that group was a fanatic of social revolution. He is dead now. He was an engraver and etcher of genius. You must have seen his work. It is much sought after by certain amateurs now. But he began by being revolutionary in his art, and ended by becoming a revolutionist, after his wife and child had died in want and misery. He used to say that the bourgeois, the smug overfed lot, had killed them. That was his real belief. He still worked at his art and led a double life. He was tall, gaunt and swarthy, with a dark beard and deep-set eyes. You must have seen him. His name was Horne.'

At this I was really amazed. Of course years ago I used to meet Horne about. He looked like a powerful, rough gipsy, with a red muffler round his throat and buttoned up in a long, shabby overcoat. He talked of art with exaltation, and gave one the impression of being strung up to the verge of insanity. A small group of connoisseurs appreciated his work. Who would have thought that this man. . . . Amazing! And yet it was not, after all, so difficult to believe.

'As you see,' X went on, 'this group was in a position to pursue its work of propaganda, and the other kind of work too, under very advantageous conditions. They were all resolute, experienced men of a superior stamp. And yet we became struck at length by the fact that plans prepared in Hermione Street almost invariably failed.'

'Who were "we"?' I asked pointedly.

'Some of us in Brussels—at the centre,' he said hastily. 'Whatever vigorous action originated in Hermione Street seemed doomed to failure. Something always happened to baffle the best-planned manifestations in every part of Europe. It was a time of general activity. You must not imagine that all our failures are of a loud sort, with arrests and trials. That is not so. Often the police work quietly, contenting themselves by defeating our combinations by a sort of counterplotting. No arrests, no noise, no alarming of the public mind and inflaming the passions. It is a wise procedure. But at that time the police were too uniformly successful from Mediterranean to the Baltic. It was annoying and began to look dangerous. At last we in Brussels came to the conclusion that there must be some untrustworthy elements amongst the London groups. And I came over to see what could be done quietly.

'My first step was to call upon our young Lady Patroness of anarchism at her private house. She received me in a flattering way. I judged that she knew nothing of the chemical and other operations going on at the top of the house in Hermione Street. The printing of anarchist literature was the only "activity" she seemed to be aware of there. She was displaying very strikingly the usual signs of severe enthusiasm, and had already written many sentimental articles with ferocious conclusions. I could see she was enjoying herself hugely, with all the gestures and grimaces of deadly earnestness. They suited her big-eyed, broad-browed face and the good carriage of her shapely head. Her black hair was done in an unusual and becoming style. Her brother was there, a serious youth, with arched eyebrows and wearing a red necktie, who struck me as being absolutely in the dark about everything in the world, including himself. By and by a tall young man came in. He was clean-shaved, with a strong jaw and something of the air of a taciturn actor or of a fanatical priest: the type with heavy black eyebrows—you know. But he was very presentable indeed. He shook hands at once vigorously with each of us in turn. The young lady came up to me and murmured sweetly, "Comrade Sevrin."

'I had never seen him before. He had little to say to us, but sat down by the side of the girl, and they fell at once into earnest conversation. She leaned forward in her deep arm-chair, and took her nicely rounded chin in her beautiful white hand. He looked attentively into her eyes. It was the attitude of love-making, serious, intense, as if on the brink of the grave. I suppose she felt it necessary to round and complete her assumption of advanced ideas, of revolutionary lawlessness, by falling in love with an anarchist. And this one, I repeat, was extremely presentable, notwithstanding his fanatical black-eyed aspect. After a few stolen glances in their direction, I had no doubt that he was in earnest. As to the lady, her gestures were unapproachable, better than the very thing itself in the blended suggestion of dignity, sweetness, condescension, fascination, surrender, and reserve. She interpreted her conception of what that precise sort of love-making should be with consummate art. And so far, she too, no doubt, was in earnest. Gestures—but so perfect!

'After I had been left alone with our Lady Patroness I informed her guardedly of the object of my visit. I hinted at our suspicions. I wanted to hear what she would have to say, and half expected some perhaps unconscious revelation. All she said was, "That's serious," looking delightfully concerned and grave. But there was a sparkle in her eyes which meant plainly, "How exciting!" After all, she knew little of anything except of words. Still, she undertook to put me in communication with Horne, who was not easy to find except in Hermione Street, where I did not wish to show myself just then.

'I met Horne. This was another kind of a fanatic altogether. I exposed to him the conclusion we in Brussels had arrived at, and pointed out to him the significant series of failures. To this he answered with exaltation:

'"I have something in hand that shall not fail to strike terror into the heart of these gorged brutes."

'And then I learned that by excavating in one of the cellars of the house he and some companions had made their way into the vaults under the great public building I have mentioned before. The blowing up of a whole wing was a certainty as soon as the materials were ready.

'I was not so appalled at the stupidity of that move as I might have been had not the usefulness of our centre in Hermione Street become already very problematical. In fact, in my opinion it was much more of a police trap by now than anything else.

'What was necessary now was to discover what, or rather who, was wrong, and I managed at last to get that idea into

Horne's head. He glared, perplexed, his nostrils working as if he were sniffing treachery in the air.

'And here comes a piece of work that will no doubt strike you as a sort of theatrical expedient. And yet what else could have been done? I wished to find out the untrustworthy member of the group. But no suspicion could be fastened on one more than another. To set a watch upon them all was not very practicable. Besides, that proceeding often fails. In any case, it takes time, and the danger was pressing. I felt certain that the premises in Hermione Street would be ultimately raided, though the police had evidently such confidence in the informer that the house, for the time being, was not even watched. Horne was positive about that point. Under the circumstances it was a bad symptom. Something had to be done quickly.

'I decided to organize a raid myself upon the group. Do you understand? A raid of other trusty comrades personating the police. A conspiracy within a conspiracy. You see the object of it, of course. When apparently about to be arrested I hoped the informer would betray himself in some way or other; either by some unguarded act or simply by his unconcerned demeanour, for instance. Of course there was the risk of complete failure and the no lesser risk of some fatal accident in the course of resistance, perhaps, or in the efforts at escape. For, as you will easily see, the Hermione Street group had to be actually and completely taken unawares, as I was sure they would be by the real police before very long. The informer was amongst them, and Horne alone could be let into the secret of my plan.

'I will not enter into the detail of my preparations. It was not very easy to arrange, but it was done very well, with a really amazing effect. The sham police invaded the restaurant, whose shutters were immediately put up. The surprise was perfect. Most of the Hermione Street party were found in the second cellar, enlarging the hole communicating with the vaults of the great public building. At the first alarm, several comrades bolted through impulsively into the aforesaid vault, where, of course, had this been a genuine raid, they would have been hopelessly trapped. We did not bother about them for the moment. They were harmless enough. The top floor caused considerable anxiety to Horne and myself. There, surrounded by tins of Stone's Dried Soup, a comrade, nicknamed the Professor* (he was an ex-science student), was engaged in perfecting some new detonators. He was an abstracted, vaguely smiling, sallow little man, armed with large round spectacles, and we were afraid that under a mistaken impression he would blow himself up and wreck the house about our ears. I rushed up-stairs and found him already at the door on the alert, listening, as he said, to "suspicious noises down below." Before I had quite finished explaining to him what was going on, he shrugged his shoulders and turned away to his balances and test-tubes. His was the true spirit of an extreme revolutionist. Explosives were his faith, his hope, his weapon, and his shield. He perished a couple of years afterwards in a secret laboratory through the premature explosion of one of his improved detonators.

'Hurrying down again, I found an impressive scene in the vast gloom of the big cellar. The man who personated the inspector (he was no stranger to the part) was speaking harshly, and giving bogus orders to his bogus subordinates for the removal of his prisoners. Evidently nothing enlightening had happened so far. Horne, saturnine and swarthy, waited with folded arms, and his patient, moody expectation had an air of stoicism well in keeping with the situation. I detected in the shadows one of the Hermione Street group surreptitiously chewing up and swallowing a small piece of paper. Some compromising scrap, I suppose; perhaps just a note of a few names and addresses. He was a true and faithful "companion." But the fund of secret malice which lurks at the bottom of our sympathies caused me to feel amused at that perfectly uncalled-for performance.

'In every other respect the risky experiment, the theatrical *coup*, if you like to call it so, seemed to have failed. The deception could not be kept up much longer; the explanation would bring about a very embarrassing and even grave situation. The man who had eaten the paper would be furious. The fellows who had bolted away would be angry too.

'To add to my vexation, the door communicating with the other cellar, where the printing-presses were, was flung open, and our young lady revolutionist appeared, a black silhouette in a close-fitting dress and a large hat, with the blaze of gas flaring in there at her back. Over her shoulder I perceived the arched eyebrows and the red necktie of her brother.

'The last people in the world I wanted to see then! They had gone that evening to some amateur concert for the delectation of the poor people, you know; but she had insisted on leaving early on purpose to call in Hermione Street on the way home, under the pretext of having some work to do. Her usual task was to correct the proofs of the Italian and French editions of the *Alarm Bell* and the *Firebrand*.'. . .*

'Heavens!' I murmured. I had been shown once copies of these publications. Nothing, in my opinion, could have been less fit for the eyes of a young lady. They were the most advanced things of the sort; advanced, I mean, beyond all bounds of reason and decency. One of them preached the dissolution of all social ties; the other advocated systematic murder. To think of a young girl calmly tracking printers' errors all along the sort of abominable sentences I remembered was intolerable to my sentiment of womanhood. And Mr X, after giving me a glance, pursued steadily:

'I think, however, that she came mostly to exercise her fascinations upon Sevrin, and to receive his homage in her queenly and condescending way. She was aware of both—fascination and homage—and enjoyed them with, I dare say, complete innocence. And we have no ground in expediency or morals to quarrel with her on that account. Charm in woman and exceptional intelligence in man are a law unto themselves. Is it not so?'

I refrained from expressing my abhorrence of that licentious doctrine because of my curiosity.

'But what happened then?' I hastened to ask.

X went on crumbling slowly a small piece of bread with a careless left hand.

'What happened, in effect,' he confessed, 'is that she saved the situation.'

'She gave you an opportunity to end your rather sinister farce,' I suggested.

'Yes,' he said, preserving his impassive bearing. 'The farce was bound to end soon. And it ended in a very few minutes. And it ended well. It might have ended badly had she not come in. Her brother, of course, did not count. They had slipped into the house quietly some time before. The printing-cellar had an entrance of its own. Not finding any one there, she sat down to her proofs, expecting Sevrin to return to his work at any moment. He did not do so. She grew impatient, heard through the door the sounds of a commotion, and naturally went to see.

'Sevrin had been with us. At first he had seemed to me the most amazed of the whole raided lot. He appeared for an instant as if paralysed with astonishment. He stood rooted to the spot. He never moved a limb. A solitary gas-jet flared near his head; all the other lights had been put out at the first alarm. And presently, from my dark corner, I observed on his shaven actor's face an expression of puzzled, vexed watchfulness, with a knitting of his heavy eyebrows. The corners of his mouth dropped scornfully. He was angry. Most likely he had seen through the game, and I regretted I had not taken him from the first into my complete confidence.

'But with the appearance of the girl he became obviously alarmed. It was plain. I could see it grow. The change of his expression was swift and startling. All other sensations and emotions were swept away by a wave of sheer terror. And I did not know why. The reason never occurred to me. I was merely astonished at the extreme alteration of the man's face. Of course he had not been aware of her presence in the other cellar. But that did not explain the shock her advent had given him. For a moment he seemed to have been scared into imbecility. He opened his mouth as if to shout, or perhaps only to gasp. At any rate, it was somebody else who shouted. This somebody else was the heroic comrade whom I had detected swallowing a piece of paper. With laudable presence of mind he let out a warning yell.

'"It's the police! Back! Back! Run back, and bolt the door behind you."

'It was an excellent hint; but instead of retreating, the girl for whom it was meant continued to advance, followed by her long-faced brother in his knickerbocker suit,* in which he had been singing comic songs for the entertainment of a joyless proletariat. She advanced not as if she had failed to understand—the word "police" has an unmistakable sound— but rather as if she could not help herself. She did not advance with the free gait and expanding presence of a distinguished amateur anarchist amongst poor, struggling professionals, but with slightly raised shoulders, and her elbows pressed close to her body, as if trying to shrink within herself. Her eyes were fixed immovably upon Sevrin. Sevrin the man, I fancy; not Sevrin the anarchist. But she advanced. And that was natural. For all their assumption of independence, girls of that class are used to the feeling of being specially protected, as, in fact, they are. This feeling accounts for nine-tenths of their audacious gestures. Her face had gone completely colourless. Ghastly. Fancy having it brought home to her so brutally that she was the sort of person who must run away from the police! I believe she was pale with indignation, mostly, though there was, of course, also the concern for her intact personality, a vague dread of some sort of rudeness. And, naturally, she turned to a man, to the man on whom she had a claim of fascination and homage—the man who could not conceivably fail her at any juncture.'

'But,' I cried, amazed at this analysis, 'if it had been serious, real, I mean—as she thought it was—what could she expect him to do for her?'

X never moved a muscle of his face.

'Goodness knows. I imagine that this charming, generous, and independent creature had never known in her life a single genuine thought; I mean a single thought detached from small human vanities, or whose source was not in some conventional perception. All I know is that after advancing a few steps she extended her hand towards the motionless Sevrin. And that at least was no gesture. It was a natural movement. As to what she expected him to do, who can tell? The impossible. But whatever she expected, it could not have come up, I am safe to say, to what he had made up his mind to do, even before that entreating hand had appealed to him so directly. It had not been necessary. From the moment he had seen her enter that cellar, he had made up his mind to sacrifice his future usefulness, to throw off the impenetrable solidly fastened mask it had been his pride to wear—'

'What do you mean?' I interrupted, puzzled. 'Was it Sevrin, then, who was—'

'He was. The most persistent, the most dangerous, the craftiest, the most systematic of informers.* A genius amongst betrayers. Fortunately for us, he was unique. The man was a fanatic, I have told you. Fortunately, again, for us, he had fallen in love with the accomplished and innocent gestures of that girl. An actor in desperate earnest himself, he must have believed in the absolute value of conventional signs. As to the grossness of the trap into which he fell, the explanation must be that two sentiments of such absorbing magnitude cannot exist simultaneously in one heart. The danger of that other and unconscious comedian robbed him of his vision, of his perspicacity, of his judgement. Indeed, it did at first rob him of his self-possession. But he regained that through the necessity—as it appeared to him imperiously—to do something at once. To do what? Why, to get her out of the house as quickly as possible. He was desperately anxious to do that. I have told you he was terrified. It could not be about himself. He had been surprised and annoyed at a move quite unforeseen and premature. I may even say he had been furious. He was accustomed to arrange the last scene of his betrayals with a deep, subtle art which left his revolutionist reputation untouched. But it seems clear to me that at the same time he had resolved to make the best of it, to keep his mask resolutely on. It was only with the discovery of her being in the house that everything—the forced calm, the restraint of his fanaticism, the mask—all came off together in a kind of panic. Why panic, do you ask? The answer is very simple. He remembered—or, I dare say, he had never forgotten the Professor alone at the top of the house, pursuing his researches, surrounded by tins upon tins of Stone's Dried Soup. There was enough in some few of them to bury us all where we stood under a heap of bricks. Sevrin, of course, was aware of that. And we must believe, also, that he knew the exact character of the man, apparently. He had gauged so many such characters! Or perhaps he only gave the Professor credit for what he himself was capable of. But, in any case, the effect was produced. And suddenly he raised his voice in authority.

'"Get the lady away at once."

'It turned out that he was as hoarse as a crow. Result, no doubt, of the intense emotion. It passed off in a moment. But these fateful words issued forth from his contracted throat in a discordant, ridiculous croak. They required no answer. The thing was done. However, the man personating the inspector judged it expedient to say roughly:

'"She shall go soon enough, together with the rest of you."

'These were the last words belonging to the comedy part of this affair.

'Oblivious of everything and everybody, Sevrin strode towards him and seized the lapels of his coat. Under his thin bluish cheeks one could see his jaws working with passion.

'"You have men posted outside. Get the lady taken home at once. Do you hear? Now. Before you try to get hold of the man up-stairs."

'"Oh! There is a man up-stairs," scoffed the other, openly. "Well, he shall be brought down in time to see the end of this."

'But Sevrin, beside himself, took no heed of the tone.

'"Who's the imbecile meddler who sent you blundering here? Didn't you understand your instructions? Don't you know anything? It's incredible. Here——"

'He dropped the lapels of the coat he had been shaking. He plunged his hand into his breast and jerked feverishly at something under his shirt. At last he produced a small square pocket of soft leather, which must have been hanging like a scapulary from his neck by the tape, whose broken ends dangled from his fist.

'"Look inside," he spluttered, flinging it in the other's face. And instantly he turned round towards the girl. She stood just behind him, perfectly still and silent. Her set, white face gave an illusion of placidity. Only her staring eyes seemed to have grown bigger and darker.

'He spoke to her rapidly, with nervous assurance. I heard him distinctly promise to make everything as clear as daylight presently. But that was all I caught. He stood close to her and never raised his hand, never attempted to touch her even with the tip of his little finger. And she stared at him stupidly. For a moment, however, her eyelids descended slowly, pathetically, and then, with the long black eyelashes lying on her white cheeks, she looked as if she were about to fall headlong in a swoon. But she never even swayed where she stood. He urged her loudly to follow him without losing an instant, and walked towards the door at the bottom of the cellar stairs without looking behind him. And, as a matter of fact, she did move after him a pace or two. But, of course, he was not allowed to reach the door. There were angry exclamations, the tumult of a short, fierce scuffle. Flung away violently, he came flying backwards upon her. She threw out her arms in a gesture of dismay and stepped aside, just clear of his head, which struck the ground heavily near her shoe.

'He grunted with the shock. By the time he had picked himself up, slowly, dazedly, he was awake to the reality of things. The man into whose hands he had thrust the leather case had extracted therefrom a narrow strip of bluish paper. He held it up above his head, and, as after the scuffle an expectant uneasy stillness reigned once more, he threw it down disdainfully with the words, "I think, comrades, that this proof was hardly necessary."

'Quick as thought, the girl stooped after the fluttering slip. Holding it spread out in both hands, she looked at it; then, without raising her eyes, opened her fingers slowly and let it fall.

'I examined that curious document afterwards. It was signed by a very high personage, and stamped and countersigned by other high officials in various countries of Europe. In his trade—or shall I say, in his mission?—that sort of talisman might have been necessary, no doubt, for even to the police itself—all but the heads—he had been known only as Sevrin the noted anarchist.

'He hung his head, biting his lower lip. A change had come over him, a sort of thoughtful, absorbed calmness. Nevertheless, he panted. His sides worked visibly, and his nostrils expanded and collapsed in weird contrast with his sombre aspect of a fanatical monk in a meditative attitude, but with something, too, in his face of an actor intent upon the terrible exigencies of his part. Before him Horne declaimed, haggard and bearded, like an inspired denunciatory prophet from a wilderness. Two fanatics. They were made to understand each other. Does this surprise you? I suppose you think that such people are given to foaming at the mouth and snarling at each other?'

I protested hastily that I was not surprised in the least; that I thought nothing of the kind; that anarchists in general were simply inconceivable to me mentally, morally, logically, sentimentally, and even physically. X received this declaration with his usual woodenness and went on.

'Horne had burst out into eloquence. While pouring out scornful invective, he let tears escape from his eyes. They fell down his black beard unheeded. Sevrin panted quicker and quicker. When he opened his mouth to speak, every one hung on his words.

' "Don't be a fool, Horne," he began. "You know very well that I have done this for none of the reasons you are throwing at me." And in a moment he became outwardly as steady as a rock under the other's livid stare. "I have been thwarting, deceiving and betraying you—from conviction."

'He turned his back on Horne, and, looking intently at the girl, repeated the words, "From conviction."

'It's extraordinary how cold she looked. I suppose she could not think of an appropriate gesture. There can have been few precedents indeed for such a situation.

' "Clear as daylight," he added. "Do you understand? From conviction."

'And still she did not stir. She did not know how to respond. But the luckless wretch was about to give her the opportunity for a beautiful and correct gesture.

' "And I had in me the power to make you share it," he protested, ardently. He had forgotten himself. He made a step towards her. Perhaps he stumbled. To me he seemed only to be stooping low before her with an extended hand. And then the appropriate gesture came. She snatched her skirt away from his polluting touch and turned her head from him with an upward tilt. It was magnificently done, this gesture of conventionally unstained honour, of an unblemished high-minded amateur.

'Nothing could have been better. And he seemed to think so, too, for once more he turned away. But this time he faced no one. He was again panting frightfully, while he fumbled hurriedly in his waistcoat pocket, and then raised his hand to his lips. There was something furtive in this movement, but directly his bearing changed visibly. His laboured breathing gave him a resemblance to a man who had just run a desperate race; a curious air of detachment, of sudden and profound indifference, replaced the strain of the striving effort. I did not want to see what would happen next. I was only too well aware. I tucked the young lady's arm under mine without a word, and made my way with her to the stairs.

'Her brother walked behind us. Half-way up she seemed unable to lift her feet high enough, and we had to pull and push to get her to the top. In the passage she dragged herself along, hanging on my arm, helplessly bent like an impotent old woman. We issued into an empty street through a half-open door, staggering like besotted revellers. At the corner we stopped a four-wheeler, and the ancient driver looked round from his box with morose contempt at our efforts to get her in. Twice during the drive I felt her collapse on my shoulder in a half faint. Facing us, the youth in knickerbockers remained as mute as a fish, and, till he jumped out with the latch-key, more still than I would have believed it possible.

'At the door of their drawing-room she left my arm and walked in first, catching at the chairs and tables. She unpinned her hat, then, as if exhausted with the effort, her cloak still hanging from her shoulders; she flung herself into the deep arm-chair, sideways, her face half buried in a cushion. The good brother appeared silently with a glass of water. She motioned it away. He drank it himself and walked to a distant corner of the room—behind the grand piano, somewhere.

All was still in this room where I had seen, for the first time, Sevrin, the anti-anarchist, captivated and spellbound by the consummate and hereditary grimaces that in a certain sphere of life take the place of feelings with an excellent effect. I suppose her thoughts were busy with the same memory. Her shoulders were shaken by dry sobs. A pure attack of nerves. When it quieted down she murmured drearily, "What will they do to him?"

'"Nothing. They can do nothing to him," I assured her, with perfect truth. I was pretty certain he had died in less than twenty minutes from the moment his hand had gone to his lips. For if his fanatical anti-anarchism went even as far as carrying poison in his pocket, only to rob his adversaries of their legitimate vengeance, I knew he would take care to provide something that would not fail him when required.

'She sighed deeply. There were red spots on her cheeks and a feverish brilliance in her eyes while she exhaled her characteristic plaint.

'"What an awful, terrible experience, to be so basely, so abominably, so cruelly deceived by a man to whom one has given one's whole confidence!" She gulped down a pathetic sob. "If I ever felt sure of anything, it was of Sevrin's high-mindedness."

'Then she began to weep quietly, which was good for her. Then through her flood of tears, half resentful, "What was it he said to me?—'From conviction!' It seemed worse than anything. What could he mean by it?"

'"That, my dear young lady," I said gently, "is more than I or anybody else can explain to you."

'Mr X flicked a crumb off the front of his coat.

'And that was strictly true as to her. Though Horne, for instance, understood very well; and so did I, especially after we had been to Sevrin's lodging in a dismal back street of an intensely respectable quarter. Horne was known there as a friend, and we had no difficulty in being admitted, the slatternly girl merely remarking, as she let us in, that "Mr Sevrin had not been home that night." We forced a couple of drawers in the way of duty, and found a little useful information. The most interesting part was his diary; for this man, engaged in such deadly work, had the weakness to keep a record of the most damnatory kind. There were his acts and also his thoughts laid bare to us. But the dead don't mind that. They don't mind anything.

' "From conviction." Yes. The vague but ardent humanitarianism which had urged him in his first youth to embrace the extreme revolutionary doctrines had ended in a sudden revulsion of feeling. You have heard of converted atheists. These turn often into dangerous fanatics. But the soul remains the same, after all. After he had got acquainted with the girl, there are to be met in that diary of his, mingled with amorous rhapsodies, bizarre, piously worded aspirations for her conversion. He took her sovereign grimace with deadly seriousness. But all this cannot interest you. For the rest, I don't know if you remember—it is a good many years ago now—the journalistic sensation of the "Hermione Street Mystery"; the finding of a man's body in the cellar of an empty house; the inquest; some arrests; many surmises—then silence—the usual end for many obscure martyrs and confessors. The fact is, he was not enough of an optimist. You must be a savage, determined, pitiless, thick-and-thin optimist, like Horne, for instance, to make a good revolutionist of the extreme type.'

He rose from the table. A waiter hurried up with his overcoat; another held his hat in readiness.

'But what became of the young lady?' I asked.

'I happen to know,' he said, buttoning himself up carefully. 'I confess to the small malice of sending her Sevrin's diary. She went into retirement; then she went to Rome; then she went into a convent. I don't know where she will go next. What does it matter? Gestures! Gestures! Mere gestures of her class.'

He fitted on his glossy high hat with extreme precision, and casting a slight glance round the room, full of well-dressed people, innocently dining, muttered between his teeth,

'And nothing else! That is why their kind is fated to perish.'

I never saw Mr X again after that evening. I took to dining elsewhere. On my next visit to Paris I found my friend all impatience to hear of the effect produced on me by this rare item of his collection. I told him all the story, and he beamed on me with the pride of his distinguished specimen.

'Isn't X well worth knowing?' he bubbled over in great delight. 'He's unique, amazing, absolutely terrific.'

His enthusiasm grated upon my finer feelings. I told him curtly that the man's cynicism was simply abominable.

'Oh, abominable! abominable!' my friend asserted effusively. 'And then, you know, he likes to have his little joke sometimes,' he added in a confidential tone.

I fail to understand the connection of this last remark. I have been utterly unable to discover where in all this the joke comes in.

THE BRUTE
A Piece of Invective

On dodging in from the rain-swept street, I exchanged a smile and a glance with Miss Blank in the bar of the Three Crows. This exchange was effected with extreme propriety. It's a shock to think that, if still alive, Miss Blank must be something over sixty now. How the time flies!

Noticing my gaze directed inquiringly at the partition of glass and varnished wood, Miss Blank was good enough to say encouragingly:

'Only Mr Jermyn and Mr Stone in the parlour, with a gentleman I've never seen before.'

I moved toward the parlour door. A voice discoursing on the other side (it was but a match-board partition) rose so loudly that the concluding words became quite plain in all their atrocity:

'That fellow Wilmot fairly dashed her brains out, and a good job, too!'

This inhuman sentiment, since there was nothing profane or improper in it, failed to so much as check the slight yawn Miss Blank was achieving behind her hand. And she remained gazing fixedly at the window-panes, which streamed with rain.

As I opened the parlour door the same voice went on in the same cruel strain:

'I was glad when I heard she got the knock from somebody at last. Sorry enough for poor Wilmot, though. That man and I used to be chums at one time. Of course, that was the end of him. A clear case, if there ever was one. No way out of it—none at all.'

The voice belonged to the gentleman Miss Blank had never seen before. He straddled his long legs on the hearthrug. Jermyn, leaning forward, held his pocket handkerchief spread out before the grate. He looked back dismally over his shoulder, and as I slipped behind one of the little wooden tables I nodded to him. On the other side of the fire, imposingly calm and large, sat Mr Stone, jammed tight into a capacious Windsor armchair.* There was nothing small about him but his short white side-whiskers. Yards and yards of extra superfine pilot-cloth (made up into an overcoat) lay piled up on a chair by his side. And he must just have brought some liner from sea, because another chair was smothered under his black water-proof, made of threefold oiled silk, double-stitched throughout. A man's hand-bag of the usual size reposing on the floor was dwarfed to a child's toy by the striking proportions of his boots.

I did not nod to him. He was too big to be nodded to in that parlour. He was a senior Trinity* pilot, and condescended to take his turn in the cutter only during the summer months. He had been many times in charge of royal yachts, in and out of Port Victoria.* Besides, it's no use nodding to a monument. And he was like one. He didn't speak, he didn't blink, he didn't budge. He just sat there, holding his handsome old head up, immovable and almost bigger than life. It was extremely fine. Mr Stone's presence reduced poor old Jermyn to a mere shabby wisp of a man, and made the talkative stranger in tweeds on the hearth-rug look absurdly boyish. This last must have been a few years over thirty, and was certainly not the sort of individual that gets abashed at the sound of his own voice, because, gathering me in, as it were, by a friendly glance, he kept it going without a check.

'I was glad of it,' he repeated emphatically. 'You may be surprised at it, but then, you haven't gone through the experience I've had of her. I can tell you, it was something to remember. Of course, I got off scot-free,—as you can see,—though she did her best to break up my pluck for me. She jolly near drove as fine a fellow as ever lived into a madhouse. What do you say to that—eh?'

Not an eyelid twitched in Mr Stone's enormous face. Monumental! The speaker looked straight into my eyes.

'It used to make me sick to think of her going about the world murdering people.'

Old Jermyn approached the handkerchief a little nearer to the grate and groaned. It was simply a habit he had.

'I've seen her once,' he declared with mournful indifference. 'She had a house—'

The stranger in tweeds turned to stare down at him, surprised.

'She had three houses,' he corrected, authoritatively. But old Jermyn was not to be contradicted.

'She had a house, I say,' he repeated, with dismal obstinacy, —'a great—big—ugly—white thing. You could see it from miles away—sticking up.'

'So you could,' assented the other readily. 'It was old Colchester's notion, though he was always threatening to give her up. He couldn't stand her any more; he declared it was too much of a good thing for him; he would wash his hands of her, if he never got another—and so on. I dare say he would have chucked her, only—it may surprise you—his missus wouldn't hear of it. Funny, eh? But, with women, you never know how they will take a thing. Mrs Colchester, with her mustaches and big eyebrows, set up for being strong-minded. She used to walk about dressed in brown silk, with a great gold cable flopping about her bosom. You should have heard her snap out "Rubbish!" or "Stuff and nonsense!" I dare say she knew when she was well off. They had no children and had never set up a home anywhere. When in England, Mrs Colchester stayed with some of her relations or just made shift to hang out anyhow in some cheap hotel or boarding-house. I dare say she liked to get back to the comforts she was used to. She knew very well she couldn't gain by a change. And, moreover, Colchester, though a first-rate man, was not what you may call in his first youth, and perhaps she may have thought that he wouldn't be able to get another (as he used to say) so easily. Anyhow, for one reason or another, it was "Rubbish" and "Stuff and nonsense" for the good lady. I once overheard Mr Lucian Apse himself say to her confidentially, "I assure you, Mrs Colchester, I am beginning to feel quite unhappy about the name she's getting for herself." "Oh!" she said, with her deep little horse-laugh, "if one took notice of all the silly talk!" And she showed Apse all her ugly false teeth at once. "It would take more than that to make me lose my confidence in her, I assure you," she says.'

At this point, without any change of facial expression, Mr Stone emitted a short, sardonic laugh. It was very impressive, but I didn't see the joke. I looked from one to the other. The stranger on the hearth-rug had an ugly smile.

'And Mr Lucian Apse shook both Mrs Colchester's hands, he was so pleased to hear a good word said for their favourite. All these Apses, young and old, you know were perfectly infatuated with that abominable, dangerous . . .'

'I beg your pardon,' I interrupted, exasperated, for he seemed to be addressing himself exclusively to me, 'but who on earth have you been talking about?'

'The Apse family,' he answered courteously.

Miss Blank put her head in and said that the cab was at the door, if Mr Stone wanted to catch the eleven-three up.*

At once the senior pilot rose in his mighty bulk and began to struggle into his coat with awe-inspiring upheavals. The stranger and I hurried impulsively to his assistance, and directly we laid our hands on him he became perfectly quiescent. We had to raise our arms very high and to make efforts. It was like caparisoning a gentle elephant. With a loud, 'Thanks, gentlemen!' Mr Stone dived under and squeezed himself through the door in a great hurry.

We smiled at each other in a friendly way.

'I wonder how he gets up a ship's side-ladder,' said the man in tweeds; and poor Jermyn, who was a mere North Sea pilot without official status or recognition of any sort, pilot only by courtesy, groaned:

'He makes eight hundred a year.'

'Are you a sailor?' I asked the stranger, who had come back to his position on the rug.

'I used to be till a couple of years ago, when I got married. I even went to sea first in that very ship we were speaking of when you came in.'

'What ship?' I asked, puzzled. 'I never heard you mention a ship.'

'I've just told you her name, my dear sir,' he replied. 'The *Apse Family*. Surely you've heard of the great firm of Apse & Sons, shipping owners. They had a pretty big fleet. There was the *Lucy Apse* and the *Harold Apse*, and *Anne*, *John*,

Malcolm, Clara, Juliet, and so on—no end of *Apse*s. Every
brother, sister, aunt, cousin, wife—and grandmother, too, for
all I know—of the firm had a ship named after them. Good,
solid, old-fashioned lot they were, too, built to carry and to
last. None of your newfangled labour-saving appliances in
them, but plenty of men and plenty of good salt beef and
hardtack* put aboard—and off you go to fight your way
out and home again.'

Old Jermyn made a sound of approval which sounded like
a groan of pain. Those were the ships for him. He pointed
out in doleful tones that you couldn't say to labour-saving
appliances, 'Jump lively now, my hearties.' No labour-saving
appliance would go aloft on a dirty night, with the sands
under your lee.*

'No,' assented the stranger, with a wink at me. 'The Apses
didn't believe in them, either, apparently. They treated their
people well—as people don't get treated nowadays—and they
were awfully proud of their ships. Nothing ever happened
to them. This last one, the *Apse Family*, was to be like the
others, only she was to be still stronger, still safer, still more
roomy and comfortable. I believe they meant her to last
forever. They had her built composite—iron, teak-wood, and
greenheart, and her scantling* was something fabulous. If ever
an order was given for a ship in a spirit of pride! Everything
of the best. The commodore-captain* of the employ was to
command her, and they planned the accommodation for him
like a house on shore under a big tall poop* that went nearly
to the mainmast. No wonder Mrs Colchester wouldn't let the
old man give her up. Why, it was the best home she ever
had in all her married days. Ah! she had nerve, that woman.

'The fuss that was made while the ship was building! "Let's
have this a little stronger, and that a little heavier, and hadn't
that other thing better be changed for something a little
thicker?" The builders entered into the spirit of the thing,
and there she was, growing into the clumsiest, heaviest ship
of her size, right before all their eyes, without anybody getting aware of it, somehow. She was to be 2,000 tons register,
or a little over; no less on any account. But see what happens.
When they came to measure her, she turned out 1,999 tons

and a fraction, and no more. General consternation! And
they say old Mr Apse was so annoyed that he took to his
bed and died. The old gentleman had retired from active
business twenty-five years before, and was ninety-six at the
time, if a day, so his death wasn't perhaps so surprising. Still,
Mr Lucian Apse was convinced that his father would have
lived to a hundred. So we may put him at the head of the
list. Next comes the poor devil of a shipwright that brute
caught and squashed as she went off the ways. They called
it the launch of a ship, but I've heard people say that, from
the wailing and yelling and scrambling out of the way, it was
more like letting a devil loose upon the river. She snapped
all the checks like pack-thread, and went for her own tugs
in attendance like a fury. Before anybody could see what she
was up to, she sent one to the bottom, and laid up another
for three months' repairs. One of her cables parted, and then,
suddenly—you couldn't tell why—she let herself be brought
up with the other as quiet as a lamb.

'That's how she was. You could never be sure what she
would be up to next. There are ships difficult to handle, but
generally you can depend on them behaving rationally. But
with that ship, whatever you did with her, you never knew
how it would end. Ah! she was a wicked beast. . . . Or perhaps she was only just insane.'

He uttered this supposition in so earnest a tone that I
could not refrain from smiling. He left off biting his lower
lip to apostrophize me.

'Eh! Why not? Why couldn't there be something in her
build, in her lines, corresponding to . . . What's madness?
Only something just a tiny bit wrong in the make of your
brain. Why shouldn't there be a mad ship?—I mean mad in
a shiplike way, so that under no circumstances could you
be sure she would do what any other sensible ship would
naturally do for you. There are ships that steer wildly, and
ships that can't be quite trusted always to stay, others that
want careful watching when running in a gale, and again
there may be a ship that will lie to badly and make heavy
weather of it in every little blow. But then you expect her to
be always so. You take it as part of her character, as a ship,

just as you take account of a man's peculiarities of temper
when you deal with him. But with her you couldn't. She
was unaccountable. If she wasn't mad, then she was the most
evil-minded, underhand savage brute that ever went afloat.
I've seen her run beautifully in a heavy gale for two days,
and, on the third, broach* to twice in the same afternoon.
The first time she flung the helmsman clean over the wheel,
but, as she didn't quite manage to kill him, she had another
try about three hours afterwards. She swamped herself fore and
aft, burst all the canvas she had set, scared all hands pretty
nearly into a panic, and even frightened Mrs Colchester down
there in those beautiful stern cabins that she was so proud
of. When we mustered the crew, there was one man missing.
Swept overboard, of course, without being either seen or heard,
poor devil; and I only wonder more of us didn't go. Another
voyage, one day—there was a little wind, but no sea to speak
of—the mate hauls down the outer jib and sends some hands
to stow it. That brute had been going along steady as a church
all the morning. Directly the first two men got out on the
boom, without any warning, she takes a confounded dive and
snaps the spar short off by the cap. All in a minute, there
she was up in the wind, with all the head-gear under her
port bow, and only an old cloth cap tangled up in the wreckage left of the two men. Gone! Never had one single glimpse
of either of them. Always something like that—always. I
heard an old mate tell Captain Colchester once that it had
come to this with him—that he was afraid to open his mouth
to give any sort of order. She was as much of a terror in
harbour as at sea. You could never be certain what would
hold her. On the slightest provocation, she would start snapping ropes, cables, wire hawsers* like carrots. She was heavy,
clumsy, unhandy—but that does not quite explain that power
for mischief she had. Not to me, anyhow. And I knew her
well. You know, somehow, when I think of her, I can't help
remembering what we hear of uncontrollable lunatics breaking loose.'

He looked at me inquisitively.

'In the ports where she was known,' he went on, 'they
dreaded the sight of her. She thought nothing of knocking

away twenty feet or so of solid stone facing off a quay or wiping off the end of a wooden wharf. She must have lost miles of chain and hundreds of tons of anchors, in her time. When she fell aboard some poor unoffending ship, it was the very devil of a job to haul her off again. And she never got hurt herself—just a few scratches or so, perhaps. Of course, they had wanted to have her strong, and she was. Strong enough to ram polar ice with. And as she began, so she went on. From the day she was launched she never let a year pass without murdering somebody. I think the owners got very worried about it. But they were a stiff-necked generation, all those Apses. They wouldn't admit there could be anything wrong with the *Apse Family*. They wouldn't even change her name. "Stuff and nonsense," as Mrs Colchester said. They ought at least to have shut her up for life in some dry-dock or other away up the river, and never let her smell salt water again. I assure you, my dear sir, that she invariably did kill some one every voyage she made. It was perfectly well known. She got a name for it far and wide.'

I expressed my surprise that a ship with such a reputation could ever get a crew.

'Then you don't know sailors, my dear sir. Let me just show you by an instance. One day in dock at home, while loafing on the forecastle-head,* I noticed two respectable salts coming along, one a middle-aged, competent, steady man evidently, the other a smart youngish chap. They read the name on the bows, and stopped, looking at her. Says the elder man: "*Apse Family*. That's the sanguinary female dog [I'm putting it in that way] of a ship, Jack, that kills a man every voyage. I wouldn't sign in her—not for Jo, I wouldn't." And the other says: "If she were mine, I'd have her towed on the mud and set on fire, blame if I wouldn't." Then the first man chimes in: "Much do they care. Men are cheap, God knows!" The younger one spat in the water alongside. "They won't have me—not for double wages." They hung about for some time, and then walked up the dock. Half an hour later I saw them both on our deck, looking round for the mate and apparently very anxious to be taken on. And they were.'

'How do you account for this?' I asked.

'What would you say?' he retorted. 'Recklessness? The vanity of boasting in the evening to all their chums: "We've just got shipped in that there *Apse Family*. Blow her! She ain't going to scare us." Sheer sailorlike perversity? A sort of curiosity? Well—a little of all that, no doubt. I put the question to them in the course of the voyage. The answer of the elderly chap was:

'"A man can die but once." The younger assured me in a mocking tone that he wanted to see "how she would do it this time." But I tell you what: there was a sort of fascination about that brute.'

Jermyn, who seemed to have seen every ship in the world, broke in sulkily:

'I saw her once out of this very window, towing up the river. A great, black, ugly thing, going along like a big hearse.'

'Something sinister about her looks, wasn't there?' said the man in tweeds, looking down at old Jermyn with a friendly eye. 'I always had a sort of horror of her. She gave me a beastly shock when I was no more than fourteen, the very first day—nay, hour—I joined her. Father came up to see me off, and was to go down to Gravesend* with us. I was his second boy to go to sea. My big brother was already an officer then. We got on board about eleven in the morning, and found the ship ready to drop out of the basin, stern first. Ten minutes afterwards the voyage began. She had not gone three times her own length when, at a little pluck the tug gave her to enter the dock-gates, she made one of her rampaging starts, and put such a weight on the deck-rope—a new six-inch hawser—that forward there they had no chance to ease it round in time and it parted. I saw the broken end fly up high in the air. Next moment she came against the pier-head with a jar that staggered everybody about her decks. She didn't hurt herself—not she. But one of her boys the mate had sent aloft on the mizen* to do something came down on the poop-deck—thump! right in front of me. He was not much older than myself. We had been grinning at each other only a few minutes before. He must have been handling himself carelessly, not expecting to get such a jerk.

I heard his startled cry, "Oh!" in a high treble, as he felt himself going, and looked up in time to see him go limp all over as he fell. Ough! Poor father was remarkably white about the gills when we shook hands in Gravesend. "Are you all right?" he says, looking hard at me. "Yes, Father." "Quite sure?" "Yes, Father." "Well, then, good-by, my boy." He told me afterwards that at half a word from me he would have carried me off home with him there and then. . . . I am the baby of the family, you know,' added the man in tweeds, stroking his mustache, with an ingenuous smile.

'This might have utterly spoiled a chap's nerve for going aloft, you know, utterly. He fell within two feet of me, cracking his head on a mooring-bitt.* Never moved. Stone-dead. Nice-looking little fellow, he was. I had just been thinking we would be great chums. . . . However, that wasn't yet the worst that brute of a ship could do. I served in her three years of my time, and then I got transferred to the *Lucy Apse* for a year. The sailmaker we had in the *Apse Family* turned up there too, and I remember him saying to me, one evening after we had been a week at sea: "Isn't she a meek little ship?" No wonder we thought the *Lucy Apse* a dear, meek little ship after getting clear of that big, rampaging, savage, brute. It was like heaven. Her officers seemed to me the restfulest lot of men on earth. To me, who had known no other ship but the *Apse Family*, the *Lucy* was like a sort of magic craft that did what you wanted her to do of her own accord. One evening we got caught aback pretty sharply from right ahead. In about ten minutes we had her full again and going along easy, sheets aft,* tacks down, decks cleared, and the officer of the watch leaning against the weather-rail peacefully. It seemed simply marvellous to me. The other, most likely, would have stuck in irons for half an hour, rolling her decks full, knocking the men about—spars cracking, braces snapping, yards* taking charge, and a confounded scare going on aft about her beastly rudder, which she had a way of flapping about fit to raise your hair on end. I couldn't get over my wonder for days.

'Well, I finished my last year of apprenticeship in that jolly little ship (she wasn't so little, either, but after that other

heavy devil she seemed but a plaything to handle)—I finished
my time and passed my exam for second mate; and then,
just as I was thinking of having three weeks of good time
on shore, I got at breakfast a letter from the firm asking me
the earliest day I could be ready to join the *Apse Family* as
third officer. I gave my plate a shove that shot it into the
middle of the table. Dad looked up over his paper; mother
raised her hands in astonishment; and I went out bareheaded
into our bit of a garden, where I walked round and round
for an hour.

'When I came in, mother was out of the dining-room and
dad had shifted berth into his big armchair by the fire. The
letter was lying on the mantelpiece.

'"It's very creditable to you and very kind of them," he
said. "And I see also that Charles has been appointed chief
mate of that ship for one voyage."

'There was a PS overleaf in Mr Apse's own handwriting
which I had overlooked. Charley was my big brother.

'"I don't like very much to have two of my boys in the
same ship," father goes on in his deliberate, solemn way;
"and I may tell you that I would not mind writing Mr Apse
a letter to that effect."

'Dear old chap! He was a wonderful father. What would
you have done? The mere notion of going back (and as an
officer, too) to be worried and bothered and kept on the
jump night and day by that brute made me feel sick. But she
wasn't a ship you could afford to be shy of openly. Besides,
the most genuine excuse could not be given without mortally
offending Apse & Sons. The firm, and I believe the whole
family down to the old unmarried sisters in Lancashire, had
grown desperately touchy about that accursed ship's character.
This was a case for answering "Ready now" from your very
deathbed if you wished to die in their good graces. And that's
precisely what I did answer—by wire.

'The prospect of being with my big brother cheered me
up considerably, though it made me a bit anxious, too. Ever
since I remember myself as a little chap he had been very
good to me, and I looked upon him as the finest fellow in
the world. And so he was. No better officer ever walked the

deck of a merchant-ship, and that's a fact. He was a fine, strong, upstanding, sun-tanned young fellow, with his brown hair curling a little, and an eye like a hawk. He was just splendid. We hadn't seen each other for many years, and even this time, though he had been in England three weeks already, he hadn't showed up at home yet, but had spent his spare time in Surrey somewhere, making up to Maggie Colchester, old Captain Colchester's niece. Her father, a great friend of my dad, was in the sugar-broking business, and Charley made a sort of second home of their house. I wondered what my big brother would think of me. There was a sort of sternness about Charley's face which never left it, not even when he was larking in his rather wild fashion.

'He received me with a great shout of laughter. He seemed to think my joining as an officer the funniest thing in the world. There were eleven years between our ages, and I suppose he remembered me best in pinafores.* I was just four when he first went to sea. It surprised me to find how boisterous he could be.

' "Now we shall see what you are made of," he cried. And he held me off by the shoulders and punched my ribs and hustled me into his berth. "Sit down, Ned. I am glad of the chance of having you with me. I'll put the finishing touch to you, my young officer, providing you're worth the trouble. And, first of all, get it well into your head that we are not going to let this brute kill anybody this voyage. We'll stop her racket."

'I perceived he was in dead earnest about it. He talked grimly of the ship, and how we must be careful and allow no carelessness of any sort: take no chances, and look after the men as if they were five-year-old kids. And we must never allow this ugly beast to catch us napping with any of her damned tricks.

'He gave me a regular lecture on special seamanship for the use of the *Apse Family*; then, changing his tone, he began to talk at large, rattling off the wildest, funniest nonsense, till my sides ached with laughing. I could see very well he was a bit above himself with high spirits. It couldn't be because of my coming—not to that extent. But, of course, I wouldn't have dreamt of asking what was the matter. I had a proper respect for my big brother, I can tell you. But it was all made plain enough a day or two afterwards when I heard that Miss Maggie Colchester was coming for the voyage. Uncle was giving her a sea trip for her health.

'I don't know what could have been wrong with her health. She had a beautiful colour and a deuce of a lot of fair hair. She didn't care a rap for wind or rain, or spray, or sun, or green seas, or anything. She was a jolly girl of the very best sort, but the way she cheeked my big brother used to frighten me. I always expected it to end in an awful row. However, nothing decisive happened till after we had been in Sydney for a week. One day, in the men's dinner-hour, Charley put his head into my cabin. I was stretched out on my back on the settee, smoking in peace.

'"Come along ashore with me, Ned," he says in his curt way.

'I jumped up, of course, and away after him down the gangway and up George Street. He strode along like a giant, and I at his elbow, panting. It was confoundedly hot. "Where on earth are you rushing me to, Charley?" I made bold to ask.

'"Here," he says.

'It was a jeweller's. I couldn't imagine what he could want there. It seemed a sort of mad freak. He thrust under my nose three rings which looked very tiny on his big brown palm, growling out:

'"For Maggie. . . . Which?"

'I got a kind of scare at this. I couldn't make a sound, but I pointed at the one that sparkled white and blue. He put it in his waistcoat pocket, paid for it, and bolted out. When we got back on board I was quite out of breath. "Shake hands, old chap!" I gasped out. He gave me a thump on the back. "Give what orders you like to the boatswain when the hands turn to," says he. "I am off duty this afternoon."

'Then he vanished from the deck for a while, but presently he came out of the cabin with Maggie, and those two went over the gangway publicly, before all hands, going for a walk together on that awful blazing hot day with clouds of dust flying about. They came back after a few hours, looking very staid, but didn't seem to have the slightest idea where they had been. Anyway, that's the answer they both made to Mrs Colchester's question at tea-time.

'And didn't she turn upon Charley with her voice like an old night cabman's: "Rubbish! Don't know where you've been! Stuff and nonsense! You've walked the girl off her legs. Don't do it again."

'It's surprising how meek Charley could be with that old woman. Only on one occasion he whispered to me, "I'm jolly glad she isn't Maggie's aunt, except by marriage. That's no sort of relationship." But I think he let Maggie have too much of her own way. She was hopping all over that ship, in her yachting-skirt and a red tam-o'-shanter, like a bright bird on a dead black tree. The old salts used to grin when they saw her coming along, and offered to teach her knots and splices. I believe she liked the men, for Charley's sake, I suppose.

'As you may imagine, the diabolic propensities of that cursed ship were never spoken of on board of her—not in her cabin, at any rate. Only once, on the homeward passage, Charley incautiously said something about bringing all her crew home this time. Old Colchester began to look uncomfortable at once, and that silly, hard-bitten old woman flew out at Charley as though he had said something indecent. I was quite confounded myself; as to Maggie, she sat completely mystified, opening her dark eyes very wide. Of course, before she was a day older she wormed it all out of me. She was a very difficult person to lie to.

'"How awful!" she said, quite solemn. "So many poor fellows! I am glad the voyage is nearly over. I won't have a moment's peace about Charley now."

'I assured her Charley was all right: it took more than that ship knew to get over a seaman like Charley; and she agreed with me.

'Next day we got the tug off Dungeness;* and when the tow-rope was fast, Charley rubbed his hands and said to me in an undertone:

'"We've baffled her, Neddy."

' "Looks like it," I said, with a grin at him. It was beautiful weather and the sea as smooth as a mill-pond. We went up the river without a shadow of trouble except once, when, off Hole Haven,* she took a sudden sheer and nearly had a barge anchored just clear of the fairway. But I was aft, and she did not catch me napping that time. Charley came up on the poop looking very concerned. "Close shave," says he.

' "Never mind, Charley," I answered cheerily. "You've tamed her."

'We were to tow right up. The river pilot boarded us well down, and the first words I heard him say were: "You may just as well take your port anchor inboard at once, Mr Mate."

'This had been done when I went forward and saw Maggie on the forecastle-head enjoying the bustle. I begged her to go aft, but she took no notice of me, of course. Then Charley, who was very busy, caught sight of her, and shouted in his biggest voice: "Get off the forecastle-head Maggie. You're in the way here." For all answer she made a funny face at him, and I saw poor Charley turn away, hiding a smile. She was flushed with the excitement of getting home again, and her eyes seemed to snap live sparks as she looked at the river. A collier-brig* had gone round just ahead of us, and our tug had to stop her engines in a hurry to avoid running slap bang into her.

'In a moment, as is usually the case, all the shipping in the reach seemed to get into a hopeless tangle. A schooner and a ketch* got up a small collision all to themselves right in the middle of the river. It was very exciting to watch. Meantime our tug remained stopped. Any other ship than that brute could have been coaxed to keep straight for a couple of minutes. But not she! Her head fell off at once; she swung athwart the stream and began to drift down, taking her tug along with her too, at that. I noticed a cluster of coasters at anchor, within a quarter of a mile of us, and I thought I had better speak to the pilot. "If you let this brute get amongst that lot," I said quietly, "she will stop there for hours, grinding some of them to bits before we get her out again."

' "Don't I know her!" cries he, stamping his foot in a perfect fury. And he out with his whistle to make that bothered tug get the ship's head up-stream again as quick as possible. He blew like mad, waving his arm to port, and presently we could see that the tug's engines had been set going ahead. Her paddles churned the water, but it was as if she had been trying to tow a rock—she couldn't get an inch out of that ship. Again the pilot blew his whistle and waved his arm to port. We could see the tug's paddles turning faster and faster, away broad on our bow.

'For a moment tug and ship seemed to hang motionless in a crowd of moving shipping, and then the terrific strain that evil, stony-hearted brute would always put on everything tore the towing-chock* clean out of her. The tow-rope surged over, snapping the iron stanchions of the head-rail, one after another, as if they had been sticks of sealing-wax. It was only then I noticed that, in order to have a better view over our heads, Maggie had stepped upon the port anchor as it lay flat on the forecastle-deck.

'It had been lowered properly into its hard-wood beds, but there had been no time to take a turn with it; anyway, it was quite secure as it was for going into dock; but I could see directly that the tow-rope would sweep under the fluke* in another second. My heart flew up right into my throat, but not before I had the time to yell out, "Jump clear of that anchor!" . . .

'But I hadn't time to shriek out her name. I don't suppose she heard me at all. The first touch of the rope against the fluke threw her down heavily; she was up on her feet again quick as lightning, but she was up on the wrong side. There came a horrid scraping sound, and then that anchor, tipping over, rose up like something alive; its great rough iron arm caught her round the waist, seemed to clasp her close with a dreadful hug, and flung itself with her downwards and over in a terrific clang of iron, followed by heavy ringing blows that shook the ship from stem to stern—because the ring-stopper held!'

'How horrible!' I said.

'I used to dream for years afterwards of live anchors catching hold of girls,' said the man in tweeds, a little wildly. He shuddered.

'With a most pitiful howl, Charley was over after her almost on the instant. But Lord! He didn't see as much as a gleam of her red tam-o'-shanter under the water. Nothing! Nothing whatever! In a moment there were half a dozen boats around us, and he got pulled into one. I, with the boat-swain and the carpenter, let go the other anchor and brought the ship up somehow. The pilot had gone silly. He walked up and down the forecastle-head, wringing his hands and muttering to himself: "Killing women now! Killing women now!" Not another word could you get out of him.

'Dusk fell, then a night black as pitch; and, peering upon the river, I heard a low, mournful hail, "Ship ahoy!" Two boatmen came alongside. They had a lantern in their boat, and looked up the ship's side, holding on to the ladder without a word. I saw a lot of loose fair hair down there. Brrrr!' He shuddered again.

'After the tide had turned, Maggie's body had floated clear of one of the mooring-buoys,' he explained. 'I crept aft, feeling half dead, and managed to send a rocket up—to let the other searchers know on the river. And then I slunk away forward like a cur, and spent the night sitting on the bowsprit,* so as to be as far as possible out of Charley's way.'

'Poor fellow!' I murmured.

'Yes; poor fellow!' he repeated musingly. 'Ah! she wouldn't let him—not even him—baffle her of her prey. But he made her fast in dock next morning. He did. We hadn't exchanged a word—not a single look, for that matter. I didn't want to look at him. When the last rope was fast, he put his hands to his head and stood gazing down at his feet as if trying to remember something. The men waited on the main-deck for the word that ends the voyage. Perhaps that was what he was trying to remember. I gave it for him: "That'll do, men."

'I never saw a crew leave a ship so quietly. They sneaked over the rail one after another, taking care not to bang their sea-chests too heavily. They looked our way, but not a single one had the stomach to come up and offer to shake hands with the mate, as is usual.

'I followed him all over the empty ship to and fro, here and there, with no living soul about but the two of us, because the old ship-keeper, who had known him from a boy, had locked himself up in the galley—both doors. Suddenly poor Charley mutters in a sort of crazy voice, "I'm done here," and strides down the gangway, with me at his heels, up the dock, out at the gate, on towards Tower Hill.* He used to take rooms with a decent old landlady in America Square, to be near his work.

'All at once he stops, turns short round, and comes straight at me. "Ned," says he, "I am going home." I had the good luck to sight a four-wheeler,* and got him in. His legs were beginning to give way. In our hall he fell down on a chair, and I'll never forget father's and mother's amazed, perfectly still faces as they stood over him. They hadn't heard, and couldn't understand what had happened to him till I blubbered out, "Maggie's drowned."

'Mother let out a little cry. Father looks from him to me and from me to him as if comparing our faces—for, upon my soul, Charley did not resemble himself at all. Nobody moved; and the poor fellow raised his two big brown hands slowly to his throat and with one single tug rips everything open—collar, shirt, waistcoat, into rags—a perfect wreck and ruin of a man. Father and I got him up-stairs somehow, and mother pretty nearly killed herself nursing him through a brain-fever.'

The man in tweeds nodded at me significantly.

'Ah! there was nothing that could be done with that brute. She had a devil in her.'

'Where's your brother now?' I asked, expecting to hear he was dead. But he was commanding a ship on the China coast and had not been home for years.

Old Jermyn fetched a heavy sigh, and, the handkerchief being now sufficiently dry, put it up tenderly to his red and dejected nose.

'You understand now,' the man in tweeds started again, 'why I was glad to hear that lunatic Wilmot had managed to dash her brains out on some rocks in Spencer Gulf.* She was a ravening beast. A ship may be given a certain latitude in her temper—but when it comes to killing women! . . . Old Colchester put his foot down and resigned; and—would you believe it?—Apse & Sons wrote to him asking whether he wouldn't reconsider his decision! Anything for the sake of the *Apse Family*! Old Colchester went to the office then and said that he would reconsider: he would take charge again, on condition of taking her out into the North Sea and scuttling her! He was nearly off his chump. He used to be iron-gray, but he had gone snow-white in a fortnight. And Mr Lucian Apse (they had known each other as young men) pretended not to notice it. Eh! Here's infatuation, if you like. Here's pride for you.

'They jumped at the first man they could get to take her, for fear of the scandal of the *Apse Family* not being able to find a skipper. He was a festive soul, I believe, but he stuck to her grim and hard. Wilmot was second mate. A harum-scarum fellow and pretending to a great scorn for all the girls. The fact is, he was really timid. But only let one of them do as much as lift her little finger in encouragement and there was nothing that could hold him. As apprentice he deserted abroad after a petticoat, once, and would have gone to the dogs then if his skipper hadn't taken the trouble to find him and lug him by the ears out of some house of perdition or other.

'It was said that one of the firm had been heard to express a hope that she would be lost soon. I can hardly credit it, unless it might have been Mr Alfred Apse, whom the family didn't think much of. They had him in the office, but he was considered a bad egg altogether, always flying off to race-meetings and coming home drunk. You would have thought that a ship so full of deadly tricks would run herself ashore some day out of sheer cussedness. But not she! She was going to last for ever. She had a nose to keep off the bottom.'

Jermyn made a grunt of approval.

'A ship after a pilot's own heart,' jeered the man in tweeds, 'eh? Well, Wilmot managed it. He was the man for it, but even he, perhaps, couldn't have done the trick without that green-eyed governess or nurse or whatever she was to the children of Mr and Mrs Pamphilius.

'They were passengers in her from Port Adelaide* to the Cape.* Well, the ship went out and anchored outside for the day. The skipper—a hospitable soul—had a lot of guests to a farewell lunch, as usual with him. It was five in the evening before the last boat-load left the side, and the weather looked ugly and dark in the gulf. There was no reason for him to get under way. However, as he had said he would go that day, he imagined it was proper to do so anyhow. But as he had no mind after all these festivities to tackle the straits in the dark with a scant wind, he gave orders at nine o'clock to keep her under the lower topsails and foresail as close as she would lie, dodging along the land till daylight. Then he sought his virtuous couch, I suppose. The mate was on deck having his face washed very clean with hard rain-squalls. Wilmot relieved him at midnight. The *Apse Family* had, as you observed, a house on her poop . . .'

'A big—white—thing—sticking up,' Jermyn murmured sadly at the fire.

'That's it; a companionway for the cabin stairs and chart-room combined. The rain drove in gusts on the sleepy Wilmot. The ship was then surging slowly to the southward along the shore, close hauled, with the coast within three miles or so on her port side. There was nothing to look out for in that part of the gulf, and Wilmot went round to dodge the squalls under the lee of the chart-room whose door on that side was open. The night was black like a barrel of coal-tar. And then he heard a woman's voice whispering to him.

'That confounded green-eyed girl of the Pamphilius people had put the kids to bed long time ago, of course, but it seems she couldn't sleep herself. She heard eight bells struck and the chief mate come below to turn in. She waited a bit, then got into her dressing-gown, and stole into the empty saloon and up the stairs into the chartroom. She sat on the settee near the open door to cool herself—perhaps. I couldn't make it out when Wilmot was telling me; he would break off to swear at every second word. We were standing on the quay, and he had an apron of sacking up to his chin and a big whip in his hand. Driver of a wool-wagon. Glad to do anything not to starve. That's what he had come to.

'I suppose it was as if somebody had struck a match in the fellow's brain. There he was with his head inside the door, on the girl's shoulder as likely as not—officer of the watch! and meantime the wind was hauling aft in gusts. The helmsman, when giving his evidence afterwards, said that he shouted several times that the binnacle-lamp* had gone out. He couldn't use the compass-card, but it didn't matter to him, because his orders were to sail her close. "I thought it funny," he said, "that the ship should keep falling off in squalls like this, but I luffed* her up every time as close as I was able. It was so dark I couldn't see my hand before my face, and the rain come in bucketfuls on my head."

'It seems that at every squall the wind hauled aft a little, till gradually the ship came to be heading straight for the coast without a single soul in her being aware of it. Wilmot himself confessed that he had not been near the standard compass for an hour. He might well have confessed! The first thing he knew was the man on the lookout shouting blue murder forward there.

'He tore his neck free, he says, and yelled back at him: "What do you say?"

'"I think I hear breakers ahead, sir," howled the man, and came rushing aft with the rest of the watch in the "awfulest blinding deluge that ever fell from the sky," Wilmot says. He wasn't a good officer, but he had in him the making of a seaman. For a second or so he was so scared and bewildered that he could not remember on which side of the gulf the ship was. But he pulled himself together at once. His first orders were: "Hard up. Shiver the main and mizen topsails!" —which was perfectly right, and it seems that he heard the sails actually fluttering. "But she was too slow in going off," Wilmot went on telling me, his dirty face twitching and the damned carter's whip shaking in his hand. "She seemed to stick fast." The flutter of the canvas above his head ceased. At this critical moment the wind hauled aft with a gust again, filling the sails, and sending the ship with a great way upon the rocks on her lee bow. She had been too slow and had overreached herself in her last little game. Her time had come —the hour, the man, the blind night, the gust of wind, the right woman to put an end to her. She deserved nothing better. Strange are the instruments of Providence! There's a sort of poetical justice, too. . . .'

The man in tweeds looked hard at me.

'The first ledge she went over stripped the false keel off her. Rip! The skipper, rushing out of his berth, found a crazy girl in a red dressing-gown flying round and round the saloon, screeching like a cockatoo—the next bump knocked her clean under the cabin table. It also started the stern-post and carried away the rudder. And then the brute ran up on to a shelving rocky shore, tearing her bottom out, till she stopped and the foremast dropped over the bows like a gangway.'

'Anybody lost?' I asked.

'No—unless that fellow Wilmot, and that's rather worse than death,' answered the gentleman unknown to Miss Blank, looking round for his cap. 'They got ashore all right. She didn't begin to break up till next day. . . . Rain left off,' he went on. 'I must get on my bike. I live in Herne Bay*—came out for a spin this morning.'

He nodded at me in a friendly way and went out with a swagger.

'Do you know who he is, Jermyn?' I asked.

The North Sea pilot shook his head dismally. 'I'm waiting for my ship to come down,' he said in a lugubrious tone, again spreading his damp handkerchief like a curtain before the glowing grate.

On going out, I exchanged a glance and a smile (strictly proper) with the respectable Miss Blank, barmaid of the Three Crows.

IL CONDE*

'Vedi Napoli e poi mori.'

THE first time we got into conversation was in the National
Museum in Naples, in the rooms on the ground floor containing the famous collection of bronzes from Herculaneum
and Pompeii: that marvellous legacy of antique art whose delicate perfection has been preserved to us by the catastrophic
fury of a volcano.

He addressed me first, over the celebrated Resting Hermes*
which we had been admiring side by side. He said the right
things about that wholly admirable piece. Nothing profound.
His taste was natural rather than cultivated. He had obviously seen many fine things in his life and appreciated them:
but he had no jargon of a dilettante or the connoisseur. A
hateful tribe. He spoke like a fairly intelligent man of the
world, a perfectly unaffected gentleman.

We had known each other by sight for some few days past.
Staying in the same hotel—good, but not extravagantly up to
date—I had noticed him in the vestibule going in and out. I
judged he was an old and valued client. The bow of the hotel-
keeper was cordial in its deference, and he acknowledged
it with familiar courtesy. For the servants he was Il Conde.
There was some squabble over a man's parasol—yellow silk
with white lining sort of thing—the waiters had discovered
abandoned outside the dining-room door. Our gold-laced door-
keeper recognised it and I heard him directing one of the lift
boys to run after Il Conde with it. Perhaps he was the only
Count staying in the hotel, or perhaps he had the distinction of being *the* Count *par excellence*, conferred upon him
because of his tried fidelity to the house.

Having conversed at the Museo (and by the by he had
expressed his dislike of the busts and statues of Roman
emperors in the gallery of marbles: their faces were too
vigorous, too pronounced for him)—having conversed already
in the morning, I did not think I was intruding when in the

evening, finding the dining-room very full, I proposed to share
his little table. Judging by the quiet urbanity of his manner he
did not think so either. His smile was very sympathetic.

He dined in an evening waistcoat and a 'smoking'* (he called
it so), with a black tie. All this of very good cut, not new—
just as these things should be. He was, morning or evening,
very correct in his dress. I have no doubt his whole existence
had been so—I mean correct, well ordered, and conventional:
undisturbed by startling events. His white hair brushed upwards
off a lofty forehead gave him the air of an idealist, of an
imaginative man. His white moustache, heavy but carefully
trimmed and arranged, was not unpleasantly tinted a golden
yellow in the middle. The faint scent of some very good per-
fume, and of good cigars (that last an odour quite remarkable
to come upon in Italy) reached me across the table. It was in
his eyes that his age showed most. They were a little watery
with creased eyelids. He must have been sixty or thereabouts.
And he was communicative. I would not go so far as to call
it garrulous—but distinctly communicative.

He had tried various climates, of Abbazia,* of the Riviera,*
of other places, too, he told me, but the only one which
suited him was the climate of the Gulf of Naples. The ancient
Romans, who were men expert in the art of living, he pointed
out to me, knew very well what they were doing when they
built their villas on these shores, in Baie, in Vico, in Capri.
They came down to this seaside to get health, bringing with
them their trains of mimes and flute-players to amuse their
leisure. He thought it extremely probable that the Romans
of the higher classes were specially predisposed to painful
rheumatic affections.

This was the only somewhat original opinion I heard him
express. It was based on no special erudition. He knew no
more of the Romans than an average informed man of the
world is expected to know. He argued from personal experience. He had suffered himself from a painful and dangerous
rheumatic affection till he found relief in this particular spot
of Southern Europe.

This was three years ago, and ever since he had taken up
his quarters on the shores of the gulf, either in one of the

hotels in Sorrento* or hiring a small villa in Capri.* He had a piano, a few books: picked up transient acquaintances of a day, week, or month in the stream of travellers from all Europe. One can imagine him going out for his walks in the streets and lanes, becoming known to beggars, shopkeepers, children, country people; talking amiably over the walls to the contadini*—and coming back to his rooms or his villa to sit before the piano, with his white hair brushed up and his thick orderly moustache, 'to make a little music for myself.' And, of course, for a change there was Naples near by—life, movement, animation, opera. A little amusement, as he said, is necessary for health. Mimes and flute-players, in fact. Only, unlike the citizens of ancient Rome, he had no affairs of the city to call him away from these moderate delights. He had no affairs at all. Probably he had never had any grave affairs to attend to in his life. It was a kindly existence, with its joys and sorrows regulated by the course of Nature—marriages, births, deaths—ruled by the prescribed usages of good society and protected by the State.

He was a widower; but in the months of July and August he ventured to cross the Alps for six weeks on a visit to his married daughter. He told me her name. It was that of a very aristocratic family. She had a castle—in Bohemia, I think. That is as near as I ever came to ascertaining his nationality. His own name, strangely enough, he never mentioned. Perhaps he thought I had seen it on the published list. Truth to say, I never looked. At any rate, he was a good European—he spoke four languages to my certain knowledge—and a man of fortune. Not of great fortune, evidently and appropriately. I imagine that to be extremely rich would have appeared to him improper, outré*—too blatant altogether. And obviously, too, the fortune was not of his making. The making of a fortune cannot be achieved without some roughness. It is a matter of temperament. His nature was too kindly for any sort of strife. In the course of conversation he mentioned his estate quite by the way, in reference to that painful and alarming rheumatic affection. One year, staying incautiously beyond the Alps as late as the middle of September, he had been laid up for three months in that lovely country house with no one but his valet and the caretaking couple to attend to him. Because, as he expressed it, he 'had no establishment there.' He had only gone for a couple of days to confer with his agent or manager. He promised himself never to be so imprudent in the future. The first weeks of September would find him on the shores of his beloved gulf.

Sometimes in travelling one comes upon such lonely men, whose only business is to wait for the unavoidable. Deaths and marriages have made a solitude round them, and one really cannot blame their endeavours to make the waiting as easy as possible. As he remarked to me, 'At my age freedom from physical pain is a very important thing.'

It must not be imagined that he was a wearisome hypochondriac. He was really much too well-bred to be a nuisance. He had an eye for the small weaknesses of humanity. But it was a good-natured eye. He made a restful, easy, pleasant companion for the hours between dinner and bedtime. We spent three evenings together, and then I had to leave Naples in a hurry to see a friend who had fallen gravely ill in Taormina.* Having nothing to do, Il Conde came to see me off at the station. I was somewhat upset, and his idleness was always ready to take a kindly form. He was by no means an indolent man.

He went along the train peering into the carriages for a good seat for me, and then remained talking to me cheerily from below. He declared he would miss me that evening very much and announced his intention of going after dinner to listen to the band in the public garden, the Villa Nazionale. He would amuse himself by hearing excellent music and looking at the best society. There would be a lot of people, as usual.

Poor fellow! I seem to see him yet—his raised face with a friendly smile under the thick moustaches, and his kind fatigued eyes. As the train pulled out, he addressed me in two languages: first in French saying, '*Bon voyage*';* then, in his very good, somewhat emphatic English, encouragingly, because he could see my concern: 'All will—be—well—yet!'

My friend's illness having taken a decidedly favourable turn, I returned to Naples on the tenth day. I cannot say I had given

much thought to Il Conde during my absence, but entering
the dining-room I looked for him in his habitual place. I had
an idea he might have gone back to Sorrento to his piano and
his books and his fishing. He was great friends with all the
boatmen, and fished a good deal with lines from a boat. But
I made out his white head in the crowd of heads, and even
from a distance noticed something unusual in his attitude.
Instead of sitting erect, gazing all round with serene urbanity,
he drooped over his plate. I stood opposite him for some
time before he looked up, a little wildly, if such a strong word
can be used in connection with his correct appearance.

'Ah, my dear sir! Is it you?' he greeted me. 'I hope all is
well.'

He was very nice about my friend. Indeed he was always
nice, with the niceness of people whose hearts are genuinely
humane. But this time it cost him an effort. His attempts at
general conversation broke down into dulness. It occurred to
me he might have been indisposed. But before I could frame
the inquiry he muttered:

'You find me here very sad.'

'I am sorry for that,' I said. 'You haven't had bad news,
I hope?'

It was very kind of me to take an interest. No. It was not
that. No bad news, thank God. And he became very still as
if holding his breath. Then, leaning forward a little, and in
an odd tone of awed embarrassment, he took me into his
confidence.

'The truth is that I have had a very—a very—how shall I
say?—abominable adventure happen to me.'

The energy of the epithet was sufficiently startling in that
man of moderate feelings and toned-down vocabulary. The
word unpleasant I thought would have fitted amply the worst
experience likely to befall a man of his stamp. And an adventure, too. It was incredible. But it is in human nature to
believe the worst; and I confess I eyed him stealthily, wondering what he had been up to. In a moment, however, my
unworthy suspicions vanished. There was a fundamental refinement of nature about the man which made me dismiss all
idea of some more or less disreputable scrape.

'It is very serious. Very serious.' He went on nervously. 'I will tell you after dinner, if you will allow me.'

I expressed my perfect acquiescence by a little bow, nothing more. I wished him to understand that I was not likely to hold him to that offer, if he thought better of it. We talked of indifferent things, but with a sense of difficulty quite unlike our former easy, gossipy intercourse. The hand raising a piece of bread to his lips, I noticed, trembled slightly. This symptom, in regard to my reading of the man, was no less than startling.

In the smoking-room he did not hang back at all. Directly we had taken our usual seats he leaned sideways over the arm of his chair and looked straight into my eyes earnestly.

'You remember,' he began, 'that day you went away? I told you then I would go to the Villa Nazionale to hear some music in the evening.'

I remembered. His handsome old face, so fresh for his age, unmarked by any trying experience, appeared haggard to me for an instant. It was like the passing of a shadow. Returning his steadfast gaze, I took a sip of my black coffee. He was very systematically minute in his narrative, simply in order, I think, not to let his excitement get the better of him.

After leaving the railway station, he had an ice, and read the paper in a café. Then he went back to the hotel, dressed for dinner and dined with a good appetite. After dinner he lingered in the hall (there were chairs and tables there) smoking his cigar; talked to the little girl of the Primo Tenore* of the San Carlo theatre, and exchanged a few words with that 'amiable lady,' the wife of the Primo Tenore. There was no performance that evening, and these people were going to the Villa also. They went out of the hotel. Very well.

At the moment of following their example—it was half-past nine already—he remembered he had a rather large sum of money in his pocket-book. He entered, therefore, the office and deposited the greater part of it with the book-keeper of the hotel. This done, he took a carozella* and drove to the sea-shore. He got out of the cab and entered the Villa on foot from the Largo di Vittoria end.

He stared at me very hard. And I understood then how really impressionable he was. Every small fact and event of that evening stood out in his memory as if endowed with mystic significance. If he did not mention to me the colour of the pony which drew the carozella, and the aspect of the man who drove, it was a mere oversight arising from his agitation, which he repressed manfully.

He had then entered the Villa Nazionale from the Largo di Vittoria end. The Villa Nazionale is a public pleasure-ground laid out in grass plots, bushes and flower-beds between the houses of the Riviera di Chiaja and the waters of the bay. Alleys of trees, more or less parallel, stretch its whole length —which is considerable. On the Riviera di Chiaja side the electric tramcars run close to the railings. Between the garden and the sea is the fashionable drive, a broad road bordered by a low wall, beyond which the Mediterranean splashes with gentle murmurs when the weather is fine.

As life goes on late in the night at Naples, the broad drive was all astir with a brilliant multitude of carriage lamps moving in pairs, some creeping slowly, others running rapidly under the rather thin motionless line of electric lights defining the shore. And a brilliant multitude of stars hung above the land humming with voices, piled up with houses, all astir with lights—and over the silent flat shadows of the sea.

The gardens themselves are not very well lit. Our friend went forward in the warm gloom, with his eyes fixed on a distant and luminous region extending nearly across the whole width of the Villa, as if the air had glowed there with its own cold, bluish but dazzling light. This magic spot, behind the black trunks of trees and masses of inky foliage, breathed out sweet sounds mingled with bursts of brassy roar, with sudden clashes of metal and grave vibrating thuds.

As he walked on, all these noises combined together into a piece of elaborate music whose harmonious phrases came persuasively through a great disorderly murmur of voices and shuffling of feet on the gravel of that open space. An enormous crowd immersed in the electric light, as if in a bath of some radiant and tenuous fluid shed on their heads by luminous globes, drifted in its hundreds round the band. Hundreds more sat on chairs in more or less concentric circles, receiving unflinchingly the great waves of sonority that ebbed out into the darkness. The Count penetrated the throng, drifted with it in tranquil enjoyment, listening and looking at the faces. All people of good society: mothers with their daughters, parents and children, young men and young women all talking, smiling, nodding to each other. Very many pretty faces, and very many pretty toilettes.* There was, of course, a quantity of diverse types: showy old fellows with white moustaches, fat men, thin men, officers in uniform; but what predominated, he told me, was the South Italian type of young man, with a colourless, clear complexion, red lips, jet-black little moustache and expressive black eyes so wonderfully effective in leering or scowling.

Withdrawing from the throng, the Count shared a little table in front of the café with a young man of just such a type. Our friend had some lemonade. The young man was sitting moodily before an empty glass. He looked up once, and then looked down again. He also tilted his hat forward. Like this——

The Count made the gesture of a man pulling his hat down over his brow, and went on.

'I think to myself: He is sad. Something is wrong with him. Young men have their troubles. I take no notice of him, of course. I pay for my lemonade, and go away.'

Strolling about in the neighbourhood of the band, the Count thinks he saw twice that young man wandering alone in the crowd. Once their eyes met. It must have been the same young man, but there were so many there of that type that he could not be certain. Moreover, he was not very much concerned except in so far that he had been struck by the marked, peevish, discontent of that face.

Presently, tired of the feeling of confinement one experiences in a crowd, the Count edged away from the band. An alley, very sombre by contrast, presented itself invitingly with its promise of solitude and coolness. He entered it, walking slowly on till the sound of the orchestra became distinctly deadened. Then he walked back and turned about once more. He did this several times before he noticed that there was somebody on one of the benches.

The spot being midway between two lamp-posts the light was faint.

The man lolled back in the corner of the seat, his legs stretched out, his arms folded and his head drooping on his breast. He never stirred, as though he had fallen asleep there, but when the Count passed by again he had changed his attitude. He sat leaning forward. His elbows were propped on his knees, and his hands were rolling a cigarette. He never looked up from that occupation.

The Count continued his stroll away from the band. He returned slowly, he said. I can imagine him enjoying to the full, but with his usual tranquillity, the balminess of this southern night and the sounds of music softened delightfully by the distance.

Presently, he approached for the third time the man on the garden seat, still leaning forward with his elbows on his knees. It was a dejected pose. In the semi-obscurity of the alley his high shirt collar and his cuffs made small patches of vivid whiteness. The Count said that he just noticed him in a casual way getting up brusquely as if to walk away, but almost before he was aware of it the man stood before him asking in a low, gentle tone whether the signor would have the kindness to oblige him with a light.

The Count answered this request by a polite 'Certainly,' and dropped his hands with the intention of exploring both pockets of his trousers for the matches.

'I dropped my hands,' he said, 'but I never put them in my pockets. I felt a pressure there——'

He put the tip of his finger on a spot close under his breast-bone, the very spot of the human body where a Japanese gentleman begins the operation of the Hara-kiri, which is a form of suicide following upon dishonour, upon an intolerable outrage to the delicacy of one's feelings.

'I glance down,' he continued in an awe-struck voice, 'and what do I see? A knife! A long knife——'

'You don't mean to say,' I exclaimed amazed, 'that you were attacked like this in the Villa at half-past ten o'clock, within a stone's throw of fifteen hundred people!'

He nodded several times, staring at me with all his might.

'The clarionet,' he declared solemnly, 'was finishing his solo, and I assure you I heard every note. Then the band crashed

fortissimo, and that creature rolled its eyes and gnashed its
teeth hissing at me with the greatest ferocity, "Be silent! No
noise or——" '

I could not get over my astonishment.

'What sort of knife was it?' I asked stupidly.

'A long blade. A stiletto—perhaps a kitchen knife. A long
narrow blade. It gleamed. And his eyes gleamed. His white
teeth, too. I could see them. He was very ferocious. I thought
to myself: "If I hit him he will kill me." How could I fight
with him? He had the knife, and I had nothing. I am nearly
seventy, and this is a young man. I seemed even to recognise
him. The moody young man of the café. The young man I
met in the crowd. But I could not tell. There are so many
like him in this country.'

The distress of that moment was reflected in his face. I
should think that physically he must have been paralysed by
surprise. His thoughts, however, remained extremely active.
They ranged over every alarming possibility. The idea of setting up a vigorous shouting occurred to him too. But he did
nothing of the kind, and the reason why he refrained gave
me a good opinion of his mental alertness. He reflected that
nothing prevented the other from shouting, too.

'This young man might in an instant have thrown away his
knife and pretended I was the aggressor. Why not? He might
have said I attacked him. Why not? It was one incredible
story against another! He might have said anything—bring
some horrible charge against me—what do I know? By his
dress he was no common robber. He seemed to belong to the
better classes. What could I say? He was an Italian—I am
a foreigner. Of course, I have a passport, and there is our
consul—but to be arrested, dragged at night to the police
office like a criminal!'

He shuddered. It was in his character to shrink from
scandal, much more than from mere death. And certainly for
many people this would have always remained—considering
certain peculiarities of Neapolitan manners—a deucedly queer
story. The Count was no fool. His belief in the respectable
placidity of life having received this rude shock, he thought
that now anything might happen. But also a notion came

into his head that this young man was perhaps merely an infuriated lunatic.

The way he said this gave me the first hint of his attitude towards this adventure. In his exaggerated delicacy of sentiment he felt that nobody need be affected in his self-esteem by what a madman may choose to do to one. It became apparent, however, that the Count was to be denied that consolation. He enlarged upon the abominably savage way in which that young man rolled his glistening eyes and gnashed his white teeth. The band was going now through a slow movement of solemn braying by all the trombones, with deliberately repeated bangs of the big drum.

'But what did you do?' I asked greatly excited.

'Nothing,' answered the Count. 'I let my hands hang down very still. I told him quietly I did not intend making a noise. He snarled like a dog, then said in an ordinary voice:

' "*Vostro portofolio.*" '*

'So I naturally,' continued the Count—and from this point acted the whole thing in pantomime. Holding me with his eyes, he went through all the motions of reaching into his inside breast pocket, taking out the pocket-book and handing it over. But that young man, still bearing steadily on the knife, refused to touch it.

He directed the Count to take the money out himself, received it into his left hand, motioned the pocket-book to be returned to the pocket, all this being done to the thrilling of flutes and clarionets sustained by the emotional drone of the hautboys. And the 'young man,' as the Count called him, said: 'This seems very little.'

'It was, indeed, only 340 or 360 lire,' the Count pursued. 'I had left my money in the hotel, as you know. I told him this was all I had on me. He shook his head impatiently and said:

' "*Vostro orologio.*" '

The Count gave me the dumb show of pulling out the watch, detaching it. But, as it happened, the valuable gold timepiece he possessed had been left at a watchmaker's for cleaning. He wore that evening (on a leather strap) the Waterbury fifty-franc thing he used to take with him on his

fishing expeditions. Perceiving the nature of this booty, the
well-dressed robber made a contemptuous clicking sound with
his tongue like this, 'Tse-Ah!' and waved it away hastily.
Then, as the Count was returning the disdained object to his
pocket, he demanded with a threateningly increased pressure
of the knife on the epigastrum, by way of reminder:

'"*Vostri anelli.*"'

'One of the rings,' went on Il Conde, 'was given me many
years ago by my wife; the other is the signet ring of my
father. I said, "No. That you shall not have!"'

Here the Count reproduced the gesture corresponding to
that declaration by clapping one hand upon the other, and
pressing both thus against his chest. It was touching in its
patient resolution. 'That you shall not have,' he repeated firmly
and closed his eyes, fully expecting—I don't know whether
I am doing right by recording that such an unpleasant word
had passed his lips—fully expecting to feel himself being—
I really hesitate to say—being disembowelled by the push of
the long sharp blade resting murderously against the pit of
his stomach—the very seat, in all human beings, of anguish-
ing sensations.

Great waves of harmony went on flowing from the band.

Suddenly the Count felt the nightmarish pressure removed
from the sensitive spot. He opened his eyes. He was alone.
He had heard nothing. It is probable that 'the young man'
had departed, with light steps, some time before, but the sense
of the horrid pressure had lingered even after the knife had
gone. A feeling of weakness came over him. He had just time
to stagger to the garden seat. He felt as though he had held
his breath for a long time. He sat all in a heap panting with
the shock of the reaction.

The band was executing the complicated finale with
immense bravura. It ended with a tremendous crash. He
heard it unreal and remote, as if his ears were stopped, and
then the hard clapping of two thousand more or less pairs
of hands like a sudden hail-shower passing away. The profound silence which succeeded recalled him to himself.

A tramcar resembling a long glass box wherein people
sat with their faces strongly lighted, ran along swiftly within

ninety yards of the spot where he had been robbed. Then another rustled by, and yet another going the other way. The audience about the band had broken up, and dark figures were entering the alley in small conversing groups. The Count sat up straight, and tried to think calmly of what had happened to him. The vileness of it took his breath away again. As far as I can make it out he was disgusted with himself. I do not mean to say with his behaviour. Indeed, if his pantomimic rendering of it for my information was to be trusted, it was the perfection of dignified composure. No, it was not that. He was not ashamed. He was shocked at being the selected victim, not of robbery so much as of contempt. It was something like this. His tranquillity had been wantonly desecrated. His lifelong, kindly, placid nicety of outlook had been defaced.

Nevertheless, at that stage, before the iron had time to sink deep, he was able to argue himself into comparative equanimity. As his agitation calmed down somewhat, he became aware that he was frightfully hungry. Yes, hungry. The sheer emotion had made him simply ravenous, he told me. He got up from the seat and, after walking for some time, found himself outside the gardens and before an arrested tramcar, without knowing very well how he got there. He got in, as if in a dream, by a sort of instinct. Fortunately, he found in his trouser-pocket a copper to satisfy the conductor. Then the car stopped, and as everybody got out he got out, too. He recognised the Piazza San Ferdinando, but apparently it did not occur to him to take a cab and drive to the hotel. He wandered aimlessly on the Piazza like a lost dog, thinking vaguely of the best way of getting something to eat at once.

Suddenly in a flash, he remembered his twenty-franc piece. He explained to me that he had that piece of French gold for something like three years, and that he used to carry it about with him as a sort of reserve in case of accident. Anybody may have his pocket picked—a quite different thing from a brazen and insulting robbery.

The monumental archway entrance of the Galleria Umberto faced him at the top of a vast flight of stairs. He climbed these without loss of time, and directed his steps towards

the Café Umberto. All the tables outside were occupied by
a lot of people who were drinking. But as he wanted something to eat, he went inside into the café, which is divided
into aisles by square pillars set all round with long looking-
glasses. The Count sat down on a red velvet settee against one
of these pillars waiting for his risotto. And his mind reverted
to his abominable adventure.

He thought of the moody, well-dressed young man, with
whom he had exchanged glances in the crowd around the
bandstand, and who, he felt confident, was the robber. Would
he recognise him again? Doubtless. But he did not want ever
to see him again. The best thing was to forget this humiliat-
ing episode.

The Count looked round anxiously for the coming of his
risotto, and, behold! to the left against the wall—there was
the young man! He sat alone at a table, with a bottle of some
sort of wine or syrup and a carafe of iced water before him.
The smooth olive cheeks, the red lips, the little jet-black moustache turned up gallantly, the fine black eyes a little heavy and
shaded by long eyelashes, that peculiar expression of cruel
discontent which is seen only in the busts of some Roman
emperors—it was he, no doubt at all. But that was a type.
The Count looked away hastily. The young officer over there
reading a paper was like that, too. Same type. Two young
men further away playing draughts also resembled——

The Count lowered his head with the fear in his heart of
being everlastingly haunted by the vision of that young man.
He began to eat his risotto. Presently he heard the young man
on his left call the waiter in a bad-tempered tone.

At the call, not only his own waiter, but two other idle
waiters belonging to quite a different row of tables, rushed
towards him with obsequious alacrity, which is not the general characteristic of the waiters in the Café Umberto. The
young man muttered something, and one of the waiters walking rapidly to the nearest door called out loudly into the
Galleria 'Pasquale!'

Everybody knows Pasquale, the sordid old fellow who,
shuffling between the tables, offers for sale cigars, cigarettes,
picture postcards, matches to the clients of the café. He is

otherwise an engaging scoundrel. The Count saw the grey-haired, unshaven, sallow ruffian enter the café in his shabby clothes, the glass case hanging from his neck by a leather strap, and, at a word from the waiter, make his shuffling way with a sudden spurt to the young man's table. The young man was in need of a cigar with which Pasquale served him fawningly. The old pedlar was going out, when the Count, on a sudden impulse, beckoned to him.

Pasquale approached, his smile of deferential recognition combining oddly with the ironic searching expression of the eyes. Leaning his case on the table, he lifted the glass lid without a word. The Count took a box of cigarettes and, urged by a fearful curiosity, asked as casually as he could:

'Tell me, Pasquale, who is that young signor over there?'

The other bent over his box at once.

'That, Signor Count,' he said begining to rearrange his wares busily and without looking up, 'that is a young cavaliere of a very good family from Bari.* He studies in the university, and is the chief, *capo*, of an association of young men—of very nice young men.'

He paused, and then, with mingled discretion and pride of knowledge, murmured the explanatory word 'camorra'* and shut down the lid. 'A very powerful camorra,' he breathed out. 'The professors themselves respect it greatly . . . *una lira e cinquante centesimi,* Signor Conde.*'

Our friend paid with the gold piece. While Pasquale was making up the change, he observed that the young man, of whom he had heard so much in so very few words, was watching the transaction covertly. After the old vagabond had withdrawn with a bow, the Count settled with the waiter and sat still. A numbness, he told me, had come over him.

The young man paid, too, got up and crossed over, apparently for the purpose of looking at himself in the mirror set in a pillar just behind the Count's seat. He was dressed all in black with a dark green bow tie. The Count looked round, and was startled by meeting a vicious glance out of the corners of the other's eyes. The young cavaliere from Bari, (according to Pasquale: but Pasquale is, of course, an accomplished liar) went on arranging his tie, settling his hat before the glass, and meantime he spoke just loud enough to be heard by the Count. He spoke through his teeth with the most insulting venom of contempt and gazing straight into the mirror.

'Ah! So you had gold on you—you old *birba**—you *furfante!** But you are not done with me yet.'

The fiendishness of his expression vanished like lightning, and he lounged out of the café with a moody, impassive face.

The poor Count, when telling me this last episode, trembled and fell back in his chair. His forehead broke into perspiration. There was an extravagance of wantonness in this outrage which appalled even me. What it was to the Count's delicacy I can't imagine. I am sure that if he had not been too refined, too correct to do such a blatantly vulgar thing as dying from apoplexy in a café, he would have had a fatal stroke there and then. But, irony apart, all my difficulty was to keep him from seeing the extent of my commiseration. He shrank from every excessive sentiment, and my commiseration was practically unbounded. It did not surprise me to hear that he had been in bed a week. Then he got up to make his arrangements for leaving Southern Italy at once and for ever.

And he was convinced that he could not live a whole twelve months in any other climate!

No argument I could advance had any effect. It was not timidity, though he did say to me once, 'You do not know what a camorra is, my dear sir. I am a marked man.' He was not afraid of what could be done to him. To be so marked hurt his delicate conception of life's ease and serenity. He couldn't stand it. No Japanese gentleman, outraged in his exaggerated sense of honour, could have gone about his preparations for Hara-kiri with greater resolution. For it really amounted to that with the Count. He was going, and there was an end of it. He was going the very next day—to die on his estate, I suppose, as if the infamy of that outrage had tainted beyond endurance the idle dignity of his life.

There is a saying of Neapolitan patriotism intended for the information of foreigners, I presume: See Naples and then die. It is a saying of excessive vanity, and everything excessive was abhorrent to the nice moderation of the poor Count.

Yet, as I was seeing him off at the railway station, I thought he was behaving with singular fidelity to its conceited spirit. He had seen Naples. He had seen it completely. He had seen it with a startling thoroughness—and now he was going to his grave. He was going to it by the *train de luxe* of the International Sleeping Car Company, *via* Trieste and Vienna. As the four long, sombre coaches pulled out of the station I raised my hat with a queer sensation of paying a last tribute of respect to a funeral *cortège*. Il Conde's profile, much aged already and stonily still, glided away from me behind the lighted pane of glass—*Vedi Napoli e poi mori*.

PRINCE ROMAN

'EVENTS which happened seventy years ago are perhaps rather too far off to be dragged aptly into a mere conversation. Of course, the year 1831 is for us an historical date, one of these fatal years when in the presence of the world's passive indignation and eloquent sympathies we had once more to murmur "*Væ victis!*"* and count the cost in sorrow. Not that we were ever very good at calculating, either in prosperity or in adversity. That's a lesson we could never learn, to the great exasperation of our enemies, who have bestowed upon us the epithet of Incorrigible. . . .'

The speaker was of Polish nationality, that nationality not so much alive as surviving, which persists in thinking, breathing, speaking, hoping and suffering in its grave railed in by a million of bayonets and triple-sealed with the seals of three great empires.

The conversation was about aristocracy. How did this now-a-days discredited subject come up? It is some years ago now, and the precise recollection has faded. But I remember that it was not considered practically, as an ingredient in the social mixture; and I verily believe that we arrived at that subject through some exchange of ideas about patriotism—a somewhat discredited sentiment, because the delicacy of modern humanitarians regards it as a relic of barbarism. Yet neither the great Florentine painter* who closed his eyes in death thinking of his city, nor St Francis blessing with his last breath the town of Assisi, were barbarians. It requires a certain greatness of soul to interpret patriotism worthily—or else a sincerity of feeling denied to the vulgar refinement of modern thought which cannot understand the august simplicity of a sentiment proceeding from the very nature of things and men.

The aristocracy we were talking about was the very highest, the great families of Europe, not impoverished, not converted, not liberalised, the most distinctive and specialised class of all classes, for which even ambition itself does not exist among the usual incentives to activity and regulators of conduct.

The undisputed right of leadership having passed away from them, we judged that their great fortunes, their cosmopolitanism brought about by wide alliances, their elevated station, in which there is so little to gain and so much to lose, must make their position difficult in times of political commotion or national upheaval. No longer born to command— which is the very essence of aristocracy—it becomes difficult for them to do aught else but hold aloof from the great movements of popular passion.

We had reached that conclusion when the remark about far-off events was made and the date of 1831 mentioned. And the speaker continued:—

I don't mean to say that I knew Prince Roman at that remote time. I begin to feel pretty ancient, but I am not so ancient as that. In fact, Prince Roman was married the very year my father was born. It was in 1828; the nineteenth century was young yet, and the prince was even younger than the century, but I don't know exactly by how much. In any case, his was an early marriage. It was an ideal alliance from every point of view. The girl was young and beautiful, an orphan, heiress of a great name and of a great fortune. The prince, then an officer in the Guards,* distinguished amongst his fellows by something reserved and reflective in his character, had fallen headlong in love with her beauty, her charm and the serious qualities of her mind and heart. He was a silent young man; but his glances, his bearing, his whole person expressed his absolute devotion to the woman of his choice, a devotion which she returned in her own frank and fascinating manner.

The flame of this pure young passion promised to burn for ever; and for a season it lit up the dry, cynical atmosphere of the great world of St Petersburg. The Emperor Nicholas* himself, the great-grandfather of the present man,* the one who died from the Crimean War,* the last, perhaps, of the autocrats with a mystical belief in the divine character of his mission, showed some interest in this pair of married lovers.

It is true that Nicholas kept a watchful eye on all the doings of the great Polish nobles.* The young people, leading the life appropriate to their station, were obviously wrapped up in each other; and society, fascinated by the sincerity of a feeling moving serenely among the artificialities of its anxious and fastidious agitation, watched them with benevolent indulgence and an amused tenderness.

The marriage was the social event of 1828, in the Capital. Just forty years afterwards I was staying in the country house of my mother's brother in our southern provinces.

It was the dead of winter. The great lawn in front was as pure and smooth as an Alpine snowfield, a white and feathery level sparkling under the sun as if sprinkled with diamond-dust, declining gently to the lake—a long sinuous piece of frozen water looking bluish and more solid than the earth. A cold, brilliant sun glided low above an undulating horizon of great folds of snow in which the villages of Ukrainian* peasants remained out of sight, like clusters of boats hidden in the hollows of a running sea. And everything was very still.

I don't know now how I had managed to escape at eleven o'clock in the morning from the school-room. I was a boy of nine. The little girl, my cousin, a few months younger than myself, though hereditarily more quick-tempered, was less adventurous. So I had escaped alone; and presently I found myself in the great stone-paved hall, warmed by a monumental stove of white tiles, a much more pleasant locality than the school-room, which, for some reason or other, perhaps hygienic, was always kept at a low temperature.

We children were aware that there was a guest staying in the house. He had arrived the night before just as we were being driven off to bed. We broke back through the line of our beaters to rush and flatten our noses against the dark window-panes; but we were too late to see him alight. We had only watched, in a ruddy glare, the big travelling carriage on sleigh-runners harnessed with six horses, a black mass against the snow, going off to the stables, preceded by a horseman carrying a blazing ball of tow and resin in an iron basket at the end of a long stick swung from his saddle-bow. Two stable boys had been sent out early in the afternoon

along the snow-tracks to meet the expected guest at dusk
and light his way with these road torches. At that time, you
must remember, there was not a single mile of railways in
our southern provinces. My little cousin and I had no knowledge of trains and engines, except from picture books as of
things rather vague, extremely remote and not particularly
interesting unless to grown-ups who travelled abroad.

Our notion of princes, perhaps a little more precise, was
mainly literary, and had a glamour reflected from the light of
fairy tales, in which princes always appear young, charming,
heroic and fortunate. Yet, as well as any other children, we
could draw a firm line between the real and the ideal. We
knew that princes were historical personages. And there was
some glamour in that fact, too. But what had driven me to
roam cautiously over the house like an escaped prisoner, was
the hope of snatching an interview with a special friend of
mine, the head forester, who generally came to make his report
at that time of the day. I yearned for news of a certain wolf.
You know, in a country where wolves are to be found, almost
every winter brings forward an individual eminent by the
audacity of his misdeeds, by his charmed life—by his more
perfect wolfishness, so to speak. I wanted to hear some new
thrilling tale of that wolf—perhaps the dramatic story of his
death. . . .

But there was no one in the hall.

Deceived in my hopes, I became suddenly very much
depressed. Unable to slip back in triumph to my studies, I
elected to stroll spiritlessly into the billiard-room, where certainly I had no business. There was no one there either, and
I felt very lost and desolate under its high ceiling, all alone
with the massive English billiard-table which seemed, in heavy,
rectilinear silence to disapprove of that small boy's intrusion.

As I began to think of retreat I heard footsteps in the
adjoining drawing-room; and before I could turn tail and flee,
my uncle and his guest appeared in the doorway. To run away
after having been seen would have been highly improper, so
I stood my ground. My uncle looked surprised to see me;
the guest by his side was a spare man, of average stature,
buttoned up in a black frock coat* and holding himself very

erect with a stiffly soldierlike carriage. From the folds of a soft, white neck-cloth peeped the points of a collar lying close against each shaven cheek. A few wisps of thin grey hair were brushed smoothly across the top of his bald head. His face, which must have been beautiful in its day, had preserved in age the harmonious simplicity of its lines. What amazed me was its even, almost deathlike pallor. He seemed to me to be prodigiously old. A faint smile, a mere momentary alteration in the set of his thin lips, acknowledged my blushing confusion; and I became greatly interested to see him reach into the inside breast-pocket of his coat. He extracted therefrom a lead pencil and a block of detachable pages, which he handed to my uncle with an almost imperceptible bow.

I was very much astonished, but my uncle received it as a matter of course. He wrote rapidly something at which the other glanced and nodded slightly. A fine wrinkled hand— the hand was older than the face—patted my cheek and then rested on my head lightly. An unringing voice, a voice as colourless as the face itself, issued from his sunken lips, while the eyes, faded and still, looked down at me kindly.

'And how old is this shy little boy?'

Before I could answer my uncle wrote down my age on the pad. I was deeply impressed. What was this ceremony? Was this personage too great to be spoken to? Again he glanced at the pad, and again gave a nod, and again that impersonal, mechanical voice was heard.

'He resembles his grandfather.'

I remembered my paternal grandfather. He had died not long before. He, too, was prodigiously old. And to me it seemed perfectly natural that two such ancient and venerable persons should have known each other in the dim ages of creation before my birth. But my uncle obviously had not been aware of the fact. So obviously that the mechanical voice explained—

'Yes, yes. Comrades in '31. He was one of those who knew. Old times, my dear sir, old times . . .'

He made a gesture as if to put aside an importunate ghost. And now they were both looking down in silence. I wondered whether anything was expected from me. To my round, questioning eyes my uncle remarked, 'He's completely deaf.' And the unrelated, inexpressive voice said: 'Give me your hand.'

Acutely conscious of inky fingers, I put it out timidly. I had never seen a deaf person before and was rather startled. He pressed it firmly and then gave me a final pat on the head.

My uncle addressed me weightily.

'You have shaken hands with Prince Roman S——.* It's something for you to remember when you grow up.'

I was impressed by his tone. I had enough historical information to know vaguely that the Princes S—— counted amongst the sovereign princes of Ruthenia* till the union of all Ruthenian lands to the kingdom of Poland, when they became great Polish magnates, sometime at the beginning of the fifteenth century. But what concerned me most was the failure of the fairy tale glamour. It was shocking to discover a prince who was deaf, bald, meagre and so prodigiously old. It never occurred to me that this imposing and disappointing man had been young, rich and beautiful. I could not know that he had been happy in the felicity of an ideal marriage uniting two young hearts, two great names and two great fortunes; happy with a happiness which, as in fairy tales, seemed destined to last for ever. . . .

But it did not last for ever. It was fated not to last very long, even by the measure of the days allotted to men's passage on this earth where enduring happiness is only found in the conclusion of fairy tales. A daughter was born to them, and shortly afterwards the health of the young princess began to fail. For a time she bore up with smiling intrepidity, sustained by the feeling that now her existence was necessary for the happiness of two lives. But at last the husband, thoroughly alarmed by the rapid changes in her appearance, obtained an unlimited leave and took her away from the Capital, to his parents in the country.

The old prince and princess were extremely frightened at the state of their beloved daughter-in-law. Preparations were at once made for a journey abroad. But it seemed as if it were already too late; and the invalid herself opposed the project with gentle obstinacy. Thin and pale in the great arm-chair, where the insidious and obscure nervous malady made her appear smaller and more frail every day, without effacing the smile of her eyes or the charming grace of her wasted face, she clung to her native land and wished to breathe her native air. Nowhere else could she expect to get well so quickly, nowhere else would it be so easy for her to die.

She died before her little girl was two years old. The grief of the husband was terrible, and the more awful to his parents because perfectly silent and dry-eyed. After the funeral, while the immense bareheaded crowd of peasants surrounding the private chapel in the grounds was dispersing, the prince, waving away his friends and relations, remained alone to watch the masons of the estate closing the family vault. When the last stone was in position he uttered a groan, the first sound of pain which had escaped him for days, and, walking away with lowered head, shut himself up again in his apartments.

His father and mother feared for his reason. His outward tranquillity appalled them. They had nothing to trust to but that very youth which made his despair so self-absorbed and so intense. Old Prince John, fretful and anxious, repeated: 'Poor Roman should be roused somehow. He's so young.' But they could find nothing to rouse him with. And the old princess, wiping her eyes, wished in her heart he were young enough to come and cry at her knee.

In time Prince Roman, making an effort, would join now and again the family circle. But it was as if his heart and his mind had been buried in the family vault with the wife he had lost. He took to wandering in the woods with a gun, watched over secretly by one of the keepers, who would report in the evening that 'His Serenity has never fired a shot all day.' Sometimes walking to the stables in the morning, he would order in subdued tones a horse to be saddled, wait switching his boot till it was led up to him, then mount without a word and ride out of the gates at a walking pace. He would be gone all day. People saw him on the roads looking neither to the right nor to the left, white-faced, sitting rigidly in the saddle like a horseman of stone on a living mount.

The peasants working in the fields, the great unhedged fields, looked after him from the distance; and sometimes some sympathetic old woman on the threshold of a low, thatched hut was moved to make the sign of the cross in the air behind his back; as though he were one of themselves, a simple village soul struck by a sore affliction.

He rode looking straight ahead, seeing no one, as if the earth were empty and all mankind buried in that grave which had opened so suddenly in his path to swallow up his happiness. What were men to him with their sorrows, joys, labours and passions from which she who had been all the world to him had been cut off so early?

They did not exist; and he would have felt as completely lonely and abandoned as a man in the toils of a cruel nightmare if it had not been for this countryside where he had been born and had spent his happy boyish years. He knew it well —every slight rise crowned with trees amongst the ploughed fields, every dell concealing a village. The dammed streams made a chain of lakes set in the green meadows. Far away to the north the great Lithuanian forest faced the sun, no higher than a hedge; and to the south, the way to the plains, the vast brown spaces of ploughed earth touched the blue sky.

And this familiar landscape, associated with the days without thought and without sorrow, this land the charm of which he felt without even looking at it, soothed his pain, like the presence of a trusted friend who sits silent and disregarded by one in some dark hour of life.

One afternoon, it happened that the prince, after turning his horse's head for home, remarked a low thick cloud of dark dust cutting off slantwise a part of the view. He reined in on a knoll and peered. There were pointed gleams of steel here and there in that cloud, and it contained moving forms which revealed themselves at last as a long line of peasant carts full of soldiers, proceeding slowly in double file under the escort of mounted Cossacks.

It was like an immense reptile creeping over the fields; its head dipped out of sight in a slight hollow and its tail went on writhing and growing shorter as though the monster were eating its way into the very heart of the land.

The prince directed his way through a village lying a little off the track. The roadside inn with its stable, byre* and barn all under one enormous thatched roof, resembled a deformed, hunchbacked, ragged giant, sprawling amongst the small huts of the peasants. The innkeeper, a portly, dignified Jew, clad in a black satin coat reaching down to his heels and girt with a red sash, stood at the door stroking his long, silvery beard.

He watched the prince approach and bowed gravely from the waist, not expecting to be noticed even, since it was well known that their young lord had no eyes for anything or anybody in his grief. It was quite a shock for him when the prince pulled up and asked: 'What's all this, Yankel?'

'That, please your Serenity, that is a convoy of foot soldiers they are hurrying down to the south.'

He glanced right and left cautiously, but as there was no one near but some children playing in the dust of the village street, he came up close to the stirrup.

'Doesn't your Serenity know? It has begun already down there. All the landowners great and small are out in arms, and even the common people have risen. Only yesterday the saddler from Grodek' (it was a tiny market-town near by) 'went through here with his two apprentices on his way to join. He left even his cart with me. I gave him a guide through our neighbourhood. You know, your Serenity, our people, they travel a lot and they see all that's going on, and they know all the roads.'

He tried to keep down his excitement, for the Jew Yankel, innkeeper and tenant of all the mills on the estate, was a Polish patriot. And in a still lower voice—

'I was already a married man when the French and all the other nations passed this way with Napoleon.* Tse! Tse! That was a great harvest for death. Nu! Perhaps this time God will help.'

The prince nodded. 'Perhaps'—and falling into deep meditation he let his horse take him home.

That night he wrote a letter, and early in the morning sent a mounted express to the post town. During the day he came out of his taciturnity, to the great joy of the family circle, and conversed with his father of recent events—the revolt in

Warsaw, the flight of the Grand duke Constantine,* the first
slight successes of the Polish army (at that time there was a
Polish army), the rising in the provinces. Old Prince John,
moved and uneasy, speaking from a purely aristocratic point
of view, mistrusted the popular origins of the movement,
regretted its democratic tendencies, and did not believe in
the possibility of success.

He was sad, inwardly agitated.

'I am judging all this calmly. There are secular principles
of legitimacy and order which have been violated in this reckless enterprise for the sake of subversive illusions. Though,
of course, the patriotic impulses of the heart . . .'

Prince Roman had listened in a thoughtful attitude. He
took advantage of the pause to tell his father quietly that he
had sent that morning a letter to St Petersburg resigning his
commission in the Guards.

The old prince remained silent. He thought that he ought
to have been consulted. His son was also ordonnance officer
to the Emperor,* and he knew that the Tzar* would never
forget this appearance of defection in a Polish noble. In a
discontented tone he pointed out to his son that as it was
he had an unlimited leave. The right thing would have been
to keep quiet. They had too much tact at court to recall a
man of his name. Or at worst, some distant mission might
have been asked for—to the Caucasus* for instance—away
from this unhappy struggle which was wrong in principle and
therefore destined to fail.

'Presently you will find yourself without any interest in life
and with no occupation. And you will need something to
occupy you, my poor boy. You have acted rashly, I fear.'

Prince Roman murmured, 'I thought it better.'

His father faltered under his steady gaze.

'Well, well—perhaps! But as ordonnance officer to the
Emperor and in favour with all the Imperial family . . .'

'Those people had never been heard of when our house
was already illustrious,' the young man let fall negligently.

This was the sort of remark to which the old prince was
sensible.

'Well—perhaps it is better,' he conceded at last.

The father and son parted affectionately for the night, but next day Prince Roman seemed to have fallen back into the depths of his indifference. He rode out as usual, and reined in on the knoll from which the day before he had seen a reptile-like convoy of soldiery, bristling with bayonets, crawl over the face of that land which was his. The woman he loved had been his too. Death had robbed him of her. Her loss had been to him a moral shock. It had opened his heart to a greater sorrow, his mind to a vaster thought, his eyes to all the past, and to the existence of another love, fraught with pain, but as mysteriously imperative as that lost one to which he had entrusted his happiness.

That evening he retired earlier than usual and rang for his personal servant.

'Go and see if there is light yet in the quarters of the master of the horse. If he is still up, ask him to come and speak to me.'

While the servant was absent on this errand, the prince tore up hastily some papers, locked the drawers of his desk and hung a medallion containing the miniature of his wife round his neck, against his breast.

The man the prince had sent for belonged to that past which the death of his love had called to life. He was of a family of small nobles who for generations had been adherents, servants and friends of the Princes S——. He remembered the times before the last partition,* and had taken part in the struggles of the last hour. He was a typical old Pole of that class, with a great capacity for emotion, for blind enthusiasm; with martial instincts and simple beliefs; and even with the old-time habit of larding his speech with Latin words. And his kindly, shrewd eyes, his ruddy face, his lofty brow and his thick, grey, pendant moustache were also very typical of his kind.

'Listen, Master Francis,' the prince said familiarly and without preliminaries. 'Listen, old friend. I am going to vanish from here quietly. I go where something louder than my grief, and yet something with a voice very like it, calls me. I confide in you alone. You will say what's necessary when the time comes.'

The old man understood. His extended hands trembled exceedingly. But as soon as he found his voice he thanked God aloud for letting him live long enough to see the descendant of the illustrious family in its youngest generation give an example *coram gentibus** of the love of his country and of valour in the field. He doubted not of his dear prince attaining a place in council and in war worthy of his high birth; he saw already that *in fulgore** of family glory *affulget patriæ serenitas.** At the end of this speech he burst into tears and fell into the prince's arms.

The prince quieted the old man, and when he had him seated in an arm-chair and comparatively composed he said—

'Don't misunderstand me, Master Francis. You know how I loved my wife. A loss like that opens one's eyes to unsuspected truths. There is no question here of leadership and glory. I mean to go alone, and to fight obscurely in the ranks. I am going to offer my country what is mine to offer, that is, my life, as simply as the saddler from Grodek who went through yesterday with his apprentices. . . .'

The old man cried out at this. That could never be. He could not allow it. But he had to give way before the arguments and the express will of the prince.

'Ha! If you say that it is a matter of feeling and conscience—so be it. But you cannot go utterly alone. Alas! that I am too old to be of any use. *Eripit verba dolor,** my dear Prince, at the thought that I am over seventy and of no more account in the world than a cripple in the church porch. It seems that to sit at home and pray to God for the nation and for you, is all that I am fit for. But there is my son, my youngest boy, Peter. He will make a worthy companion for you. And as it happens he's staying with me here. There has not been for ages a Prince S——hazarding his life without a companion of our name to ride by his side. You must have by you somebody who knows who you are, if only to let your parents and your old servant hear what is happening to you. And when does your Princely Mightiness intend to start?'

'In an hour,' said the prince; and the old man hurried off to warn his son.

Prince Roman took up a candlestick and walked quietly through many dark rooms in the silent house. The head nurse said afterwards that, waking up suddenly, she saw the prince looking at his child, one hand shading the light from its eyes. He gazed at her for some time, and then, putting the candlestick on the floor, bent over the cot and kissed lightly the little girl, who did not wake. He went out noiselessly, taking the light away with him. She saw his face perfectly well, but she could read nothing of his purpose on it. It was pale but perfectly calm. After he turned away from the cot he never looked back at it once.

The only other trusted person, besides the old man and his son Peter, was the Jew Yankel. When he asked the prince where precisely he wanted to be guided, the prince answered, 'To the nearest party.' A grandson of the Jew, a lanky youth, conducted the two young men by little-known paths, across woods and morasses, and led them in sight of the few fires of a small detachment of Polish insurgents camped in a hollow. Some invisible horses neighed, a voice in the dark cried: 'Who goes there?' . . . and the young Jew departed hurriedly, explaining that he must make haste home to be in time for keeping the Sabbath.

Thus humbly and in accord with the simplicity of the vision of duty beheld when death had removed the brilliant bandage of happiness from his eyes, did Prince Roman bring his offering to his country. His companion made himself known as the son of the master of the horse to the Princes S——, and declared him to be a relation, a distant cousin from the same parts as himself and, as people presumed, of the same name. In truth no one inquired much. Two more young men, clearly of the right sort, had joined. Nothing more natural.

Prince Roman did not remain long in the south. One day, while scouting with several others, the party was ambushed near the entrance of a village by some Russian infantry. The first discharge laid low a good many, and the rest scattered in all directions. The Russians, too, did not stay, being afraid of a return in force. After some time, the peasants coming to view the scene extricated Prince Roman from under his dead horse. He was unhurt, but his faithful companion had been one of the first to fall. The prince helped the peasants to bury him and the other dead.

Then alone, not certain where to find the main body of partisans which was constantly moving about, he resolved to try and join the main Polish army facing the Russians on the borders of Lithuania. Disguised in peasant clothes, in case of meeting some marauding Cossacks, he wandered for a couple of weeks before he came upon a village occupied by a regiment of Polish cavalry on outpost duty.

On a bench, before a peasant hut of the better sort, sat an elderly officer whom he took for the colonel. The prince approached respectfully, told his story shortly and stated his desire to enlist; and when asked his name by the officer, who had been looking him over carefully, he gave on the spur of the moment the name of his dead companion.

The elderly officer thought to himself: 'Here's the son of some peasant proprietor of the liberated class.' He liked his appearance.

'And can you read and write, my dear fellow?' he asked.

'Yes, your honour, I can,' said the prince.

'Good. Come along inside the hut; the regimental adjutant is there. He will enter your name and administer the oath to you.'

The adjutant stared very hard at the new-comer, but said nothing. When all the forms had been gone through and the recruit gone out, he turned to his superior officer.

'Do you know who that is?'

'Who? That Peter? A likely chap.'

'That's Prince Roman S——'

'Nonsense!'

But the adjutant was positive. He had seen the prince several times, about two years before, in the Castle in Warsaw. He had even spoken to him once at a reception of officers held by the Grand Duke.

'He's changed. He seems much older, but I am certain of my man. I have a good memory for faces.'

The two officers looked at each other in silence.

'He's sure to be recognised sooner or later,' murmured the adjutant. The colonel shrugged his shoulders.

'It's no affair of ours—if he has a fancy to serve in the ranks. As to being recognised, it's not so likely. All our officers and men come from the other end of Poland.'

He meditated gravely for a while, then smiled. 'He told me he could read and write. There's nothing to prevent me making him a sergeant at the first opportunity. He's sure to shape all right.'

Prince Roman, as a non-commissioned officer, surpassed the colonel's expectations. Before long Sergeant Peter became famous for his resourcefulness and courage. It was not the reckless courage of a desperate man; it was a self-possessed, as if conscientious, valour which nothing could dismay; a boundless but equable devotion, unaffected by time, by reverses, by the discouragement of endless retreats, by the bitterness of waning hopes and the horrors of pestilence added to the toils and perils of war. It was in this year that the cholera made its first appearance in Europe.* It devastated the camps of both armies, affecting the firmest minds with the terror of a mysterious death stalking silently between the piled-up arms and around the bivouac fires.

A sudden shriek would wake up the harassed soldiers, and they would see in the glow of embers one of themselves writhe on the ground like a worm trodden on by an invisible foot. And before the dawn broke he would be stiff and cold. Parties so visited have been known to rise like one man, abandon the fire and run off into the night in mute panic. Or a comrade talking to you on the march would stammer suddenly in the middle of a sentence, roll affrighted eyes, and fall down with distorted face and blue lips, breaking the ranks with the convulsions of his agony. Men were struck in the saddle, on sentry duty, in the firing line, carrying orders, serving the guns. I have been told that in a battalion, forming under fire with perfect steadiness for the assault of a village, three cases occurred within five minutes at the head of the column; and the attack could not be delivered because the leading companies scattered all over the fields like chaff before the wind.

Sergeant Peter, young as he was, had a great influence over his men. It was said that the number of desertions in the squadron in which he served was less than in any other in the whole of that cavalry division. Such was supposed to be the compelling example of one man's quiet intrepidity in facing every form of danger and terror.

However that may be, he was liked and trusted generally. When the end came and the remnants of that army corps, hard pressed on all sides, were preparing to cross the Prussian frontier, Sergeant Peter had enough influence to rally round him a score of troopers. He managed to escape, with them, at night, from the hemmed-in army. He led this band through two hundred miles of country covered by numerous Russian detachments and ravaged by the cholera. But this was not to avoid captivity, to go into hiding and try to save themselves. No. He led them into a fortress which was still occupied by the Poles, and where the last stand of the vanquished revolution was to be made.

This looks like mere fanaticism. But fanaticism is human. Man has adored ferocious divinities. There is ferocity in every passion—even in love itself. The religion of undying hope resembles the mad cult of despair, of death, of annihilation. The difference lies in the moral motive springing from the secret needs and the unexpressed aspirations of the believers. It is only to vain men that all is vanity; and all is deception only to those who have never been sincere with themselves.

It was in the fortress that my grandfather found himself together with Sergeant Peter. My grandfather was a neighbour of the S——family in the country, but he had never met Prince Roman, who, however, knew his name perfectly well. The Prince introduced himself one night as they both sat on the ramparts, leaning against a gun-carriage.

The service he wished to ask for was, in case of his being killed, to have the intelligence conveyed to his parents.

They talked in low tones, the other servants of the piece lying about near them. My grandfather gave the required promise, and then asked frankly—for he was greatly interested by the disclosure so unexpectedly made—

'But tell me, Prince, why this request? Have you any evil forebodings as to yourself?'

'Not in the least; I was thinking of my people. They have no idea where I am,' answered Prince Roman. 'I'll engage to do as much for you, if you like. It's certain that half of the garrison at least will be killed before the end, so there's an even chance of one of us surviving the other.'

My grandfather told him where, as he supposed, his wife and children were then. From that moment till the end of the siege, the two were much together. On the day of the great assault my grandfather received a severe wound. The town was taken. Next day the citadel itself, its hospital full of dead and dying, its magazines empty, its defenders having burnt their last cartridges, opened its gates.

During all the campaign the prince, exposing his person conscientiously on every occasion, had not received a scratch. No one had recognised him, or, at any rate, had betrayed his identity. Till then, as long as he did his duty, it had mattered nothing who he was.

Now, however, the position was changed. As ex-guardsman and as late ordonnance-officer to the Emperor, this rebel ran a serious risk of being given special attention in the shape of a firing squad at ten paces. For more than a month he remained lost in the miserable crowd of prisoners packed in the casemates* of the citadel, with just enough food to keep body and soul together, but otherwise allowed to die from wounds, privation and disease at the rate of forty or so a day.

The position of the fortress being central, new parties, captured in the open in the course of a thorough pacification, were being sent in frequently. Amongst such new-comers there happened to be a young man, a personal friend of the prince from his school days. He recognised him, and in the extremity of his dismay cried aloud: 'My God! Roman—you here!'

It is said that years of life embittered by remorse paid for this momentary lack of self-control. All this happened in the main quadrangle of the citadel. The warning gesture of the Prince came too late. An officer of the gendarmes* on guard had heard the exclamation. The incident appeared to him worth inquiring into. The investigation which followed was not very arduous, because the prince, asked categorically for his real name, owned up at once.

The intelligence of a Prince S——being found amongst the prisoners was sent to St Petersburg. His parents were already there, living in sorrow, incertitude and apprehension. The Capital of the Empire was the safest place to reside in for a noble whose son had disappeared so mysteriously from home in a time of rebellion. The old people had not heard from him, or of him, for months. They took care not to contradict the rumours of suicide from despair circulating in the great world, which remembered the interesting love-match, the charming and frank happiness brought to an end by death. But they hoped secretly that their son survived, and that he had been able to cross the frontier with that part of the army which had surrendered to the Prussians.

The news of his captivity was a crushing blow. Directly, nothing could be done for him. But the greatness of their name, of their position, their wide relations and connections in the highest spheres, enabled his parents to act indirectly; and they moved heaven and earth, as the saying is, to save their son from the 'consequences of his madness,' as poor Prince John did not hesitate to express himself. Great personages were approached by society leaders, high dignitaries were interviewed, powerful officials were induced to take an interest in that affair. The help of every possible secret influence was enlisted. Some private secretaries got heavy bribes. The mistress of an influential senator obtained a large sum of money.

But, as I have said, in such a glaring case no direct appeal could be made and no open steps taken. All that could be done was to incline by private representations the mind of the President of the Military Commission to the side of clemency. That superior officer ended by being impressed by the hints and suggestions, some of them from very high quarters, which he received from St Petersburg. After all, the gratitude of such great nobles as the Princes S——was something worth having from a worldly point of view. He was a good Russian, but he was also a good-natured man. Moreover, the hate of Poles was not at that time a cardinal article of patriotic creed, as it became some thirty years later. He felt well disposed at first sight towards that young man, bronzed, thin-faced, worn out by months of hard campaigning, the hardships of the siege and the rigours of captivity.

The Commission was composed of three officers. It sat in the citadel in a bare, vaulted room behind a long, black table. Some clerks occupied the two ends; besides the gendarmes who brought in the prince, there was no one else there.

Within those four sinister walls, shutting out from him all the sights and sounds of liberty, all hopes of the future, all consoling illusions—alone in the face of his enemies erected judges, who can tell how much love of life there was in Prince Roman? How much remained of that sense of duty, revealed to him in sorrow? How much of his awakened love for his native country?—that country which demands to be loved as no other country has ever been loved, with the mournful affection one bears to the unforgotten dead and with the unextinguishable fire of a hopeless passion which only a living, breathing, warm ideal can kindle in our breasts, for our pride, for our weariness, for our exultation, for our undoing.

There is something monstrous in the thought of such an exaction till it stands before us embodied in the shape of a fidelity without fear and without reproach. Nearing the supreme moment of his life, the prince could only have had the feeling that it was about to end. He answered the questions put to him clearly, concisely, with the most profound indifference. After all those tense months of action, to talk was a weariness to him. But he concealed it, lest his foes should suspect in his manner the apathy of discouragement or the numbness of a crushed spirit. The details of his conduct could have no importance one way or another; with his thoughts these men had nothing to do. He preserved a scrupulously courteous tone. He had refused the permission to sit down.

What happened at this preliminary examination is only known from the presiding officer. Pursuing the only possible course in that glaringly bad case, he tried from the first to bring to the prince's mind the line of defence he wished him to take. He absolutely framed his questions so as to put the right answers in the culprit's mouth, going so far as to suggest the very words—how, distracted by excessive grief after his young wife's death, rendered irresponsible for his conduct by his despair, in a moment of blind recklessness, without realising the highly reprehensible nature of the act, nor yet its danger and its dishonour, he went off to join the nearest rebels on a sudden impulse. And that now, penitently . . .

But the culprit was silent. The military judge looked at him hopefully. In silence Prince Roman reached for a pen and wrote on a sheet of paper he found under his hand: 'I joined the national rising from conviction.'

He pushed the paper across the table. The president took it up, showed it in turn to his two colleagues sitting to the right and left, then, looking fixedly at Prince Roman, let it fall from his hand. And the silence remained unbroken till he spoke to the gendarmes ordering them to remove the prisoner.

Such was the written testimony of Prince Roman in the supreme moment of his life. I have heard that the Princes of the S——family, in all its branches, adopted the last two words, '*From conviction*,' for the device under the armorial bearings of their house. I don't know whether this report is true. My uncle could not tell me. He remarked only that, naturally, it was not to be seen on Prince Roman's own seal.

He was condemned for life to Siberian mines. Emperor Nicholas, who always took personal cognisance of all sentences on Polish nobility, wrote with his own hand in the margin: 'The authorities are severely warned to take care that this convict walks in chains like any other criminal every step of the way.'

It was a sentence of deferred death. Very few survived entombment in these mines for more than three years. Yet as he was reported as still alive at the end of that time, he was allowed, on a petition of his parents and by way of exceptional grace, to serve as common soldier in the Caucasus. All communication with him was forbidden. He had no civil rights. For all practical purposes except that of suffering he was a dead man. The little child he had been so careful not to wake up when he kissed her in her cot, inherited all the fortune after Prince John's death. Her existence saved those immense estates from confiscation.

It was twenty-five years before Prince Roman, stone deaf, his health broken, was permitted to return to Poland. His daughter, married splendidly to a Polish-Austrian *grand seigneur** and moving in the cosmopolitan sphere of the highest European aristocracy, lived mostly abroad in Nice and Vienna. He, settling down on one of her estates, not the one with the palatial residence but another where there was a modest little house, saw very little of her.

But Prince Roman did not shut himself up as if his work were ended. There was hardly anything done in the private and public life of the neighbourhood in which Prince Roman's advice and assistance were not called upon, and never in vain. It was well said that his days did not belong to himself but to his fellow-citizens. And especially he was the particular friend of all returned exiles, helping them with purse and advice, arranging their affairs and finding them means of livelihood.

I heard from my uncle many tales of his devoted activity, in which he was always guided by a simple wisdom, a high sense of honour and the most scrupulous conception of private and public probity. He remains a living figure for me because of that meeting in a billiard-room, when, in my anxiety to hear about a particularly wolfish wolf, I came in momentary contact with a man who was pre-eminently a man amongst all men capable of feeling deeply, of believing steadily, of loving ardently.

I remember to this day the grasp of Prince Roman's bony, wrinkled hand closing on my small, inky paw, and my uncle's half-serious, half-amused way of looking down at his trespassing nephew.

They moved on and forgot that little boy. But I did not move; I gazed after them, not so much disappointed as disconcerted by this prince, so utterly unlike a prince in a fairy tale. They moved very slowly across the room. Before reaching the other door the prince stopped; and I heard him —I seem to hear him now—saying: 'I wish you would write to Vienna about filling up that post. He's a most deserving fellow—and a word from you would be decisive with my daughter.'

My uncle's face turned to him expressed genuine wonder. It said as plainly as any speech could say: What better
recommendation than a father's can be needed? The prince
was quick at reading expressions. Again he spoke with the
toneless accent of a man who has not heard his own voice
for years, for whom the soundless world is like an abode of
silent shades. And to this day I remember the very words.

'I ask you to write, because, you see, my daughter and my
son-in-law don't believe me to be a good judge of men. They
think that I let myself be guided too much by sentiment.'

THE INN OF THE TWO WITCHES
A Find

THIS tale, episode, experience—call it how you will—was
related in the fifties of the last century by a man who, by
his own confession, was sixty years old at the time. Sixty is
not such a bad age—unless in perspective, when no doubt
it is contemplated by the majority of us with mixed feelings.
It is a calm age; the game is practically over by then; and
standing aside one begins to remember with a certain vividness what a fine fellow one used to be. I have observed that,
by an amiable attention of Providence, most people begin at
sixty to take a romantic view of themselves.

I suppose it was the romanticism of growing age which
set our man to relate his experience for his own satisfaction
or for the wonder of his posterity. It could not have been for
his glory, because the experience was simply that of an abominable fright—terror he calls it. You will have guessed that the
relation alluded to in the very first lines was in writing.

This writing constitutes the Find declared in the sub-title.
It was made in a box of books bought in London, in a street
which no longer exists, from a second-hand bookseller in the
last stage of decay. As to the books themselves, they were at
least twentieth-hand, and on inspection turned out not worth
the very small sum of money disbursed. It might have been
some premonition of that fact which made me say: 'But I
must have the box too.' The decayed bookseller assented
with the careless, tragic gesture of a man already doomed
to extinction.

A litter of loose pages at the bottom of the box excited
my curiosity but faintly. The close, neat, regular handwriting was not attractive at first sight. But the statement that
in AD 1813 the writer was twenty-two years old caught my
eye. Two-and-twenty is an interesting age, in which one is
easily reckless and easily frightened, the faculty of reflection
being weak and the power of imagination strong.

In another place the phrase 'At night we stood in again'*
arrested my languid attention, because it was a sea phrase.
'Let's see what it is all about,' I thought, without excitement.

Oh! but it was a dull-faced MS, each line resembling every
other line in their close-set and regular order. It was like the
drone of a monotonous voice. A treatise on sugar-refining
(the dreariest subject I can think of) could have been given a
more lively appearance. 'In AD 1813 I was twenty-two years
old,' he begins earnestly, and goes on with every appearance
of calm, horrible industry. Don't imagine, however, that there
is anything archaic in my find. Diabolic ingenuity in invention, though as old as the world, is by no means a lost art.
Look at the telephones for shattering the little peace of mind
given to us in this world, or at the machine guns for letting
with dispatch life out of our bodies. Nowadays any blear-eyed
old witch, if only strong enough to turn an insignificant little
handle, could lay low a hundred young men of twenty in
the twinkling of an eye.

If this isn't progress! . . . Why, immense! We have moved
on, and so you must expect to meet here a certain naïve-
ness of contrivance and simplicity of aim appertaining to the
remote epoch. And of course no motoring tourist can hope
to find such an inn anywhere now. This one, the one of the
title, was situated in Spain. That much I discovered only
from internal evidence, because a good many pages of that
relation were missing—perhaps not a great misfortune after
all. The writer seemed to have entered into a most elaborate
detail of the why and wherefore of his presence on that coast
—presumably the north coast of Spain. His experience has
nothing to do with the sea, though. As far as I can make
it out, he was an officer on board a sloop-of-war.* There's
nothing strange in that. At all stages of the long Peninsular
campaign* many of our men-of-war, of the smaller kind, were
cruising off the north coast of Spain—as risky and disagreeable a station as can be well imagined.

It looks as though that ship of his had had some special
service to perform. A careful explanation of all the circumstances was to be expected from our man, only, as I've said,
some of his pages (good tough paper too) were missing: gone

in covers for jampots or in wadding for the fowling-pieces of his irreverent posterity. But it is to be seen clearly that communication with the shore and even the sending of messengers inland was part of her service, either to obtain intelligence from or to transmit orders or advice to patriotic Spaniards, guerilleros or secret juntas of the province. Something of the sort. All this can be only inferred from the preserved scraps of his conscientious writing.

Next we come upon the panegyric of a very fine sailor, a member of the ship's company, having the rating of the captain's coxswain.* He was known on board as Cuba Tom; not because he was a Cuban, however. He was indeed the best type of a genuine British tar of that time, and a man-of-war's* man for years. He came by the name on account of some wonderful adventures he had in that island in his young days—adventures which were the favourite subject of the yarns he was in the habit of spinning to his shipmates of an evening on the forecastle* head. He was intelligent, very strong and of proved courage. Incidentally we are told, so exact is our narrator, that Tom had the finest pigtail for thickness and length of any man in the Navy. This appendage, much cared for and sheathed tightly in a porpoise skin, hung half-way down his broad back, to the great admiration of all beholders and to the great envy of some.

Our young officer dwells on the manly qualities of Cuba Tom with something like affection. This sort of relation between officer and man was not then very rare. A youngster on joining the service was put under the charge of a trustworthy seaman, who slung his first hammock for him, and often, later on became a sort of humble friend to the junior officer. This man the narrator on joining the sloop had found on board after some years of separation. There is something touching in the warm pleasure he remembers and records at this meeting with the professional mentor of his boyhood.

We discover then that no Spaniard being forthcoming for the service, this worthy seaman with the unique pigtail and a very high character for courage and steadiness, had been selected as messenger for one of these missions inland which have been mentioned. One gloomy autumn morning the sloop ran close to a shallow cove where a landing could be made on that iron-bound shore. A boat was lowered and pulled in, Tom Corbin (Cuba Tom) perched in the bow and our young man (Mr Edgar Byrne was his name on this earth which knows him no more) sitting in the stern-sheets.*

A few inhabitants of a hamlet whose grey stone houses could be seen a hundred yards or so up a shallow ravine had come down to the shore and watched the approach of the boat. The two Englishmen leaped ashore. Either from dullness or astonishment the peasants gave no greeting, and only fell back in silence.

Mr Byrne had made up his mind to see Tom Corbin started fairly on his way. He looked round at the heavy, surprised faces. 'We won't get much out of them,' he said. 'Let us walk up to the village. There will be a wine-shop for sure where we may find somebody more promising to talk to and get some information from.'

'Aye, aye, sir,' said Tom, falling into step behind his officer. 'A bit of palaver as to courses and distances can do no harm; I crossed the broadest part of Cuba by the help of my tongue, though knowing far less Spanish than I do now. As they say themselves, it was "four words and no more" with me, that time when I got left behind on shore by the *Blanche* frigate.'

He made light of what was before him, which was but a day's journey into the mountains. It is true that there was another day's journey before striking the mountain path, but that was nothing for a man who had crossed the island of Cuba on his two legs, and with no more than four words of the language to begin with.

The officer and the man were walking now on a thick sodden bed of dead leaves which the peasants thereabouts accumulate in the streets of their villages to rot during the winter for field manure. Turning his head Mr Byrne perceived that the whole male population of the hamlet was following them on the noiseless springy carpet. Women stared from the doors of the houses, and the children had apparently gone into hiding. The village knew the ship by sight, afar off, but no stranger had landed on that spot perhaps for a hundred years or more. The cocked hat of Mr Byrne, the bushy whiskers and the enormous pigtail of the sailor filled them with mute wonder. They pressed behind the two Englishmen, staring like those islanders discovered by Captain Cook in the South Seas.

It was then that Byrne had his first glimpse of the little cloaked man in a yellow hat. Faded and dingy as it was, this covering for his head made him noticeable.

The entrance to the wine-shop was like a rough hole in a wall of flints. The owner was the only person who was not in the street, for he came out from the darkness at the back, where the inflated forms of wine-skins hung on nails could be vaguely distinguished. He was a tall, one-eyed Asturian* with scrubby, hollow cheeks; a grave expression of countenance contrasted enigmatically with the roaming restlessness of his solitary eye. On learning that the matter in hand was the sending on his way of that English mariner toward a certain Gonzales in the mountains, he closed his good eye for a moment as if in meditation. Then opened it, very lively again.

'Possibly, possibly. It could be done.'

A friendly murmur arose in the group in the doorway at the name of Gonzales, the local leader against the French. Inquiring as to the safety of the road, Byrne was glad to learn that no troops of that nation had been seen in the neighbourhood for months. Not the smallest little detachment of these impious *polizones*.* While giving these answers the owner of the wine-shop busied himself in drawing into an earthenware jug some wine which he set before the heretic English, pocketing with grave abstraction the small piece of money the officer threw upon the table in recognition of the unwritten law that none may enter a wine-shop without buying drink. His eye was in constant motion, as if it were trying to do the work of the two; but when Byrne made inquiries as to the possibility of hiring a mule it became immovably fixed in the direction of the door, which was closely besieged by the curious. In front of them, just within the threshold, the little man in the large cloak and yellow hat had taken his stand. He was a diminutive person, a mere homunculus, Byrne describes him, in a ridiculously mysterious yet assertive attitude, a corner of his cloak thrown cavalierly over his left shoulder, muffling his chin and mouth; while the broad-brimmed yellow hat hung sideways on a corner of his square little head. He stood there taking snuff repeatedly.

'A mule,' repeated the wine-seller, his eye fixed on that quaint and snuffy figure. . . . 'No, señor officer! Decidedly no mule is to be got in this poor place.'

The coxswain, who stood by with the true sailor's air of unconcern in strange surroundings, struck in quietly: 'If your honour will believe me, Shank's pony's* the best for this job. I would have to leave the beast somewhere, anyhow, since the captain has told me that half my way will be along paths fit only for goats.'

The diminutive man made a step forward, and spoke through the folds of the cloak, which seemed to muffle a sarcastic intention: 'Si, señor. They are too honest in this village to have a single mule amongst them for your worship's service. To that I can bear testimony. In these times it's only rogues or very clever men who can manage to have mules or any other four-footed beasts and the wherewithal to keep them. But what this valiant mariner wants is a guide; and here, señor, behold my brother-in-law Bernardino, wine-seller and Alcade* of this most Christian and hospitable village, who will find you one.'

This, Mr Byrne says in his relation, was the only thing to do. A youth in a ragged coat and goatskin breeches was produced after some more talk. The English officer stood treat to the whole village, and as the peasants crowded in to drink he and Cuba Tom took their departure accompanied by the guide. The diminutive man in the cloak had disappeared.

Byrne went along with the coxswain out of the village. He wanted to see him fairly on his way; and he would have gone a greater distance even, if the seaman had not suggested respectfully the advisability of return so as not to keep the ship a moment longer than necessary so close in with the shore on such an unpromising-looking morning. A wild, gloomy sky hung over their heads when they took leave of each other, and their surroundings of rank bushes and stony fields were dreary.

'In four days' time,' were Byrne's last words, 'the ship will stand in and send a boat on shore if the weather permits. If not, you'll have to make it out on shore the best you can till we come along to take you off.'

'Right you are, sir,' answered Tom, and strode on. Byrne watched him step out on a narrow path. In a thick pea-jacket,* with a pair of pistols in his belt, a cutlass by his side and a stout cudgel in his hand, he looked a sturdy figure and well able to take care of himself. He turned round for a moment to wave his hand, giving to Byrne one more view of his honest bronzed face with bushy whiskers. The lad in goatskin breeches, looking, Byrne says, like a faun or a young satyr leaping ahead, stopped to wait for him and then went off at a bound. Both disappeared.

Byrne turned back. The hamlet was hidden in a fold of the ground, and the spot seemed the most lonely corner of the earth, and as if accursed in its uninhabited desolate barrenness. Before he had walked many yards, however, there appeared very suddenly from behind a bush the muffled-up diminutive Spaniard. Naturally Byrne stopped short.

The other made a mysterious gesture with a tiny hand peeping from under his cloak. His hat hung very much at the side of his head. 'Señor,' he said, without any preliminaries, 'caution! It is a positive fact that one-eyed Bernardino, my brother-in-law, has at this moment a mule in his stable. And why he who is not clever has a mule there? Because he is a rogue, a man without conscience. Because I had to give up the *macho** to him to secure for myself a roof to sleep under and a mouthful of *olla** to keep my soul in this insignificant body of mine. Yet, señor, it contains a heart many times bigger than the mean thing which beats in the breast of that brute connection of mine, of whom I am ashamed, though I opposed that marriage with all my power. Well, the mis-guided woman suffered enough. She had her purgatory on this earth—God rest her soul.'

Byrne says he was so astonished by the sudden appearance of that sprite-like being, and by the sardonic bitterness of the speech, that he was unable to disentangle the significant fact from what seemed but a piece of family history fired out at him without rhyme or reason. He was confounded, and at the same time he was impressed by the rapid, forcible delivery, quite different from the frothy, excited loquacity of an Italian. So he stared while the homunculus, letting his cloak fall about him, aspired an immense quantity of snuff out of the hollow of his palm.

'A mule,' exclaimed Byrne, seizing at last the real aspect of the discourse. 'You say he has got a mule? That's queer! Why did he refuse to let me have it?'

The diminutive Spaniard muffled himself up again with great dignity. '*Quien sabe?*'* he said coldly, with a shrug of his draped shoulders. 'He is a great *politico* in everything he does. But one thing your worship may be certain of—that his intentions are always rascally. This husband of my *defunta** sister ought to have been married a long time ago to the widow with the wooden legs.'[1]

'I see. But remember that, whatever your motives, your worship countenanced him in this lie.'

The bright, unhappy eyes on each side of a predatory nose confronted Byrne without wincing, while with that testiness which lurks so often at the bottom of Spanish dignity: 'No doubt the señor officer would not lose an ounce of blood if I were stuck under the fifth rib,' he retorted. 'But what of this poor sinner here?' Then changing his tone: 'Señor, by the necessities of the times I live here in exile, a Castilian,* and an old Christian, existing miserably in the midst of these brute Asturians, and dependent on the worst of them all, who has less conscience and scruples than a wolf. And being a man of intelligence I govern myself accordingly. Yet I can hardly contain my scorn. You have heard the way I spoke. A *caballero** of parts like your worship might have guessed that there was a cat in there.'

'What cat?' said Byrne uneasily. 'Oh, I see. Something suspicious. No, señor. I guessed nothing. My nation are not

---

[1] The gallows, supposed to be widowed of the last executed criminal and waiting for another.

good guessers at that sort of thing; and therefore I ask you plainly whether that wine-seller has spoken the truth in other particulars.'

'There are certainly no Frenchmen anywhere about,' said the little man, with a return to his indifferent manner.

'Or robbers—*ladrones?*'

'*Ladrones en grande**—no! Assuredly not,' was the answer in a cold philosophical tone. 'What is there left for them to do after the French? And nobody travels in these times. But who can say? Opportunity makes the robber. Still, that mariner of yours has a fierce aspect, and with the son of a cat rats will have no play. But there is a saying too, that where honey is, there will soon be flies.'

This oracular discourse exasperated Byrne. 'In the name of God,' he cried, 'tell me plainly if you think my man is reasonably safe on his journey.'

The homunculus, undergoing one of his rapid changes, seized the officer's arm. The grip of his little hand was astonishing. 'Bernardino has taken notice of him. What more do you want, señor? And listen—men have disappeared on this road—on a certain portion of this road, when Bernardino kept a *meson*, an inn, and I, his brother-in-law, had coaches and mules for hire. Now there are no travellers, no coaches. The French have ruined me. Bernardino has retired here for reasons of his own after my sister died. They were three to torment the life out of her, he and Erminia and Lucilla, two aunts of his—all affiliated to the devil. And now he has robbed me of my last mule. You are an armed man. Demand the *macho* from him, with a pistol to his head, señor—it is not his, I tell you—and ride after your man who is so precious to you. And then you shall both be safe, for no two travellers have been ever known to disappear together in those days. As to the beast, I, its owner, I confide it to your honour.'

They were staring hard at each other, and Byrne nearly burst into a laugh at the ingenuity and transparency of the little man's plot to regain possession of his mule. But he had no difficulty to keep a straight face, because he felt deep within himself a strange inclination to do that very thing. He did not laugh, but his lip quivered; at which the diminutive Spaniard, detaching his black, glittering eyes from Byrne, turned his back on him brusquely with a gesture and a fling of the cloak which somehow expressed contempt, bitterness and discouragement all at once. He turned away and stood still, his hat aslant, muffled up to the ears. But he was not offended to the point of refusing the silver *duro** which Byrne offered him with a non-committal speech as if nothing extraordinary had passed between them.

'I must make haste on board now,' said Byrne then.

'*Vaya usted con Dios*,'* muttered the gnome. And this interview ended with a sarcastic low sweep of the hat, which was replaced at the same perilous angle as before.

Directly the boat had been hoisted the sloop's sails were filled on the offshore tack, and Byrne imparted the whole story to his captain, who was but a very few years older than himself. There was some amused indignation at it—but while they laughed they looked gravely at each other. A Spanish dwarf trying to induce an officer of His Majesty's Navy to steal a mule for him—that was too funny, too ridiculous, too incredible. Those were the exclamations of the captain. He couldn't get over the grotesqueness of it.

'Incredible. That's just it,' murmured Byrne at last, in a significant tone.

They exchanged a long stare. 'It's as clear as daylight,' affirmed the captain impatiently, because in his heart he was not certain. And Tom, the best seaman in the ship for one, the good-humouredly deferential friend of his boyhood for the other, was becoming endowed with a compelling fascination, like a symbolic figure of loyalty appealing to their feelings and their conscience, so that they could not detach their thoughts from his safety. Several times they went up on deck, only to look at the coast as if it could tell them something of his fate. It stretched away, lengthening in the distance, mute, naked and savage, veiled now and then by the slanting, cold shafts of rain. The westerly swell rolled its interminable angry lines of foam, and big dark clouds flew over the ship in a sinister procession.

'I wish to goodness you had done what your little friend in the yellow hat wanted you to do,' said the commander of the sloop, late in the afternoon, with visible exasperation.

'Do you, sir?' answered Byrne, bitter with positive anguish. 'I wonder what you would have said afterwards? Why! I might have been kicked out of the Service for looting a mule from a nation in alliance with His Majesty. Or I might have been battered to a pulp with flails and pitchforks—a pretty tale to go home about one of your officers—while trying to steal a mule. Or chased ignominiously to the boat—for you would not expect me to shoot unoffending people for the sake of a mangy mule. . . . And yet,' he added in a low voice, 'I almost wish myself I had done it.'

Before dark those two young men had worked themselves up into a highly complex psychological state of scornful scepticism and alarmed credulity. It tormented them exceedingly; and the thought that it would have to last for six days at least and possibly be prolonged further for an indefinite time was not to be borne. The ship was therefore put on the inshore tack* at dark. All through the gusty night she went towards the land to look for her man, at times lying over* in the heavy puffs, at others rolling idle in the swell, nearly stationary, as if she too had a mind of her own to swing perplexed between cool reason and warm impulse.

Then just at daybreak a boat put off from her and went on, tossed by the seas, towards the shallow cove, where, with considerable difficulty, a man in a thick coat and a round hat managed to land on a strip of shingle.

'It was my wish,' writes Mr Byrne, 'a wish of which my captain approved, to land secretly if possible. I did not want to be seen either by my aggrieved friend in the yellow hat, whose motives were not clear, or by the one-eyed wine-seller, who may or may not have been affiliated to the devil, or indeed by any other dweller in that primitive village. But the cove was the only possible landing-place for miles; and from the steepness of the ravine I couldn't make a circuit to avoid the houses.

'Fortunately,' he goes on, 'all the people were yet in their beds. It was barely daylight when I found myself walking on the thick layer of sodden leaves filling the only street. No soul was stirring abroad, no dog barked. The silence was profound, and I had concluded with some wonder that apparently no dogs were kept in the hamlet, when I heard a low snarl, and from a noisome alley between two hovels emerged a vile cur with its tail between its legs. He slunk off silently, showing me his teeth as he ran ahead, and disappeared so suddenly that he might have been the unclean incarnation of the Evil One. There was, too, something so weird in the manner of his coming and vanishing, that my spirits, already by no means very high, became further depressed by the revolting sight of this creature, as if by an unlucky presage.'

Byrne got away from the coast unobserved as far as he knew, and then struggled manfully to the west against wind and rain, on a barren dark upland, under a sky of ashes. Far away the harsh and desolate mountains raising their scarped and denuded ridges seemed to wait for him menacingly. The evening found him fairly near to them, but, in sailor language, uncertain of his position, hungry, wet and tired out by a day of steady tramping over broken ground, during which he had seen very few people, and had been unable to obtain the slightest intelligence of Tom Corbin's passage. 'On! on! I must push on,' he had been saying to himself through the hours of solitary effort, spurred more by an anxious feeling than by any definite fear or definite hope.

The lowering daylight died out quickly, leaving him faced by a broken bridge. He descended into the ravine, forded a narrow stream of rapid water by the last gleam, and clambering out on the other side was met by the night, which fell like a bandage over his eyes. The wind, sweeping in the darkness the broadside of the Sierra,* worried his ears by a continuous roaring noise as of a maddened sea. He suspected that he had lost the road. Even in daylight, with its ruts and mud-holes and ledges of outcropping stone, it was difficult to distinguish from the dreary waste of the moor, interspersed with boulders and clumps of naked bushes. But as he says, 'he steered his course by the feel of the wind,' his hat rammed low on his brow, his head down, stopping now and again from mere weariness of mind rather than of body—as if not his strength but his resolution were being overtaxed by the strain of endeavour, half suspected to be vain, and by the unrest of his feelings.

In one of these pauses, borne on the wind faintly as if from very far away, he heard a sound of knocking, just knocking on wood. He noticed that the wind had lulled suddenly.

His heart started beating tumultuously, because in himself he carried the impression of the desert solitudes he had been traversing for the last six hours—the oppressive sense of an uninhabited world. When he raised his head a gleam of light, illusory as it often happens in dense darkness, swam before his eyes. While he peered, the sound of feeble knocking was repeated—and suddenly he felt, rather than saw, the existence of a massive obstacle in his path. What was it? The spur of a hill? Or was it a house? Yes. It was a house right close, as though it had risen from the ground or had come gliding to meet him, dumb and pallid, from some dark recess of the night. It towered loftily. He had come up under its lee; another three steps and he could have touched the wall with his hand. It was no doubt a *posada*,* and some other traveller was trying for admittance. He heard again the sound of cautious knocking.

Next moment a broad band of light fell into the night through the opened door. Byrne stepped eagerly into it, whereupon the person outside leaped away into the night with a stifled cry. An exclamation of surprise was heard too, from within. Byrne, flinging himself against the half-closed door, forced his way in against some considerable resistance.

A miserable candle, a mere rushlight, burned at the end of a long deal table, and in its light Byrne saw, staggering yet, the girl he had driven from the door. She had a short black skirt, an orange shawl, a dark complexion—and the escaped single hairs from the mass, sombre and thick like a forest and held up by a comb, made a black mist about her low forehead. A shrill, lamentable howl of 'Misericordia!'* came in two voices from the further end of the long room, where the firelight of an open hearth played between heavy shadows. The girl, recovering herself, drew a hissing breath through her set teeth.

It is unnecessary to report the long process of questions and answers by which he soothed the fears of two old women who sat on each side of the fire, on which stood a large earthenware pot. Byrne thought at once of two witches watching the brewing of some deadly potion. But all the same, when one of them, raising forward painfully her broken form, lifted the cover of the pot, the escaping steam had an appetising smell. The other did not budge, but sat hunched up, her head trembling all the time.

They were horrible. There was something grotesque in their decrepitude. Their toothless mouths, their hooked noses, the meagreness of the active one and the hanging yellow cheeks of the other (the still one, whose head trembled), would have been laughable if the sight of their dreadful physical degradation had not been appalling to one's eyes, had not gripped one's heart with poignant amazement at the unspeakable misery of age, at the awful persistency of life becoming at last an object of disgust and dread.

To get over it Byrne began to talk, saying that he was an Englishman and that he was in search of a countryman who ought to have passed this way. Directly he had spoken, the recollection of his parting with Tom came up in his mind with amazing vividness: the silent villagers, the angry gnome, the one-eyed wine-seller Bernardino. Why! These two unspeakable frights must be that man's aunts—affiliated to the devil.

Whatever they had been once, it was impossible to imagine what use such feeble creatures could be to the devil, now, in the world of the living. Which was Lucilla and which was Erminia? They were now things without a name.

A moment of suspended animation followed Byrne's words. The sorceress with the spoon ceased stirring the mess in the pot, the very trembling of the other's head stopped for the space of breath. In this infinitesimal fraction of a second Byrne had the sense of being really on his quest, of having reached the turn of the path, almost within hail of Tom.

'They have seen him,' he thought with conviction. Here was at last somebody who had seen him. He made sure they would deny all knowledge of the *Ingles*;* but on the contrary, they were eager to tell him that he had eaten and slept the night in the house. They both started talking together, describing his appearance and behaviour. An excitement quite fierce in its feebleness possessed them. The doubled-up sorceress waved about her wooden spoon, the puffy monster got off her stool and screeched, balancing herself from one foot to the other, while the trembling of her head was accelerated to positive vibration. Byrne was quite disconcerted by their excited behaviour. Yes! The big, fierce Englishman went away in the morning after eating a piece of bread and drinking some wine. And if the *caballero* wished to follow the same path nothing could be easier—in the morning.

'You will give me somebody to show me the way?' said Byrne.

'Si, señor. A proper youth. The man the caballero saw going out.'

'But he was knocking at the door,' protested Byrne. 'He only bolted when he saw me. He was coming in.'

'No! no!' the two horrid witches screamed out together. 'Going out! Going out!'

After all it may have been true. The sound of knocking had been faint, elusive, reflected Byrne. Perhaps only the effect of his fancy. He asked: 'Who is that man?'

'Her *novio*!'* they screamed, pointing to the girl. 'He is gone home to a village far away from here. But he will return in the morning. Her *novio*! And she is an orphan—the child of poor Christian people. She lives with us for the love of God—for the love of God.'

The orphan, crouching on the corner of the hearth, had been looking at Byrne. He thought that she was more like a child of Satan kept there by these two weird harridans for the love of the devil. Her eyes were a little oblique, her mouth rather thick but admirably formed; she had a sort of wild beauty, and the whole expression of her dark face was voluptuous and untamed. As to the character of her steadfast gaze attached upon him with a sensuously savage attention, 'to know what it was like,' says Mr Byrne, 'you have only to observe a hungry cat watching a bird in a cage or a mouse inside a trap.'

It was she who served him the food, of which he was glad; though with those big, slanting black eyes examining him at close range, as if he had something curious written on his face, she gave him an uncomfortable sensation. But anything was better than being approached by those bleareyed night-marish witches. His apprehensions somehow had been soothed; perhaps by the sensation of warmth after severe exposure, and the ease of resting after the exertion of fighting the gale inch by inch all the way. He had no doubt of Tom's safety. He was now sleeping in the mountain camp, having been met by Gonzales' men.

Byrne rose, filled a tin goblet with wine out of a skin hanging on the wall, and sat down again. The witch with the mummy face began to talk to him, rambling of old times; she boasted of the inn's fame in those better days. Great people in their own coaches stopped there. An archbishop slept once in the *casa*,* a long, long time ago.

The witch with the puffy face seemed to be listening from her stool, motionless, except for the trembling of her head. The girl (Byrne was certain she was a casual gipsy admitted there for some reason or other) sat on the hearthstone in the glow of the embers. She hummed a tune very low, rattling a pair of castanets slightly now and then. At the mention of the archbishop she chuckled impiously and moved her head to look at Byrne, so that the red glow of the fire flashed in her black eyes and on her white teeth under the dark cowl of the enormous overmantel. And he smiled at her.

He rested now in the ease of security. His advent not having been expected, there could be no plot against him in existence. Drowsiness stole upon his senses. He enjoyed it, but keeping a hold, so he thought at least, on his wits; but he must have been gone further than he thought, because he was startled beyond measure by a fiendish uproar. He had never heard anything so pitilessly strident in his life. The witches had started a fierce quarrel about something or other. What-ever it was, they were now only abusing each other violently, without arguments; their senile, guttural screams expressed nothing but wicked anger and ferocious dismay. The gipsy girl's black eyes flew from one to the other. Never before had Byrne felt himself so removed from fellowship with human beings. Before he had really time to understand the subject of the quarrel, the girl jumped up, rattling her castanets loudly. A silence fell. She came up to the table and bent over, her eyes in his.

'Señor,' she said, with decision, 'you shall sleep in the arch-bishop's room.'

Neither of the witches objected. The dried-up one, bent double, waited, propped on a stick. The puffy-faced one had now a crutch.

Byrne got up, walked to the door, and turning the key in the enormous lock, put it coolly in his pocket. This was clearly the only entrance, and he did not mean to be taken unawares by whatever danger there might have been lurking outside. When he turned from the door he saw the two witches, 'affiliated to the devil,' and the Satanic girl looking at him in silence. He wondered if Tom Corbin took the same precaution last night. And thinking of him he had again that queer impression of his nearness. The world was perfectly dumb. And in this stillness he heard the blood beating in his ears with a confused rushing noise in which there seemed to be a voice uttering the words: 'Mr Byrne, look out, sir.' Tom's voice. He shuddered; for the delusions of the sense of hearing are the most vivid of all, and from their nature have a compelling character.

It seemed impossible that Tom should not be there. Again a slight chill as of stealthy draught penetrated through his very clothes and passed over all his body. He shook off the impression with an effort.

It was the girl who preceded him upstairs, carrying an iron lamp from the naked flame of which ascended a thin thread of smoke. Her soiled white stockings were full of holes.

With the same quiet resolution with which he had locked the door below, Byrne threw open one after another the doors in the corridor. All the rooms were empty except for some nondescript lumber in one or two. And the girl, seeing what he would be at, stopped every time, raising the smoky light in each doorway patiently. Meantime she observed him with sustained attention. The last door of all she threw open herself.

'You sleep here, señor,' she murmured in a voice light as a child's breath, offering him the lamp.

'Good night señorita,' he said politely, taking it from her. She didn't return the wish audibly, though her lips did move a little, while her gaze, black like a starless night, never for a moment wavered before him. He stepped in, and as he turned to close the door she was still there motionless and disturbing, with her voluptuous mouth and slanting eyes, with the expression of expectant sensual ferocity of an eager cat. He hesitated for a moment, and in the dumb house he heard again the blood pulsating ponderously in his ears, while once more the illusion of Tom's voice speaking earnestly somewhere near by was specially terrifying because this time he could not make out the words.

He slammed the door in the girl's face at last, leaving her in the dark; and he opened it again almost on the instant. Nobody. She had vanished without the slightest sound. He closed the door quickly and bolted it with two heavy bolts.

A profound mistrust possessed him suddenly. Why did the witches quarrel about letting him sleep in that room? And what meant that stare of the girl, as if she wanted to impress his features for ever in her mind? His own nervousness alarmed him. He seemed to himself to be removed very far from mankind.

He examined the room. It was not very high, just high enough to take the bed, which stood under an enormous baldaquin-like canopy from which fell heavy curtains at foot and head; a bed certainly worthy of an archbishop. There was a heavy table carved all round the edges, some arm-chairs of enormous weight, like the spoils of a grandee's palace; a tall, shallow wardrobe placed against the wall and with double doors. He tried them. Locked. A suspicion came into his mind, and he snatched up the lamp to make a closer examination. No; it was not a disguised entrance. That heavy, tall piece of furniture stood clear of the wall by quite an inch. He glanced at the bolts of his room-door. No! No one could get at him treacherously while he slept. But would he be able to sleep? he asked himself anxiously. If only he had Tom there—the trusty seaman who had fought at his right hand in a cutting-out affair or two and had always preached to him the necessity of taking care of himself. 'For it's no great trick,' he used to say, 'to get yourself killed in a hot fight. Any fool can do that. The proper fashion is to fight the Frenchies and then live to fight another day.'

Byrne found it a hard matter not to fall into listening to the silence. Somehow he had the conviction that nothing would break it unless he heard again the haunting sound of Tom's voice. He had heard it twice before. Odd! And yet no wonder, he argued with himself reasonably, since he had been thinking of the man for over thirty hours continuously and, what's more, inconclusively. For his anxiety for Tom had never taken a definite shape. 'Disappear' was the only word connected with the idea of Tom's danger. It was very vague and awful. 'Disappear!' What did that mean?

Byrne shuddered, and then said to himself that he must be a little feverish. But Tom had not disappeared. Byrne had just heard of him. And again the young man felt the blood beating in his ears. He sat still expecting every moment to hear through the pulsating strokes the sound of Tom's voice. He waited, straining his ears, but nothing came. Suddenly the thought occurred to him, 'He has not disappeared, but he cannot make himself heard.'

He jumped up from the arm-chair. How absurd! Laying his pistols and his hanger* on the table, he took off his boots and, feeling suddenly too tired to stand, flung himself on the bed, which he found soft and comfortable beyond his hopes.

He had felt very wakeful, but he must have dozed off after all, because the next thing he knew he was sitting up in bed and trying to recollect what it was that Tom's voice had said. Oh! He remembered it now. It had said: 'Mr Byrne! Look out, sir!' . . . A warning this. But against what?

He landed with one leap in the middle of the floor, gasped once, then looked all round the room. The window was shuttered and barred with an iron bar. Again he ran his eyes slowly all round the bare walls and even looked up at the ceiling. Afterwards he went to the door to examine the fastenings. They consisted of two enormous iron bolts sliding into holes made in the wall; and as the corridor outside was too narrow to admit of any battering arrangement or even to permit an axe to be swung, nothing could burst the door

open—unless gunpowder. But while he was still making sure
that the lower bolt was pushed well home, he received the
impression of somebody's presence in the room. It was so
strong that he spun round quicker than lightning. There was
no one. Who could there be? And yet. . . .

It was then that he lost the decorum and restraint a man
keeps up for his own sake. He got down on his hands and
knees, with the lamp on the floor, to look under the bed, like
a silly girl. He saw a lot of dust and nothing else. He got
up, his cheeks burning, and walked about, discontented with
his own behaviour and unreasonably angry with Tom for not
leaving him alone. The words 'Mr Byrne! Look out, sir!' kept
on repeating themselves in his head in a tone of warning.

'Hadn't I better just throw myself on the bed and try to go
to sleep?' he asked himself. But his eyes fell on the tall wardrobe, and he went towards it, feeling irritated with himself
and yet unable to desist. How he could explain to-morrow
the burglarious misdeed to the two odious witches he had no
idea. Nevertheless he inserted the point of his hanger between
the two halves of the door and tried to prise them open.
They resisted. He swore, sticking now hotly to his purpose.
His mutter, 'I hope you will be satisfied, confound you!' was
addressed to the absent Tom. Just then the doors gave way
and flew open.

He was there.

He, the trusty, sagacious and courageous Tom, was there,
drawn up shadowy and stiff, in a prudent silence which his
wide-open eyes by their fixed gleam seemed to command Byrne
to respect. But Byrne was too startled to make a sound.
Amazed, he stepped back a little—and on the instant the seaman flung himself forward headlong as if to clasp his officer
round the neck. Instinctively Byrne put out his faltering arms;
he felt the horrible rigidity of the body, and then the coldness of death as their heads knocked together and their faces
came into contact. They reeled, Byrne hugging Tom close to
his breast in order not to let him fall with a crash. He had
just strength enough to lower the awful burden gently to the
floor—then his head swam, his legs gave way, and he sank
on his knees, leaning over the body with his hands resting

on the breast of that man once full of generous life and now as insensible as a stone.

'Dead! My poor Tom, dead!' he repeated mentally. The light of the lamp standing near the edge of the table fell from above straight on the stony, empty stare of those eyes which in life had a mobile and merry expression.

Byrne turned his own away from them. Tom's black silk neckerchief was not knotted on his breast. It was gone. The murderers had also taken off his shoes and stockings. And noticing this spoliation, the exposed throat, the bare, up-turned feet, Byrne felt his eyes run full of tears. In other respects the seaman was fully dressed; neither was his clothing disarranged, as it must have been in a violent struggle. Only his checked shirt had been pulled a little out at the waistband in one place, just enough to ascertain whether he had a money-belt fastened round his body. Byrne began to sob into his handkerchief.

It was a nervous outburst which passed off quickly. Remaining on his knees, he contemplated sadly the athletic body of as fine a seaman as ever had drawn a cutlass, laid a gun or passed the weather earing in a gale, lying stiff and cold, his cheery, fearless spirit departed—perhaps turning to him, his boy chum, to his ship out there rolling on the grey seas off an iron-bound coast, at the very moment of its flight.

He perceived that the six brass buttons of Tom's jacket had been cut off. He shuddered at the notion of the two miserable and repulsive witches busying themselves ghoulishly about the defenceless body of his friend. Cut off. Perhaps with the same knife which . . . The head of one trembled, the other was bent double, and their eyes were red and bleared, their infamous claws unsteady. It must have been in this very room too, for Tom could not have been killed in the open and brought in here afterwards. Of that Byrne was certain. Yet those devilish crones could not have killed him themselves, even by taking him unawares—and Tom would be always on his guard, of course. Tom was a very wide-awake, wary man when engaged on any service. And in fact how did they murder him? Who did? In what way?

Byrne jumped up, snatched the lamp off the table and stooped swiftly over the body. The light revealed on the clothing no stain, no trace, no spot of blood anywhere. Byrne's hands began to shake so that he had to set the lamp on the floor and turn away his head in order to recover from this agitation.

Then he began to explore that cold, still and rigid body for a stab, a gunshot wound, for the trace of some killing blow. He felt all over the skull anxiously. It was whole. He slipped his hand under the neck. It was unbroken. With terrified eyes he peered closely under the chin and saw no marks of strangulation on the throat.

There were no signs anywhere. He was just dead.

Impulsively Byrne got away from the body, as if the mystery of an incomprehensible death had changed his pity into suspicion and dread. The lamp on the floor near the set, still face of the seaman showed it staring at the ceiling as if despairingly. In the circle of light Byrne saw by the undisturbed patches of thick dust on the floor that there had been no struggle in that room.

'He has died outside,' he thought. Yes, outside in that narrow corridor, where there was hardly room to turn, the mysterious death had come to his poor dear Tom. The impulse of snatching up his pistols and rushing out of the room abandoned Byrne suddenly. For Tom too had been armed, with just such powerless weapons as he himself possessed—pistols, a cutlass! And Tom had died a nameless death, by incomprehensible means.

A new thought came to Byrne. That stranger knocking at the door, and fleeing so swiftly at his appearance, had come there to remove the body. Aha! That was the guide the withered witch had promised would show the English officer the shortest way of rejoining his man. A promise, he saw it now, of dreadful import. He who had knocked would have two bodies to deal with next night. Man and officer would go forth from the house together. For Byrne was certain now that he would have to die before the morning—and in the same mysterious manner, leaving behind him an unmarked body.

The sight of a smashed head, of a throat cut, of a gaping gunshot wound, would have been an inexpressible relief. It would have soothed all his fears. His soul cried within him to that dead man whom he had never found wanting in danger. 'Why don't you tell me what I am to look out for, Tom! Why don't you?' But in rigid immobility, extended on his back, the seaman seemed to preserve an austere silence, as if disdaining in the finality of his awful knowledge to hold converse with the living.

Suddenly Byrne flung himself on his knees by the side of the body and, dry-eyed, fierce, opened the shirt wide on the breast, as if to tear the secret forcibly from that cold heart which had been so loyal to him in life. Nothing! Nothing! Nothing! He raised the lamp, and all the sign vouchsafed him by that face which used to be so kindly in expression was a small bruise on the forehead—the least thing, a mere mark. The skin even was not broken. He stared at it a long time, as if lost in a dreadful dream. Then he observed that Tom's hands were clenched, as though he had fallen facing somebody in a fight with fists. His knuckles on closer view appeared somewhat abraded—both hands.

The discovery of these slight signs was more appalling to Byrne than the absolute absence of every mark would have been. So Tom had died striking against something which could be hit, and yet could kill one without leaving a wound—by a breath.

Terror, hot terror, began to play about Byrne's heart like a tongue of flame that touches and withdraws before it turns a thing to ashes. He backed away from the body as far as he could, then came forward stealthily, casting fearful glances, to steal another look at the bruised forehead. There would perhaps be such a faint bruise on his own forehead—before the morning.

'I can't bear it,' he whispered to himself. Tom was for him now an object of horror, a sight at once tempting and revolting to his fear. He couldn't bear to look at him.

At last, desperation getting the better of his increasing horror, he stepped forward from the wall against which he had been leaning, seized the corpse under the armpits, and began to lug it over to the bed. The bare heels of the seaman trailed on the floor noiselessly. He was heavy with the dead weight of inanimate objects. With a last effort Byrne landed him face downwards on the edge of the bed, rolled him over, snatched from under this stiff, passive thing a sheet, with which he covered it over. Then he spread the curtains at head and foot so that, joining together as he shook their folds, they hid the bed altogether from his sight.

He stumbled towards a chair, and fell on it. The perspiration poured from his face for a moment, and then his veins seemed to carry for a while a thin stream of half-frozen blood. Complete terror had possession of him now, a nameless terror which had turned his heart to ashes.

He sat upright in the straight-backed chair, the lamp burning at his feet, his pistols and his hanger at his left elbow on the end of the table, his eyes turning incessantly in their sockets round the walls, over the ceiling, over the floor, in the expectation of a mysterious and appalling vision. The thing which could deal death in a breath was outside that bolted door. But Byrne believed neither in walls nor bolts now. Unreasoning terror turning everything to account, his old-time boyish admiration of the athletic Tom, the undaunted Tom (he had seemed to him invincible), helped to paralyse his faculties, added to his despair.

He was no longer Edgar Byrne. He was a tortured soul suffering more anguish than any sinner's body had ever suffered from rack or boot. The depth of his torment may be measured when I say that this young man, as brave at least as the average of his kind, contemplated seizing a pistol and firing into his own head. But a deadly, chilly languor was spreading over his limbs. It was as if his flesh had been wet plaster stiffening slowly about his ribs. Presently, he thought, the two witches will be coming in, with crutch and stick— horrible, grotesque, monstrous—affiliated to the devil—to put a mark on his forehead, the tiny little bruise of death. And he wouldn't be able to do anything. Tom had struck out at something, but he was not like Tom. His limbs were dead already. He sat still, dying the death over and over again; and the only part of him which moved was his eyes, turning round and round in their sockets, running over the walls, the floor, the ceiling, again and again, till suddenly they became motionless and stony—starting out of his head, fixed in the direction of the bed.

He had seen the heavy curtains stir and shake, as if the dead body they concealed had turned over and sat up. Byrne, who thought the world could hold no more terrors in store, felt his hair stir at the roots. He gripped the arms of the chair, his jaw fell and the sweat broke out on his brow, while his dry tongue clove suddenly to the roof of his mouth. Again the curtains stirred, but did not open. 'Don't, Tom!' Byrne made effort to shout, but all he heard was a slight moan such as an uneasy sleeper may make. He felt that his brain was going, for, now, it seemed to him that the ceiling over the bed had moved, had slanted, had come level again—and once more the closed curtains swayed gently as if about to part.

Byrne closed his eyes not to see the awful apparition of the seaman's corpse, coming out animated by an evil spirit. In the profound silence of the room he endured a moment of frightful agony, then opened his eyes again. And he saw at once that the curtains remained closed still, but that the ceiling over the bed had risen quite a foot. With the last gleam of reason left to him he understood that it was the enormous baldaquin over the bed which was coming down, while the curtains attached to it swayed softly, sinking gradually to the floor.

His drooping jaw snapped to—and half rising in his chair he watched mutely the noiseless descent of the monstrous canopy. It came down in smooth, short rushes till lowered half-way or more, when it took a run and settled swiftly, its turtle-back shape with the deep border-piece fitting exactly the edge of the bedstead. A slight crack or two of wood was heard, and the overpowering stillness of the room resumed its sway.*

Byrne stood up, gasped for breath, and let out a cry of rage and dismay, the first sound which he is perfectly certain did make its way past his lips on this night of terrors. This, then, was the death he had escaped! This was the devilish artifice of murder poor Tom's soul had perhaps tried from beyond the border to warn him of. For this was how he had died. Byrne was certain he had heard the voice of the seaman, faintly distinct in his familiar phrase 'Mr Byrne! Look out, sir!' and then again uttering words he could not make out. But then the distance separating the living from the dead is so great! Poor Tom had tried. Byrne ran to the bed and attempted to lift up, to push off the horrible lid smothering the body. It resisted his efforts, heavy as lead, immovable like a tombstone. The rage of vengeance made him desist; his head buzzed with chaotic thoughts of extermination, he turned round the room as if he could find neither his weapons nor the way out, and all the time he stammered awful menaces. . . .

A violent battering at the door of the inn recalled him to his soberer senses. He flew to the window, pulled the shutters open and looked out. In the faint dawn he saw below him a mob of men. Ha! He would go and see at once this murderous lot, collected no doubt for his undoing. After his struggle with nameless terrors he yearned for an open fray with armed enemies. But he must have remained yet bereft of his reason, because, forgetting his weapons, he rushed down-stairs with a wild cry, unlocked the door while blows were raining on it outside, and flinging it open flew with his bare hands at the throat of the first man he saw before him. They rolled over together. Byrne's hazy intention was to break through, to fly up the mountain path and come back presently with Gonzales' men to exact an exemplary vengeance. He fought furiously till a tree, a house, a mountain, or heaven itself seemed to crash down upon his head—and he knew no more.

Here Mr Byrne describes in detail the skilful manner in which he found his broken head bandaged, informs us that he had lost a great deal of blood, and ascribes the preservation of his sanity to that circumstance. He sets down Gonzales' profuse apologies in full too. For it was Gonzales who, tired of waiting for news from the English, had come down to the inn with half his band, on his way to the sea. 'His Excellency,' he explained, 'rushed out with fierce impetuosity, and moreover was not known to us for a friend, and so we,' etc., etc., etc. When asked what had become of the witches, he only pointed his finger silently to the ground, then voiced calmly a moral reflection: 'The passion for gold is pitiless in the very old, señor,' he said. 'No doubt in former days they put many a solitary traveller to sleep in the archbishop's bed.'

'There was also a gipsy girl there,' said Byrne feebly from the improvised litter on which he was being carried to the coast by a squad of guerilleros.

'It was she who winched up that infernal machine, and it was she too who lowered it that night,' was the answer.

'But why? Why?' exclaimed Byrne. 'Why should she wish for my death?'

'No doubt for the sake of your Excellency's coat buttons,' said politely the saturnine Gonzales. 'We found those of the dead mariner concealed on her person. But your Excellency may rest assured that everything that is fitting has been done on this occasion.'

Byrne asked no more questions. There was still another death which was considered by Gonzales as 'fitting to the occasion.' The one-eyed Bernardino, stuck against the wall of his wine-shop, received the charge of six escopettas* into his breast. As the shots rang out, the rough bier with Tom's body on it, carried by a bandit-like gang of Spanish patriots, passed down the ravine to the cove, where two boats from the ship were waiting for what was left on earth of her best seaman.

Mr Byrne, very pale and weak, stepped into the boat which carried the body of his humble friend. For it was decided that Tom Corbin should be sent down to his rest far out in the Bay of Biscay. The officer took the tiller and, turning his head for a last look at the shore, saw, moving diagonally on the grey hillside, something which he made out to be a little man in a yellow hat mounted on a mule—that mule without which the fate of Tom Corbin would have remained for ever an insoluble mystery.

LAUGHING ANNE

WHILE we were hanging about near the water's edge, as sailors idling ashore like to do (it was in the open space before the Harbour Office of a great Eastern Port),* a man came toward us from the 'front' of business houses, aiming obliquely at the landing steps. He attracted my attention because in the movement of figures in white drill suits on the pavement from which he stepped, his costume, the usual tunic and trousers, being made of light grey flannel, made him noticeable.

I had time to observe him. He was stout, but he was not grotesque. His face was round and smooth, his complexion very fair. On his nearer approach I saw a little mustache made all the fairer by a good many white hairs. And he had, for a stout man, quite a good chin. In passing us he exchanged nods with the friend I was with and smiled.

My friend was Hollis, the fellow who had so many adventures and had known so many queer people in that part of the (more or less) gorgeous East in the good old days. He said:

'That's a good man. I don't mean good in the sense of smart or skilful in his trade. I mean a really *good* man.'

I turned round at once to look at the phenomenon. The 'really *good* man' had a very broad back. I saw him signal a sampan* to come alongside, get into it and go off in the direction of a cluster of local steamers anchored close inshore.

I said: 'He's a seaman, isn't he?'

'Yes. Commands that biggish dark-green painted steamer, *Sissie**—Glasgow. He has never commanded anything else but the *Sissie*—Glasgow,* only it wasn't always the same *Sissie*. The first he had was about half the length of this one, and we used to tell poor Davidson that she was a size too small for him. Even at that time Davidson had bulk. We warned him he would get callouses on his shoulders and elbows because of the tight fit of his command. And Davidson could well afford the smiles he gave us for our chaff. He made lots

of money in her. She belonged to a portly Chinaman who
resembled a Mandarin* in a picture book, with goggles and
thin, drooping mustaches, and as dignified as only a Celestial*
knows how to be.

'The best of Chinamen as employers is that they have such
gentlemanly instincts. Once they become convinced that you
are a straight man, they give you their unbounded confidence.
You simply can't do wrong, then. And they are pretty quick
judges of character, too. Davidson's Chinaman was the first
to find out his worth, on some theoretical principle. One day
in his counting-house, before several white men he was heard
to declare: "Captain Davidson is a good man." And that
settled it. After that you couldn't tell if it was Davidson who
belonged to the Chinaman or the Chinaman who belonged
to Davidson. It was he who shortly before he died ordered
in Glasgow the new *Sissie* for Davidson to command.

'She was really meant to comfort poor Davidson. Can you
fancy anything more naïvely touching than this old Mandarin
spending several thousand pounds to console his white man.
Well, there she is. The old Madarin's sons have inherited her
and Davidson with her; and he commands her; and what with
his salary and trading privileges he makes a lot of money; and
everything is as before; and Davidson even smiles—you have
seen it? Well, the smile's the only thing which isn't as before.'

'Tell me, Hollis,' I asked, 'what do you mean by good—
in this connection?'

'Well—there are men who are born good just as others
are born witty. What I mean is his nature. No simpler, more
scrupulously delicate soul had ever lived in such a—a—
comfortable envelope. How we used to laugh at Davidson's
fine scruples! In short, he's thoroughly humane, and I don't
imagine there can be much of any other sort of goodness
that counts on this earth. And as he's that, with a shade
of particular refinement, I may well call him a "*really* good
man."'

I knew from old that Hollis was a firm believer in the
final value of shades. And I said, 'I see,' because I really did
see Hollis's Davidson in the man who had passed us a little
while before. But I remembered that at the very moment he

smiled his placid face appeared veiled in melancholy—a sort of spiritual shadow. I went on:

'Who on earth has paid him off for being so fine by spoiling his smile?'

'That's quite a story and I will tell it to you if you like. Confound it! it's quite a surprising one, too. Surprising in every way, but mostly in the way it knocked over poor Davidson—and apparently only because he is such a good sort. He was telling me all about it only a few days ago. He said that when he saw these four fellows with their heads in a bunch over the table, he at once didn't like it. He didn't like it at all. You mustn't suppose that Davidson is a soft fool. These men—

'But I had better begin at the beginning. We must go back to the first time the trade dollars* had been called in by our government in exchange for a new issue. Just about the time when I left these parts to go home and stay there. Every trader in the islands was thinking of getting his old dollars sent up here in time and the demand for empty French wine cases—you know, the dozen of vermouth or claret size—was something unprecedented. The custom was to pack the dollars in little bags of a hundred each. I don't know how many bags each case would hold. A good lot. Pretty tidy sums must have been moving afloat just then. Davidson. . . . But let us get away from here. Won't do to stay in the sun. Where could we . . . I know! . . . let us go to those tiffin-rooms* over there. . . .'

We moved over accordingly. Our appearance in the long, empty room at that early hour caused visible consternation among the China boys. But Hollis led the way to one of the tables between the windows, screened by rattan blinds. A brilliant half-light trembled on the ceiling, on the white-washed walls, bathed the multitude of vacant chairs and tables in a peculiar, stealthy glow.

'All right. We will get something to eat when it's ready,' he said, waving the anxious Chinaman waiter aside. He took his temples, touched with grey, between his hands, leaning over the table to bring his face, his dark, keen eyes, closer to mine.

'Davidson then was commanding the steamer *Sissie*—the little one which we used to chaff him about. Well, she was so small that he ran her alone, with only the Malay serang* for a deck officer. The nearest approach to another white man on board of her was his engineer, a Portuguese half-caste, as thin as a lath and quite a youngster at that. For all practical purposes Davidson was managing that command of his single-handed, and of course this was known in the port. I am telling you of it because the fact had its influence on the development you shall hear of presently.

'His steamer, being so small, could go up tiny creeks and into shallow bays and through reefs and over sandbanks, collecting produce where no other vessel but native craft would think of venturing. It is a paying game often. Davidson was known to visit places that no one else could find and that hardly anybody had ever heard of.

'The old dollars being called in, Davidson's Chinaman thought that the *Sissie* would be just the thing to collect them from small traders in the less frequented parts of the Archipelago. Davidson, too, thought it was a good idea, and together they made up a list of his calls on his next trip. Then Davidson (he had naturally the chart of his voyages in his head) remarked that on his way back he might look in at a certain settlement up a mere creek, where a poorer sort of white man lived in a native village. Davidson pointed out to his Chinaman that the fellow was certain to have some rattans* to ship.

'This was sound talk, and the Chinaman owner could not but agree. But if it hadn't been sound it would have been just the same. Davidson did what he liked. He was a man that could do no wrong. However, this suggestion of his was not merely a business matter. There was in it a touch of Davidsonian kindness. For you must know that the man could not have continued to live quietly up that creek if it had not been for Davidson's willingness to call there from time to time. And Davidson's Chinaman knew that perfectly well, too. So he only smiled his dignified bland smile and said:

' "All right Captain. You do what you like."

'I will explain presently how this connection between Davidson and that fellow came about. Now I want to tell you about the part of this affair which happened here. The preliminaries of it.

'You know as well as I do that these tiffin-rooms where we are sitting now have been in existence for many years. Well, next day, about twelve o'clock, Davidson dropped in here to get something to eat.

'And here comes the only moment in this story where accident—mere accident—plays a part. If Davidson had gone home that day for tiffin there would be now, after twelve years or more, nothing changed in his kindly, placid smile.

'But he came in here, and perhaps it was sitting at this very table that he remarked to a friend of mine that his next trip was to be a dollar-collecting trip. He added, laughing, that his wife was making rather a fuss about it. She had begged him to stay ashore and get somebody else to take his place for a voyage. She thought there was some danger on account of the dollars. He told her, he said, that there were no Java-sea* pirates nowadays except in boys' books. He had laughed at her fears, but he was very sorry, too, for when she took any notion into her head it was impossible to argue her out of it. She would be worrying herself all the time he was away. Well, he couldn't help it. There was no one ashore fit to take his place for the trip.

'This friend of mine and I went home together on the same mail-boat, and he mentioned that conversation one evening in the Red Sea while we were talking over the things and people we had just left, with more or less regret.

'I can't say that Davidson occupied a very prominent place. Moral excellence seldom does. He was quietly appreciated by those who knew him well, but his more obvious distinction consisted in this—that he was married. Ours, as you remember, was a bachelor crowd; in spirit anyhow, if not absolutely in fact. There might have been a few wives in existence, but if so they were invisible, distant, never alluded to. For what would have been the good? Davidson alone was visibly married.

'Being married suited him exactly. It fitted him so well that the wildest of us did not resent the fact when it was disclosed. Directly he felt his feet out here Davidson had sent for his wife. She came out (from West Australia) in the *Somerset** under the care of Captain Ritchie—you, know, Monkey-face Ritchie—who couldn't praise enough her sweetness, he gentleness and her charm. She seemed to be the heaven-born mate for Davidson. She found on arrival a very pretty bungalow on the hill, ready for her and the little girl they had.

'We used to admire her from a distance. It was a girlish head out of a keepsake. We had not many opportunities for a closer view because she did not care to give them to us. We would have been glad to drop in at the Davidson bungalow, but we were made to feel somehow that we were not very welcome there. Not that she ever said anything ungracious. She never had much to say for herself. I was, perhaps, the one who saw most of the Davidsons at home. What I noticed most in the general aspect of vapid sweetness was her convex, obstinate forehead and her small, red, pretty, ungenerous mouth. But then I am an observer with strong prejudices. Most of us were fetched by her white, swanlike neck, by that drooping, pure, innocent profile. There was a lot of latent devotion to Davidson's wife hereabouts, at that time, I can tell you. But my idea was that she repaid it by a profound suspicion of the sort of men we were, a mistrust which extended, I fancied, to her very husband at times.

'I observed to this friend I have been telling you of that Davidson must have been vexed by this display of wifely anxiety.

'My friend said, "No. He seemed rather touched and distressed. There really was no one he could ask to relieve him, mainly because he intended to make a call in some God-forsaken creek to look up a fellow of the name of Bamtz, who apparently had settled there."

'And again my friend wondered.

'"Tell me," he cried, "what connection can there be between Davidson and such a creature as Bamtz?"

'I don't remember now what answer I made. A sufficient one could have been given in two words: "Davidson's goodness." That never boggled at unworthiness if there was the slightest reason for compassion. I don't want you to think that Davidson had no discrimination at all. Bamtz could not have imposed on him. Moreover, everybody knew what Bamtz was. He was a loafer, with a beard. When I think of Bamtz, the first thing I see is that long, black beard and a lot of propitiatory wrinkles at the corners of two little eyes. There was no such beard from here to Polynesia, where a beard is a valuable property. It was a unique beard, and so was the bearer of the same. A unique loafer. He made a fine art of it, or rather a sort of craft and mystery. One can understand a fellow living by cadging and small swindles in towns, in large communities of people; but Bamtz managed to do that trick in the wilderness, to loaf on the outskirts of the virgin forest.

'He understood how to ingratiate himself with the natives. He would arrive in some settlement up a river, make a present of a cheap carbine or a pair of shoddy binoculars, or something of that sort, to the Rajah, or the head man, or the principal trader, and on the strength of that gift ask for a house, posing mysteriously as a very special trader. He would spin them no end of yarns, live on the fat of the land for a while, and then do some mean swindle or other—or else they would get tired of him and ask him to quit. He had been known to loaf up and down the wilderness as far north as the Gulf of Tonkin.* Neither did he disdain a spell of civilization from time to time. And it was while loafing and cadging in Saïgon, bearded and dignified (he gave himself out there as a bookkeeper), that he came across Laughing Anne.

'The less said of her history the better, but something must be said. We may safely suppose there was very little heart left in her famous laugh when Bamtz spoke first to her in some low café. She was stranded in Saïgon with precious little money and in great trouble about a kid she had, a boy of five or six.

'A fellow I just remember, whom they called Pearler Harry, had brought her out into those parts—from Australia, I believe. He brought her out and then dropped her, and she remained knocking about here and there, known to most of us by sight, at any rate. Everybody in the Archipelago had heard of Laughing Anne. She had really a pleasant silvery laugh always at her disposal, so to speak, but it wasn't enough apparently to make her fortune. The poor creature was ready to stick to any half-decent man if he would only let her, but she always got dropped, as it might have been expected.

'To pick up with Bamtz was coming down pretty low in the world even from a material point of view. She had been always decent, in her way, whereas Bamtz was, not to mince words, an abject sort of creature. On the other hand that bearded loafer, who looked much more like a pirate than a bookkeeper, was not a brute. He was gentle, rather, even in his speech. And then despair, like misfortune, makes us acquainted with strange bedfellows. For she may well have despaired. She was no longer young—you know. They vanished from Saïgon together. And, of course, nobody cared what had become of them.

'Six months later Davidson experienced a shock. It was that, no less. He came in to the Mirrah Settlement. It was the very first time he had been up that creek, where no European vessel had ever been seen before. A Javanese passenger he had on board offered him fifty dollars to call in there—it must have been some very particular business—and Davidson consented to try. It was a small settlement. Some sixty houses, most of them built on piles over the river, the rest scattered in the long grass; the usual pathway at the back; the forest hemming in the clearing and smothering what there might have been of air into a dead, hot, stagnation.

'All the population was on the river bank staring silently, as Malays will do, at the *Sissie* anchored in the stream. She was as wonderful to them as an angel's visit. Many of the old people had only heard vaguely of "fire-ships", and none of the children had ever seen a white man. On the back path Davidson strolled in perfect solitude. But he became aware of a bad smell and concluded he would go no farther.

'While he stood wiping his forehead he heard from somewhere the exclamation, "My God! It's Davy!"

'Davidson's lower jaw, as he expressed it, came unhooked at the crying of this excited voice. Davy was the name used by the associates of his young days; he hadn't heard it for many years. He stared about with his mouth open and saw a white woman issue from the long grass in which a small hut stood buried nearly up to the roof.

'Try to imagine the shock: in that wild place that you couldn't find on a map, and more squalid than the most poverty-stricken Malay Settlement had a right to be, this European woman coming swishing out of the long grass, in a fanciful tea-gown* thing, with a long train, dingy pink satin and frayed lace trimmings; her eyes like black coals in a pasty-white face. . . . Davidson thought that he was asleep, that he was delirious.

'The woman came forward, her arms extended, and laid her hands on Davidson's shoulders, exclaiming:

' "Why! You have hardly changed at all. The same good Davy. . . ." And she laughed a little wildly. This sound was to Davidson like a galvanic shock to a corpse. He started in every muscle.

' "Laughing Anne," he said in an awe-struck voice.

' "All that's left of her, Davy. . . . All that's left of her."

'Davidson looked up at the sky, but there was to be seen no balloon from which she could have fallen on that spot. When he brought his distracted gaze down it rested on a child holding on with a brown little paw to the pink satin gown. He had run out of the grass after her. Had Davidson seen a real hobgoblin his eyes could not have bulged more than at this small boy in a dirty white blouse and ragged knickers. He had a round head of tight chestnut curls, very sunburnt legs, a freckled face and merry eyes.

'Davidson, overcome, looked up at the woman in silence. She sent the child back to the hut and when he had disappeared in the grass she turned to Davidson, tried to speak, but after getting out the words, "That's my Tony," burst into a long fit of crying. She had to lean on Davidson's shoulder. He, distressed in the goodness of his heart, stood rooted to the spot where she had come upon him.

'What a meeting—eh? Bamtz had sent her out to see what white man it was who had landed. And she had recognized him from that time when Davidson, who had been pearling himself in his youth, had been associating with Harry the Pearler and others, the quietest of a rather rowdy set.

'Before Davidson retraced his steps to go on board his steamer, he had heard much of Laughing Anne's story and had even an interview, on the path, with Bamtz himself. She went to the hut to fetch him, and he come out lounging, with his hands in his pockets with that detached, casual manner under which he concealed his propensity to cringe.

'Bamtz wanted Davidson to promise to call more or less regularly. He thought he saw an opening to do business with rattans there, if only he could depend on some craft to bring out trading goods and take away his produce.

' "I have a few dollars to make a start on. The people are all right. The Orang Kaya* has given me that empty house there to live in as long as I will stay," added Bamtz.

' "Do it, Davy," cried the woman suddenly. "Think of that poor kid."

' "Seen him? Cute little customer," said the reformed loafer in such a tone of interest as to surprise Davidson into a kindly glance.

' "I certainly can do it," he declared. Anne went a little distance down the path with him, talking anxiously.

' "It's for the kid. How could I have kept him with me if I had to knock about in towns? Here he will never know that his mother was a painted woman. And that Bamtz likes him. He's real fond of him. I suppose I ought to thank God for that. . . ."

'Davidson attempted a veiled warning as to Bamtz, but she interrupted him. She knew what men were. She knew what this man was like. But he had taken wonderfully to the kid. And Davidson desisted willingly, saying to himself that surely poor Laughing Anne could have no illusions by this time. She wrung his hand hard at parting.

' "It's for the kid, Davy. It's for the kid. Isn't he a bright little chap?"

'All this happened about two years before the day when Davidson, sitting in this very room, talked to my friend. You will see presently how this room can get full. Every seat'll be occupied, and, as you notice, the tables are set close, so that the backs of the chairs are almost touching. There is also a good deal of noisy talk here about one o'clock.

'I don't suppose Davidson was talking very loudly, but very likely he had to raise his voice across the table to my friend. And here accident, mere accident, put in its work by providing a pair of fine ears close behind Davidson's chair. It was ten to one against the owner of the same having enough change in his pockets to get his tiffin here. But he had. Most likely had rooked somebody of a few dollars at cards over night. He was a bright creature of the name of Fector, a spare, short, jumpy fellow with a red face and muddy eyes. He described himself as a journalist, as certain kind of women give themselves out as actresses when in the dock of a police court. It's not likely that he overheard every word that Davidson said, but he heard enough about the dollars to set his wits at work.

'He let Davidson go out and then hastened away himself down to the native slums to a sort of lodging-house kept in partnership by the usual sort of Portuguese and a very disreputable Chinaman. Macao Hotel, it was called, but it was mostly a gambling den that one used to warn fellows against. Perhaps you remember.

'There he had met a precious couple, a partnership even more queer than the Portuguese and the Chinaman. One of the two was Niclaus—you know. Why! The fellow with a Tartar mustache and a yellow complexion, like a Mongolian, only that his eyes were set straight and his features were European. One couldn't tell what breed he was. A nondescript beggar. From a certain angle you would think a very bilious white man. And I dare say he was. He owned a Malay prau and called himself The Nakhoda, as one would say: The Captain. Aha! now you remember. He couldn't apparently speak any other language than English, but he flew the Dutch flag on his prau.*

'The other was the Frenchman without hands. Yes. The very same we used to know in '79 in Sydney, keeping a little tobacco shop at the lower end of George Street. You remember the huge carcass hunched up behind the counter, the big white face and the long black hair brushed back off a high forehead like a bard's. He was always rolling cigarettes on his knee with his stumps, telling endless yarns of Polynesia

and whining and cursing in turns about *"mon malheur."** His
hands had been blown away by a dynamite cartridge while
fishing in some lagoon. This accident, I believe, had made
him more wicked than before, which is saying a good deal.
No one knew then that he had fastened himself on Niclaus
and was living in his prau. I daresay he put Niclaus up to
a thing or two.

'That very evening the three of them departed on a visit to
Bamtz in Niclaus's prau. They must have passed under the
bows of the *Sissie*, and no doubt looked at her with interest
as the scene of their future exploit.

'Three weeks later, having collected a good many cases of
old dollars (they were stowed aft in the lazaretto,* with an
iron bar and a padlock securing the hatch under his cabin-
table)—yes, with a bigger lot than he had expected to collect, Davidson found himself homeward bound and off the
entrance of the creek where Bamtz lived and even, in a sense,
flourished.

'It was so late in the day that Davidson actually hesitated
whether he should not pass by this time. He had no regard
for Bamtz, who was a degraded but not a really unhappy
man. His pity for Laughing Anne was no more than her case
deserved. But his goodness was of a particularly delicate sort.
He realized how these people were dependent on him, and
how they would feel their dependence (if he failed to turn
up) through a long month of anxious waiting. Prompted by
his sensitive humanity, Davidson, in the gathering dusk, turned
the *Sissie*'s head toward the hardly discernible coast and
navigated her safely through a maze of shallow patches. But
by the time he got to the mouth of the creek the night had
come.

'The narrow waterway lay like a black cutting through
the forest. And as there were always grounded snags in the
channel which it would be impossible to make out, Davidson
very prudently turned the *Sissie* round and with only enough
steam on the boilers to give her a touch ahead, if necessary,
let her drift up with the tide, silent and invisible in the impenetrable darkness and in the dumb stillness.

'It was a long job and when at the end of two hours David-son thought he must be up to the clearing, the settlement slept already—the whole land of forests and rivers was asleep.

'Davidson, seeing a solitary light in the massed darkness of the shade, knew that it was burning in Bamtz's house. This was unexpected at this time of the night, but convenient as a guide. By a turn of the screw and a touch of the helm Davidson sheered the *Sissie* alongside Bamtz's wharf—a miserable structure of a dozen piles and a few planks, of which the ex-vagabond was very proud. A couple of Kalashes* jumped on it, took a turn with the ropes thrown to them round two posts, and the *Sissie* came to rest without a single loud word or the slightest noise. And just in time, too, for the tide turned even before she was properly moored.

'Davidson stepped carefully over the shaky planks, not being anxious to get a sprained ankle, and picked his way across the waste ground to the foot of the house ladder. The house was but a glorified hut on piles, unfenced and lonely.

'Like many a stout man he is very light-footed. He walked up the seven steps or so, stepped across the bamboo platform quietly, but what he saw through the doorway stopped him short.

'Four men were sitting by the light of a solitary candle. There was a bottle, a jug and glasses on the table, but they were not engaged in drinking. Two packs of cards were lying there, too, but they were not preparing to play. They were talking together in whispers, and remained quite unaware of him. He himself was too astonished to make a sound for some time. The world was still, except for the sibilation of the whispers from these four heads bunched together over the table.

' "And Davidson, as I have quoted him to you before, didn't like it. He didn't like it at all."

'The situation ended with a scream proceeding from the distant, dark part of the room. "Oh, Davy! You've given me a turn."

'Davidson made out beyond the table Anne's very pale face. She laughed, a little hysterically, out of the deep shadows between the dark mat walls. "Ha! Ha! Ha!"

'The four heads sprang apart at the first sound and four pairs of eyes became fixed stonily on Davidson. The woman came forward having little more on than a loose chintz wrapper and straw slippers on her bare feet. Her head was tied up Malay fashion in a red handkerchief, with a mass of loose hair hanging under it behind. Her professional, gay, European feathers had literally dropped from her in the course of these two years, but a long necklace of what looked like amber beads hung round her uncovered neck. It was the only ornament she had left. Bamtz had sold all her poor-enough trinkets during the flight from Saïgon—when their association began.

'She came forward then, past the table into the light, with her usual groping gesture of extended arms, as though her soul, poor thing, had gone blind long ago, her white cheeks hollow, her eyes darkly wild—distracted, as Davidson thought. She came on swiftly, grabbed him by the arm, dragging him in. "It's heaven itself that sent you to-night. My Tony's so bad—come and see him. Come along—do!"

'Davidson submitted. The only one of the men to move was Bamtz, who made as if to get up, but dropped back in his chair again. Davidson in passing heard him mutter confusedly something that sounded like, "cute little beggar."

'The child lying, very flushed, in a miserable cot knocked up out of gin-cases, stared at Davidson with wide unseeing eyes. It was a bad bout of fever, clearly. But while Davidson was promising to go on board and fetch some medicines, and generally trying to say reassuring things, he could not help being struck by the extraordinary manner of the woman standing by his side. Gazing with despairing, still eyes down at the cot, she would suddenly throw a quick startled glance at Davidson and then toward the other room.

' "Yes, my poor girl," he whispered, interpreting her distraction in his own way, though he had nothing precise in mind. "I am afraid this bodes no good to you. How is it they are here?"

'She seized his forearm and breathed out forcibly: "No good to me! Oh, no! But what about you? They are after the dollars they think you have on board."

'Davidson let out an astounded, "How do they know there are any dollars?" She clapped her hands lightly, in distress.

' "So it's true! You have them on board? Then look out for yourself." They stood gazing down at the boy in the cot, aware that they might be observed from the other room.

' "We must get him to perspire as soon as possible," said Davidson in his ordinary voice. "You'll have to give him hot drink of some kind. I will go on board and bring you a spirit kettle among other things. . . ." And he added under his breath, "Do they actually mean murder?"

'She made no sign; she never took her desolate eyes off the boy. Davidson thought she had not heard him even when, with an unchanged expression, she spoke under her breath.

' "The Frenchman would, in a minute. The others shirk it —unless you resist. He's a devil. He keeps them going. Without him they would have done nothing but talk. I've chummed with him. What can you do when you are with a man like the one I am with now? Bamtz is terrified of them, and they know it. He's in it. Oh, Davy! Take your ship away—quick!"

' "Too late," said Davidson. "She's in the mud already."

' "If the kid hadn't been in this state I would have run off with him—to you—into the woods—anywhere. Oh! Davy, will he die?" she cried aloud suddenly.

'Davidson saw three men in the doorway. They made way for him without actually daring to meet his eyes. But Bamtz was the only one who looked down with an air of guilt. The Frenchman had remained lolling in his chair; he kept his stumps in his pockets and addressed Davidson.

' "Isn't it unfortunate about that child? The distress of that woman there upsets me, but I am of no use in the world. I couldn't smoothe the pillow of my dearest friend. I have no hands. Would you mind sticking one of these cigarettes there into the mouth of a poor, harmless cripple. My nerves want soothing—upon my honour, they do."

'Davidson complied, with his naturally kind smile. As his outward placidity becomes only more pronounced, if possible, the more reason there is for excitement; and as Davidson's eyes, when his wits are hard at work, get very still and as if sleepy, the huge Frenchman might have been justified in

concluding that the man there was a mere sheep—a sheep
ready for slaughter. With a *merci bien** he uplifted his huge
carcass to reach the light of the candle with his cigarette and
Davidson left the house.

'Going down to the ship and returning, he had the time to
consider his position. At first he was inclined to believe that
these men (Niclaus—the white Nakhoda—was the only one
he knew by sight before besides Bamtz) were not of the stamp
to proceed to extremities. This was partly the reason why he
never attempted to take any measures on board. His pacific
Kalashes were not to be thought of as against white men. His
wretched engineer would have had a fit from fright at the mere
idea of any sort of combat. Davidson knew that he would
have to depend on himself in this affair if it ever came off.

'All the four were sitting again round the table when he
returned. Bamtz not having the pluck to open his mouth,
it was Niclaus who, as a collective voice, called out to him
thickly to come out soon and join in a drink.

' "I think I'll have to stay some little time in there, to help
her look after the boy," Davidson answered, without stopping.

'This was a good thing to say to allay a possible suspicion. And, as it was, Davidson felt that he must not stay very
long.

'He sat down on an old empty nail-keg near the improvised
cot and looked at the child; while Laughing Anne, moving
to and fro, preparing the hot drink, giving it to the boy in
spoonfuls, or motionless gazing at the flushed face, whispered
disjointed bits of information. She had succeeded in making
friends with that French devil. Davy would understand that
she knew how to make herself pleasant to a man.

'And Davidson nodded without looking at her.

'The big beast had got quite chummy with her. She held his
cards for him when they were having a game. Bamtz! Oh!
Bamtz in his funk was only too glad to see the Frenchman
humoured. And the Frenchman had come to believe that she
was a woman who didn't care what she did. That's how it
came about they got to talk before her openly. For a long
time she could not make out what game they were up to.
The new arrivals, not expecting to find a woman with Bamtz,
had been very startled and annoyed at first.

'Davidson felt a profound pity for her. She laid her hand on his knee and whispered an earnest warning against the Frenchman. Davy must never let him come to close quarters. Naturally Davidson wanted to know the reason, for a man without hands did not strike him as very formidable under any circumstances.

'"Mind you don't let him—that's all," she said anxiously, hesitated, and then confessed that the Frenchman had got her away from the others that afternoon and had asked her to tie a seven-pound weight (out of the set of weights Bamtz used in his business) to his right stump. She had to do it for him. She had been afraid of his awful temper. Bamtz was such a craven that he would have let the brute kick her or the child to death. Neither of the men would have cared what was done to her. The Frenchman, however, with many awful threats had warned her not to let the others know what she had done for him.

'Davidson asked her again if they really meant to do it. It was, he told me, the hardest thing to believe he had run up against, as yet, in his life. Anne nodded. The Frenchman's heart was set on this robbery. Davy might expect them, about midnight, creeping on board his ship, to steal anyhow—to murder, perhaps. Her voice sounded weary, and her eyes remained fastened on her child.

'And still Davidson could not accept it somehow; his contempt for these men was too great.

'"I'll be on the lookout," he murmured. "Let them creep."

'"Look here, Davy," she said. "I'll go outside with them when they start, and it will be hard luck if I don't find something to laugh at. They are used to that from me. Laugh or cry—what's the odds. You will be able to hear me on board this quiet night. Dark it is, too. Oh! It's dark, Davy! It's dark!"

'"Don't you run any risks," said Davidson. Presently he called her attention to the boy, who, less flushed now, had dropped into a sound sleep. "Look. He'll be all right."

'She made as if to snatch the child to her breast, but restrained herself. Davidson prepared to go. She whispered hurriedly:

'"Mind, Davy! I've told them that you generally sleep aft in a hammock under the awning over the cabin. They have been asking me about your ways and about your ship, too. I told them all I knew. I had to keep in with them. And Bamtz would have told them if I hadn't—you understand?"

'He made her a friendly sign and went out. The men about the table (except Bamtz) looked at him. This time it was Fector who spoke. "Won't you join us in a quiet game, Captain?"

'Davidson said that now the boy was better he thought he would go on board and turn in. Fector was the only one of the four whom he had, so to speak, never seen, for he had had a good look at the Frenchman. He observed his muddy eyes, his mean, bitter mouth. His contempt for those men rose in his gorge, while his placid smile, his gentle tones and general air of innocence put heart into them. They exchanged meaning glances.

'"We shall be sitting late over the cards," Fector said in his harsh, low voice.

'"Don't make more noise than you can help."

'"Oh! We are a quiet lot. And if the invalid shouldn't be so well she will be sure to send one of us down to call you, so that you may play the doctor again. So don't shoot at sight."

'"He isn't a shooting man," struck in Niclaus.

'"I never shoot before making sure there's a reason for it—at any rate," said Davidson.

'Bamtz let out a sickly snicker. The Frenchman alone got up to make a bow to Davidson's careless nod. His stumps were immovably stuck in his pockets. Davidson understood now the reason.

'He went down to the ship. His wits were working actively and he was thoroughly angry. He smiled, he says (it must have been the first grim smile of his life), at the thought of the seven-pound weight at the end of the Frenchman's stump. The ruffian had taken that precaution in case of a quarrel that might arise over the division of the spoil. A man with an unsuspected power to deal killing blows could take his own part in a sudden scrimmage round a heap of money even against adversaries armed with revolvers, especially if he himself started the row.

'"He's ready to face any of his friends with that thing. But he will have no use for it. There will be no occasion to quarrel about these dollars here," thought Davidson, getting on board quietly. He never paused to look if there was anybody about the decks. As a matter of fact, most of his crew were on shore, and the rest slept, stowed away in dark corners.

'He had his plan, and he went to work methodically.

'He brought a lot of clothing from below and disposed it in his hammock in such a way as to distend it to the shape of a human body; then he threw over all the light cotton sheet he used to draw over himself when sleeping on deck. Having done this, he loaded his two revolvers and clambered into one of the quarter boats the *Sissie* carried right aft, swung out on their davits.* Then he waited.

'And again the doubt of such a thing happening to him crept into his mind. He was almost ashamed of this ridiculous vigil in a boat. He became bored. And then he became drowsy. The stillness of the black universe wearied him. There was not even the lapping of the water to keep him company, for the tide was out and the *Sissie* was lying on soft mud. Suddenly in the breathless, soundless, hot night, an argus pheasant screamed in the woods across the stream. Davidson started violently, all his senses on the alert at once.

'The light was still burning in the house. Everything was quiet again, but Davidson felt drowsy no longer. An uneasy premonition of evil oppressed him.

' "Surely I am not afraid," he said to himself.

'The silence was like a seal on his ears, and his nervous inward impatience grew intolerable. He commanded himself to keep still. But all the same he was just going to jump out of the boat when a faint ripple on the immensity of silence, a mere tremor in the air, the shadow, the ghost of a silvery laugh, reached his ears.

'Illusion.

'He kept very still. He had no difficulty now in emulating the stillness of the mouse—a grimly determined mouse. But he could not shake off that premonition of evil unrelated to his situation. Nothing happened. It had been an illusion!

'A curiosity came to him to learn how they would go to work. He wondered and wondered, till the whole thing seemed more absurd than ever.

'He had left the lamp in the cabin burning as usual. It was part of his plan that everything should be as usual. In the dim glow of the skylight panes he saw a shadowy, bulky form coming up the ladder without a sound, make two steps toward the hammock (it hung right over the skylight) and remain motionless. The Frenchman!

'The minutes began to slip away. Davidson understood that the Frenchman's part (the poor cripple) was to watch his (Davidson's) slumbers, while the others were, no doubt, in the cabin busy forcing off the lazaretto hatch.

'What was the course they meant to pursue once they got hold of the silver (there were ten cases, and each could be carried easily by two men) nobody can tell now. But so far Davidson was right. They were in the cabin. He expected to hear the sounds of breaking in every moment. But the fact was that one of them (perhaps Fector, who had stolen papers out of desks in his time) knew how to pick a lock and apparently was provided with the tools. Thus while Davidson expected every moment to hear them begin down there, they had the bar off already and two cases actually up in the cabin out of the lazaretto.

'In the diffused faint glow of the skylight the Frenchman moved no more than a statue. Davidson could have shot him with the greatest ease—but he was not homicidally inclined. Moreover, he wanted to make sure before opening fire that the others had gone to work. Not hearing the sounds he expected to hear, he felt uncertain whether they all were on board yet.

'While he listened the Frenchman, whose immobility might have but cloaked an internal struggle, moved forward with a pace, then another. Davidson, entranced, saw him advance one leg, withdraw his right stump, the armed one, out of his pocket and, swinging his body back to put greater force into the blow, bring the seven-pound weight down on the hammock where the head of the sleeper ought to have been.

'Davidson admitted to me that his hair stirred at the roots then. But for Anne his unsuspecting head would have been there. The Frenchman's surprise must have been simply overwhelming. He staggered away from the lightly swinging hammock and before Davidson could make a movement he had vanished, bounding down the ladder to warn and alarm the other fellows.

'Davidson sprang out of the boat, threw up the skylight flap and had a glimpse of the men down there crouching round the hatch. They looked up scared and at that moment the Frenchman outside bellowed out *"Trahison! Trahison!"** They bolted out of the cabin, falling over each other and swearing. The three shots Davidson fired down the skylight had hit no one, but he ran to the edge of the cabin-top and at once opened fire at the dark shapes rushing about the deck. These shots were returned, and a rapid fusillade burst out, reports and flashes, Davidson dodging behind a ventilator and pulling the trigger till his revolver clicked, and then throwing it down to take the other in his right hand.

'He had been hearing in the din the Frenchman's infuriated yells, *"Tuez-le!** Tuez-le"* above the fierce cursing of the others. But though they fired at him they were only thinking of clearing out. In the flashes of the last shots Davidson saw them scrambling over the rail. That he had hit more than one he was certain. Two different voices had cried out in pain. But apparently none of them was disabled.

'Davidson leaned against the bulwark reloading his revolver without haste. He had not the slightest apprehension of their coming back. On the other hand, he had no intention of pursuing them on shore in the dark. What they were doing he had no idea. Looking to their hurts probably. But he could hear one of them. Not very far from the bank the Frenchman was blaspheming and cursing his associates, his luck and all the world. He ceased—then with a sudden vengeful yell, "It's that woman! It's that woman that has done it," was heard running off in the night.

'Davidson caught his breath in a sudden pang of remorse. He perceived with dismay that the stratagem of his defence had given Anne away. He did not hesitate a moment. He leaped ashore. It was for him to save her now. But even as he landed on the wharf he heard a shrill shriek which pierced his very soul.

'The light was still burning in the house. Davidson, revolver in hand, was making for it when another shriek, away to the left, made him change his direction.

'He changed his direction—but very soon he stopped. It was then that he hesitated in cruel perplexity. He guessed what had happened. The woman had managed to escape from the house in some way and now was being chased in the open by the infuriated Frenchman. He trusted she would try to run on board for protection.

'All was still around Davidson. Whether she had run on board or not this silence meant that the Frenchman had lost her in the dark.

'Davidson, relieved but still very anxious, turned towards the river-side. He had not made two steps in that direction when another shriek burst out behind him, again close to the house.

'He thinks now that the Frenchman had lost sight of that poor woman right enough. Then came that period of silence. But the horrible ruffian had not given up his murderous purpose. He reasoned that she would try to steal back to her child and went to lie in wait for her near the house.

'It must have been something like that. As she entered the light falling about the house ladder, he had rushed at her too soon, impatient for vengeance. She had let out that scream of mortal fear when she caught sight of him, and turned to run for her life again.

'This time he's sure she was making for the river, but not in a straight line. Her shrieks circled about Davidson. He turned on his heels following the horrible trail of sounds in the darkness. He wanted to shout, "This way, Anne! I am here!" But he couldn't. In the horror of this chase, more ghastly in his imagination than if he could have seen it, the perspiration broke out on his forehead, while his throat was dry as tinder. A last supreme scream was cut short suddenly.

'The silence which ensued was terrible. Davidson felt sick. He tore his feet from the spot and walked straight before him, gripping the revolver and peering into the obscurity fearfully. Suddenly a bulky shape rose from the ground within a few yards of him and bounded away. He fired at it, started to run in pursuit, and stumbled against something soft which threw him down headlong.

'Even as he pitched forward on his head he knew it could be nothing else but Laughing Anne's body. He picked himself up and, remaining on his knees, tried to lift her in his arms. He felt her so limp that he gave it up. She was lying on her face, her long hair scattered on the ground. Some of it was wet. Davidson, feeling about her head, came to a place where the crushed bone gave way under his fingers. But even before that discovery he knew that she was dead. The pursuing Frenchman had flung her down with a kick from behind, and squatting down was battering in her skull, with the weight she herself had fashioned to his stump, when the totally unexpected Davidson loomed up in the night and scared him away.

'Davidson kneeling by the side of that woman done so miserably to death was overcome by remorse. For she had died, in a way, for him. His manhood was as if stunned. For the first time he felt afraid. He might have been pounced upon in the dark at any moment by the murderer of Laughing Anne. He confesses to the impulse of creeping away from that pitiful corpse on his hands and knees to the refuge of his ship. He even says that he actually began to do so. . . .

'One can hardly picture to one's self Davidson crawling away on all fours from the murdered woman—Davidson unmanned and crushed by the idea that she had died for him in a sense. But he could not have gone very far. What stopped him was the thought of the boy, Laughing Anne's child, that (Davidson remembered her very words) would not have a dog's chance.

'This life the woman had left behind her appeared to Davidson in the light of a sacred trust. He assumed an erect attitude and, quaking inwardly still, turned about and walked towards the house.

'For all his tremors, he was very determined; but that smashed skull had affected his imagination and he felt very defenceless in the darkness, in which he seemed to hear faintly, now here, now there, the prowling footsteps of the murdering brute. But he never faltered in his purpose.

'He got away with the boy safely after all. The house he found empty. A profound silence encompassed him all the time, except once, just as he got down the ladder with Tony in his arms, when a faint groan reached his ears. It seemed to come from the pitch black space between the posts on which the house was built, but he did not stop to investigate.

'It's no use telling you in detail how Davidson got on board with the burden Anne's miserably cruel fate had thrust into his arms; how next morning his scared crew, after observing from a distance the state of affairs on board, rejoined with alacrity; how Davidson went ashore and, aided by his engineer (still half dead with fright), rolled up Laughing Anne's body in a cotton sheet and brought it on board for burial at sea later. While busy with those pitiful remains, Davidson, glancing about, perceived plainly a huge heap of white clothes huddled up against the corner post of the house. That it was the Frenchman lying there he could not doubt. Taking it in connection with the dismal groan he heard in the night, Davidson is pretty sure that his random shot gave a mortal hurt to the murderer of poor Anne.

'As to the others, Davidson never set eyes on a single one of them. Whether they had concealed themselves in the scared settlement, or bolted into the forest, or were hiding on board Niclaus' prau, which could be seen lying on the mud a hundred yards or so higher up the creek, the fact is that they vanished; and Davidson did not trouble his head about them. He lost no time in getting out of the creek directly the *Sissie* floated. After steaming some twenty miles clear of the coast he (in his own words) consigned the body to the deep. He did everything himself. He weighted her down with a few fire-bars,* he read the service, he lifted the plank, he was the only mourner. And he certainly felt, while rendering these last services to the dead, the desolation of that life and the atrocious wretchedness of its end.

'He could not look back on it without remorse. He ought to have handled the warning she had given him in another way. He was convinced that a simple display of watchfulness would have been enough to restrain that vile and cowardly crew. But the fact was, as he told me himself, that he had not quite believed that anything would be attempted.

'"I've been amusing myself by playing at being jolly clever without thinking of the consequences," he said to me mournfully.

'The body of Laughing Anne having been committed to the deep some eighteen miles SSW from Cape Selatan,* the task before Davidson was to commit Laughing Anne's child to the care of his wife. And there poor, good Davidson made a fatal move. He didn't want to tell her the whole awful story, since it involved the knowledge of the danger from which he, Davidson, had escaped. And this, too, after he had been laughing at her unreasonable fears only a short time before.

'"I thought that if I told her everything," Davidson explained to me, "she would never have a moment's peace while I was away on my trips."

'He simply stated that the boy was an orphan, the child of some people to whom he, Davidson, was under the greatest obligation, and that he felt morally bound to look after him. Some day he would tell her more, he said, and meantime he trusted in the goodness and warmth of her heart, in her woman's natural compassion.

'He didn't know that her heart was about the size of a parched pea and had about the proportional amount of warmth; and that her faculty of compassion was mainly directed to herself. He was only startled and disappointed at the air of cold surprise and the suspicious look with which she received his imperfect tale. But she did not say much. She never had much to say. She was a fool of the silent, hopeless kind.

'What story Davidson's crew thought fit to set afloat in Malay town is neither here nor there. Davidson himself took some of his friends into his confidence, besides giving the full story officially to the Harbour Master.

'The Harbour Master was considerably astonished. He didn't think, however, that a formal complaint should be made to the Dutch Government. They would probably do nothing

in the end, after a lot of trouble and correspondence. Better
let the matter drop.

'This was good common sense. But he was impressed.

' "Sounds a terrible affair, Captain Davidson."

' "Aye. Terrible enough," agreed the remorseful Davidson.
But the most terrible thing for him, though he didn't know
it yet then, was that his wife's silly brain was slowly coming
to the conclusion that Tony was Davidson's child, and that
he had invented that lame story to introduce him into her pure
home in defiance of decency, of virtue—of her most sacred
feelings.

'Davidson was aware of some constraint in his domestic
relation. But at the best of times she was not demonstrative;
and perhaps that very coldness was part of her charm in the
placid Davidson's eyes. Women are loved for all sorts of
reasons, and even for characteristics which one would think
repellent. She was watching him and nursing her suspicions.

'Then, one day, Monkey-faced Ritchie called on that sweet,
shy, Mrs Davidson. She had come out under his care and
he considered himself a privileged person—her oldest friend
in the tropics. He posed for a great admirer of hers. He was
always a great chatterer. He had got hold of the story rather
vaguely, and he started chattering on that subject, thinking
she knew all about it. And in due course he let out something about Laughing Anne.

' "Laughing Anne," said Mrs Davidson with a start. "What's
that?"

'Ritchie plunged into circumlocution at once, but she very
soon stopped him. "Is that creature dead?" she asked.

' "I believe so," stammered Ritchie. "Your husband says so."

' "But you don't know for certain?"

' "No! How could I, Mrs Davidson."

' "That's all I wanted to know," said she, and went out
of the room.

'When Davidson came home she was ready to go for him,
not with common voluble indignation, but as if trickling a
stream of cold water down his back. She talked of his base
intrigue with a vile woman, of being made a fool of, of the
insult to her dignity. . . .

'Davidson begged her to listen to him and told her all the story, thinking that it would move a heart of stone. He tried to make her understand his remorse. She heard him to the end, said "Indeed!" and turned her back on him.

'Davidson's home after this was like a frozen hell for him. A stupid woman with a sense of grievance is worse than an unchained devil. He sent the boy to the White Fathers in Malacca.* This was not a very expensive sort of education, but she could not forgive him for not casting the offensive child away utterly. She worked up her sense of her wifely wrongs and of her injured purity to such a pitch that one day, when poor Davidson was pleading with her to be reasonable and not to make an impossible existence for them both, she turned on him in a chill passion and told him that his very sight was odious to her.

'Davidson, with scrupulous delicacy, was not the man to assert his rights over a woman who could not bear the sight of him. He bowed his head; and shortly afterward he arranged for her to go to her people. That was what she wanted in her outraged dignity. And then she had always disliked the tropics and had detested secretly the people she had to live among as Davidson's wife. She took her pure, sensitive, mean little soul away to Fremantle* or somewhere in that direction. And of course the little girl went away with her too. What could poor Davidson have done with a little girl on his hands, even if she had consented to leave her with him, which is unthinkable.

'This is the story which has spoiled Davidson's smile for him—which perhaps it wouldn't have done so thoroughly had he been less of a good fellow.'

Hollis ceased. But before we rose from the table I asked him if he knew what had become of Laughing Anne's boy.

He counted carefully the change handed him by the China-man waiter and raised his head.

'Oh! yes. That's the finishing touch. He was a bright, taking little chap, as you know, and the Fathers took very special pains with his bringing up. Davidson expected in his heart to have some comfort out of him. In his placid way he's a man who needs affection. Well, Tony has grown into a fine

youth—but there you are! He wants to be a priest; he wants
to work as a missionary. The Fathers assure Davidson that
it is a serious vocation. They tell him he has a special dis-
position for mission work, too. So Laughing Anne's boy will
lead a saintly life in China somewhere; he may even become
a martyr; but poor Davidson is left out in the cold. He will
have to go down hill without a single human affection near
him because of those old dollars.'

THE WARRIOR'S SOUL

THE old officer with the long white moustaches gave rein to his indignation.

'Is it possible that you youngsters have no more sense than that? Some of you had better wipe the milk off your upper lip before you pass judgment on the few poor stragglers of a generation which has done and suffered not a little in its time.'

His hearers having expressed much compunction the ancient warrior became appeased, but he was not silenced.

'I am one of them—the survivors I mean,' he began patiently. 'And what did we do? What have we achieved? He—the great Napoleon*—started upon us to emulate the Macedonian Alexander,* with a ruck of nations behind him. We opposed empty spaces to French impetuosity, then we offered them an interminable battle so that their army went at last to sleep in its positions lying down on the heaps of its dead. Then came the wall of fire in Moscow. It toppled down on them.

'Then began the long rout of the Grand Army.* I have, seen it go on, like the doomed flight of haggard, spectral sinners across the innermost frozen circle of Dante's Inferno* ever widening before their despairing eyes.

'The lot that escaped must have had their souls doubly riveted inside their bodies, to carry them out of Russia through that frost fit to split rocks. But to say that it was our fault that a single one of them got away is mere ignorance. Why! Our own men suffered nearly to the limit of their strength. Their Russian strength.

'Of course our spirit was not broken, and then our cause was good—it was Holy. But that did not temper the wind much to men and horses.

'The flesh is weak. Good or evil purpose, humanity has to pay the price. Why, in that very fight for that little village of which I have been telling you, we were fighting for the shelter of these old houses as much as for victory. And with the French it was the same.

'It wasn't for the sake of glory or for the sake of strategy. The French knew that they would have to retreat before morning and we knew perfectly well that they would go. As far as the war was concerned there was nothing to fight about. Yet our infantry and theirs fought like wild cats, or like heroes if you like that better, amongst the houses—hot work enough—while the supports out in the open stood freezing in a tempestuous north wind which drove the snow on earth and the great masses of clouds in the sky at a terrific pace. The very air was inexpressibly sombre by contrast with the white earth. I've never seen God's creation look more sinister than on that day.

'We, the cavalry (were only a handful) had not much to do except turn our backs to the wind and receive some stray French round shot. This I may tell you was the last of the French guns, and it was the last time they had their artillery in position. These guns never went away from there either. We found them abandoned next morning. But that afternoon they were keeping up a truly infernal fire on our attacking columns; the furious wind carried away the smoke and even the noise, but we could see the constant flicker of darting fire along the French front. Then a driving flurry of snow would hide everything except the dark red flashes in the white swirl.

'At intervals when the air cleared, we could see away across the plain to our right, a sombre column moving endlessly; the column of the great rout creeping on all the time, while the fight on our left went on with a great din and fury. The cruel whirlwinds of snow swept over that broken mob time after time. And then the wind fell as suddenly as it had risen in the morning.

'Presently we got orders to charge the retreating column; I don't know why, unless to prevent us from getting frozen in our saddles, by giving us something to do. The order was welcome enough. So we changed front slightly to the right and got in motion at a walk to take that dark line in the distance in flank. It might have been half-past two in the afternoon then.

'You must know that in all this campaign, my regiment had not been on the main line of Napoleon's advance. All these months the army we belonged to had been wrestling with Oudinot* in the north. We had come only lately, driving him before us down to the Beresina.*

'It was on this occasion then that I and my comrades came for the first time near to Napoleon's Grand Army. It was an amazing and terrible sight. I had heard of it from others. I had seen the stragglers from it, some small bands of marauders, parties of prisoners in the distance. But this was the very column itself! A mere starving, half-demented mob. It issued from the forest two miles away and its head was lost in the murk of the fields. We rode into it at a trot, which was the most we could get out of our horses, and we stuck in that human mass as if in a bog. There was no resistance. I heard only a few shots, half a dozen perhaps. Their very senses seemed frozen within them. I had time to have a good look while riding at the head of my squadron. Well, I assure you, there were men walking on the outer edges so lost to everything but their own misery that they never looked our way. Soldiers!

'My horse pushed over one of them with his chest. He had a dragoon's* blue cloak all torn and scorched and he didn't even put his hand to snatch at my bridle to save himself. Perhaps his hands had been frostbitten. He just went down. Our troopers were pointing and slashing; well, and of course, I myself . . . What will you have! An enemy is an enemy. Yet a sort of awe crept into my heart. There was no noise— only a low deep murmur dwelt over them interspersed with louder cries and groans, while that mob kept on pushing and surging past us as if sightless and without feeling. A smell of scorched rags hung in the cold air. My horse staggered in the eddies of swaying men. But it was like cutting down galvanised corpses that did not care. Invaders! Yes. God was already dealing with them.

'I touched my horse with the spurs to get clear. There was a sudden rush and an angry growl, when our second squadron got into them on our right. My horse plunged and snorted and somebody got hold of my leg. As I had no mind to get pulled out of the saddle I gave a back-handed slash without looking. I heard a cry and my leg was let go suddenly.

'Just then I caught sight of the subaltern* of my troop, at some little distance from me. His name was Tomassov. That multitude of resurrected bodies with glassy eyes was seething round his horse blindly, with stifled growls and crazy curses. I saw him sitting erect in his saddle, not looking down at them, and sheathing his sword deliberately.

'This Tomassov, well, he had a beard. Of course we all had beards then. Circumstances, lack of leisure, want of razors too. No, seriously, we were a wild-looking lot in those unforgotten days which so many, so very many of us did not survive. You know our losses were awful too. Yes, we looked wild. *Des Russes sauvages*—what?

'So he had a beard—this Tomassov I mean; but he did not look *sauvage*. He was the youngest of us all. And that meant real youth. At a distance he passed muster fairly well, what with the grime and the general stamp of that campaign. But directly you were near enough to have a good look into his eyes, that was where his lack of age showed, though he was not a boy.

'Those same eyes were blue, something like the blue of our autumn skies, dreamy and gay too—credulous eyes. A topknot of fair hair decorated his brow like a diadem, in what you may call normal times.

'You may think I am talking of him as though he were the hero of a novel. Why, that's nothing to what the adjutant* of the regiment discovered about him. He discovered that he had a "lover's lips"—whatever that may be. If the adjutant meant a nice mouth, why it was nice enough. But I think it was meant for a sneer. That adjutant of ours was not a very delicate fellow. "Look at those lover's lips," he would remark in a loudish undertone while Tomassov was talking.

'Tomassov didn't quite like those murmurs. But to a certain extent he had laid himself open to banter by the lasting character of his impressions.

'They were connected with the passion of love and, perhaps, not so very unique as he seemed to think them. What made us, his comrades, tolerant of his allusions to them, was the fact that they were connected with France, with Paris.

'You can't conceive now how much prestige there was in these names, for the whole world. It was the centre of wonder for all human beings gifted with reason and imagination. There we were, the majority of us young and well connected, but not long out of our hereditary nests in the provinces, simple servants of God; rustics, if I may say so. So we were only too ready to listen to the tale of travels from our comrade Tomassov. He had been attached to our military mission in Paris the year before the war. High protections* no doubt—or maybe sheer luck.

'I don't think he could have been a very useful member of the mission. It could not have been expected from his youth and complete inexperience. Apparently all his time in Paris was his own. The use he made of it was to fall in love, to remain in that state, to cultivate it, to exist only for it, in a manner of speaking.

'Thus it was something more than a mere memory that he had brought with him from France. Memory is a fugitive thing. It can be falsified. It can be effaced. It can be even doubted. Why! I myself come to doubt sometimes that I, too, have been in Paris in my turn. And the very long road there with battles for its stages would appear still more incredible if it were not for a certain musket ball which I have been carrying about my person ever since a little cavalry affair which happened in Silesia,* at the very beginning of the Leipsic* campaign.

'Passages of love, however, are more impressive perhaps than passages of danger. You don't go affronting love in troops as it were. They are more unique, more personal and more intimate. And of course with Tomassov all that was very fresh yet. He had not been home from France four months when the war began.

'His heart, his mind were full of that experience. He was a little awed by it. And he was simple enough to let it appear in his speeches. He considered himself a sort of privileged person, not because she had looked at him with favour, but simply because—how shall I say it—he had had the wonderful illumination of that worship as if it were heaven itself which had done this for him.

'Oh yes! He was very simple. A nice youngster, yet no fool; and with that utterly inexperienced, unsuspicious and even unthinking. You find one like that here and there—in the provinces. He had a lot of poetry in him too. It could be only natural, something quite his own, not acquired. I suppose Father Adam had some poetry in him too of that natural sort. For the rest *un Russe sauvage* as the French sometimes call us, but not of that kind which, they maintain, eats tallow candles* for a delicacy.

'As to the woman, the Frenchwoman, well, though I also have been in Paris with a hundred thousand other Russians, I have never seen her. Very likely she was not in Paris then. And in any case hers were not the doors that would fly open before simple fellows of my sort, you understand. Gilded saloons were never in my way. I could not tell you how she looked, even from description, which is strange considering that I was, if I may say so, Tomassov's confidant.

'He very soon got shy of talking before the others. I suppose camp-fire comments jarred his finer feelings. But I was left to him and truly I had to submit. You can't very well expect a fellow in that state to hold his tongue altogether; and I—I suppose, you'll find it difficult to believe—I am in reality a rather silent sort of person.

'Very likely my silences appeared to him sympathetic. Goodness only knows. All the month of September our regiment quartered in villages had an easy time. It was then that I heard most of that—you can't call it a story. The story I have in my mind is not in that. Outpourings, let us call them.

'I would sit, quite content to hold my peace, a whole hour perhaps, while Tomassov talked with exaltation. And when he was done I would still hold my peace. And there would be produced a solemn effect of silence which, I imagine, pleased Tomassov in a way.

'She was of course not a woman in her first youth. A widow maybe. At any rate I have never heard Tomassov mention a husband. She had a salon.* Something very distinguished. A social centre in which that admirable lady queened it with great splendour.

'Somehow, I fancy her court was composed mostly of men. But Tomassov, I must say, kept such details out of his discourses wonderfully well. Upon my word, I don't know whether her hair was dark or fair, her eyes brown, black or blue, what was her stature, her features or her complexion. His love soared above mere physical impressions. He never described her to me in set terms.

'But he was ready to swear that in her presence, everybody's thoughts and feelings were bound to circle round her. She was that sort of woman. Conversations on all sorts of subjects went on in her salon. Most wonderful conversations, but through them all there flowed like an unheard, mysterious, strain of music the assertion, the power, the tyranny of sheer beauty. So, apparently, she was beautiful. It detached all these talking people from their life-interests, and even from their vanities. She was a secret delight and a secret torment. Even the old men when they looked at her seemed to brood, as if struck by the thought that their lives had been wasted. She was the very joy and shudder of felicity and she brought only sadness and torment to the hearts of men.

'In short, she must have been an extraordinary woman or else Tomassov was an extraordinary young fellow to feel in that way and talk like this about her. I told you the fellow had some poetry in him. And observe that all this sounded true enough. It would be just about the effect a woman very much out of the common would produce, you know. Poets do get close to the truth, somehow; there's no denying that.

'There's no poetry in my composition, I know; but I have my share of common shrewdness, and I have no doubt that the lady was kind to the youngster, once he did find his way inside her salon. His getting in is the real marvel for me. However he did get in, the innocent, and he found himself in distinguished company there, amongst men of considerable position. And you know what that means: thick waists, bald heads, teeth that are not—as some poet puts it. Imagine amongst them a nice boy, fresh and simple like an apple just off the tree. A modest, good-looking, impressionable, adoring young barbarian. My word! What a change! What a relief for jaded feelings. And with that a dose of poetry in his nature too, which saves even a simpleton from being a fool.

'He became an artlessly, unconditionally devoted slave. He was rewarded by being smiled on kindly, and in time admitted to the intimacy of the house. It may be that the unsophisticated barbarian amused the exquisite lady. Perhaps —since he didn't feed on tallow candles—he satisfied some need of tenderness in the woman? You know there are many kinds of tenderness highly civilized women are capable of. Women with heads and imaginations, I mean, and no temperament to speak of; you understand. But who's going to fathom their needs or their fancies. Most of the time they themselves don't know much about their innermost moods and blunder out of one into another, sometimes with catastrophic results. And then who's more surprised than they? However Tomassov's case was in its nature quite idyllic. The fashionable world was amused. It made for him a kind of social success. But he didn't care. There was one divinity and there was the shrine where he was permitted to go in and out without regard for official reception-hours.

'He took advantage of that privilege freely. Well, he had no official duties you know. The military mission* was supposed to be more complimentary than anything else—the head of it being a personal friend of our Emperor Alexander, and he, too, was laying himself out for successes in fashionable life exclusively—as it seemed. As it seemed.

'One afternoon Tomassov called on the mistress of his thoughts rather earlier than usual. She was not alone. There was a man with her, not one of the thick-waisted, bald-headed personages but a somebody all the same, a man of over thirty, a French officer who to some extent was also a privileged intimate. Tomassov was not jealous of him. Such a sentiment would have appeared presumptuous to the simple fellow.

'On the contrary—he admired the officer. You have no idea of the French military man's prestige in those days, even with us Russian soldiers who had managed to face them perhaps better than the rest. Victory had marked them on the forehead—it seemed for ever. They would have been more than human if they had not been conscious of it, but they were good comrades, and had a sort of brotherly feeling for all who bore arms, even if it was against them.

'And this was quite a superior example, an officer on the Major-General's staff and a man of the best society besides. He was powerfully built and thoroughly masculine though he was as carefully groomed as a woman. He had the courteous self-possession of a man of the world. His forehead, white as alabaster, contrasted impressively with the healthy colour of his face.

'I don't know whether he was jealous of Tomassov, but I suspect that he may have been a little annoyed at him as at a sort of walking absurdity of the sentimental order. But those men of the world are impenetrable; and outwardly he condescended to recognise Tomassov's existence even more distinctly than was strictly necessary. Once or twice he offered him some useful worldly advice with perfect tact and measure. Tomassov became completely conquered by that kindness piercing through the cold polish of the best society.

'Tomassov, introduced into the *petit salon*,* found these two exquisite people sitting together, and became aware that he had interrupted some special conversation. They looked at him strangely he thought; but he was not made to feel that he had intruded. After a time the lady said to the officer— his name was de Castel, "I wish you would take the trouble to ascertain the exact truth as to that rumour."

'"It's rather more than a rumour" remarked the officer. But he got up submissively and went out. She turned to Tomassov and said "You must stay."

'This express command made him supremely happy, though as a matter of fact he had had no idea of going.

'She regarded him with her still kindly glances, which made something grow and expand within his chest. It was a delicious feeling, even if it did cut one's breath short now and then. Ecstatically he drank in the sound of her tranquil seductive talk full of innocent gaiety and spiritual quietude. His passion appeared to him to flame up and envelop her in blue fiery tongues, from head to foot and over her head, while her soul reposed in the centre like a big white rose . . .

'H'm. Good this. He told me many other things like that, but this is the one I remember. As to himself he remembered everything because these were his last memories of that woman. He was seeing her for the last time, though he did not know it then.

'Mr de Castel returned, breaking into that atmosphere of sortilege Tomassov had been drinking in even to complete unconsciousness of the external world. Even at that painful moment Tomassov could not help being struck by the distinction of his movements, the ease of his manner, his superiority to himself. And he suffered from it. It occurred to him that these brilliant beings were made for each other.

'De Castel sat down by the side of the lady and said to her: "There's not the slightest doubt of it," and they both turned their eyes to Tomassov. Roused thoroughly from his enchantment he began to wonder; and a feeling of shyness came over him. He sat smiling faintly at them—the very picture of attractive innocence.

'The lady, without taking her eyes off his blushing face, said with a gravity quite unusual to her,

' "I should like to know that your generosity is perfect —without a flaw. Love at its highest should be the cult of perfection."

'Tomassov opened his eyes wide with admiration at this as though her lips had been dropping real pearls. The sentiment, however, was not uttered for the primitive Russian youth but for the exquisitely superior man of the world, de Castel.

'Tomassov could not see the effect it produced because the Frenchman lowered his head and sat there contemplating his exquisitely polished boots. The woman suggested in a sympathetic tone:

' "You have scruples?"

'The Frenchman without looking up murmured: "It could be turned into a nice point of honour."

'She said vivaciously: "That's surely artificial. I am all for natural feelings. I believe in nothing else. But perhaps your conscience . . ."

'He interrupted her. "Not at all. My conscience is not childish. The fate of these people is of no military importance to us. What can it matter? The fortune of France is invincible. If I didn't believe I wouldn't care to live."

' "Well then . . ." she uttered meaningly, and rose from her couch. The French officer stood up too. Tomassov hastened to follow their example. He suffered from a disconcerting state of mental darkness. While he was raising her white hand to his lips he heard the French officer say with a strange intonation:

' "If he has the soul of a warrior" (at that time, you know, people really talked in that way) "if he has the soul of a warrior he ought to fall at your feet in gratitude."

'Tomassov felt himself plunged into even denser darkness than before. He followed the French officer out of the room and out of the house. For he imagined that this was expected of him.

'It was getting dusk, the weather was very bad and the street quite deserted. The Frenchman lingered in it strangely. And Tomassov lingered too, without impatience. He was never in a hurry to get away from the house in which she lived. And besides something wonderful had happened to him. The hand he had reverently raised by the tips of its fingers had been pressed strongly to his lips. He had received a secret favour. He was almost frightened. The world had reeled. It had hardly steadied itself yet.

'The lingering Frenchman stopped short at the corner.

' "I don't care much to be seen with you in the lighted thoroughfares, Monsieur Tomassov," he said in an unusual grim tone.

' "Why?" asked the young man too startled to be offended.

' "From prudence," answered the other curtly. "So we'll have to part here; but before we part I'll disclose to you something of which you will see at once the importance."

'This, please note, was an evening in late March of the year 1812. For a long time already there had been talk of growing coolness between Russia and France. The word war was being whispered in drawing-rooms louder and louder and at last was heard in official circles. Thereupon the Parisian police discovered that our military envoy had corrupted some clerks at the Ministry of War and had obtained from them some very important confidential documents. The wretched men (there were two of them) had confessed their crime and were to be shot that night. To-morrow all the town would be talking of the affair. But the worst was that the Emperor Napoleon was furiously angry at the discovery and had made up his mind to have the Russian envoy arrested.

'Such was this de Castel's disclosure; and though he had spoken in low tones Tomassov remained for a moment stunned as by a great crash.

' "Arrested," he murmured dazedly.

' "Yes. And kept as a State prisoner—with everybody belonging to him . . ."

'The French officer seized Tomassov's arm above the elbow and pressed it with force.

' "And kept," he repeated into Tomassov's very ear, and then letting him go, stepped back a space and remained silent.

' "And it's you! You! who are telling me this . . ." cried Tomassov. His gratitude was inexpressible though hardly greater than his admiration for the generosity of his future foe. Could a brother have done for him more? He sought the hand of the French officer, but the latter remained wrapped up closely in his cloak. Possibly in the dark he had not noticed the attempt. He moved back a bit and in his self-possessed voice of a man of the world, as though he were speaking across a card-table or something of the sort, he called Tomassov's attention to the fact that if he meant to make use of the warning the moments were precious.

' "They are," agreed the awed Tomassov. "Good bye, then. I have no words of thanks adequate to your generosity; but if ever I have an opportunity, I swear it . . . *You may command my life* . . ."

'But the Frenchman had retreated, had already vanished in the dark lonely street. Tomassov was alone. And then he didn't waste any of the precious minutes of that night.

'See how people's idle talk and mere gossip pass into history. In all the memoirs of the time, if you read them, you will find it stated that our envoy was warned by some highly-placed woman who was in love with him. Of course it's known that he had successes with women, and in the highest spheres too. Yet the person who warned him was no other but our simple Tomassov—an altogether different sort of lover from himself.

'This is then the secret of our Emperor's representative's escape from arrest. He and all his official household got out of France all right—as history records.

'And amongst that household there was our Tomassov of course. He had, in the words of the French officer, the soul of a warrior. And what more desolate prospect to a man with such a soul than to be imprisoned on the eve of a war; to be cut off from his country in danger, from his military family, from his duty, from honour, and—well—from glory too.

'Tomassov used to shudder at the mere thought of the moral torture he had escaped; and he nursed in his heart an admiring gratitude for the two people who had saved him from that cruel ordeal. They were wonderful. For him love and friendship were but two aspects of the cult of perfection. He had found these fine examples of it and he vowed them indeed a sort of cult. It affected his attitude towards Frenchmen in general, great patriot as he was. He was indignant at the invasion of his country, but this indignation had no personal animosity in it. His was altogether a fine nature. He grieved at the appalling amount of human suffering he saw around him. Yes, he was compassionate to all forms of suffering in a manly way.

'Less fine natures than his own did not understand this very well. In the regiment they had nicknamed him the Humane Tomassov.

'He didn't take offence at it. There's nothing incompatible between humanity and a warrior's soul. People without compassion are the civilians, Government officials and such like. As to the ferocious talk one hears from a lot of people in war time—well, the tongue is an unruly member at best, and when there's some excitement going on there's no curbing its furious activity.

'So I had not been very surprised to see our Tomassov sheathe his sword before the end of the charge. As we rode away from there he was very silent. He was not talkative as a rule, but it was evident that this close view of the Grand

Army had affected him deeply, like some sight not of this earth. You know I had always been a pretty tough individual —well even I . . . And there was that fellow with a lot of poetry in his nature! You may imagine what *he* made of it, to himself. We rode side by side in silence. I was simply beyond words.

'We established our bivouac* along the edge of the wood so as to get some shelter for our horses. However, the boisterous north wind had dropped as quickly as it had sprung up, and the great winter stillness lay on the land from the Baltic to the Black sea. One could almost feel its cold lifeless immensity reaching up to the stars.

'Our men had lighted several fires for their officers and had cleared the snow around them. There were logs of wood for seats. It was a very tolerable bivouac upon the whole, even without the exultation of victory. That we were to feel later, but at present we felt it but a stern and arduous task.

'There were three of us round my fire. The third one was the adjutant. He was perhaps a well-meaning chap but not so nice as he might have been had he been less rough in manner and less crude in his perceptions. He would reason about people's conduct as though a man were as simple a figure, as, say, two sticks laid across each other; whereas a man's much more like the sea, whose movements are too complicated to explain and whose depths may bring up God only knows what at any time.

'We talked a little about that charge. Not much. That sort of thing does not lend itself to conversation. Tomassov muttered a few words about "a mere butchery." I had nothing to say. As you know I had very soon let my sword hang idle at my wrist. That helpless crowd had not even *tried* to defend itself. Just a few shots. We had two men wounded. Two! And we had charged the main column of Napoleon's Grand Army!

'Tomassov muttered wearily: "What was the good of it?" I did not wish to argue so I only just mumbled: "Ah! well" but the adjutant struck in unpleasantly.

' "Why! It warmed the men a bit. That's something. It has made me warm. A good enough reason. But our Tomassov is so humane! And besides he has been in love with a French-woman and thick as thieves with a lot of Frenchmen, so he's sorry for them. Never mind, my boy, we are on the Paris road now, and you shall soon see her."

'We let that pass for one of his foolish speeches. None of us but believed that getting to Paris would be a matter of years—of years. And lo! Less than eighteen months after-wards I was rooked of a lot of money in a gambling hall in the Palais Royal.

'Truth, being often the most senseless thing in the world, is sometimes revealed to fools. I don't think that adjutant of ours believed in his own words. He wanted just to tease Tomassov from habit. Purely from habit. We of course said nothing, and so he took his head in his hands and fell into a doze as he sat on a log on the other side of the fire.

'Our cavalry was on the extreme right wing of the army, and I must confess that we guarded it very badly. We had lost all sense of insecurity by this time. But still we did keep up a pretence of doing it, in a way. Presently a trooper rode up leading a horse and Tomassov mounted stiffly and went off on a round of the outposts. Of the perfectly use-less outposts.

'The night was still. The bivouac was still, except for the crackling of the fires. The raging wind had lifted above the earth and not the faintest breath of it could be heard. Only the full moon swam out with a rush into the sky and sud-denly hung high and motionless overhead. I remember raising my hairy face to it for a moment. Then I verily believe, I dozed off too, bent double on my log with my head towards the fierce ablaze.

'It could not have been for long; you know what an imper-manent thing such slumber is. One moment you drop into an abyss and the next you are back again in the world out of an oblivion that you would think too deep for any noise but the trumpet of the Last Judgment. And then off you go again. Your very soul seems to drop out of you into a bottomless black pit. Then up once more into a startled, slippery con-sciousness. A mere plaything of cruel sleep, one is then. Tormented both ways.

'However, when my orderly appeared before me with some porridge repeating "Won't your Honour be pleased to eat . . . Won't your Honour be pleased to eat," I managed to keep my hold of it . . . I mean that slippery consciousness. He was holding out to me a sooty pot containing some grain boiled in water with a pinch of salt. A wooden spoon was stuck in it.

'At that time these were the only rations we were getting regularly. Mere chicken food, confound it. But the Russian soldier is wonderful. Well, my fellow waited till I had feasted and then went away carrying off the empty pot.

'I was no longer sleepy. Indeed I had become specially awake with a full mental consciousness of existence extending beyond my immediate surroundings. Those are but exceptional moments with mankind, I am glad to say.

'Casting my eye round I had the sense of the earth in all its enormous expanse lapped in snow with nothing showing on it but the forest of pines with their straight stalk-like trunks in their funereal verdure; and in this aspect of general mourning I seemed to hear the sighs of mankind falling to die in the midst of a nature without life.

'They were Frenchmen. We didn't hate them; they did not hate us. We had existed far apart—and suddenly they had come rolling in with arms in their hands, without fear of God, carrying with them other nations, and all to perish together in a long, long, trail of frozen corpses. I had a sort of vision of that trail. A pathetic multitude of small dark mounds stretching away under the moonlight in a clear, still and pitiless atmosphere—a sort of horrible peace.

'But what other peace could there be for them? What else did they deserve? I don't know by what connection of emotions there came into my head the thought that the earth was a pagan planet and not a fit abode for Christian virtues.

'You may be surprised that I should remember all this so well. What is a passing emotion or a half-formed thought to last in the memory for so many years of a man's changing inconsequential life? But what fixed the emotions of that evening in my recollection so that the slightest shadows remain indelible, is an event of strange finality, an event not likely to be forgotten in a life-time as you shall see.

'I don't suppose I had been entertaining those thoughts more than five minutes when something induced me to look over my shoulder. I don't suppose it was a noise; the snow deadened all the sounds. Something it must have been, some sort of signal reaching my consciousness. Anyway I turned my head, and there was the event approaching me. Not that I knew it or had the slightest premonition. What I saw in the distance were two figures approaching in the moonlight. One of them was our Tomassov. A dark mass behind him moved across my sight; the horses which his orderly was leading away.

'Of course I had recognised Tomassov instantly. A very familiar appearance in long boots, tall and ending in a pointed hood. But by his side advanced another figure. And it was amazing! I mistrusted my eyes at first. It had a shining crested helmet on its head and was muffled up in a white cloak. The cloak was not as white as snow. Nothing in the world is. It was white more like mist. And the whole aspect was ghostly and martial to an extraordinary degree. It was as if Tomassov had captured the god of war himself. I perceived at once that he was holding this resplendent vision by the arm. Then I saw that he was holding it up.

'While I stared and stared, they crept on—for indeed they were creeping—and at last they crept into the light of our bivouac fire and passed beyond the log I was sitting on. The blaze played on the helmet. It was extremely battered and the face under it was wrapped in bits of mangy fur. No god of war this, but a Frenchman. The great white cuirassier's* cloak was scorched, burnt full of holes. The man's feet were wrapped up in old sheepskins, over rags or remnants of boots. They were monstrous and he tottered on them, sustained by Tomassov who most carefully lowered him on to the log on which I sat.

'My amazement knew no bounds.

' "You have brought in a prisoner," I said to Tomassov, as if I could not believe my eyes.

'You must understand that unless they surrendered in bodies we made no prisoners. But what was the good. Our Cossacks* either killed the stragglers or else let them alone, just as it happened. And it came really to the same thing in the end.

'Tomassov turned to me with a very troubled look.

' "He sprang up from the ground somewhere, as I was leaving the outpost. I believe he was making for it, but he walked blindly into my horse. He got hold of my leg and of course none of our chaps dared touch him then."

' "He had a narrow escape," I said.

' "He didn't appreciate it," returned Tomassov, looking even more troubled than before. "He came along holding on to my leg. That's what made me so late. He told me he is a staff officer. And then talking in a voice such, I suppose, as the damned alone use, a croaking of rage and pain, he said he had a favour to beg of me. A supreme favour. 'Do you understand me,' he says in a sort of fiendish whisper.

' "Of course I told him I did. I said: 'Oui! Je vous comprends.'*

' " 'Then,' says he—'do it. Now! At once—at once—in the pity of your heart.' "

'Tomassov ceased and stared queerly at me above the head of the prisoner.

'I said, "What did he mean?"

' "That's what I asked him," answered Tomassov in a dazed tone. "He wanted me to do him the favour to blow his brains out. As a fellow soldier he said. As a man of feeling —as—as—a humane man."

'Between us two the prisoner sat like an awful black mummy as to the face, a martial scarecrow, a grotesque horror of rags and dirt with awful living eyes, full of vitality, full of unquenchable fire in a body of horrible affliction, a skeleton at the feast of glory. And suddenly those shining, inextinguishable eyes of his became fixed upon Tomassov. He poor fellow, fascinated, returned that ghastly stare of a suffering soul in that mere husk of a man. The prisoner croaked at him in French.

' "I recognise you now. You are her Russian youngster. You were very grateful. I call on you to pay the debt. Pay it, I say, with one liberating shot. You promised. You are a man of honour. I have not even a broken sabre. All my being recoils from my own degradation. You know me."

'Tomassov said nothing.

'"Haven't you got the soul of a warrior," the Frenchman asked in an angry whisper but with something of a mocking intention in it.

'"I don't know," said poor Tomassov.

'What a look of contempt that tragic scarecrow gave him out of his unquenchable eyes! It was awful to discover so much vigour yet in that body that seemed to live only by the force of infuriated and impotent despair. Suddenly he gave a gasp and fell forward writhing in the agony of cramp in his overtaxed limbs; a not unusual effect of the heat of a camp fire. It looked like the application of a horrible torture. But the Frenchman fought against the pain at first. He only moaned low while we bent over him so as to prevent him rolling into the fire, and muttered feverishly at intervals:

'"*Tuez moi, tuez moi*"* . . . Then vanquished by the pain he screamed aloud time after time, each cry bursting out through his compressed lips.

'The adjutant woke up on the other side of the fire and started swearing awfully at the "beastly row" that Frenchman was making.

'"What's this? More of your infernal humanity, Tomassov?" he yelled at us. "Why don't you have him thrown out on the snow, to the devil out of this beyond earshot."

'As we paid not the slightest attention to his angry shouts he got up, cursing shockingly, and went from us to another fire. Presently the Frenchman became easier. We propped him up against the log and sat silent on each side of him till the cavalry trumpets started their calls at the first break of day. The big flame kept up all through the night paled on the livid light of the snows, while the frozen air all round rang with the brazen notes of the trumpets. The Frenchman's eyes, fixed in a glassy stare that for a moment made us hope that he had died quietly sitting there between us two, stirred slowly to the right and left, looking at each of our faces in turn. We exchanged glances of dismay. Then his voice, unexpected in its renewed strength and ghastly self-possession, made us shudder inwardly.

'"Bonjour, Messieurs."

'His head drooped on his chest. Tomassov addressed me in Russian.

' "It is he, the man himself" . . . I nodded and Tomassov went on in a tone of anguish! "Yes he! Brilliant, accomplished, envied by men, loved by that woman—this horror—this miserable thing that cannot die. Look at his eyes. It's terrible."

'I did not look. But I understood what Tomassov meant. We could do nothing for him. The desolation of this avenging winter of fate held both the fugitives and the pursuers in its iron grip. Compassion was but a vain word before that unrelenting destiny. I tried to say something about the convoy of prisoners being no doubt collected in the village —but I faltered at the mute glance Tomassov gave me. We knew what these convoys were like; appalling companies of hopeless wretches driven on by the butts of Cossacks' lances, back through the frozen inferno but with their faces away from their home.

'Our two squadrons had been formed along the edge of the wood. The desolate minutes were passing. The Frenchman suddenly struggled to his feet. We helped him almost without knowing what we were doing.

' "Come," he said in measured tones. "This is the moment." He paused for a whole minute, then with the same distinctness went on. "On my word of honour all faith is dead in me."

'His voice lost suddenly its self-possession, and after waiting a little he added in a murmur—"and even my courage. Yes. Upon my honour!"

'Another long pause ensued. With an effort he whispered hoarsely, "Isn't this enough to move a heart of stone? Am I to go on my knees to you?"

'Again a deep silence fell upon the three of us. Then the French officer uttered his last word of anger.

' "Milksop!"

'Tomassov didn't budge a feature. I made up my mind to go and fetch a couple of our troopers to lead that miserable Frenchman away to the village. There was nothing else for it. I had not made ten paces towards the group of horses and orderlies in front of our squadron when . . . But you have guessed it. Of course. And so did I. For I give you my word that the report of Tomassov's pistol was the most insignificant thing imaginable. The snow certainly seems to absorb sounds. It was a mere feeble pop. Of the orderlies holding our horses I don't think one turned his head.

'Yes. He had done it. Destiny had led that Frenchman to the only man who could understand him perfectly. But it was poor Tomassov's lot to be the predestined victim. You know what the world's justice is and mankind's judgment. It fell heavily on him, with a sort of inverted hypocrisy. Why that brute of an adjutant himself was the first to set going horrified allusions to the shooting of a prisoner in cold blood! Tomassov was not dismissed from the service of course. But after the siege of Dantzic* he asked for permission to resign from the army, and went away to bury himself in the depths of his province where a vague story of some dark deed clung to him for years.

'Yes. He had done it. And what was it? One warrior's soul paying its debt a hundredfold to another warrior's soul by releasing it from a fate worse than death—the loss of all faith and courage. You may look on it in that way. I don't know. And perhaps poor Tomassov did not know himself. But I was the first to approach that appalling dark group of two: the Frenchman extended rigidly on his back, Tomassov down on one knee rather nearer to the feet than to the Frenchman's head. He had taken his cap off and his hair shone like gold through the light snow that had begun to fall. He was stooping over the dead in a tenderly protecting attitude; and his young, ingenuous face with lowered eyelids expressed no grief, no sternness, no pity; but was set in the repose of a profound, as if endless and endlessly silent meditation.'

THE TALE

OUTSIDE the large single window the crepuscular light was dying out slowly in a great square gleam without colour, framed rigidly in the gathering shades of the room.

It was a long room. The irresistible tide of the night ran into the most distant part of it, where the whispering of a man's voice, passionately interrupted and passionately renewed, seemed to plead against the answering murmurs of infinite sadness.

At last no answering murmur came. His movement when he rose slowly from his knees by the side of the deep, shadowy couch holding the shadowy suggestion of a reclining woman revealed him tall under the low ceiling, and sombre all over except for the crude discord of the white collar under the shape of his head and the faint, minute spark of a brass button here and there on his uniform.

He stood over her a moment masculine and mysterious in his immobility before he sat down on a chair near by. He could see only the faint oval of her upturned face and, extended on her black dress, her pale hands, a moment before abandoned to his kisses and now as if too weary to move.

The silence was profound. The wave of passion had broken against a murmured sadness, thin air, passing mood—by its own accumulated momentum of desire; by its own towering strength sinking into the level repose that seems the end of all things under heaven, but only marks the rhythm of the swelling heart-waves running the circuit of the habitable globe.

He dared not make a sound, shrinking as a man would do from the prosaic necessities of existence. As usual, it was the woman who had the courage. Her voice was heard first —almost conventional while her being vibrated yet with conflicting emotions.

'Tell me something,' she said.

The darkness hid his surprise and then his smile. Had he not just said to her everything worth telling in the world— and that not for the first time!

'What am I to tell you?' he asked, in a voice creditably steady. He was beginning to feel grateful to her for that something final in her tone which had eased the strain.

'Why not tell me a tale?'

'A tale!' He was really amazed.

'Yes. Why not?'

These words came with a slight petulance, the hint of a loved woman's capricious will, which is capricious only because it feels itself to be a law, embarrassing sometimes and always difficult to elude.

'Why not?' he repeated, with a slightly mocking accent, as though he had been asked to give her the moon. But now he was feeling a little angry with her for that feminine mobility that slips out of an emotion as easily as out of a splendid gown.

He heard her saying, a little unsteadily with a sort of fluttering intonation which made him think suddenly of a butterfly's flight:

'You used to tell—your—your simple and—and professional —tales very well at one time. Or well enough to interest me. You had a—a sort of art—in the days—the days before the war.'*

'Really?' he said, with involuntary gloom. 'But now, you see, the war is going on,' he continued in such a dead, equable tone that she felt a slight chill fall over her shoulders. And yet she persisted. For there's nothing more unswerving in the world than a woman's caprice.

'It could be a tale not of this world,' she explained.

'You want a tale of the other, the better world?' he asked, with a matter-of-fact surprise. 'You must evoke for that task those who have already gone there.'

'No. I don't mean that. I mean another—some other— world. In the universe—not in heaven.'

'I am relieved. But you forget that I have only five days' leave.'

'Yes. And I've also taken a five days' leave from—from my duties.'

'I like that word.'

'What word?'

'Duty.'

'It is horrible—sometimes.'

'Oh, that's because you think it's narrow. But it isn't. It contains infinities, and—and so——'

'What is this jargon?'

He disregarded the interjected scorn. 'An infinity of absolution, for instance,' he continued. 'But as to this "another world"—who's going to look for it and for the tale that is in it?'

'You,' she said, with a strange, almost rough, sweetness of assertion.

He made a shadowy movement of assent in his chair, the irony of which not even the gathered darkness could render mysterious.

'As you will. In that world, then, there was once upon a time a Commanding Officer and a Northman.* Put in the capitals, please, because they had no other names. It was a world of seas and continents and islands——'

'Like the earth,' she murmured, bitterly.

'Yes. What else could you expect from sending a man made of our common, tormented clay on a voyage of discovery? What else could he find? What else could you understand or care for, or feel the existence of even? There was comedy in it and slaughter.'

'Always like the earth,' she murmured.

'Always. And since I could find in the universe only what was deeply rooted in the fibres of my being there was love in it too. But we won't talk of that.'

'No. We won't,' she said, in a neutral tone which concealed perfectly her relief—or her disappointment. Then after a pause she added: 'It's going to be a comic story.'

'Well——' he paused, too. 'Yes. In a way. In a very grim way. It will be human, and, as you know, comedy is but a matter of the visual angle. And it won't be a noisy story. All the long guns in it will be dumb—as dumb as so many telescopes.'

'Ah, there are guns in it, then! And may I ask—where?'

'Afloat. You remember that the world of which we speak had its seas. A war was going on in it. It was a funny world and terribly in earnest. Its war was being carried on over the land, over the water, under the water, up in the air, and even under the ground. And many young men in it, mostly in wardrooms and mess-rooms, used to say to each other— pardon the unparliamentary word—they used to say, "It's a damned bad war, but it's better than no war at all." Sounds flippant, doesn't it?'

He heard a nervous, impatient sigh in the depths of the couch while he went on without a pause.

'And yet there is more in it than meets the eye. I mean more wisdom. Flippancy, like comedy, is but a matter of visual first-impression. That world was not very wise. But there was in it a certain amount of common working sagacity. That, however, was mostly worked by the neutrals in diverse ways, public and private, which had to be watched; watched by acute minds and also by actual sharp eyes. They had to be very sharp indeed, too, I assure you.'

'I can imagine,' she murmured, appreciatively.

'What is there that you can't imagine?' he pronounced, soberly. 'You have the world in you. But let us go back to our Commanding Officer, who, of course, commanded a ship of a sort. My tales if often professional (as you remarked just now) have never been technical. So I'll just tell you that the ship was of a very ornamental sort once,* with lots of grace and elegance and luxury about her. Yes, once! She was like a pretty woman who had suddenly put on a suit of sackcloth and stuck revolvers in her belt. But she floated lightly, she moved nimbly, she was quite good enough.'

'That was the opinion of the Commanding Officer?' said the voice from the couch.

'It was. He used to be sent out with her along certain coasts to see—what he could see. Just that. And sometimes he had some preliminary information to help him, and sometimes he had not. And it was all one, really. It was about as useful as information trying to convey the locality and intentions of a cloud, of a phantom taking shape here and there and impossible to seize, would have been.

'It was in the early days of the war. What at first used to amaze the Commanding Officer was the unchanged face of the waters, with its familiar expression, neither more friendly nor more hostile. On fine days the sun strikes sparks upon the blue; here and there a peaceful smudge of smoke hangs in the distance, and it is impossible to believe that the familiar clear horizon traces the limit of one great circular ambush.

'Yes, it is impossible to believe, till some day you see a ship not your own ship (that isn't so impressive), but some ship in company, blow up all of a sudden and plop under almost before you know what had happened to her. Then you begin to believe. Henceforth you go out for the work to see—what you can see, and you keep on at it with the conviction that some day you will die from something you have not seen. One envies the soldiers at the end of the day, wiping the sweat and blood from their faces, counting the dead fallen to their hands, looking at the devastated fields, the torn earth that seems to suffer and bleed with them. One does, really. The final brutality of it—the taste of primitive passion—the ferocious frankness of the blow struck with one's hand—the direct call and the straight response. Well, the sea gave you nothing of that, and seemed to pretend that there was nothing the matter with the world.'

She interrupted, stirring a little.

'Oh, yes. Sincerity—frankness—passion—three words of your gospel. Don't I know them!'

'Think! Isn't it ours—believed in common?' he asked, anxiously, yet without expecting an answer, and went on at once. 'Such were the feelings of the Commanding Officer. When the night came trailing over the sea, hiding what looked like the hypocrisy of an old friend, it was a relief. The night blinds you frankly—and there are circumstances when the sunlight may grow as odious to one as falsehood itself. Night is all right.

'At night the Commanding Officer could let his thoughts get away—I won't tell you where. Somewhere where there was no choice but between truth and death. But thick weather, though it blinded one, brought no such relief. Mist is deceitful, the dead luminosity of the fog is irritating. It seems that you *ought* to see.

'One gloomy, nasty day the ship was steaming along her beat in sight of a rocky, dangerous coast that stood out intensely black like an Indian-ink drawing on grey paper. Presently the Second in command spoke to his chief. He thought he saw something on the water, to seaward. Small wreckage, perhaps.

'"But there shouldn't be any wreckage here, sir," he remarked.

'"No," said the Commanding Officer. "The last reported submarined ships were sunk a long way to the westward. But one never knows. There may have been others since then not reported nor seen. Gone with all hands."

'That was how it began. The ship's course was altered to pass the object close: for it was necessary to have a good look at what one could see. Close, but without touching: for it was not advisable to come in contact with objects of any form whatever floating casually about. Close, but without stopping or even diminishing speed: for in those times it was not prudent to linger on any particular spot, even for a moment. I may tell you at once that the object was not dangerous in itself. No use in describing it. It may have been nothing more remarkable than, say, a barrel of a certain shape and colour. But it was significant.

'The smooth bow-wave hove it up as if for a closer inspection, and then the ship, brought again to her course, turned her back on it with indifference, while twenty pairs of eyes on her deck stared in all directions trying to see—what they could see.

'The Commanding Officer and his Second in command discussed the object with understanding. It appeared to them to be not so much a proof of the sagacity as of the activity of certain neutrals. This activity had in many cases taken the form of replenishing the stores of certain submarines at sea. This was generally believed, if not absolutely known. But the very nature of things in those early days pointed that way. The object, looked at closely and turned away from with apparent indifference, put it beyond doubt that something of the sort had been done somewhere in the neighbourhood.

'The object in itself was more than suspect. But the fact of its being left in evidence roused other suspicions. Was it the result of some deep and devilish purpose? As to that all speculation soon appeared to be a vain thing. Finally the two officers came to the conclusion that it was left there most likely by accident, complicated possibly by some unforeseen necessity: such, perhaps, as the sudden need to get away quickly from the spot, or something of that kind.

'Their discussion had been carried on in curt, weighty phrases, separated by long, thoughtful silences. And all the time their eyes roamed about the horizon in an everlasting, almost mechanical effort of vigilance. The younger man summed up grimly:—

' "Well, it's evidence. That's what this is. Evidence of what we were pretty certain of before. And plain, too."

' "And much good it will do to us," retorted the Commanding Officer. "The parties are miles away; the submarine, devil only knows where, ready to kill; and the noble neutral slipping away to the eastward, ready to lie!"

'The Second in command laughed a little at the tone. But he guessed that the neutral wouldn't even have to lie very much. Fellows like that, unless caught in the very act, felt themselves pretty safe. They could afford to chuckle. That fellow was probably chuckling to himself. It's very possible he had been before at the game and didn't care a rap for the bit of evidence left behind. It was a game in which practice made one bold and successful too.

'And again he laughed faintly. But his Commanding Officer was in revolt against the murderous stealthiness of methods and the atrocious callousness of complicities that seemed to taint the very source of men's deep emotions and noblest activities; to corrupt their imagination which builds up the final conceptions of life and death. He suffered——'

The voice from the sofa interrupted the narrator.

'How well I can understand that in him!'

He bent forward slightly.

'Yes. I too. Everything should be open in love and war. Open as the day, since both are the call of an ideal which it is so easy, so terribly easy, to degrade in the name of Victory.'

He paused; then went on:—

'I don't know that the Commanding Officer delved so deep as that into his feelings. But he did suffer from them—a sort of disenchanted sadness. It is possible, even, that he suspected himself of folly. Man is various. But he had no time for much introspection, because from the south-west a wall of fog had advanced upon his ship. Great convolutions of vapours flew over, swirling about masts and funnel, which looked as if they were beginning to melt. Then they vanished.

'The ship was stopped, all sounds ceased, and the very fog became motionless, growing denser and as if solid in its amazing dumb immobility. The men at their stations lost sight of each other. Footsteps sounded stealthy; rare voices, impersonal and remote, died out without resonance. A blind white stillness took possession of the world.

'It looked, too, as if it would last for days. I don't mean to say that the fog did not vary a little in its density. Now and then it would thin out mysteriously, revealing to the men a more or less ghostly presentment of their ship. Several times the shadow of the coast itself swam darkly before their eyes through the fluctuating opaque brightness of the great white cloud clinging to the water.

'Taking advantage of these moments, the ship had been moved cautiously nearer the shore. It was useless to remain out in such thick weather. Her officers knew every nook and cranny of the coast along their beat. They thought that she would be much better in a certain cove. It wasn't a large place, just ample room for a ship to swing at her anchor. She would have an easier time of it till the fog lifted up.

'Slowly, with infinite caution and patience, they crept closer and closer, seeing no more of the cliffs than an evanescent dark loom with a narrow border of angry foam at its foot. At the moment of anchoring the fog was so thick that for all they could see they might have been a thousand miles out in the open sea. Yet the shelter of the land could be felt. There was a peculiar quality in the stillness of the air. Very faint, very elusive, the wash of the ripple against the encircling land reached their ears, with mysterious sudden pauses.

'The anchor dropped, the leads were laid in. The Commanding Officer went below into his cabin. But he had not been there very long when a voice outside his door requested his presence on deck. He thought to himself: "What is it now?" He felt some impatience at being called out again to face the wearisome fog.

'He found that it had thinned again a little and had taken on a gloomy hue from the dark cliffs which had no form, no outline, but asserted themselves as a curtain of shadows all round the ship, except in one bright spot, which was the entrance from the open sea. Several officers were looking that way from the bridge. The Second in command met him with the breathlessly whispered information that there was another ship in the cove.

'She had been made out by several pairs of eyes only a couple of minutes before. She was lying at anchor very near the entrance—a mere vague blot on the fog's brightness. And the Commanding Officer by staring in the direction pointed out to him by eager hands ended by distinguishing it at last himself. Indubitably a vessel of some sort.

'"It's a wonder we didn't run slap into her when coming in," observed the Second in command.

'"Send a boat on board before she vanishes," said the Commanding Officer. He surmised that this was a coaster. It could hardly be anything else. But another thought came into his head suddenly. "It is a wonder," he said to his Second in command, who had rejoined him after sending the boat away.

'By that time both of them had been struck by the fact that the ship so suddenly discovered had not manifested her presence by ringing her bell.

'"We came in very quietly, that's true," concluded the younger officer. "But they must have heard our leadsmen* at least. We couldn't have passed her more than fifty yards off. The closest shave! They may even have made us out, since they were aware of something coming in. And the strange thing is that we never heard a sound from her. The fellows on board must have been holding their breath."

'"Aye," said the Commanding Officer, thoughtfully.

'In due course the boarding-boat returned, appearing suddenly alongside, as though she had burrowed her way under the fog. The officer in charge came up to make his report, but the Commanding Officer didn't give him time to begin. He cried from a distance:—

'"Coaster, isn't she?"

'"No, sir. A stranger—a neutral," was the answer.

'"No. Really! Well, tell us all about it. What is she doing here?"

'The young man stated then that he had been told a long and complicated story of engine troubles. But it was plausible enough from a strictly professional point of view and it had the usual features: disablement, dangerous drifting along the shore, weather more or less thick for days, fear of a gale, ultimately a resolve to go in and anchor anywhere on the coast, and so on. Fairly plausible.

'"Engines still disabled?" inquired the Commanding Officer.

'"No, sir. She has steam on them."*

'The Commanding Officer took his Second aside. "By Jove!" he said, "you were right! They were holding their breaths as we passed them. They were."

'But the Second in command had his doubts now.

'"A fog like this does muffle small sounds, sir," he remarked. "And what could his object be, after all?"

'"To sneak out unnoticed," answered the Commanding Officer.

'"Then why didn't he? He might have done it, you know. Not exactly unnoticed, perhaps. I don't suppose he could have slipped his cable without making some noise. Still, in a minute or so he would have been lost to view—clean gone before we had made him out fairly. Yet he didn't."

'They looked at each other. The Commanding Officer shook his head. Such suspicions as the one which had entered his head are not defended easily. He did not even state it openly. The boarding officer finished his report. The cargo of the ship was of a harmless and useful character. She was bound to an English port. Papers and everything in perfect order. Nothing suspicious to be detected anywhere.

'Then passing to the men, he reported the crew on deck as the usual lot. Engineers of the well-known type, and very full of their achievement in repairing the engines. The mate surly. The master rather a fine specimen of a Northman, civil enough, but appeared to have been drinking. Seemed to be recovering from a regular bout of it.

'"I told him I couldn't give him permission to proceed. He said he wouldn't dare to move his ship her own length out in such weather as this, permission or no permission. I left a man on board, though."

'"Quite right."

'The Commanding Officer, after communing with his suspicions for a time, called his Second aside.

'"What if she were the very ship which had been feeding some infernal submarine or other?" he said in an undertone.

'The other stared. Then, with conviction:—

'"She would get off scot-free. You couldn't prove it, sir."

'"I want to look into it myself."

'"From the report we've heard I am afraid you couldn't even make a case for reasonable suspicion, sir."

'"I'll go on board all the same."

'He had made up his mind. Curiosity is the great motive power of hatred and love. What did he expect to find? He could not have told anybody—not even himself.

'What he really expected to find there was the atmosphere, the atmosphere of gratuitous treachery, which in his view nothing could excuse; for he thought that even a passion of unrighteousness for its own sake could not excuse that. But could he detect it? Sniff it? Taste it? Receive some mysterious communication which would turn his invincible suspicions into a certitude strong enough to provoke action with all its risks?

'The master met him on the after-deck, looming up in the fog amongst the blurred shapes of the usual ship's fittings. He was a robust Northman, bearded, and in the force of his age. A round leather cap fitted his head closely. His hands were rammed deep into the pockets of his short leather jacket. He kept them there while he explained that at sea he lived in the chart-room, and led the way there, striding carelessly.

Just before reaching the door under the bridge he staggered a little, recovered himself, flung it open, and stood aside, leaning his shoulder as if involuntarily against the side of the house, and staring vaguely into the fog-filled space. But he followed the Commanding Officer at once, flung the door to, snapped on the electric light, and hastened to thrust his hands back into his pockets, as though afraid of being seized by them either in friendship or in hostility.

'The place was stuffy and hot. The usual chart-rack overhead was full, and the chart on the table was kept unrolled by an empty cup standing on a saucer half-full of some spilt dark liquid. A slightly-nibbled biscuit reposed on the chronometer-case. There were two settees, and one of them had been made up into a bed with a pillow and some blankets, which were now very much tumbled. The Northman let himself fall on it, his hands still in his pockets.

' "Well, here I am," he said, with a curious air of being surprised at the sound of his own voice.

'The Commanding Officer from the other settee observed the handsome, flushed face. Drops of fog hung on the yellow beard and moustaches of the Northman. The much darker eyebrows ran together in a puzzled frown, and suddenly he jumped up.

' "What I mean is that I don't know where I am. I really don't," he burst out, with extreme earnestness. "Hang it all! I got turned around somehow. The fog has been after me for a week. More than a week. And then my engines broke down. I will tell you how it was."

'He burst out into loquacity. It was not hurried, but it was insistent. It was not continuous for all that. It was broken by the most queer, thoughtful pauses. Each of these pauses lasted no more than a couple of seconds, and each had the profoundity of an endless meditation. When he began again nothing betrayed in him the slightest consciousness of these intervals. There was the same fixed glance, the same unchanged earnestness of tone. He didn't know. Indeed, more than one of these pauses occurred in the middle of a sentence.

'The Commanding Officer listened to the tale. It struck him as more plausible than simple truth is in the habit of being.

But that, perhaps, was prejudice. All the time the Northman was speaking the Commanding Officer had been aware of an inward voice, a grave murmur in the depth of his very own self, telling another tale, as if on purpose to keep alive in him his indignation and his anger with that baseness of greed or of mere outlook which lies often at the root of simple ideas.

'It was the story that had been already told to the boarding officer an hour or so before. The Commanding Officer nodded slightly at the Northman from time to time. The latter came to an end and turned his eyes away. He added, as an afterthought:—

' "Wasn't it enough to drive a man out of his mind with worry? And it's my first voyage to this part, too. And the ship's my own. Your officer has seen the papers. She isn't much, as you can see for yourself. Just an old cargo-boat. Bare living for my family."

'He raised a big arm to point at a row of photographs plastering the bulkhead.* The movement was ponderous, as if the arm had been made of lead. The Commanding Officer said, carelessly:—

' "You will be making a fortune yet for your family with this old ship."

' "Yes, if I don't lose her," said the Northman, gloomily.

' "I mean—out of this war," added the Commanding Officer.

'The Northman stared at him in a curiously unseeing and at the same time interested manner, as only eyes of a particular blue shade can stare.

' "And you wouldn't be angry at it," he said, "would you? You are too much of a gentleman. We didn't bring this on you. And suppose we sat down and cried. What good would that be? Let those cry who made the trouble," he concluded, with energy. "Time's money, you say. Well—*this* time *is* money. Oh! isn't it!"

'The Commanding Officer tried to keep under the feeling of immense disgust. He said to himself that it was unreasonable. Men were like that—moral cannibals feeding on each other's misfortunes. He said aloud:—

' "You have made it perfectly plain how it is that you are here. Your log-book confirms you very minutely. Of course, a log-book may be cooked. Nothing easier."

'The Northman never moved a muscle. He was gazing at the floor; he seemed not to have heard. He raised his head after a while.

' "But you can't suspect me of anything," he muttered, negligently.

'The Commanding Officer thought: "Why should he say this?"

'Immediately afterwards the man before him added: "My cargo is for an English port."

'His voice had turned husky for the moment. The Commanding Officer reflected: "That's true. There can be nothing. I can't suspect him. Yet why was he lying with steam up* in this fog—and then, hearing us come in, why didn't he give some sign of life? Why? Could it be anything else but a guilty conscience? He could tell by the leadsmen that this was a man-of-war."

'Yes—why? The Commanding Officer went on thinking: "Suppose I ask him and then watch his face. He will betray himself in some way. It's perfectly plain that the fellow *has* been drinking. Yes, he has been drinking; but he will have a lie ready all the same." The Commanding Officer was one of those men who are made morally and almost physically uncomfortable by the mere thought of having to beat down a lie. He shrank from the act in scorn and disgust, which was invincible because more temperamental than moral.

'So he went out on deck instead and had the crew mustered formally for his inspection. He found them very much what the report of the boarding officer had led him to expect. And from their answers to his questions he could discover no flaw in the log-book story.

'He dismissed them. His impression of them was—a picked lot; have been promised a fistful of money each if this came off; all slightly anxious, but not frightened. Not a single one of them likely to give the show away. They don't feel in danger of their life. They know England and English ways too well!

'He felt alarmed at catching himself thinking as if his vaguest suspicions were turning into a certitude. For, indeed, there was no shadow of reason for his inferences. There was nothing to give away.

'He returned to the chart-room. The Northman had lingered behind there; and something subtly different in his bearing, more bold in his blue, glassy stare, induced the Commanding Officer to conclude that the fellow had snatched at the opportunity to take another swig at the bottle he must have had concealed somewhere.

'He noticed, too, that the Northman on meeting his eyes put on an elaborately surprised expression. At least, it seemed elaborated. Nothing could be trusted. And the Englishman felt himself with astonishing conviction faced by an enormous lie, solid like a wall, with no way round to get at the truth, whose ugly murderous face he seemed to see peeping over at him with a cynical grin.

' "I dare say," he began, suddenly, "you are wondering at my proceedings, though I am not detaining you, am I? You wouldn't dare to move in this fog?"

' "I don't know where I am," the Northman ejaculated, earnestly. "I really don't."

'He looked around as if the very chart-room fittings were strange to him. The Commanding Officer asked him whether he had not seen any unusual objects floating about while he was at sea.

' "Objects! What objects? We were groping blind in the fog for days."

' "We had a few clear intervals," said the Commanding Officer. "And I'll tell you what we have seen and the conclusion I've come to about it."

'He told him in a few words. He heard the sound of a sharp breath indrawn through closed teeth. The Northman with his hand on the table stood absolutely motionless and dumb. He stood as if thunderstruck. Then he produced a fatuous smile.

'Or at least so it appeared to the Commanding Officer. Was this significant, or of no meaning whatever? He didn't know, he couldn't tell. All the truth had departed out of the world as if drawn in, absorbed in this monstrous villainy this man was—or was not—guilty of.

'"Shooting's too good for people that conceive neutrality in this pretty way," remarked the Commanding Officer, after a silence.

'"Yes, yes, yes," the Northman assented, hurriedly—then added an unexpected and dreamy-voiced "Perhaps."

'Was he pretending to be drunk, or only trying to appear sober? His glance was straight, but it was somewhat glazed. His lips outlined themselves firmly under his yellow moustache. But they twitched. Did they twitch? And why was he drooping like this in his attitude?

'"There's no perhaps about it," pronounced the Commanding Officer sternly.

'The Northman had straightened himself. And unexpectedly he looked stern too.

'"No. But what about the tempters? Better kill that lot off. There's about four, five, six million of them," he said, grimly; but in a moment changed into a whining key. "But I had better hold my tongue. You have some suspicions."

'"No, I've no suspicions," declared the Commanding Officer.

'He never faltered. At that moment he had the certitude. The air of the chart-room was thick with guilt and falsehood braving the discovery, defying simple right, common decency, all humanity of feeling, every scruple of conduct.

'The Northman drew a long breath. "Well, we know that you English are gentlemen. But let us speak the truth. Why should we love you so very much? You haven't done anything to be loved. We don't love the other people, of course. They haven't done anything for that either. A fellow comes along with a bag of gold . . . I haven't been in Rotterdam* my last voyage for nothing."

'"You may be able to tell something interesting, then, to our people when you come into port," interjected the Officer.

'"I might. But you keep some people in your pay at Rotterdam. Let them report. I am a neutral—am I not? . . . Have you ever seen a poor man on one side and a bag of gold on the other? Of course, I couldn't be tempted. I haven't the nerve for it. Really I haven't. It's nothing to me. I am just talking openly for once."

' "Yes. And I am listening to you," said the Commanding Officer, quietly.

'The Northman leaned forward over the table. "Now that I know you have no suspicions, I talk. You don't know what a poor man is. I do. I am poor myself. This old ship, she isn't much, and she is mortgaged, too. Bare living, no more. Of course, I wouldn't have the nerve. But a man who has nerve! See. The stuff he takes aboard looks like any other cargo—packages, barrels, tins, copper tubes—what not. He doesn't see it work. It isn't real to him. But he sees the gold. That's real. Of course, nothing could induce me. I suffer from an internal disease. I would either go crazy from anxiety—or—or—take to drink or something. The risk is too great. Why—ruin!"

' "It should be death." The Commanding Officer got up, after this curt declaration, which the other received with a hard stare oddly combined with an uncertain smile. The Officer's gorge rose at the atmosphere of murderous complicity which surrounded him, denser, more impenetrable, more acrid than the fog outside.

' "It's nothing to me," murmured the Northman, swaying visibly.

' "Of course not," assented the Commanding Officer, with a great effort to keep his voice calm and low. The certitude was strong within him. "But I am going to clear all you fellows off this coast at once. And I will begin with you. You must leave in half an hour."

'By that time the Officer was walking along the deck with the Northman at his elbow.

' "What! In this fog?" the latter cried out, huskily.

' "Yes, you will have to go in this fog."

' "But I don't know where I am. I really don't."

'The Commanding Officer turned round. A sort of fury possessed him. The eyes of the two men met. Those of the Northman expressed a profound amazement.

' "Oh, you don't know how to get out." The Commanding Officer spoke with composure, but his heart was beating with anger and dread. "I will give you your course. Steer south-by-east-half-east for about four miles and then you will be clear to haul to the eastward for your port. The weather will clear up before very long."

'"Must I? What could induce me? I haven't the nerve."

'"And yet you must go. Unless you want to——"

'"I don't want to," panted the Northman. "I've enough of it."

'The Commanding Officer got over the side. The Northman remained still as if rooted to the deck. Before his boat reached his ship the Commanding Officer heard the steamer beginning to pick up her anchor. Then, shadowy in the fog, she steamed out on the given course.

'"Yes," he said to his officers, "I let him go."'

The narrator bent forward towards the couch, where no movement betrayed the presence of a living person.

'Listen,' he said, forcibly. 'That course would lead the Northman straight on a deadly ledge of rock. And the Commanding Officer gave it to him. He steamed out—ran on it —and went down. So he had spoken the truth. He did not know where he was. But it proves nothing. Nothing either way. It may have been the only truth in all his story. And yet . . . He seems to have been driven out by a menacing stare—nothing more.'

He abandoned all pretence.

'Yes, I gave that course to him. It seemed to me a supreme test. I believe—no, I don't believe. I don't know. At the time I was certain. They all went down; and I don't know whether I have done stern retribution—or murder; whether I have added to the corpses that litter the bed of the unreadable sea the bodies of men completely innocent or basely guilty. I don't know. I shall never know.'

He rose. The woman on the couch got up and threw her arms round his neck. Her eyes put two gleams in the deep shadow of the room. She knew his passion for truth, his horror of deceit, his humanity.

'Oh, my poor, poor——'

'I shall never know,' he repeated, sternly, disengaged himself, pressed her hands to his lips, and went out.

EXPLANATORY NOTES

'The Idiots'

3 *Treguier to Kervanda . . . Ploumar*: the place-names and geo-
graphy of the story are suggested by the peninsula to the
north-west of Lannion in the département of Côtes du Nord
(Brittany, north-west France), the region where the Conrads
honeymooned. There is a town called Tréguier, but it is more
than thirty miles from l'Île Grande, where the Conrads were
staying. Conrad possibly had in mind the road from Trébeurden
to Trégastel. A second road crosses it, going westward to l'Île
Grande, where the story reaches its climax, and eastward to
Pleumeur-Bodou, the original of Ploumar. Kervanda is unidentified, but there are several villages in the area beginning with
'Ker' (like 'Tre' and 'Plou', a common initial syllable among
Breton place-names). The originals for the children of the title
were to be seen on the road from Lannion to Pleumeur-Bodou.

6 *biniou*: Breton bagpipe.

7 *republican*: the events of this story take place in the early
1880s. Following the national disaster of the Franco-Prussian
War of 1870–1, the French political world was dominated
by republicans, who tended to be left of centre and intent on
reducing the power of the Church, and royalists, ultra-
conservatives who hoped to see the restoration of the French
monarchy.

8 *tallow candle*: candle made from animal fat.

sabots: wooden clogs.

10 *Parisian toilette*: fashionable clothes from Paris.

marquise: wife of the Marquis (a peer between duke and count).

royalist: see note to p. 7.

ma chère amie: (Fr.) my beloved; literally, my dear friend.

Chamber: the Chamber of Deputies. The lower house of the
French National Assembly.

Channel Islands: these British-owned islands are less than
seventy-five miles from the region where the action of the story
is laid.

11 *soutane*: a black cassock. This long, dress-like garment was the characteristic garb of a Roman Catholic priest at this time.

12 *schooner*: a small seagoing vessel, usually with two masts.

13 *Allez! Houp!*: (Fr.) [loosely] Get on out of it!

Malheur!: (Fr.) worst luck! Literally, unhappiness.

15 *Kervanion*: unidentified. See note to p. 3.

17 *Lotharios*: libertines, amorous deceivers. From a character in Nicholas Rowe's play *Fair Penitent* (1703).

cut your neck: decapitate you with the guillotine.

18 *gendarmes*: police.

22 *Raven islet . . . Molène . . . Fougère Bay*: these names suggest that Susan is on l'Île Grande, a small peninsula. Le Corbeau (the Raven) is to the east, while l'Île Fougère lies to the west, with l'Île Molène beyond.

23 *Morbihan*: the *département* (county) immediately to the south of Côtes du Nord (see note to p. 3).

26 *Curé*: parish priest.

'The Lagoon'

29 *juragan*: (Malay) master of a small boat.

sampan: small boat of Chinese pattern.

sarong: (Malay) cloth wrapping worn round the waist.

Tuan: (Malay) a term of address to men of some position; perhaps the equivalent of 'Mr' or 'Sir'. Conrad translates it as 'Lord' in his novel *Lord Jim*.

33 *Si Dendring*: the Ruler.

Mara bahia!: (Malay, from Sanskrit) a warning of a danger, risk.

34 *Rajahs*: princes, rulers.

36 *sumpitan*: (Malay) blowpipe.

37 *prau*: a Malay boat (*perahu*) propelled by sail or paddles. It was about 30 feet long and narrow, and was often fitted with an outrigger on one side.

40 *In the searching clearness . . . hopeless darkness of the world*: Conrad changed this last sentence when he republished the story. See 'Note on the Texts'.

'To-morrow'

41 *Colebrook*: there is no place of this name on the coast of
   Britain. 'Amy Foster', a story that Conrad wrote in 1901, is
   also set in Colebrook.

42 *tap-room*: a room in a tavern where the beverages are kept on
   tap and readily available.

   broadcloth: fine, plain-woven, double-width, black cloth of
   high quality, used mostly for men's garments.

46 *collier*: coal-carrying ship.

59 *South Shields*: port in the north-east of England, near New-
   castle upon Tyne, about 250 miles from where Captain Hagberd
   lived, on the coast of East Anglia.

62 *off his chump*: mad (chump = head).

   humped my swag: shouldered my kit.

   Gambucinos: gold and silver prospectors; a Mexican term,
   more often spelled 'Gambusinos'.

   Rio Gila: the river Gila in Arizona, USA.

   Mazatlan: on the coast of Sinaloa state, Mexico.

67 *no terrific inscription*: see Dante, *Inferno*, canto iii. l. 9, in
   which 'Abandon hope all you who enter here' is written above
   the gate of hell.

'An Anarchist'

69 *An Anarchist*: anarchism was an influential political philosophy
   in Europe and the USA from the 1840s until about 1920.
   There are many sorts of anarchism, but all are in agreement
   in their rejection of state and other forms of authority and
   their emphasis on individual judgement and choice. In the 1870s
   some anarchists began to argue that theorizing and verbal
   proselytizing were ineffective, so they advocated violent action
   —'propaganda by deed'. While periods of public violence
   occurred in various European countries from the mid-1870s to
   the early 1920s, the major period of 'propaganda by deed' was
   between 1892 and 1897. Other groups, such as nationalists
   or Communists, were sometimes willing to resort to violence
   and were often confused in the public mind with anarchists,
   even though they might be strongly opposed to the anarchist
   position.

Many leading theorists of anarchism came, like Conrad himself, from the minor aristocracy. Conrad's father had been a revolutionary nationalist, but his son claimed to have no faith in revolutions, yet many of his stories are deeply critical of established governments. In about 1905 he became interested in the anarchist movement. This story, 'An Informer', and *The Secret Agent* were the result.

Bos: (Lat.) ox.

stamping upon a yellow snake: in his allegorical cartoons for the magazine *Punch*, Sir John Tenniel often represented anarchism as a snake, lizard, or dragon (see James F. English, 'Anarchy in the Flesh: Conrad's "Counterrevolutionary" Modernism and the *Witz* of the Political Unconscious', *Modern Fiction Studies*, 38 (1992), 615–30).

Vino-bos, Jelly bos . . . Tribos: there were a number of meat extracts—or beef teas—available in early twentieth-century Britain: Eiffel Tower Ox-Cup (in jelly tablet form), later known at Ju-Vis; Brand's essence of Beef; Bovril; and Oxo.

70 *Cayenne*: the Île Royale is the largest of the three Îles de Salut, French convict islands off Cayenne, the capital city of French Guiana.

Marañon: not identified, but Conrad possibly had in mind the Ilha de Marajó, at the estuary of the Amazon river, in Brazil. It is 500 miles down the coast from Cayenne.

71 *Horta*: not identified. Conrad might have been thinking of Belém, which is to the east of Marajó, or Macapá to the north-west.

72 *anarchist from Barcelona*: Barcelona (a city in north-eastern Spain) had a reputation as the centre of Spanish anarchism. In 1896, when a bomb was thrown at a religious procession in Barcelona, the Spanish government arrested and tortured 400 suspects. There were protests at their treatment all over Europe, and in 1897 an anarchist assassinated the Spanish president. On 31 May 1906, between the time when Conrad wrote 'An Anarchist' and its publication, a bomb was thrown in Madrid at the newly married King and Queen of Spain. Twenty deaths and many more injuries were reported, and the Spanish police immediately arrested 800 suspected anarchists.

73 *spanner*: wrench.

74 *Monsieur! Monsieur. Arrêtez!*: (Fr.) Sir! Sir! Stop!

75 *Ouvrier*: (Fr.) workman.

Mécanicien, monsieur: (Fr.) mechanic, sir.

76 *vaqueros*: (Sp.) cow hand, cowboy.

Anarchisto de Barcelona: (Sp.) Anarchist of Barcelona.

77 *Il ne faut pas beaucoup pour perdre un homme*: (Fr.) a little thing may bring about the undoing of a man.

mon atelier: (Fr.) my workshop, or my studio.

Le sommeil me fuit: (Fr.) sleep eludes me.

79 *sacrée boutique*: (Fr.) literally, sacred shop; figuratively, damned system.

Vive l'anarchie!: (Fr.) long live anarchy! Norman Sherry, in *Conrad's Western World* (Cambridge: Cambridge University Press, 1971), 424, cites a report in an 1894 number of the *Torch*, an anarchist journal, of a French workman abusing the government in a bar and of another who was sentenced to a year's imprisonment for shouting 'Vive l'anarchie'.

patron: (Fr.) boss.

80 *estaminet*: (Fr.) bar or coffee-house.

compagnon: (Fr.) comrade.

Des exaltés—quoi!: (Fr.) some enthusiasts, huh!

81 *n'est-ce pas, monsieur?*: (Fr.) isn't that so, sir?

a black bag with the bomb inside: the most violent period of French anarchism was between March 1892 and June 1894: eleven dynamite explosions killed nine people, an anarchist attacked and wounded the Serbian minister in Paris, and the President of France was assassinated.

82 *Iles de Salut*: see note to Cayenne, p. 70.

the convicts planned a mutiny: an actual mutiny of anarchist convicts took place on St Joseph's Island on 21 October 1894. None escaped. At least three anarchist publications gave accounts of the mutiny (Sherry, *Conrad's Western World*, 220).

85 *sous-officiers*: (Fr.) non-commissioned officers.

87 *Allez! En route!*: (Fr.) go on! Get going!

88 *Vive la liberté! . . . Mort aux bourgeois*: (Fr.) long live liberty! Death to the bourgeois!

89 *Calmez vous*: (Fr.) calm yourself.

90 *pontoon*: large flat-bottomed barge or lighter furnished with cranes, capstans, and tackles, used for overhauling ships, raising weights, etc.

'The Informer'

92 *Number One*: P. J. P. Tynan was known as Number One. He was not an anarchist but the leader of 'the Irish Invincibles', an insurrectionary organization (Sherry, *Conrad's Western World*, 423).

étagères: pieces of furniture fitted with shelves for displaying items.

imperial: a short tuft of hair growing beneath the lower lip, made fashionable by Emperor Napoleon III.

porcelain: a London anarchist called Parmeggiani was a collector and dealer in porcelain and antiques (Sherry, *Conrad's Western World*, 209).

97 *distinguished government official*: William Michael Rossetti, brother of the poets Dante Gabriel and Christina, was a not particularly distinguished clerk in the Excise Office.

his grown-up children: in 1891, while still teenagers, W. M. Rossetti's three eldest children, Olivia, Arthur, and Helen, started a journal of revolutionary anarchism. *Torch: A Journal of International Socialism* (renamed *Torch of Anarchy* in 1895) was initially produced on a duplicating machine in the Rossetti family home at 3 St Edmund's Terrace, London. In 1894 the Rossettis acquired an old printing-press, which they moved across London to 127 Ossulston Street, a single-storey, two-room house near King's Cross. Their connection with the journal ended in 1896, but the following year Olivia married Antonio Agresti, a prominent anarchist and an engraver, whom she had met through his regular contributions to the *Torch*. (See H. Oliver, *The International Anarchist Movement in Late Victorian London* (London: Croom Helm, 1983), 120–4.)

The daughter of this story is an amalgam of Olivia and Helen. Conrad met Helen Rossetti Angeli in 1903 or 1904, when she was about 20 (Sherry, *Conrad's Western World*, 212–13).

appropriate gestures: Conrad's preferred title for the story was 'Gestures'.

98 *bombe glacée*: (Fr.) a frozen dessert of spherical shape, containing two layers of ice-cream.

103 *the Professor*: this character reappears in *The Secret Agent*. Arthur Rossetti was interested in chemistry, but he was no terrorist, even though he experimented with explosives.

104 *the Alarm Bell and the Firebrand*: *Alarm* (1896) was a short-lived moderate anarchist journal. *Firebrand* was advertised regularly in the *Torch*.

106 *knickerbocker suit*: knickerbockers were loose-fitting breeches, gathered in at the knee.

107 *the most systematic of informers*: anarchists were constantly concerned about police spies, and not without good reason. The most famous, Serreaux, was in the pay of the French police. He was the editor of *La Révolution sociale*, one of the leading anarchist journals of the 1880s. H. Oliver, in *The International Anarchist Movement*, describes a Home Office memorandum of 1903 suggesting that Michele Angiolillo, who assassinated President Antonio Cánovas del Castillo of Spain, had been denounced by his comrades as a police spy and so felt impelled to violent action in order to prove himself (p. 116).

'The Brute'

116 *Windsor armchair*: a type of wooden armchair.

Trinity: the Corporation of Trinity House is the British licensing authority for maritime pilots and is responsible for lighthouses.

Port Victoria: in *The Mirror of the Sea* (1906) Conrad writes about the approach to London by sea and 'the entrance to the [river] Medway, with its men-of-war moored in a line, and the long wooden jetty of Port Victoria, with its few low buildings like the beginning of a hasty settlement upon a wild and unexplored shore' (*The Mirror of the Sea, and A Personal Record*, ed. Zdzisław Najder (Oxford: Oxford University Press, 1988), 104).

118 *eleven-three up*: 11.03 train to London.

119 *salt beef and hardtack*: typical sailors' food. Hard tack is ship's biscuit.

lee: the side of a ship or promontory sheltered from the wind.

scantling: dimension, size.

commodore-captain: the senior captain in a fleet of merchant ships.

poop: raised deck at the rear of a sailing ship.

121 *broach*: veer suddenly so as to turn the side of ship to windward, or to meet the sea.

ropes, cables, wire hawsers: ropes are all cordage of over one inch in diameter; cables are heavy ropes usually used with anchors; hawsers are larger than ropes but smaller than cables.

122 *forecastle*: the forward part of a ship, traditionally the crew's living space.

123 *Gravesend*: town on the south shore of the Thames estuary in England.

mizen: the third mast from the bows in a vessel with three or more masts.

124 *mooring-bitt*: a frame composed of two strong pillars, fixed upright in the forward part of the ship and bolted to the deck beams; the mooring cable is secured to it.

sheets . . . tacks: types of rigging.

spars . . . braces . . . yards: spars are any wooded supports used in the rigging of ship; yards are large spars crossing the masts of a ship horizontally or diagonally; braces are ropes secured to ends of all yards of a square-rigged ship by which the yards are braced, or swung, at different angles.

126 *pinafores*: coveralls or aprons worn by small children to keep their clothes from being soiled.

128 *Dungeness*: headland on the coast of south-east England, facing into the Straits of Dover.

129 *Hole Haven*: on Canvey Island, off the north shore of the Thames estuary.

collier-brig: two-masted vessel used for carrying coal on short coastal voyages.

a schooner and a ketch: two types of small, two-masted seagoing vessels. A schooner has a smaller mast in front of the main mast; a ketch has a smaller mast behind the main mast.

130 *towing-chock*: a heavy wooden or metal fitting secured on deck, with jaws through which a towing cable passes.

fluke: the triangular shape at the end of each arm of an anchor which digs into the seabed or the ground.

131 *bowsprit*: a large spar or boom running out from the front stem of a sailing vessel.

132 *Tower Hill*: street in east London, adjacent to the Tower of London.

four-wheeler: a four-wheeled, horse-drawn cab.

Spencer Gulf: off the coast of South Australia.

133 *Port Adelaide*: the port of Adelaide in South Australia.

the Cape: Cape Province, South Africa.

135 *binnacle-lamp*: the binnacle is a receptacle for the ship's compass, fitted with lights for sailing at night.

luffed: to luff is to bring a ship's head closer to the wind.

136 *Herne Bay*: on the north coast of Kent, about sixty miles from London.

'Il Conde'

137 *'Il Conde'*: the title means 'The Count', but it is a mixture of Italian and Spanish. In Italian it would be 'Il Conte', in Spanish, 'El Conde'. In the preface to *A Set of Six*, Conrad acknowledges the mistake, and in later letters he sometimes spells the noun 'Conte', but it was never changed in any of the editions. Jocelyn Baines reports that the story was based upon the experience of Count Zygmunt Szembek, a fellow Pole whom Conrad met in Capri.

'Vedi Napoli e poi mori': (It.) see Naples and then die.

Hermes: a Greek god.

138 *smoking*: a French version of 'smoking-jacket', a dinner-jacket or tuxedo.

Abbazia: Italian name for Opatija, a coastal resort in Istria, Croatia. It was under Austrian rule at this time.

the Riviera: the northern Mediterranean coast between Cannes (France) and La Spezia (Italy). A popular resort area, particularly for the winter months.

139 *Sorrento*: city on the southern shore of the Gulf of Naples.

Capri: island in the Gulf of Naples.

contadini: (It.) country people, peasants.

outré: (Fr.) exaggerated, excessive.

140 *Taormina*: city on the east coast of Sicily, about 300 miles from Naples.

Bon voyage: (Fr.) a pleasant journey to you; goodbye.

142 *Primo Tenore*: (It.) first tenor.

carozella: (It.) *carrozzella*, a Neapolitan term for a cab.

144 *toilettes*: (Fr.) dresses, clothing.

147 *vostro portofolio*: (It.) your wallet.

151 *Bari*: the major city in Puglia, at the 'heel' of Italy.

camorra: Neapolitan equivalent of the Mafia.

una lira e cinquanti centesimi: (It.) one lira and fifty cents.

152 *birba*: (It.) rascal, rogue, villain.

furfante: (It.) scoundrel, knave.

'Prince Roman'

154 *Væ victis!*: (Lat.) woe to the conquered! See Livy, *History*, book v, sect. 48.

great Florentine painter: Michelangelo. Giorgio Vasari reports that before dying, the artist begged that his body be returned to Florence (*The Lives of the Painters, Sculptors and Architects*, iv, ed. William Gaunt (London: Everyman, 1963), 182).

155 *Guards*: an élite army regiment.

Emperor Nicholas: Nicholas I, who ruled Russia from 1825 to 1855.

the present man: Nicholas II, the last emperor of Russia, who was killed following the Communist revolution of 1917.

Crimean War: 1853–6. Russia was defeated by France, Britain, and Turkey.

156 *Polish nobles*: in the middle of the eighteenth century, the western boundaries of Poland were much as they are today, but to the east they included most of present-day Lithuania, Belorus, and the western half of Ukraine. By 1795, following three partitions, Poland had ceased to exist as an independent state. Austria and Prussia, its neighbours to the south-west and north-west, divided up the region of the ethnic Poles, while Russia to the east appropriated Lithuania, Belorus, and the Polish Ukraine. Napoleon created the Duchy of Warsaw out of the lands seized by Prussia and Austria, but after 1815 Russia gained control of much of this entity. Most of the old Polish nobility now became subject to the Russian emperor. This situation did not change until the end of the First World War, after this story was first published.

Ukrainian: the Ukraine was then the territory around the southern reaches of the river Dnieper, extending 200–300 miles to the west and some 100 miles to the east of the river. It is now an independent republic.

157   *frock coat*: a double-breasted black coat extending almost to the knee. It was standard male attire in the second half of the nineteenth century.

159   *Prince Roman S——*: Prince Roman Sanguszko.

Ruthenia: the non-Russian Ukraine.

162   *byre*: cow-house.

the French . . . with Napoleon: refers to the French invasion of Russia in 1812, after which the French army was destroyed. See notes to p. 231.

163   *the revolt in Warsaw, the flight of the Grand duke Constantine*: in November 1830 some officers of the Polish army led an insurrection in Warsaw. Much of the army and many civilians rose in support, and Nicholas I's brother Constantine, the imperial governor of Poland, fled to Russia. The Russians did not manage to suppress the rebellion until September 1831. Conrad met Prince Roman Sanguszko in 1867, four years after the century's second Polish uprising. Conrad's parents were exiled in 1862, and both died as a result of the hardships they endured.

ordonnance officer: from the French *officier d'ordonnance*, an assisting officer, aide-de-camp.

Tzar: emperor of Russia.

Caucasus: mountains between the Black and Caspian seas, marking one of the southern borders of Russia.

164   *the last partition*: the last partition of Poland, 1795, which followed an uprising against the second partition, 1793.

165   *coram gentibus*: (Lat.) in the presence of the people.

in fulgore: (Lat.) in a flash.

affulget patriæ serenitas: (Lat.) the brightness of the native land shines forth.

Eripit verba dolor: (Lat.) grief denies me words.

168   *cholera made its first appearance in Europe*: part of a worldwide pandemic that first came to the attention of European physicians in Bengal in 1817. It had reached Poland's borders before the end of 1830, but European opinion, particularly among Poland's supporters, associated the spread of the disease with the Russian campaign there. In the course of 1831 the Russian army suffered even more severely than the Poles.

170 *casemates*: vaulted chambers built into the ramparts of a fortress, normally used as a barrack or battery or both.

   gendarmes: soldiers on police duty.

174 *grand seigneur*: (Fr.) great aristocrat.

'The Inn of the Two Witches'

177 *we stood in again*: we came towards the shore.

   sloop-of-war: a small naval vessel, two- or three-masted.

   Peninsular campaign: Britain and France were at war for much
   of the period 1792–1815. When Napoleon I, the Emperor of
   France, made his brother King of Spain in 1808, both Spain
   and Portugal revolted. The British then sent help under the
   Duke of Wellington; the allies succeeded in driving the French
   out of the Iberian peninsula and by 1814 had carried the war
   into French territory.

178 *captain's coxswain*: the coxswain was the helmsman and senior
   rating on a ship's boat—the captain's boat would be the most
   important. On a small warship, such as a sloop-of-war, the
   senior petty officer (naval equivalent of a sergeant) was known
   as the coxswain.

   man-of-war's: warship.

   forecastle: see note to p. 122.

179 *stern-sheets*: the part of an open boat between the stern and
   the last oarsman's position.

180 *Asturian*: from Asturias, a coastal region of northern Spain.

   polizones: (Sp.) idlers, tramps.

181 *Shank's pony's*: travelling on foot.

   Alcade: a sheriff or justice in Spain, mayor. Variant of the
   Spanish *alcalde*.

182 *pea-jacket*: a short, double-breasted coat made of thick cloth.

   macho: (Sp.) male mule.

   olla: (Sp.) stew.

183 *Quien sabe?*: (Sp.) who knows?

   defunta: (Sp. *difunta*) late, dead.

   Castilian: from Castile, a central region of Spain.

   caballero: (Sp.) gentleman.

184 *Ladrones en grande*: thieves on a large scale.

185 *duro*: dollar, a Spanish coin worth five pesetas.

Vaya usted con Dios: (Sp.) go with God.

186 *inshore tack*: a course towards the shore.

lying over: leaning over with the wind.

187 *Sierra*: mountain range.

188 *posada*: (Sp.) wayside inn.

Misericordia!: (Sp.) mercy!

189 *Ingles*: (Sp.) Englishman.

190 *novio*: (Sp.) fiancé.

191 *casa*: (Sp.) house.

194 *hanger*: short sword.

200 *the overpowering stillness of the room resumed its sway*: Wilkie Collins's story 'A Terribly Strange Bed' (1852) highlights the same means of murder, but Conrad denied knowledge of it and claimed that such a bed was discovered at the end of the eighteenth century at an inn between Rome and Naples. Collins acknowledged a debt to the artist W. S. Herrick for the story. Such beds were probably a common feature of travellers' tales.

202 *escopettas*: carbines, short muskets used by mounted troops. From the Spanish *escopeta*.

'Laughing Anne'

203 *a great Eastern Port*: probably Singapore.

sampan: small boat of Chinese pattern.

Sissie: a charged name for Conrad. In March of 1883 he was second mate on the barque *Palestine*. When the cargo of coal caught fire, the crew abandoned ship and came ashore at Muntok on the island of Bangka, off the coast of Sumatra. The SS *Sissie* took them to Singapore for a court of enquiry, which cleared the crew and officers of all blame. Conrad used the incident in 'Youth' (1898).

Glasgow: the second city of Scotland, a major shipbuilding centre in the nineteenth century. It was the *Sissie*'s port of registration.

204 *Mandarin*: a Chinese official, educated and of high social status.

Celestial: from the second half of the nineteenth century, a word used in English to designate a Chinese person. 'Celestial Empire' is the literal translation of a Chinese term for 'China'.

205 *trade dollars*: responding to a general currency shortage, from 1895 the British government permitted the minting of British trade dollars for use in the Far Eastern trade. In 1903 the Straits Settlements (roughly, the Malay peninsula) introduced their own dollars, and the British trade dollars were demonetized in 1904 and 1905. Mexican trade dollars were also in wide use and were withdrawn at the same time.

tiffin-rooms: lunch-rooms.

206 *Malay serang*: Malays are one of the peoples of the Malay peninsula and archipelago. *Serang* is a Hindi term used for the boatswain or senior crewman.

rattans: climbing plants, notable for their long, thin, jointed and pliable stems. They are used for furniture, blinds, etc.

207 *Java-sea*: in Indonesia, between the islands of Java (Jawa) and Borneo.

Somerset: a steamship called the *Somerset* took the *Palestine* (see note to p. 203) in tow until the fire became too fierce.

209 *Gulf of Tonkin*: Beibu Wan, between Vietnam and the Chinese island of Hainan.

211 *tea-gown*: a semi-formal gown of fine material in graceful, flowing lines, worn especially in the afternoon for entertaining at home.

212 *the Orang Kaya*: (Malay) the rich or powerful man. Here it probably means the head man of the village.

213 *prau*: Malay boat (*perahu*), propelled by sail or paddles. Long (about 30 feet) and narrow, often fitted with an outrigger on one side.

214 *mon malheur*: (Fr.) my misfortune.

lazaretto: a space between decks, used as a storeroom.

215 *Kalashes*: (Hindi) natives employed as seamen.

218 *merci bien*: (Fr.) thank you very much.

221 *davits*: a pair of cranes on the side or stern of a ship, used for raising and lowering a boat.

223 *Trahison!*: (Fr.) treachery!

Tuez-le!: (Fr.) kill him!

226 *fire-bars*: bars of a boiler furnace.

227 *Cape Selatan*: on the south-east coast of Borneo.

229 *Malacca*: British (previously Dutch) settlement on the west coast of the Malay peninsula.

Fremantle: town near Perth, Western Australia.

'The Warrior's Soul'

231 *Napoleon*: Emperor of France from 1804 to 1814. In June 1812 he led an army into Russia, and following the Battle of Borodino in September, the Russians abandoned the defence of Moscow. After five weeks in Moscow, however, Napoleon, finding his lines of communication and supply overstretched, began the retreat from Russia. Harassed by the Russian army and starved and frozen by the winter, fewer than one man in five returned to Europe.

Macedonian Alexander: Alexander the Great, conqueror of Greece and most of the middle east. He led his army on a march of conquest that took them from Macedon in northern Greece to the northern plains of India. His name is a byword for military success.

Grand Army: *La Grande Armée*, the great army that Napoleon led into Russia in 1812. Originally consisting of about 420,000 men—600,000 with reinforcements—it was only partly French: there were large contingents from other parts of Europe, including Poland.

Dante's Inferno: in the *Inferno* (written in the early fourteenth century) Dante represents the most egregious sinners in a realm of ice rather than fire.

233 *Oudinot*: Charles Oudinot (1767–1847), Duc de Reggio. The son of a French businessman, he became a marshal of France under Napoleon.

Beresina: a river in north-eastern Belorus. Oudinot and Ney's contingent suffered severe losses when crossing the river against a larger Russian force.

dragoon's: a mounted infantryman, armed with a carbine or short musket.

234 *subaltern*: a junior army officer, below the rank of Captain.

Des Russes sauvages: (Fr.) savage Russians.

adjutant: an officer who assists the senior officers in the details of military duty.

235 *protections*: influence, connections.

Silesia: area on the west bank of the upper reaches of the Oder river. Now in south-west Poland, it was part of Prussia in 1812.

Leipsic: Leipzig, a city in eastern Germany. In 1812 it was in Saxony.

236 *tallow candles*: see note to p. 8.

salon: a large room used for receiving guests. In eighteenth-century Paris it became common for fashionable women to receive guests regularly, and the salons became centres for the exchange of the latest intellectual and political ideas.

238 *military mission*: military embassy.

239 *petit salon*: small salon, drawing-room.

244 *bivouac*: temporary field camp.

247 *cuirassier's*: cavalry soldier wearing a breastplate.

Cossacks: a people of the Ukraine. Celebrated horsemen, they were employed as cavalry by the imperial Russian government and were notorious for their savagery.

248 *Oui! Je vous comprends*: (Fr.) yes, I understand you.

249 *Tuez moi, tuez moi*: (Fr.) kill me, kill me.

251 *Dantzic*: Danzig or Gdansk, a port city in northern Poland. It was in Prussia in 1812.

'The Tale'

253 *the war*: World War I (1914–18). In early 1915 Germany instituted a submarine blockade of Great Britain and began attacking passenger ships as well as cargo vessels. By late 1916, when Conrad wrote 'The Tale', German submarines were sinking 300,000 tons of allied shipping a month, and in April 1917 alone they destroyed more than 650,000 tons. There seemed to be a distinct possibility that Britain would be starved into submission. By October 1917, when the story appeared, Britain had lost eight million tons of shipping, but the new convoy system of merchant ship protection was already taking effect.

254 *Northman*: probably a Norwegian or Swede. Norway, Sweden, Denmark, and the Netherlands were all neutral during World War I. Some neutral ships undertook the supplying of German submarines at sea.

255 *the ship was of a very ornamental sort once*: private yachts were hired by the Admiralty and fitted out with guns and wireless equipment for auxiliary patrol duties. By the end of April 1915 an auxiliary patrol of about sixty yachts and more than 500 trawlers had been established.

260 *leadsmen*: sailors responsible for taking depth soundings with a lead weight on the end of a measured rope.

261 *she has steam on them*: i.e. she is ready to depart.

264 *bulkhead*: one of the upright partitions serving as the walls of a cabin.

265 *steam up*: see note to p. 261.

267 *Rotterdam*: the principal port of Holland, which was a neutral country in World War I.